# THE MYTHICS

PAPERCUT**Z**

MORE GREAT GRAPHIC NOVEL SERIES AVAILABLE FROM

# PAPERCUTZ™

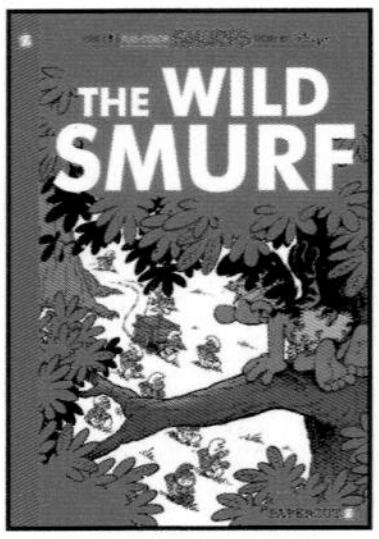
THE WILD SMURF
PAPERCUTZ

THE SMURFS #21

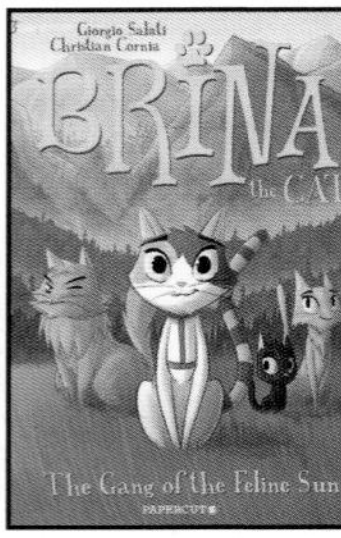
Giorgio Salati
Christian Cornia
BRINA the CAT
The Gang of the Feline Sun
PAPERCUTZ

BRINA THE CAT #1

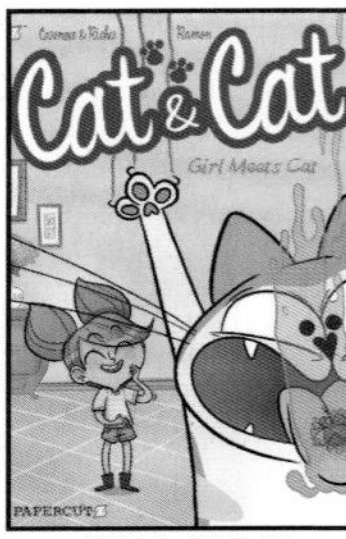
Cat & Cat
Girl Meets Cat
PAPERCUTZ

CAT & CAT #1

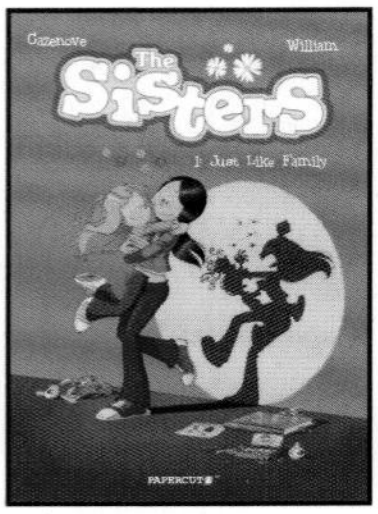
Cazenove
William
The Sisters
1 Just Like Family

THE SISTERS #1

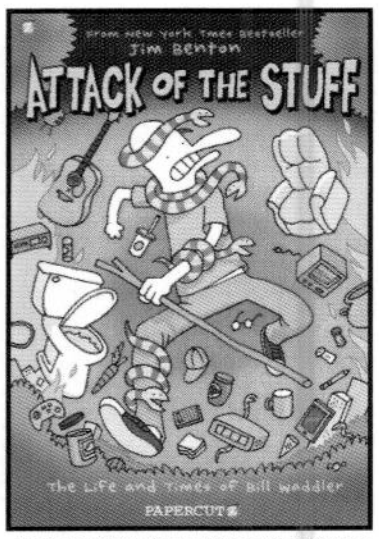
From New York Times Bestseller
Jim Benton
ATTACK OF THE STUFF
The Life and Times of Bill Waddler
PAPERCUTZ

ATTACK OF THE STUFF

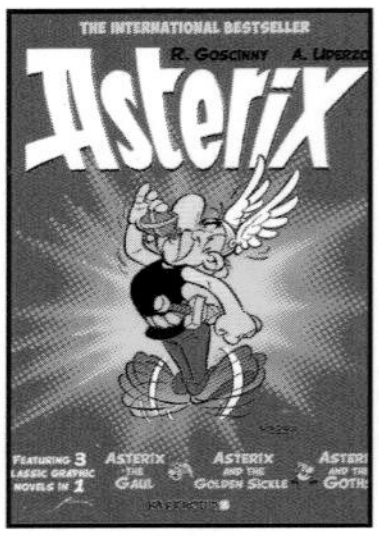
THE INTERNATIONAL BESTSELLER
R. GOSCINNY
A. UDERZO
Asterix

ASTERIX #1

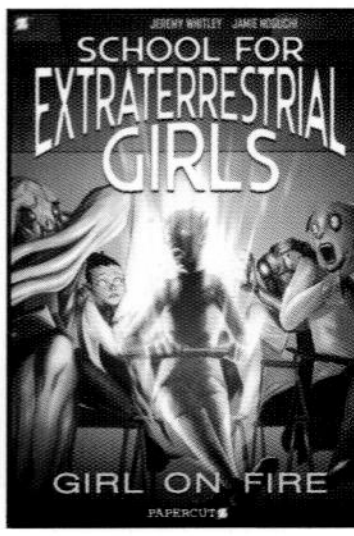
JEREMY WHITLEY
JAMIE NOGUCHI
SCHOOL FOR EXTRATERRESTRIAL GIRLS
GIRL ON FIRE
PAPERCUTZ

SCHOOL FOR EXTRATERRESTRIAL GIRLS #1

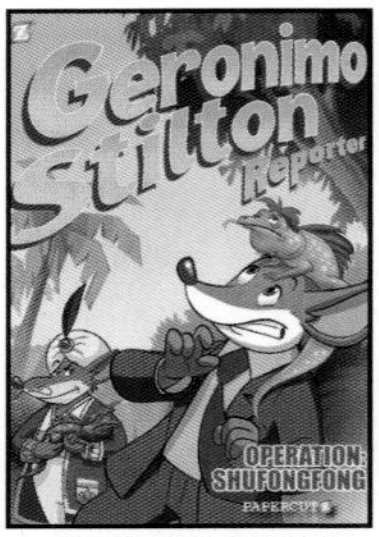
Geronimo Stilton
Reporter
OPERATION: SHUFONGFONG
PAPERCUTZ

GERONIMO STILTON REPORTER #1

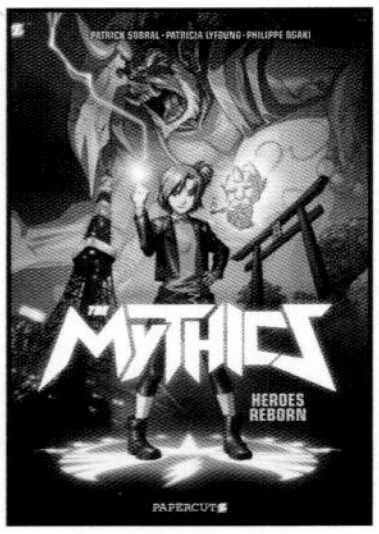
THE MYTHICS
HEROES REBORN
PAPERCUTZ

THE MYTHICS #1

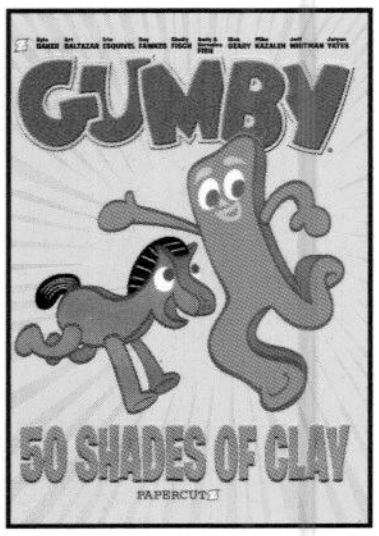
GUMBY
50 SHADES OF CLAY
PAPERCUTZ

GUMBY #1

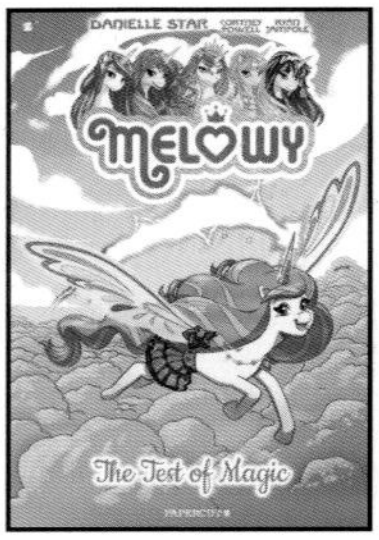
DANIELLE STAR
Melowy
The Test of Magic
PAPERCUTZ

MELOWY #1

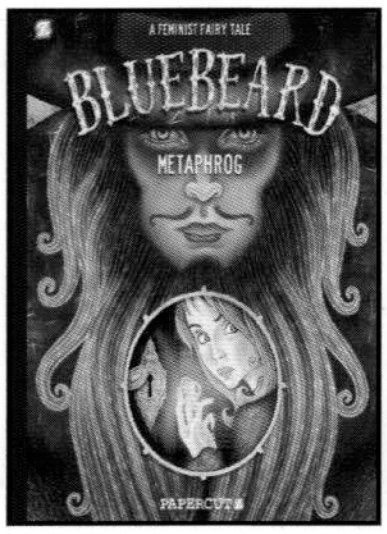
A FEMINIST FAIRY TALE
BLUEBEARD
METAPHROG
PAPERCUTZ

BLUEBEARD

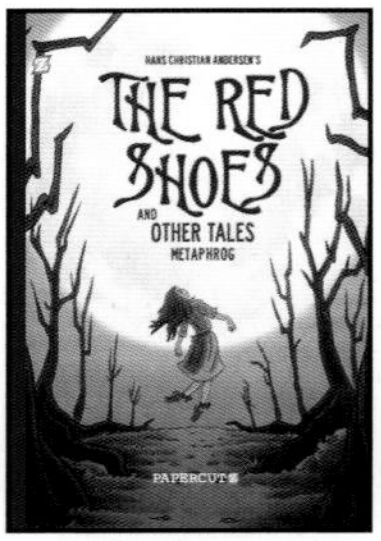
HANS CHRISTIAN ANDERSEN'S
THE RED SHOES
AND OTHER TALES
METAPHROG
PAPERCUTZ

THE RED SHOES

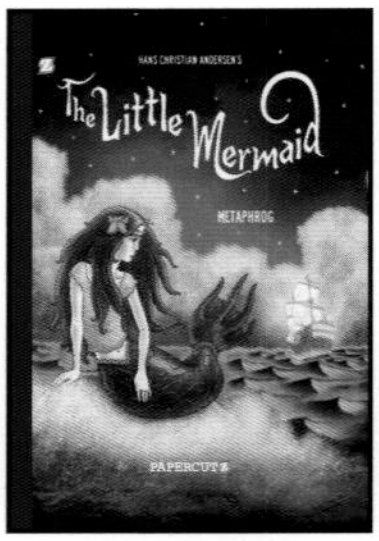
HANS CHRISTIAN ANDERSEN'S
The Little Mermaid
METAPHROG
PAPERCUTZ

THE LITTLE MERMAID

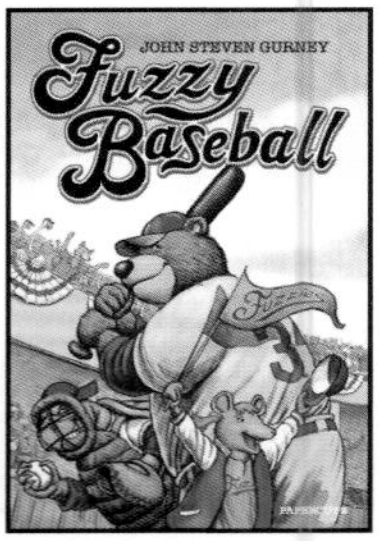
JOHN STEVEN GURNEY
Fuzzy Baseball

FUZZY BASEBALL #1

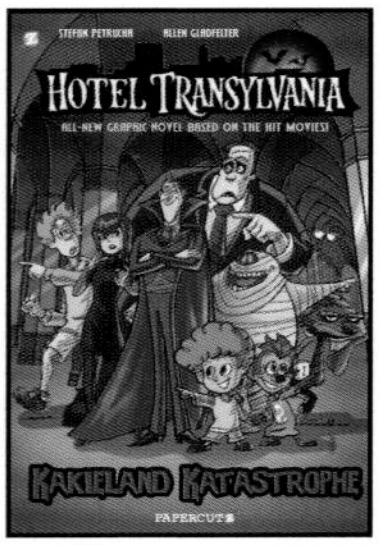
STEFAN PETRUCHA
KELLEN GLADFELTER
HOTEL TRANSYLVANIA
ALL-NEW GRAPHIC NOVEL BASED ON THE HIT MOVIES!
KAKIELAND KATASTROPHE
PAPERCUTZ

HOTEL TRANSYLVANIA #1

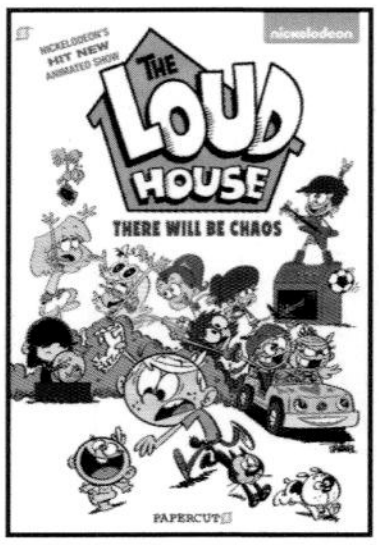
nickelodeon
THE LOUD HOUSE
THERE WILL BE CHAOS
PAPERCUTZ

THE LOUD HOUSE #1

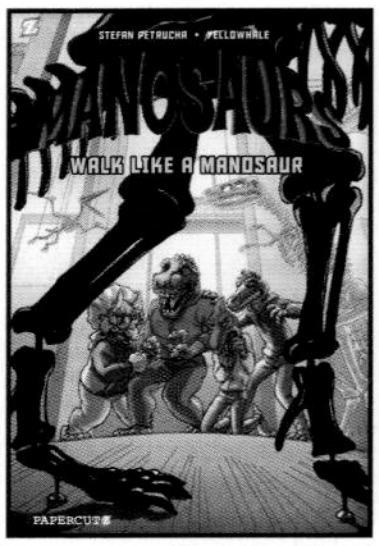
STEFAN PETRUCHA
MANOSAURS
WALK LIKE A MANOSAUR
PAPERCUTZ

MANOSAURS #1

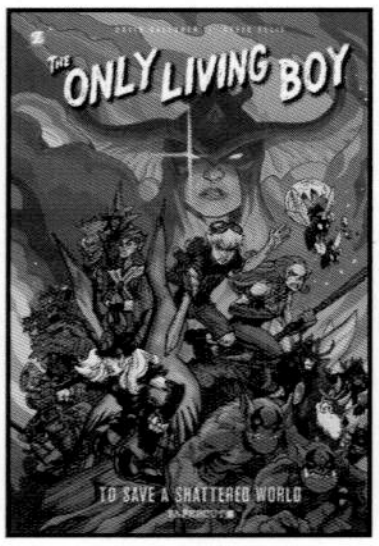
THE ONLY LIVING BOY
TO SAVE A SHATTERED WORLD
PAPERCUTZ

THE ONLY LIVING BOY #5

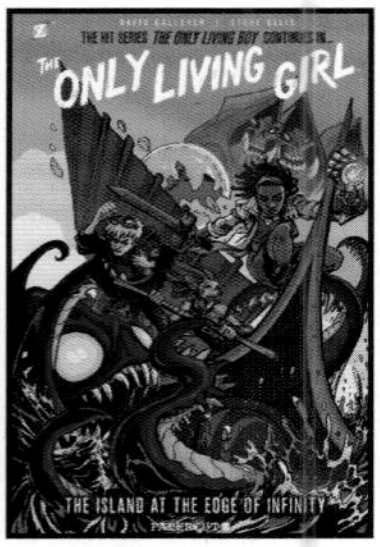
THE ONLY LIVING GIRL
THE ISLAND AT THE EDGE OF INFINITY
PAPERCUTZ

THE ONLY LIVING GIRL #1

**papercutz.com**

Also available where ebooks are sold.

# 3. APOCALYPSE AHEAD

## PATRICK SOBRAL • PATRICIA LYFOUNG
## PHILIPPE OGAKI • ALICE PICARD • JÉRÔME ALQUIÉ
## ZIMRA • NICOLAS JARRY

PAPERCUTZ™
New York

Originally published in French under the following titles:
*Les Mythics*, volume 7 *"Hong Kong,"* de P. Sobral, P. Lyfoung, P. Ogaki, and A. Picard
*Les Mythics*, volume 8 *"Saint-Pétersbourg,"* de P. Sobral, P. Lyfoung, P. Ogaki, and Zimra
*Les Mythics*, volume 9 *"Stonehenge,"* de P. Sobral, P. Lyfoung, P. Ogaki, N. Jarry, and J. Alquié
© Editions Delcourt, 2019/2020
English Translation and all other editorial material © 2021 Papercutz. All rights reserved.
Created by PATRICK SOBRAL, PATRICIA LYFOUNG, and PHILIPPE OGAKI

**Part 7- Hong Kong**
Script — PHILIPPE OGAKI
Art — ALICE PICARD
Color—MAGALI PAILLAT

**Part 8- Saint Petersburg**
Script— PATRICIA LYFOUNG
Art — ZIMRA
Color—MAGALI PAILLAT

**Part 9- Stonehenge**
Script—PATRICK SOBRAL with help from NICOLAS JARRY
Art and Color— JÉRÔME ALQUIÉ

Original editor — THIERRY JOOR

Special thanks to SÉVERINE AUPERT, LUCIE MASSENA, and LINA DI FLAMMINIO

Papercutz books may be purchased for business or promotional use.
For information on bulk purchases please contact Macmillan Corporate and
Premium Sales Department at (800) 221-7945 x5442

Translation — ELIZABETH S. TIERI
Lettering — WILSON RAMOS JR.
Editor — JEFF WHITMAN
Editorial Intern — INGRID RIOS
JIM SALICRUP
Editor-in-Chief

PB ISBN: 978-1-5458-0556-5
HC ISBN: 978-1-5458-0555-8

Printed in China
April 2021

Distributed by Macmillan
First Papercutz Printing

# THE MYTHICS

## PART 7: HONG KONG

Story by
**PHILIPPE OGAKI**

Art by
**ALICE PICARD**

Color by
**MAGALI PAILLAT**

Here we are in "Phase 2" (as the Americans say) of THE MYTHICS. Thank you to Jerôme Alquié who again agreed to put his hands (and his talent) to the service of the universe of THE MYTHICS. A great thank you to Nicolas Jarry who helped me develop this storyline and obviously, thank you to the original Dream Team for this fabulous saga, Patricia, Phillippe, and the Delcourt editors. And let's not forget the talented artists and colorists who have agreed to let us borrow their talent again or those who are just joining the adventure that's in progress. Thank you for your excellent work. THE MYTHICS is a superb example of collaboration and it shows.
But above all, a big thank you to you, dear readers, for having permitted us to get here and for having trusted in us. We will not fail you; that's a promise! Beautiful and new adventures await you, dear readers.
Long live THE MYTHICS!
–*Patrick Sobral*

Thanks to you, dear readers! Because of you, we hope that the adventures of THE MYTHICS will continue for a long time! An enormous thanks to Rachel and Magali, for having illustrated this book so well! You went above and beyond my hopes! What talent! Thanks also to Philippe, Patrick, Nicolas, and Jerome. Thanks to Mina, who served as the test reader! Thanks to the entire Delcourt team who have supported us since the beginning. And finally, thank you for having this book in your hands and for bringing it to life.
–*Patricia Lyfoung*

I thank all the collaborators and the whole formidable team who have given life (and spared no effort) to our young heroes, THE MYTHICS and thanks to the readers who always show such enthusiasm in following their adventures.
–*Philippe Ogaki*

Thank you, readers, for accompanying THE MYTHICS since the start of their adventures.
Thank you to team Mythics!
Thanks for everything to my Cher and Tendre!
–*Alice Picard*

Thanks to Patrick Sobral and Nicolas Jarry for this excellent, colorful story in the streets of London and at the mythical site of Stonehenge. Thanks to all those authors, editors, and booksellers who keep this very beautiful young adult series alive all over. Thanks to Cricri, Remi, Maeline and Antonin, my parents, and all my close family and friends, and a special thought to Carine... Finally, thank you to all of you readers for all your growing enthusiasm for the adventures of THE MYTHICS!
–*Jerôme Alquié*

Thank you to all our readers for their loyalty, and to all the beautiful people who surround me.
Thank you to Patricia and Rachel for this beautiful story and this super collaboration!
–*Magali Paillat*

Thank you to Patricia for having invited me to participate in THE MYTHICS adventure, and to Magali for the shimmering colors!
Thanks as well to Patrick, Philippe, Thierry, and the whole Delcourt team for their trust and their support.
And thanks to Alex for supporting me during the deadlines (and Gish!)!
–*Zimra*

Editor's note: THE MYTHICS was originally published in France by Delcourt, which should explain why they're being thanked by THE MYTHICS creators.

# PREVIOUSLY IN
# THE MYTHICS

An ancient evil has returned to Earth after being banished to Mars for millennia. The old gods who thought they had defeated Evil found their descendants to become the new young protectors of Earth. Six children from all over the world were chosen.

First, *Yuko*, a Japanese schoolgirl in a rock band discovered she has electrifying lightning powers. She met her ancestor, *Raijin*, the God of Ligtning himself, who led Yuko to her legendary weapon. Yuko learned to hone her newfound powers of electricity to defeat *Fujin*, the evil God of Wind, before he could destroy all of Japan with nuclear warfare.

Meanwhile, in Egypt, young *Amir*, a recently orphaned boy taking over his father's successful company and landholdings, encountered *Horus*, the Sun and Moon God. Horus and Amir struggled to vanquish Evil in the form of *Seth* (aided by Amir's wicked half-brother) before they could reanimate all the dead mummies and take over the world in Evil's image.

Then, a young Opera hopeful, *Abigail*, faced a blizzard freezing all of Germany orchestrated by *Loki*, the God of Mischief, disguised as a wolf in sheep's clothing in the form of Abigail's charismatic professor. Under the guidance of *Freyja*, the Norse God of Beauty, Abigail learned to find her voice, and control her supersonic vocal powers to wield her mythic weapon to stop Evil in its tracks.

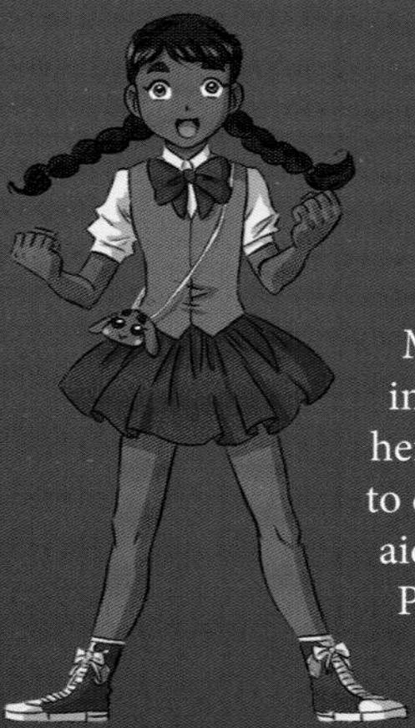

Meanwhile, in India, young adolescent *Parvati* is very involved as a volunteer at her local health clinic. But when her whole town comes down with a zombie bug, Parvati had to channel her newfound powers to save everyone. With the aid of her new tiger companion and ancient ancestor *Durga*, Parvarti was able to put a stop to the evil *Kali*, Goddess of Destruction, who was out to destroy the whole world with her zombie virus.

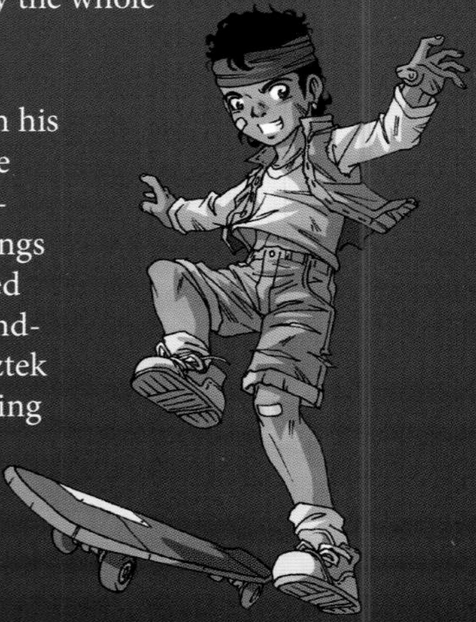

Then, in the slums of Mexico, young *Miguel*, who lives with his father and little sister, was in need of an awakening in more ways than one. After running with the wrong crowd, working with a shady businessman to provide for his family, things soon got out of the young teen's control and Evil resurrected in *Neococ Yaotl*, the God of Death, taking Miguel's old friend-turned-rival hostage. Miguel, under the guidance of the Aztek God of Wind, *Quetzalcoatl*, had to rise up and stop him using the power of the winds bestowed on him and the ancient weapon, the Serpent's Tail. It was a bloody battle to the finish, but Miguel managed to save his friend, and save the whole world.

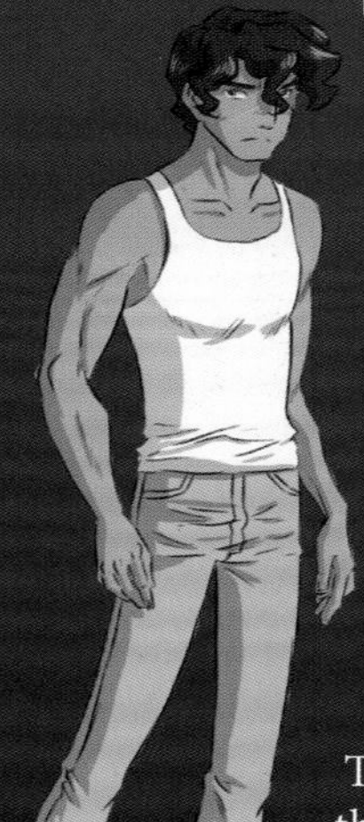

Finally, the last ancient hero summoned, is *Neo*, a teen from Greece struggling to support his impoverished single mother and triplet siblings. Neo and his demi-god mentor, *Hercules*, were tasked to stop *Ares*, the Greek God of War, in his path of chaos and destruction. To make matters even worse, Neo's family were smack dab in the middle of that path. After an epic sea battle, Neo's path as a hero was forged.

These children are Earth's last hope in the war against Evil. Using their powers and strengths, they might just have what it takes to be the new Gods of today. Now they are prepared to meet each other for the first time…

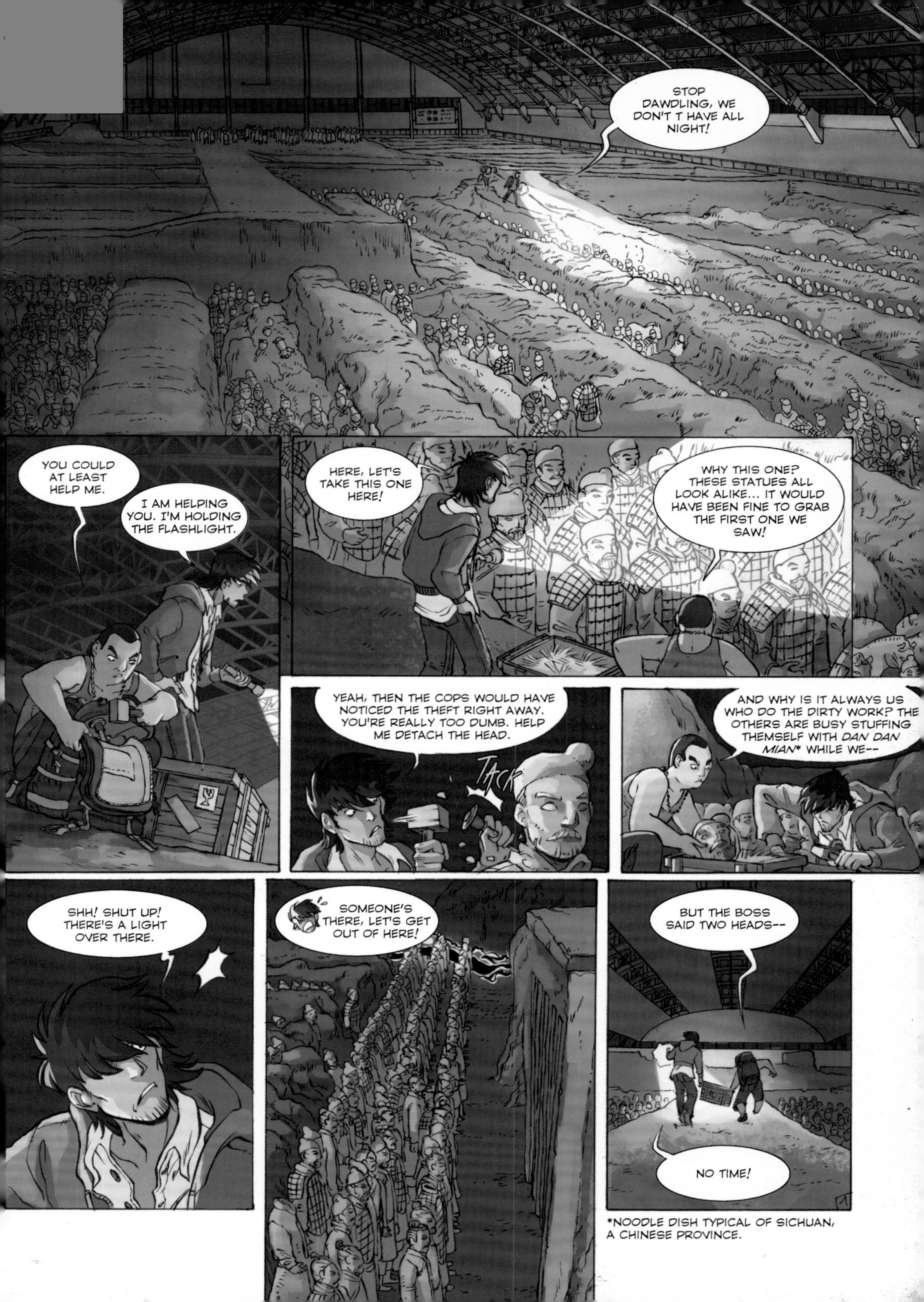
STOP DAWDLING, WE DON'T T HAVE ALL NIGHT!
YOU COULD AT LEAST HELP ME.
I AM HELPING YOU. I'M HOLDING THE FLASHLIGHT.
HERE, LET'S TAKE THIS ONE HERE!
WHY THIS ONE? THESE STATUES ALL LOOK ALIKE... IT WOULD HAVE BEEN FINE TO GRAB THE FIRST ONE WE SAW!
YEAH, THEN THE COPS WOULD HAVE NOTICED THE THEFT RIGHT AWAY. YOU'RE REALLY TOO DUMB. HELP ME DETACH THE HEAD.
TACK
AND WHY IS IT ALWAYS US WHO DO THE DIRTY WORK? THE OTHERS ARE BUSY STUFFING THEMSELF WITH *DAN DAN MIAN** WHILE WE--
SHH! SHUT UP! THERE'S A LIGHT OVER THERE.
SOMEONE'S THERE, LET'S GET OUT OF HERE!
BUT THE BOSS SAID TWO HEADS--
NO TIME!

*NOODLE DISH TYPICAL OF SICHUAN, A CHINESE PROVINCE.

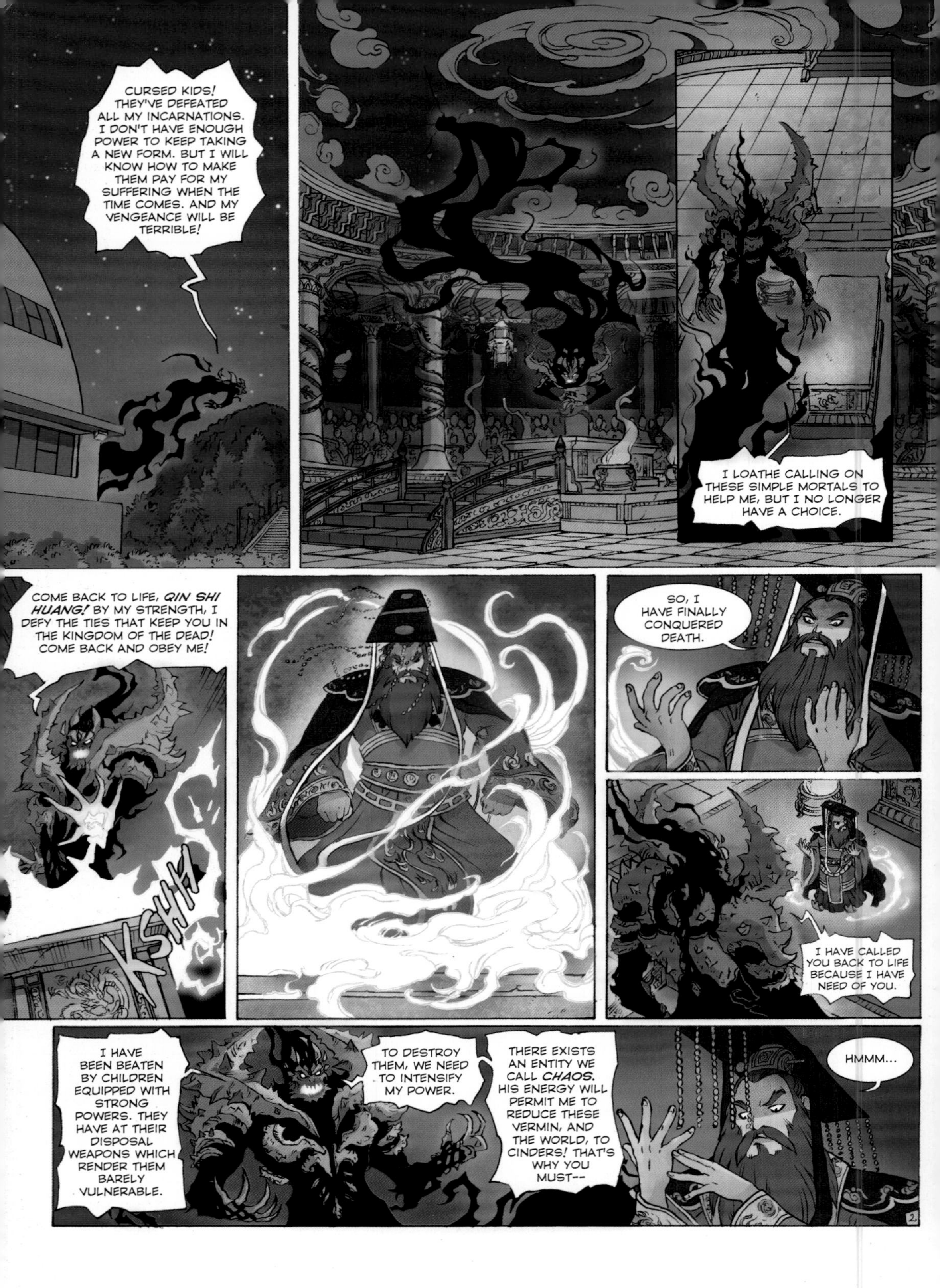
CURSED KIDS! THEY'VE DEFEATED ALL MY INCARNATIONS. I DON'T HAVE ENOUGH POWER TO KEEP TAKING A NEW FORM. BUT I WILL KNOW HOW TO MAKE THEM PAY FOR MY SUFFERING WHEN THE TIME COMES. AND MY VENGEANCE WILL BE TERRIBLE!
I LOATHE CALLING ON THESE SIMPLE MORTALS TO HELP ME, BUT I NO LONGER HAVE A CHOICE.
COME BACK TO LIFE, QIN SHI HUANG! BY MY STRENGTH, I DEFY THE TIES THAT KEEP YOU IN THE KINGDOM OF THE DEAD! COME BACK AND OBEY ME!
KSHHH
SO, I HAVE FINALLY CONQUERED DEATH.
I HAVE CALLED YOU BACK TO LIFE BECAUSE I HAVE NEED OF YOU.
I HAVE BEEN BEATEN BY CHILDREN EQUIPPED WITH STRONG POWERS. THEY HAVE AT THEIR DISPOSAL WEAPONS WHICH RENDER THEM BARELY VULNERABLE.
TO DESTROY THEM, WE NEED TO INTENSIFY MY POWER.
THERE EXISTS AN ENTITY WE CALL CHAOS. HIS ENERGY WILL PERMIT ME TO REDUCE THESE VERMIN, AND THE WORLD, TO CINDERS! THAT'S WHY YOU MUST--
HMMM...

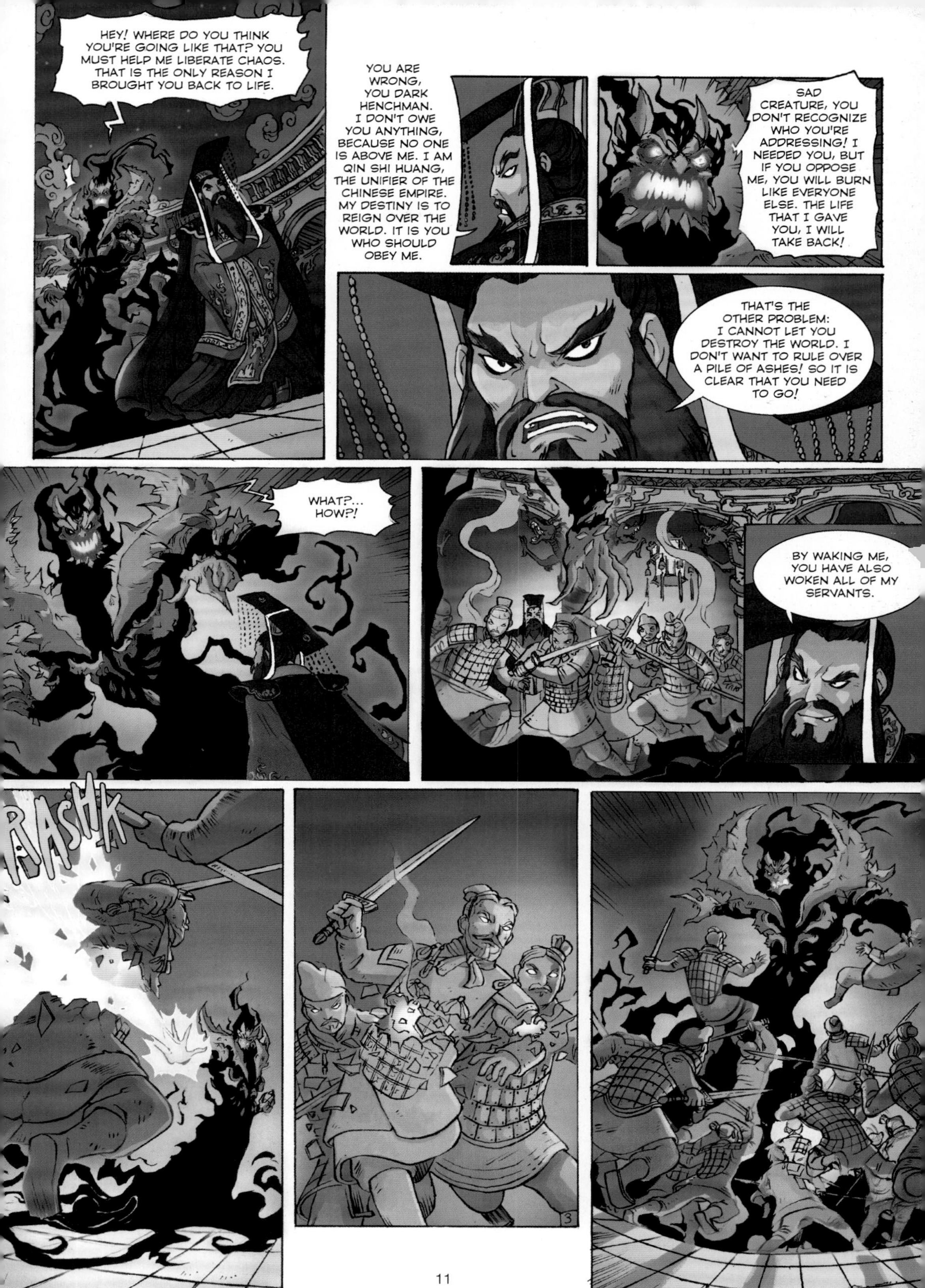
HEY! WHERE DO YOU THINK YOU'RE GOING LIKE THAT? YOU MUST HELP ME LIBERATE CHAOS. THAT IS THE ONLY REASON I BROUGHT YOU BACK TO LIFE.
YOU ARE WRONG, YOU DARK HENCHMAN. I DON'T OWE YOU ANYTHING, BECAUSE NO ONE IS ABOVE ME. I AM QIN SHI HUANG, THE UNIFIER OF THE CHINESE EMPIRE. MY DESTINY IS TO REIGN OVER THE WORLD. IT IS YOU WHO SHOULD OBEY ME.
SAD CREATURE, YOU DON'T RECOGNIZE WHO YOU'RE ADDRESSING! I NEEDED YOU, BUT IF YOU OPPOSE ME, YOU WILL BURN LIKE EVERYONE ELSE. THE LIFE THAT I GAVE YOU, I WILL TAKE BACK!
THAT'S THE OTHER PROBLEM: I CANNOT LET YOU DESTROY THE WORLD. I DON'T WANT TO RULE OVER A PILE OF ASHES! SO IT IS CLEAR THAT YOU NEED TO GO!
WHAT?... HOW?!
BY WAKING ME, YOU HAVE ALSO WOKEN ALL OF MY SERVANTS.
RASHK

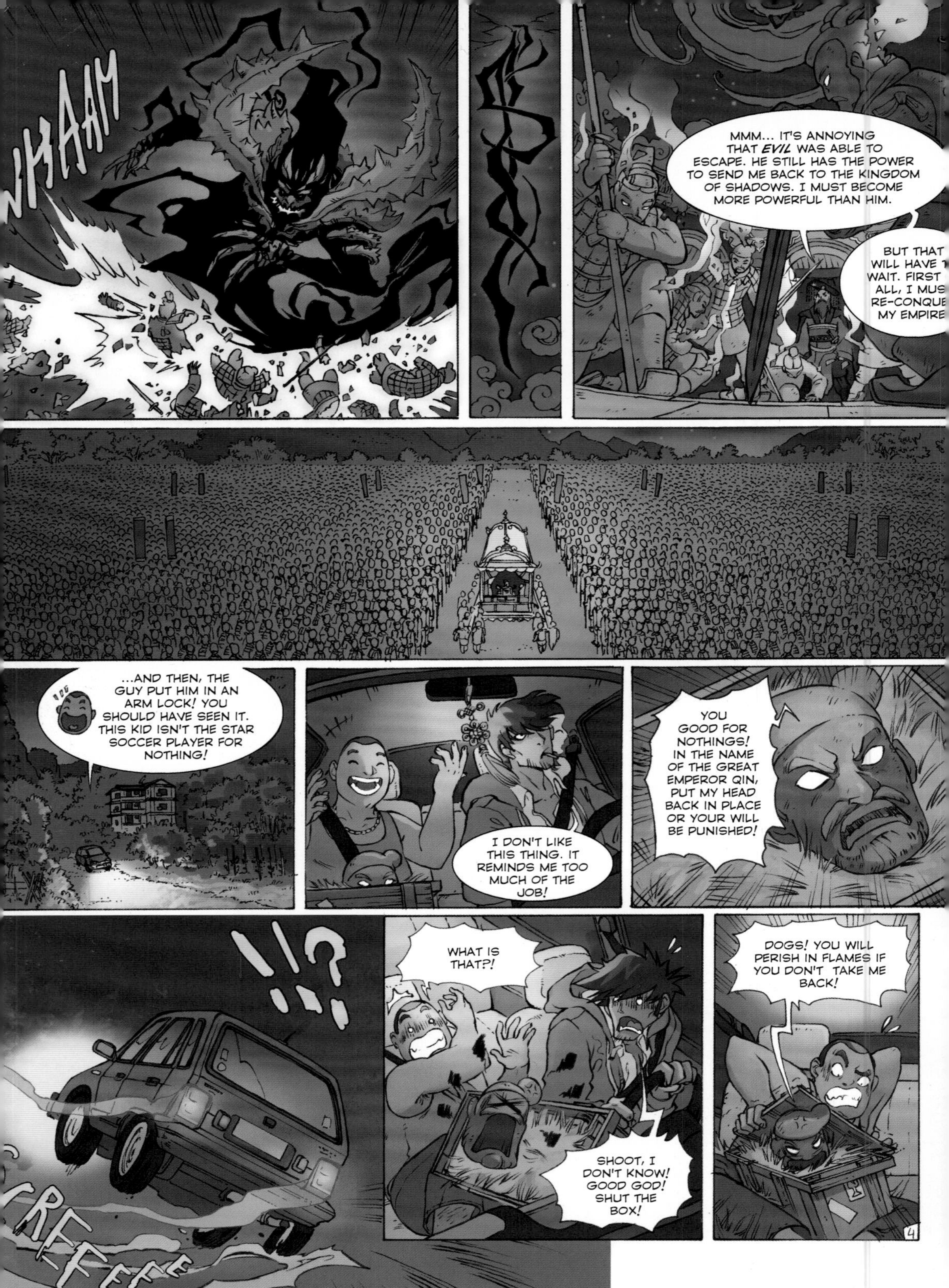
WHAAAM
MMM... IT'S ANNOYING THAT EVIL WAS ABLE TO ESCAPE. HE STILL HAS THE POWER TO SEND ME BACK TO THE KINGDOM OF SHADOWS. I MUST BECOME MORE POWERFUL THAN HIM.
BUT THAT WILL HAVE T WAIT. FIRST ALL, I MUS RE-CONQUE MY EMPIRE
...AND THEN, THE GUY PUT HIM IN AN ARM LOCK! YOU SHOULD HAVE SEEN IT. THIS KID ISN'T THE STAR SOCCER PLAYER FOR NOTHING!
I DON'T LIKE THIS THING. IT REMINDS ME TOO MUCH OF THE JOB!
YOU GOOD FOR NOTHINGS! IN THE NAME OF THE GREAT EMPEROR QIN, PUT MY HEAD BACK IN PLACE OR YOUR WILL BE PUNISHED!
!!?
WHAT IS THAT?!
SHOOT, I DON'T KNOW! GOOD GOD! SHUT THE BOX!
DOGS! YOU WILL PERISH IN FLAMES IF YOU DON'T TAKE ME BACK!
4

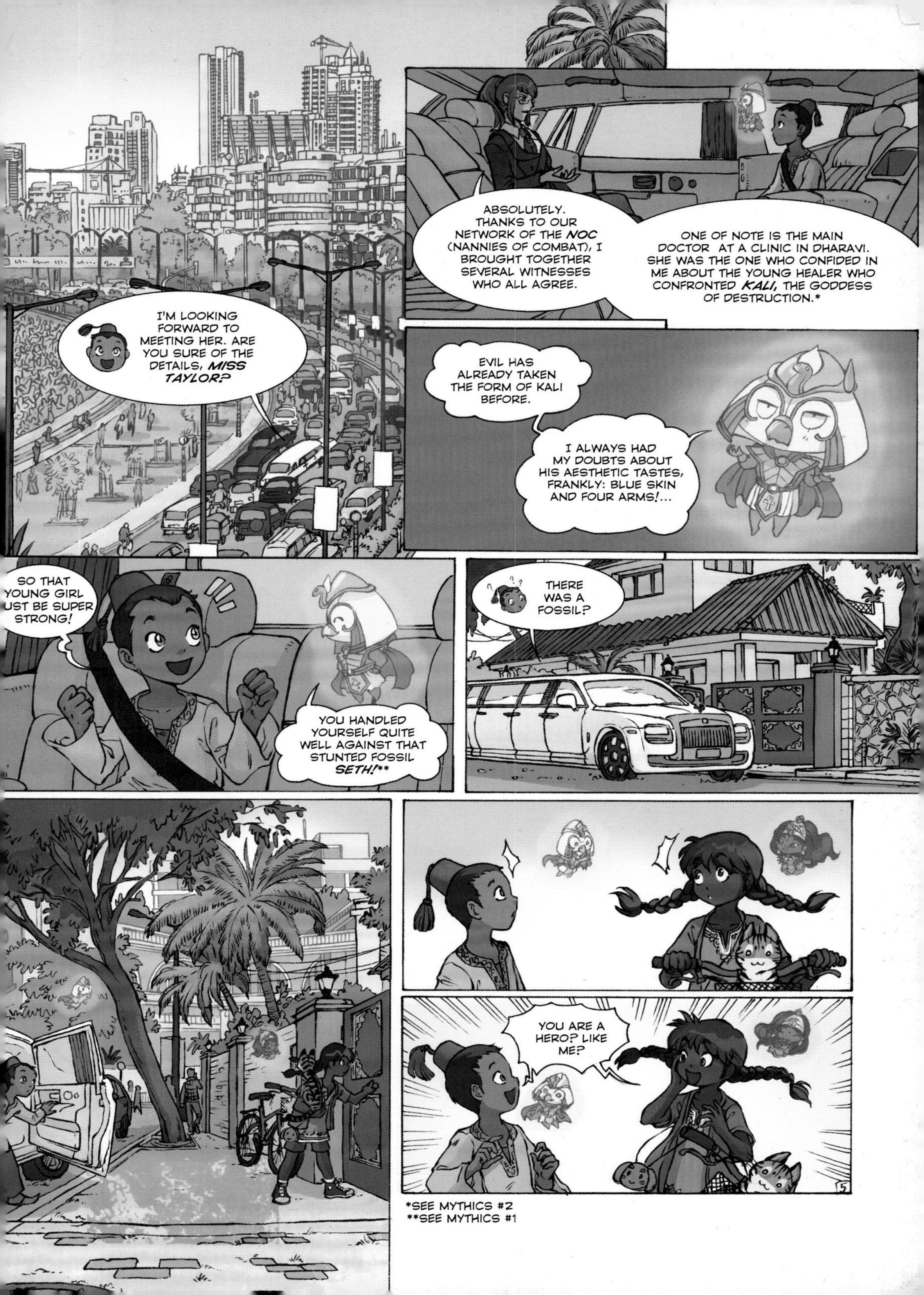
I'M LOOKING FORWARD TO MEETING HER. ARE YOU SURE OF THE DETAILS, MISS TAYLOR?
ABSOLUTELY. THANKS TO OUR NETWORK OF THE NOC (NANNIES OF COMBAT), I BROUGHT TOGETHER SEVERAL WITNESSES WHO ALL AGREE.
ONE OF NOTE IS THE MAIN DOCTOR AT A CLINIC IN DHARAVI. SHE WAS THE ONE WHO CONFIDED IN ME ABOUT THE YOUNG HEALER WHO CONFRONTED KALI, THE GODDESS OF DESTRUCTION.*
EVIL HAS ALREADY TAKEN THE FORM OF KALI BEFORE.
I ALWAYS HAD MY DOUBTS ABOUT HIS AESTHETIC TASTES, FRANKLY: BLUE SKIN AND FOUR ARMS!...
SO THAT YOUNG GIRL UST BE SUPER STRONG!
YOU HANDLED YOURSELF QUITE WELL AGAINST THAT STUNTED FOSSIL SETH!**
THERE WAS A FOSSIL?
YOU ARE A HERO? LIKE ME?

*SEE MYTHICS #2
**SEE MYTHICS #1

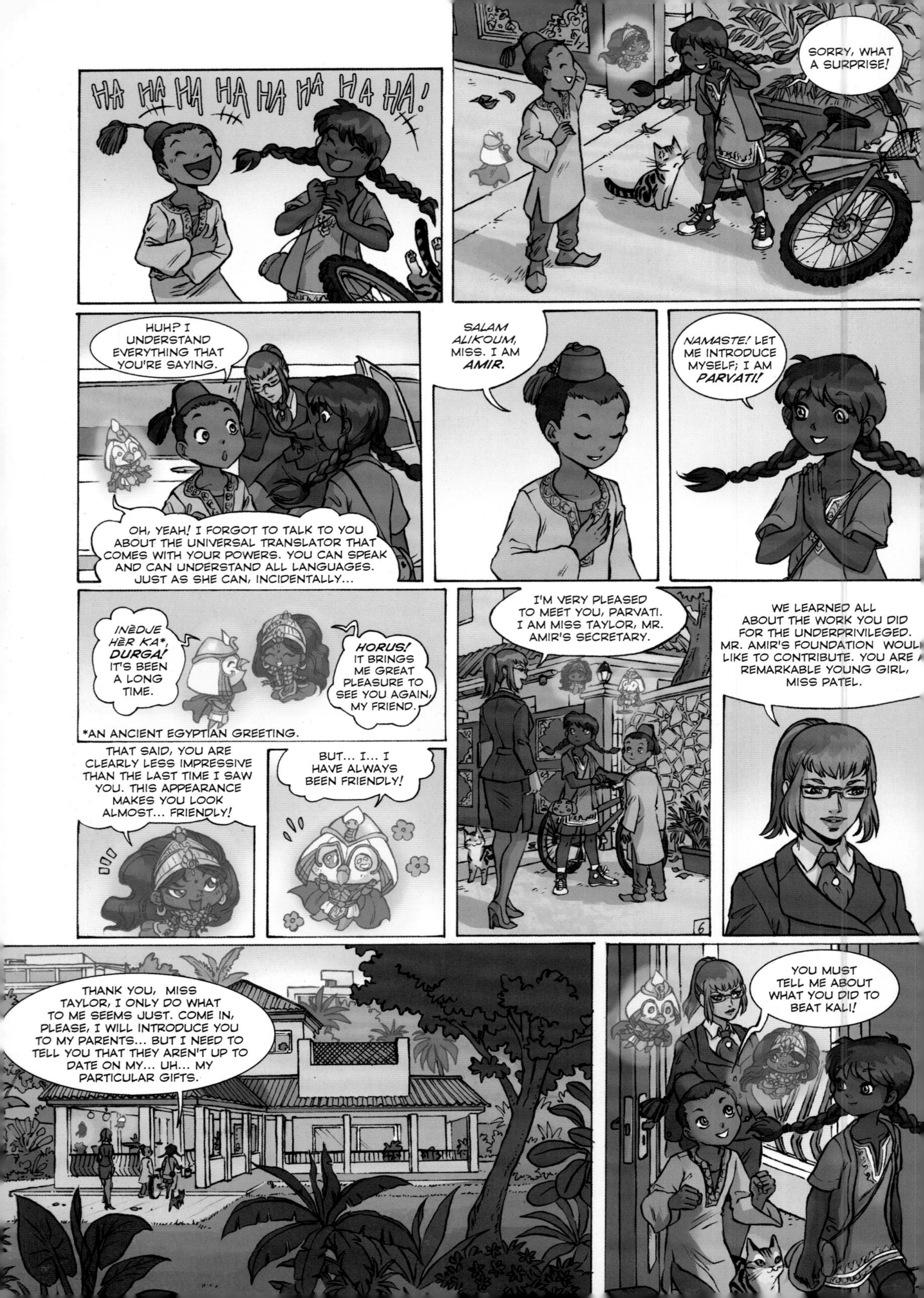
HA HA HA HA HA HA HA HA!
SORRY, WHAT A SURPRISE!
HUH? I UNDERSTAND EVERYTHING THAT YOU'RE SAYING.
OH, YEAH! I FORGOT TO TALK TO YOU ABOUT THE UNIVERSAL TRANSLATOR THAT COMES WITH YOUR POWERS. YOU CAN SPEAK AND CAN UNDERSTAND ALL LANGUAGES. JUST AS SHE CAN, INCIDENTALLY...
SALAM ALIKOUM, MISS. I AM AMIR.
NAMASTE! LET ME INTRODUCE MYSELF; I AM PARVATI!
INÈDJE HÈR KA*, DURGA! IT'S BEEN A LONG TIME.
HORUS! IT BRINGS ME GREAT PLEASURE TO SEE YOU AGAIN, MY FRIEND.
*AN ANCIENT EGYPTIAN GREETING.
THAT SAID, YOU ARE CLEARLY LESS IMPRESSIVE THAN THE LAST TIME I SAW YOU. THIS APPEARANCE MAKES YOU LOOK ALMOST... FRIENDLY!
BUT... I... I HAVE ALWAYS BEEN FRIENDLY!
I'M VERY PLEASED TO MEET YOU, PARVATI. I AM MISS TAYLOR, MR. AMIR'S SECRETARY.
6
WE LEARNED ALL ABOUT THE WORK YOU DID FOR THE UNDERPRIVILEGED. MR. AMIR'S FOUNDATION WOUL LIKE TO CONTRIBUTE. YOU ARE A REMARKABLE YOUNG GIRL, MISS PATEL.
THANK YOU, MISS TAYLOR, I ONLY DO WHAT TO ME SEEMS JUST. COME IN, PLEASE, I WILL INTRODUCE YOU TO MY PARENTS... BUT I NEED TO TELL YOU THAT THEY AREN'T UP TO DATE ON MY... UH... MY PARTICULAR GIFTS.
YOU MUST TELL ME ABOUT WHAT YOU DID TO BEAT KALI!

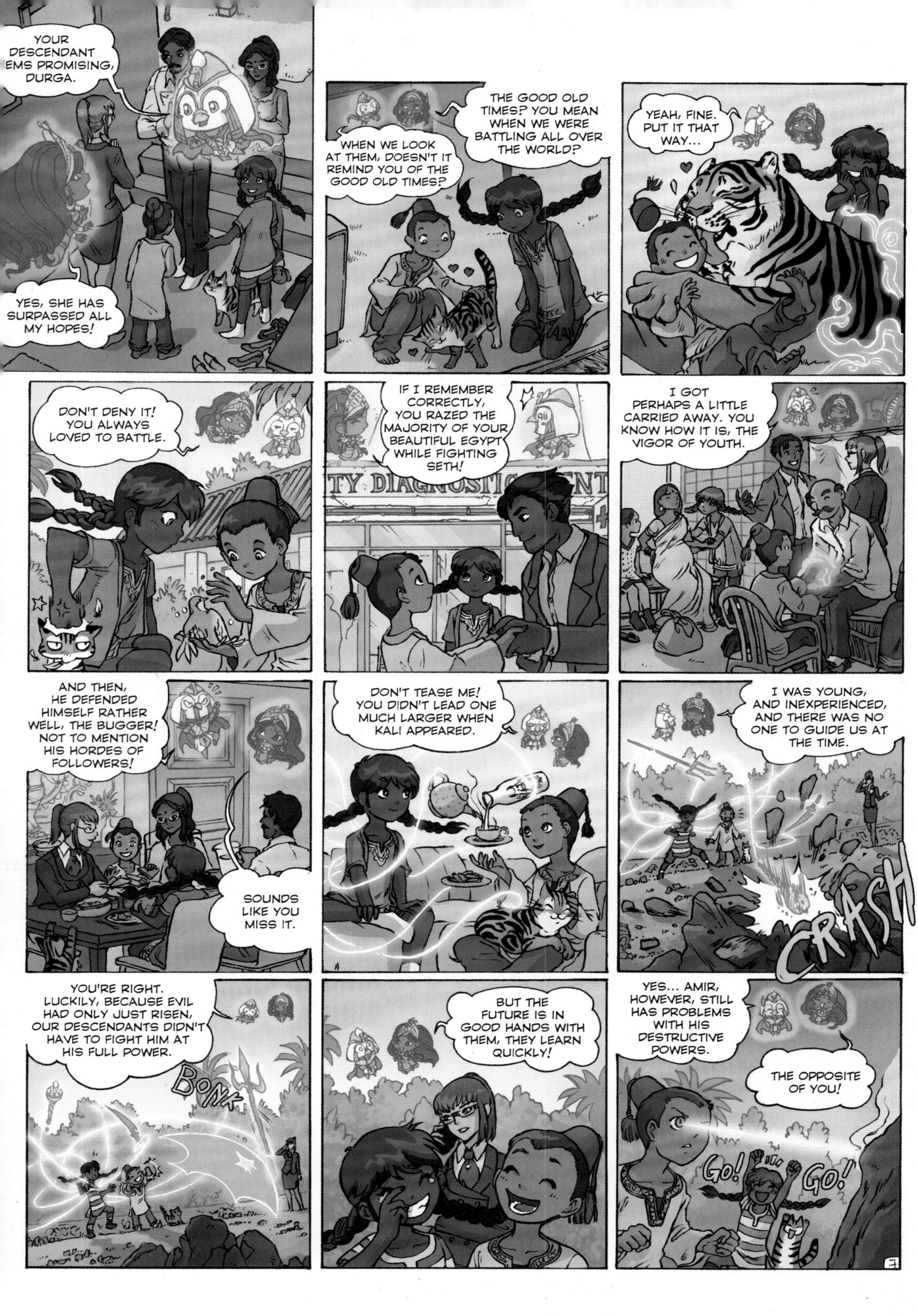
YOUR DESCENDANT EMS PROMISING, DURGA.
YES, SHE HAS SURPASSED ALL MY HOPES!
WHEN WE LOOK AT THEM, DOESN'T IT REMIND YOU OF THE GOOD OLD TIMES?
THE GOOD OLD TIMES? YOU MEAN WHEN WE WERE BATTLING ALL OVER THE WORLD?
YEAH, FINE. PUT IT THAT WAY...
DON'T DENY IT! YOU ALWAYS LOVED TO BATTLE.
IF I REMEMBER CORRECTLY, YOU RAZED THE MAJORITY OF YOUR BEAUTIFUL EGYPT WHILE FIGHTING SETH!
TY DIAGNOSTIC CENT
I GOT PERHAPS A LITTLE CARRIED AWAY. YOU KNOW HOW IT IS, THE VIGOR OF YOUTH.
AND THEN, HE DEFENDED HIMSELF RATHER WELL, THE BUGGER! NOT TO MENTION HIS HORDES OF FOLLOWERS!
SOUNDS LIKE YOU MISS IT.
DON'T TEASE ME! YOU DIDN'T LEAD ONE MUCH LARGER WHEN KALI APPEARED.
I WAS YOUNG, AND INEXPERIENCED, AND THERE WAS NO ONE TO GUIDE US AT THE TIME.
CRASH
YOU'RE RIGHT. LUCKILY, BECAUSE EVIL HAD ONLY JUST RISEN, OUR DESCENDANTS DIDN'T HAVE TO FIGHT HIM AT HIS FULL POWER.
BONK
BUT THE FUTURE IS IN GOOD HANDS WITH THEM, THEY LEARN QUICKLY!
YES... AMIR, HOWEVER, STILL HAS PROBLEMS WITH HIS DESTRUCTIVE POWERS.
THE OPPOSITE OF YOU!
GO! GO!

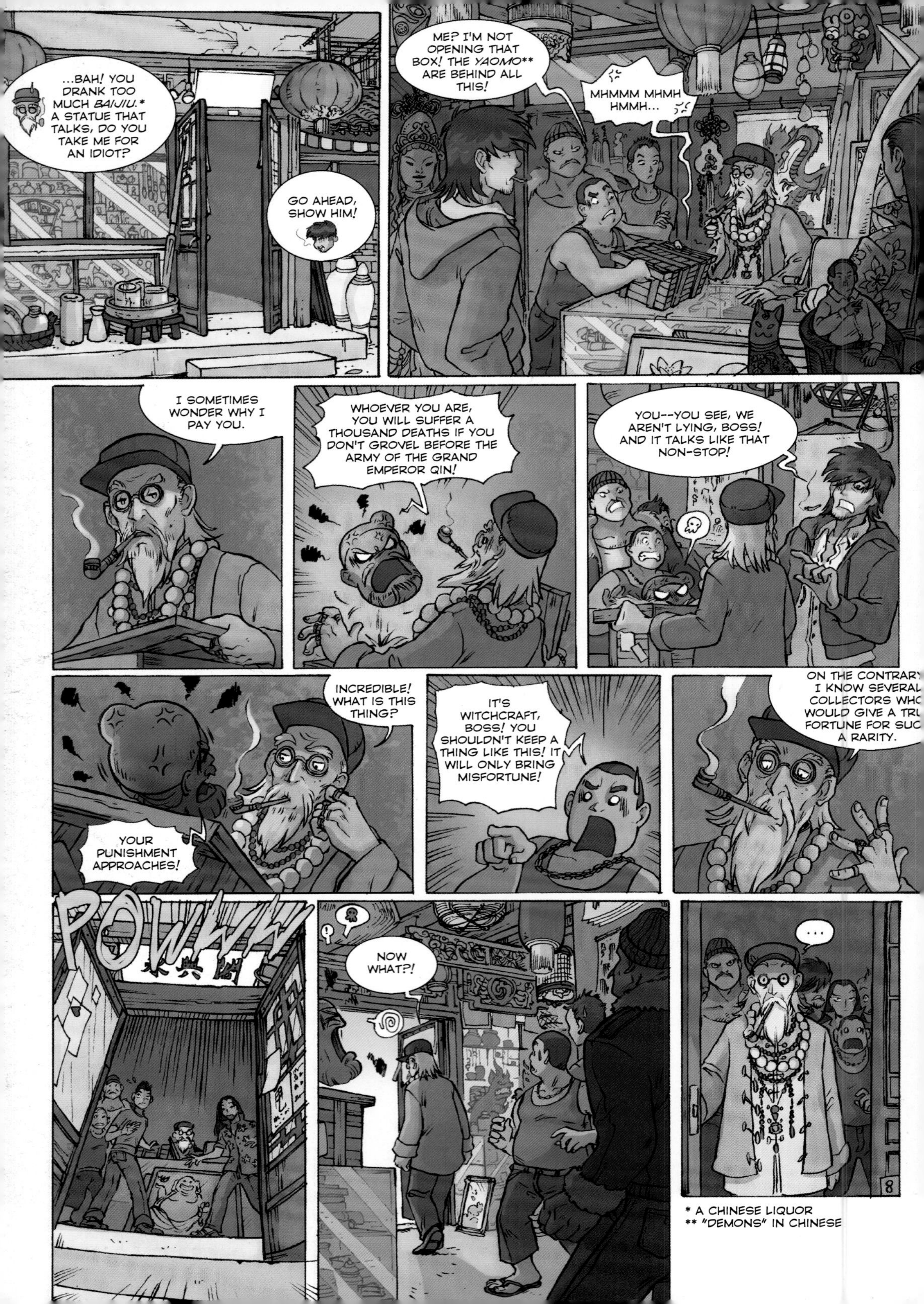
...BAH! YOU DRANK TOO MUCH BAIJIU.* A STATUE THAT TALKS, DO YOU TAKE ME FOR AN IDIOT?
GO AHEAD, SHOW HIM!
ME? I'M NOT OPENING THAT BOX! THE YAOMO** ARE BEHIND ALL THIS!
MHMMM MHMH HMMH...
I SOMETIMES WONDER WHY I PAY YOU.
WHOEVER YOU ARE, YOU WILL SUFFER A THOUSAND DEATHS IF YOU DON'T GROVEL BEFORE THE ARMY OF THE GRAND EMPEROR QIN!
YOU--YOU SEE, WE AREN'T LYING, BOSS! AND IT TALKS LIKE THAT NON-STOP!
INCREDIBLE! WHAT IS THIS THING?
YOUR PUNISHMENT APPROACHES!
IT'S WITCHCRAFT, BOSS! YOU SHOULDN'T KEEP A THING LIKE THIS! IT WILL ONLY BRING MISFORTUNE!
ON THE CONTRARY I KNOW SEVERAL COLLECTORS WHO WOULD GIVE A TRU FORTUNE FOR SUC A RARITY.
POWWW
NOW WHAT?!
...



* A CHINESE LIQUOR
** "DEMONS" IN CHINESE

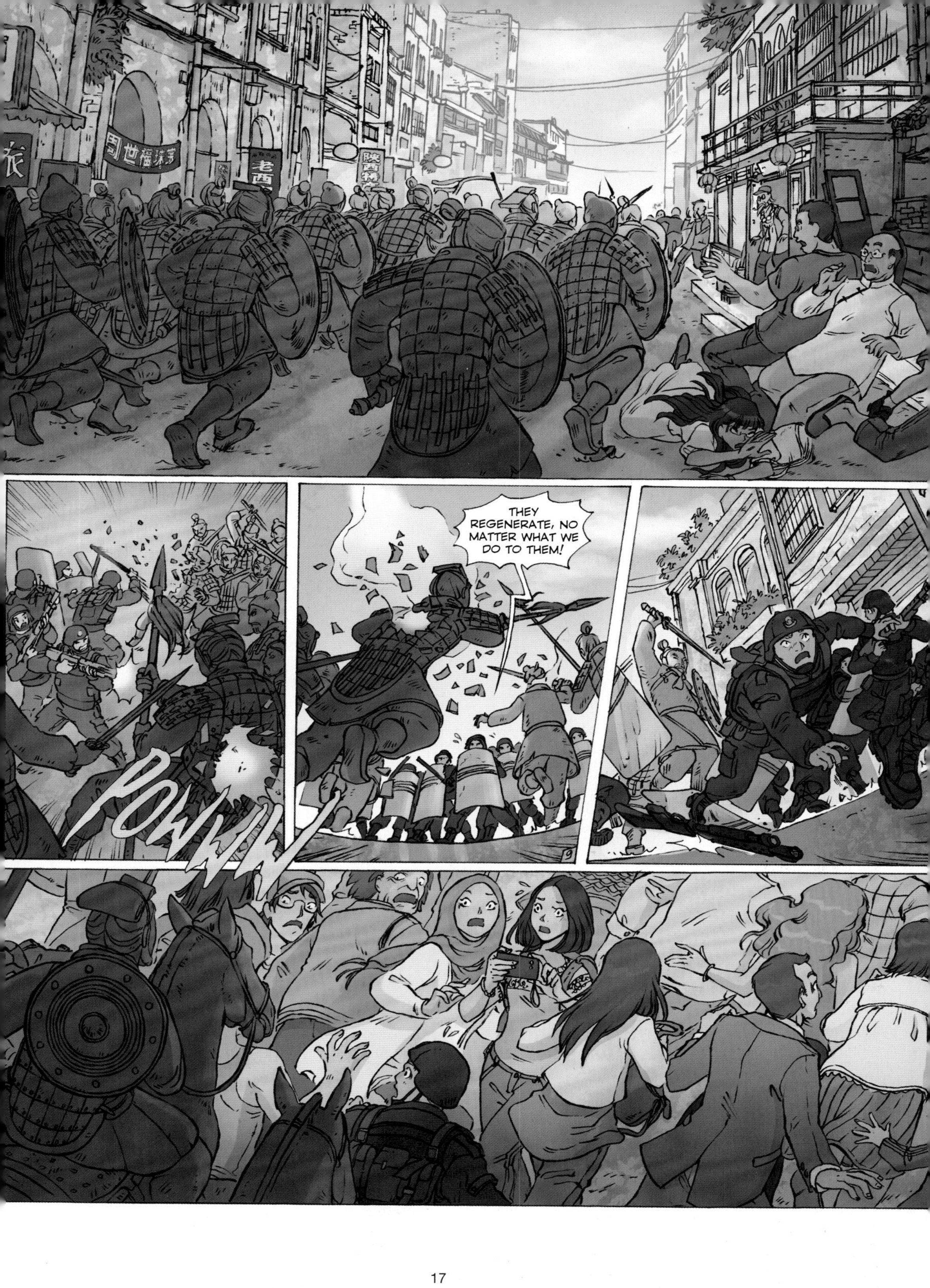
THEY REGENERATE, NO MATTER WHAT WE DO TO THEM!
POWWW

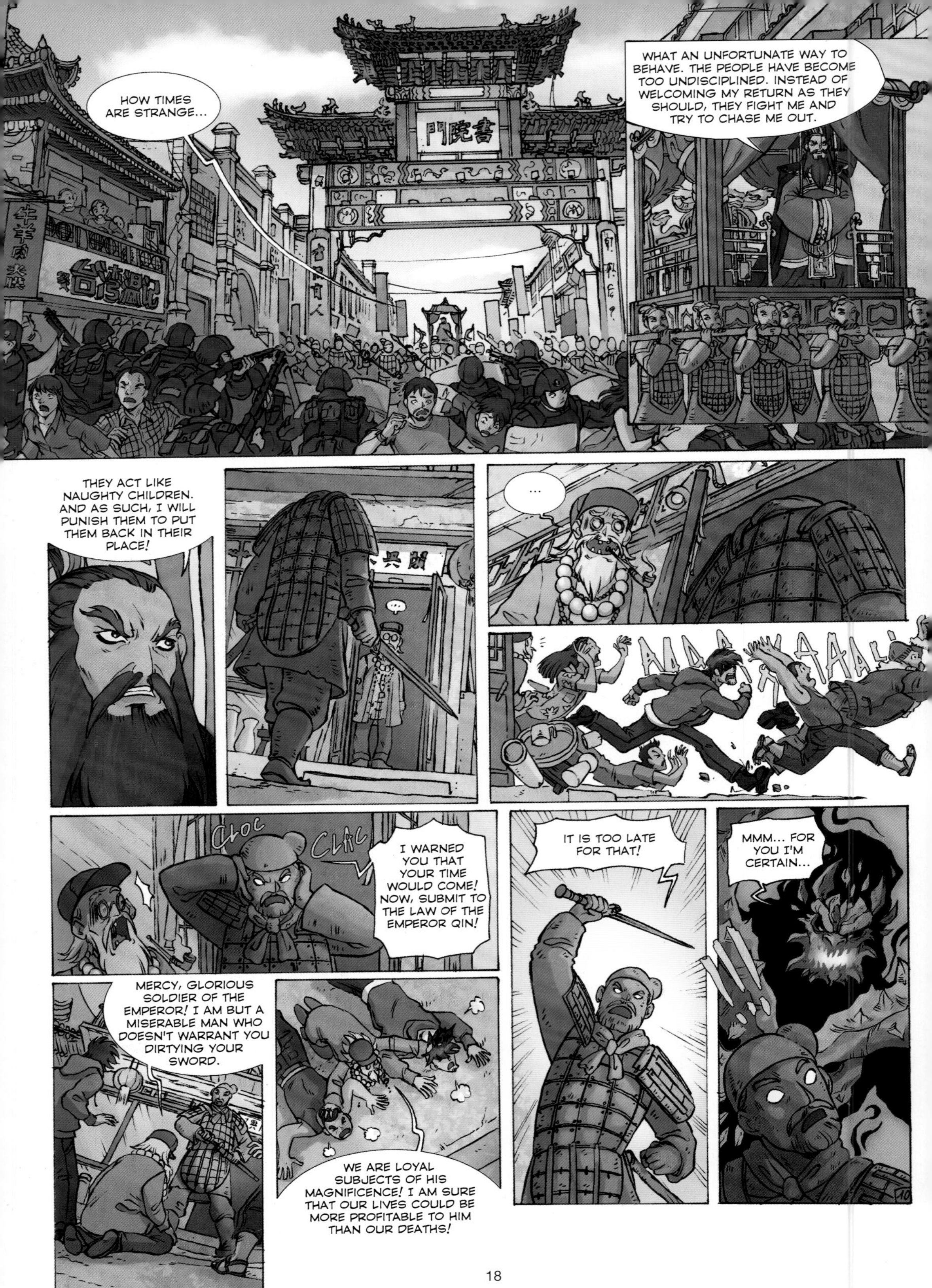
HOW TIMES ARE STRANGE...
WHAT AN UNFORTUNATE WAY TO BEHAVE. THE PEOPLE HAVE BECOME TOO UNDISCIPLINED. INSTEAD OF WELCOMING MY RETURN AS THEY SHOULD, THEY FIGHT ME AND TRY TO CHASE ME OUT.
THEY ACT LIKE NAUGHTY CHILDREN. AND AS SUCH, I WILL PUNISH THEM TO PUT THEM BACK IN THEIR PLACE!
...
AAAA AAAAAAAL!
CLOC
CLAC
I WARNED YOU THAT YOUR TIME WOULD COME! NOW, SUBMIT TO THE LAW OF THE EMPEROR QIN!
MERCY, GLORIOUS SOLDIER OF THE EMPEROR! I AM BUT A MISERABLE MAN WHO DOESN'T WARRANT YOU DIRTYING YOUR SWORD.
WE ARE LOYAL SUBJECTS OF HIS MAGNIFICENCE! I AM SURE THAT OUR LIVES COULD BE MORE PROFITABLE TO HIM THAN OUR DEATHS!
IT IS TOO LATE FOR THAT!
MMM... FOR YOU I'M CERTAIN...

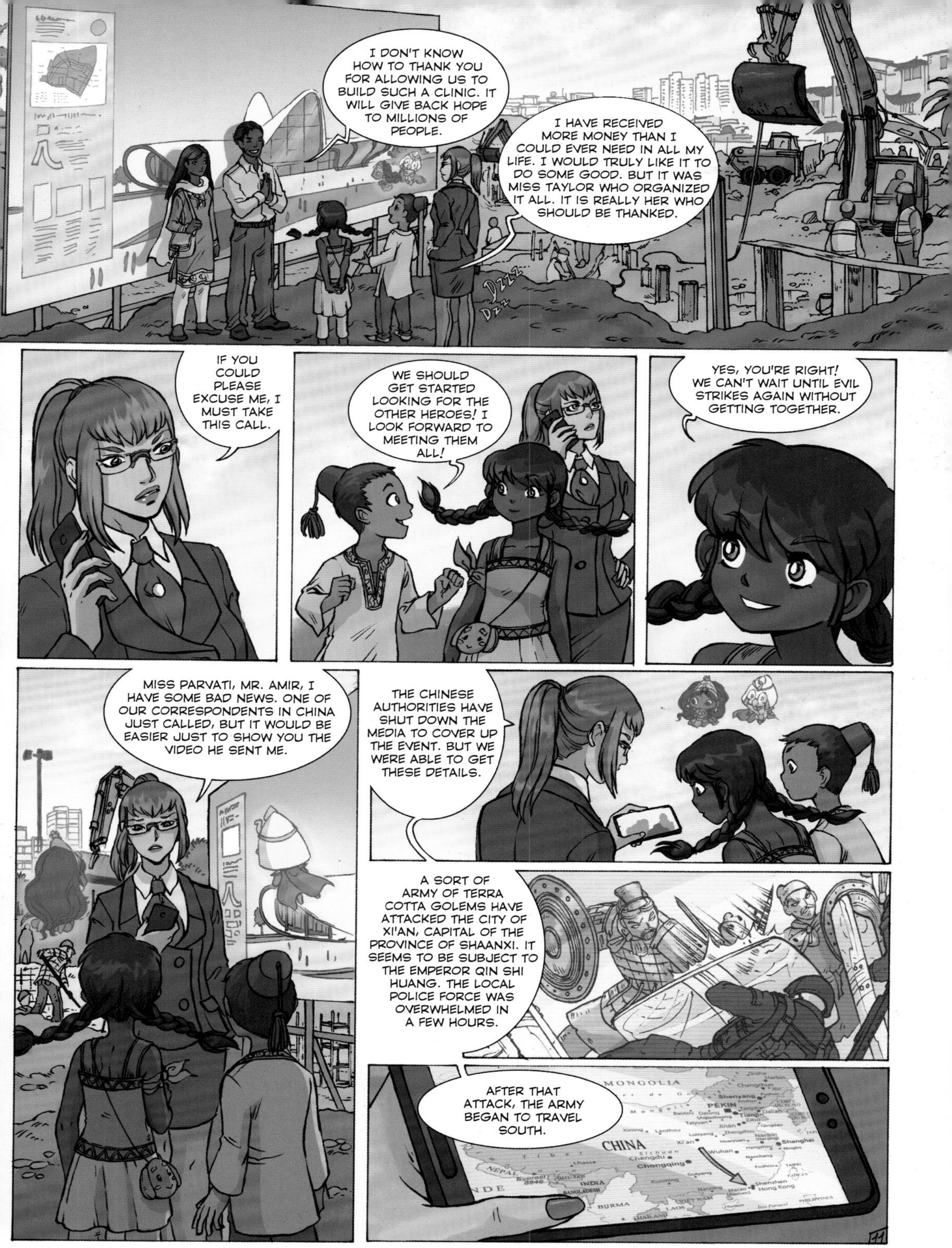
I DON'T KNOW HOW TO THANK YOU FOR ALLOWING US TO BUILD SUCH A CLINIC. IT WILL GIVE BACK HOPE TO MILLIONS OF PEOPLE.
I HAVE RECEIVED MORE MONEY THAN I COULD EVER NEED IN ALL MY LIFE. I WOULD TRULY LIKE IT TO DO SOME GOOD. BUT IT WAS MISS TAYLOR WHO ORGANIZED IT ALL. IT IS REALLY HER WHO SHOULD BE THANKED.
Dzzz
Dzz
IF YOU COULD PLEASE EXCUSE ME, I MUST TAKE THIS CALL.
WE SHOULD GET STARTED LOOKING FOR THE OTHER HEROES! I LOOK FORWARD TO MEETING THEM ALL!
YES, YOU'RE RIGHT! WE CAN'T WAIT UNTIL EVIL STRIKES AGAIN WITHOUT GETTING TOGETHER.
MISS PARVATI, MR. AMIR, I HAVE SOME BAD NEWS. ONE OF OUR CORRESPONDENTS IN CHINA JUST CALLED, BUT IT WOULD BE EASIER JUST TO SHOW YOU THE VIDEO HE SENT ME.
THE CHINESE AUTHORITIES HAVE SHUT DOWN THE MEDIA TO COVER UP THE EVENT. BUT WE WERE ABLE TO GET THESE DETAILS.
A SORT OF ARMY OF TERRA COTTA GOLEMS HAVE ATTACKED THE CITY OF XI'AN, CAPITAL OF THE PROVINCE OF SHAANXI. IT SEEMS TO BE SUBJECT TO THE EMPEROR QIN SHI HUANG. THE LOCAL POLICE FORCE WAS OVERWHELMED IN A FEW HOURS.
AFTER THAT ATTACK, THE ARMY BEGAN TO TRAVEL SOUTH.
MONGOLIA
CHINA
PEKIN
Chengdu
Chongqing
11

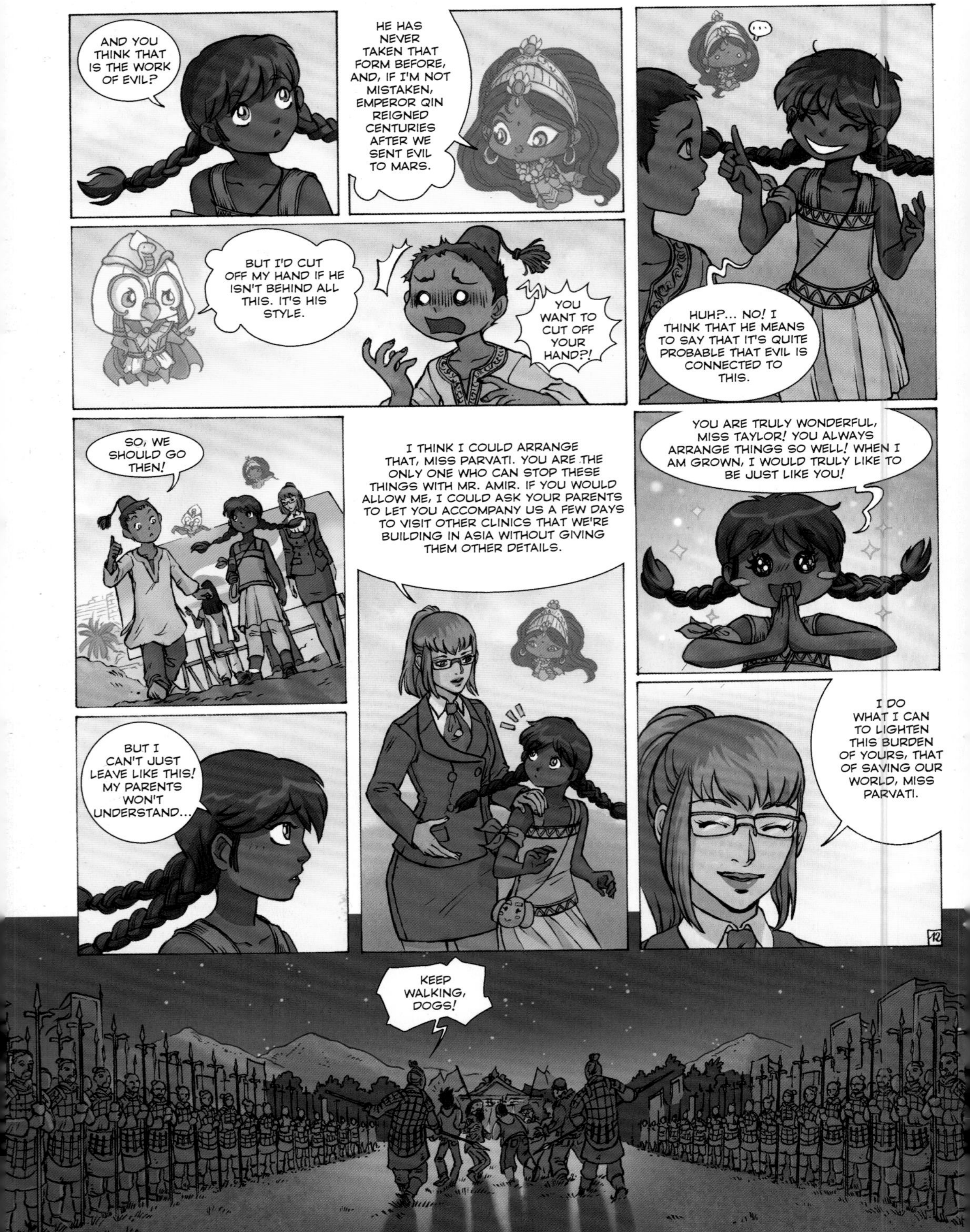
AND YOU THINK THAT IS THE WORK OF EVIL?
HE HAS NEVER TAKEN THAT FORM BEFORE, AND, IF I'M NOT MISTAKEN, EMPEROR QIN REIGNED CENTURIES AFTER WE SENT EVIL TO MARS.
BUT I'D CUT OFF MY HAND IF HE ISN'T BEHIND ALL THIS. IT'S HIS STYLE.
YOU WANT TO CUT OFF YOUR HAND?!
...
HUH?... NO! I THINK THAT HE MEANS TO SAY THAT IT'S QUITE PROBABLE THAT EVIL IS CONNECTED TO THIS.
SO, WE SHOULD GO THEN!
BUT I CAN'T JUST LEAVE LIKE THIS! MY PARENTS WON'T UNDERSTAND...
I THINK I COULD ARRANGE THAT, MISS PARVATI. YOU ARE THE ONLY ONE WHO CAN STOP THESE THINGS WITH MR. AMIR. IF YOU WOULD ALLOW ME, I COULD ASK YOUR PARENTS TO LET YOU ACCOMPANY US A FEW DAYS TO VISIT OTHER CLINICS THAT WE'RE BUILDING IN ASIA WITHOUT GIVING THEM OTHER DETAILS.
YOU ARE TRULY WONDERFUL, MISS TAYLOR! YOU ALWAYS ARRANGE THINGS SO WELL! WHEN I AM GROWN, I WOULD TRULY LIKE TO BE JUST LIKE YOU!
I DO WHAT I CAN TO LIGHTEN THIS BURDEN OF YOURS, THAT OF SAVING OUR WORLD, MISS PARVATI.
KEEP WALKING, DOGS!

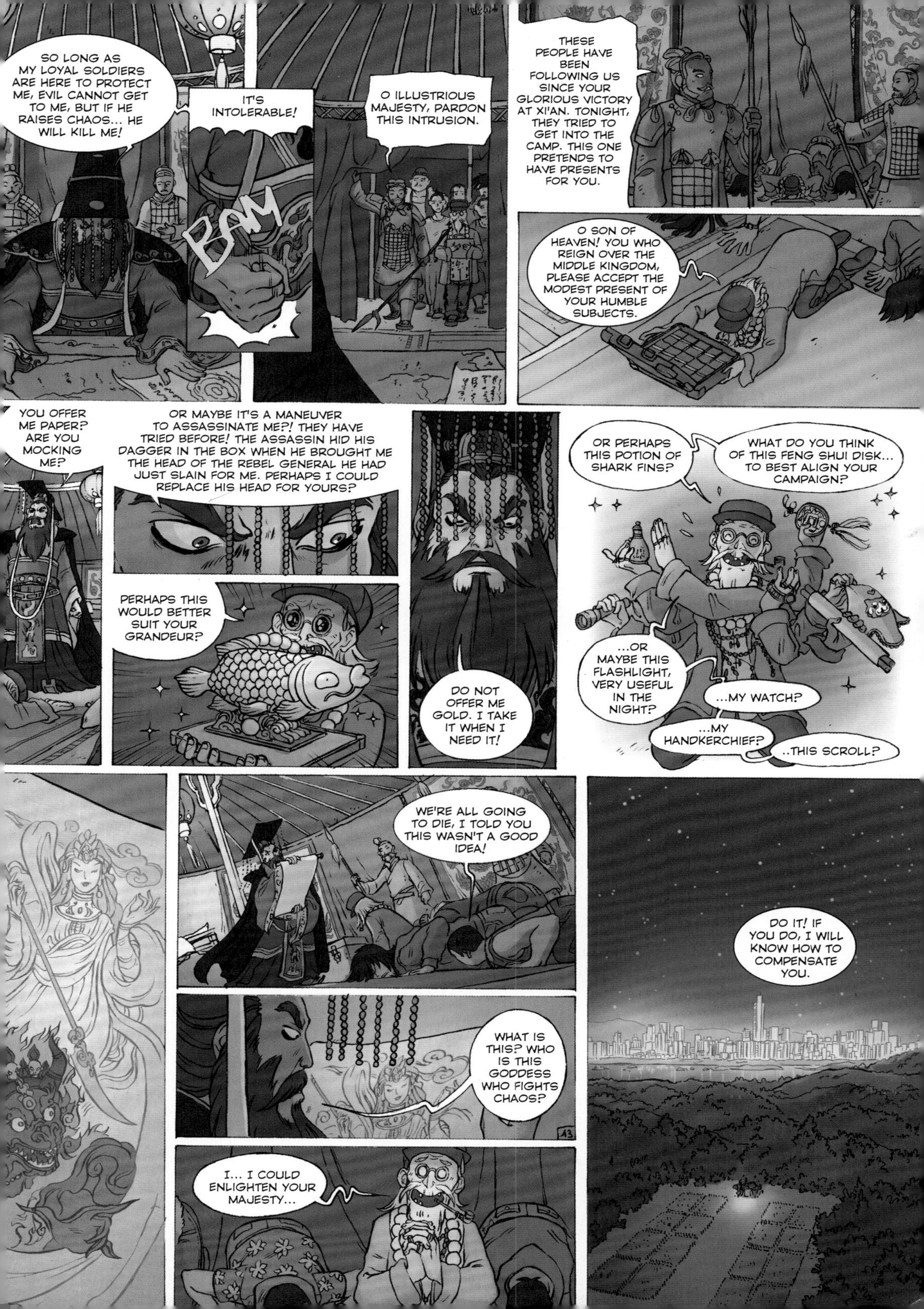
SO LONG AS MY LOYAL SOLDIERS ARE HERE TO PROTECT ME, EVIL CANNOT GET TO ME, BUT IF HE RAISES CHAOS... HE WILL KILL ME!
IT'S INTOLERABLE!
BAM
O ILLUSTRIOUS MAJESTY, PARDON THIS INTRUSION.
THESE PEOPLE HAVE BEEN FOLLOWING US SINCE YOUR GLORIOUS VICTORY AT XI'AN. TONIGHT, THEY TRIED TO GET INTO THE CAMP. THIS ONE PRETENDS TO HAVE PRESENTS FOR YOU.
O SON OF HEAVEN! YOU WHO REIGN OVER THE MIDDLE KINGDOM, PLEASE ACCEPT THE MODEST PRESENT OF YOUR HUMBLE SUBJECTS.
YOU OFFER ME PAPER? ARE YOU MOCKING ME?
OR MAYBE IT'S A MANEUVER TO ASSASSINATE ME?! THEY HAVE TRIED BEFORE! THE ASSASSIN HID HIS DAGGER IN THE BOX WHEN HE BROUGHT ME THE HEAD OF THE REBEL GENERAL HE HAD JUST SLAIN FOR ME. PERHAPS I COULD REPLACE HIS HEAD FOR YOURS?
PERHAPS THIS WOULD BETTER SUIT YOUR GRANDEUR?
DO NOT OFFER ME GOLD. I TAKE IT WHEN I NEED IT!
OR PERHAPS THIS POTION OF SHARK FINS?
WHAT DO YOU THINK OF THIS FENG SHUI DISK... TO BEST ALIGN YOUR CAMPAIGN?
...OR MAYBE THIS FLASHLIGHT, VERY USEFUL IN THE NIGHT?
...MY WATCH?
...MY HANDKERCHIEF?
..THIS SCROLL?
WE'RE ALL GOING TO DIE, I TOLD YOU THIS WASN'T A GOOD IDEA!
WHAT IS THIS? WHO IS THIS GODDESS WHO FIGHTS CHAOS?
13
I... I COULD ENLIGHTEN YOUR MAJESTY...
DO IT! IF YOU DO, I WILL KNOW HOW TO COMPENSATE YOU.

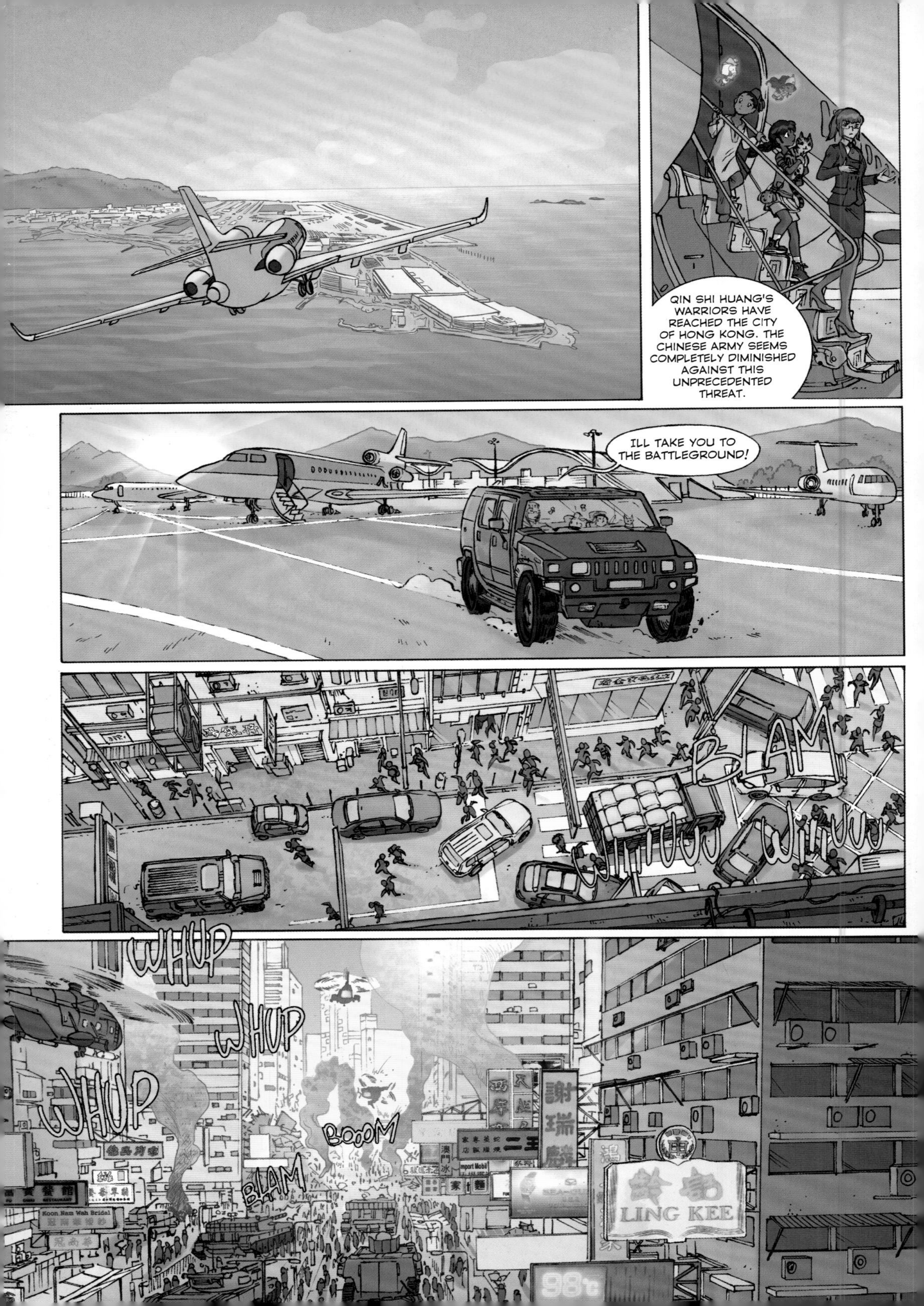
QIN SHI HUANG'S WARRIORS HAVE REACHED THE CITY OF HONG KONG. THE CHINESE ARMY SEEMS COMPLETELY DIMINISHED AGAINST THIS UNPRECEDENTED THREAT.
ILL TAKE YOU TO THE BATTLEGROUND!
BLAM
WHUP
WHUP
WHUP
BOOOM
BLAM
LING KEE

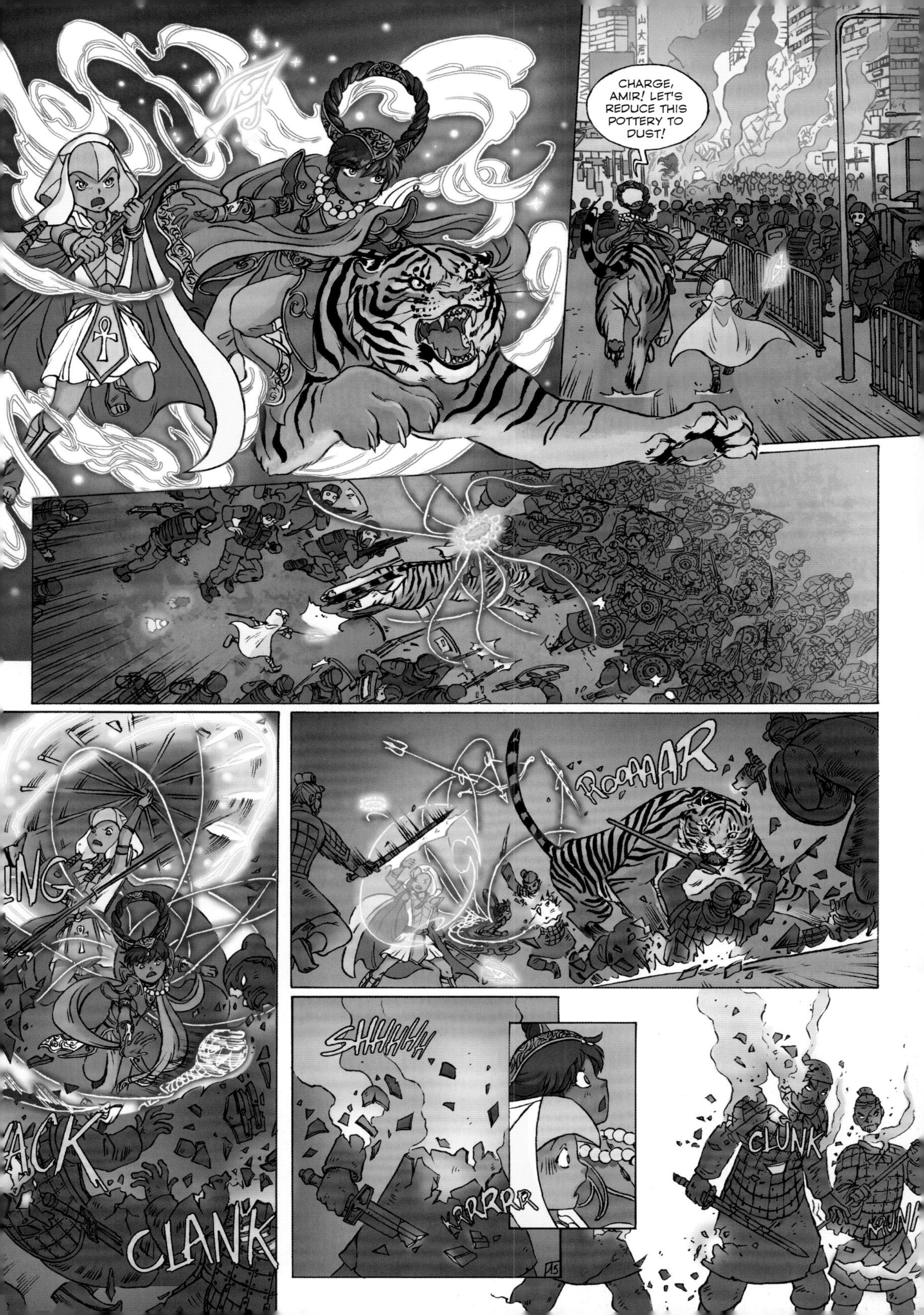
CHARGE, AMIR! LET'S REDUCE THIS POTTERY TO DUST!
ING
ACK
CLANK
ROOAAAR
SHHHHH
KRRRRR
CLUNK
KRUN

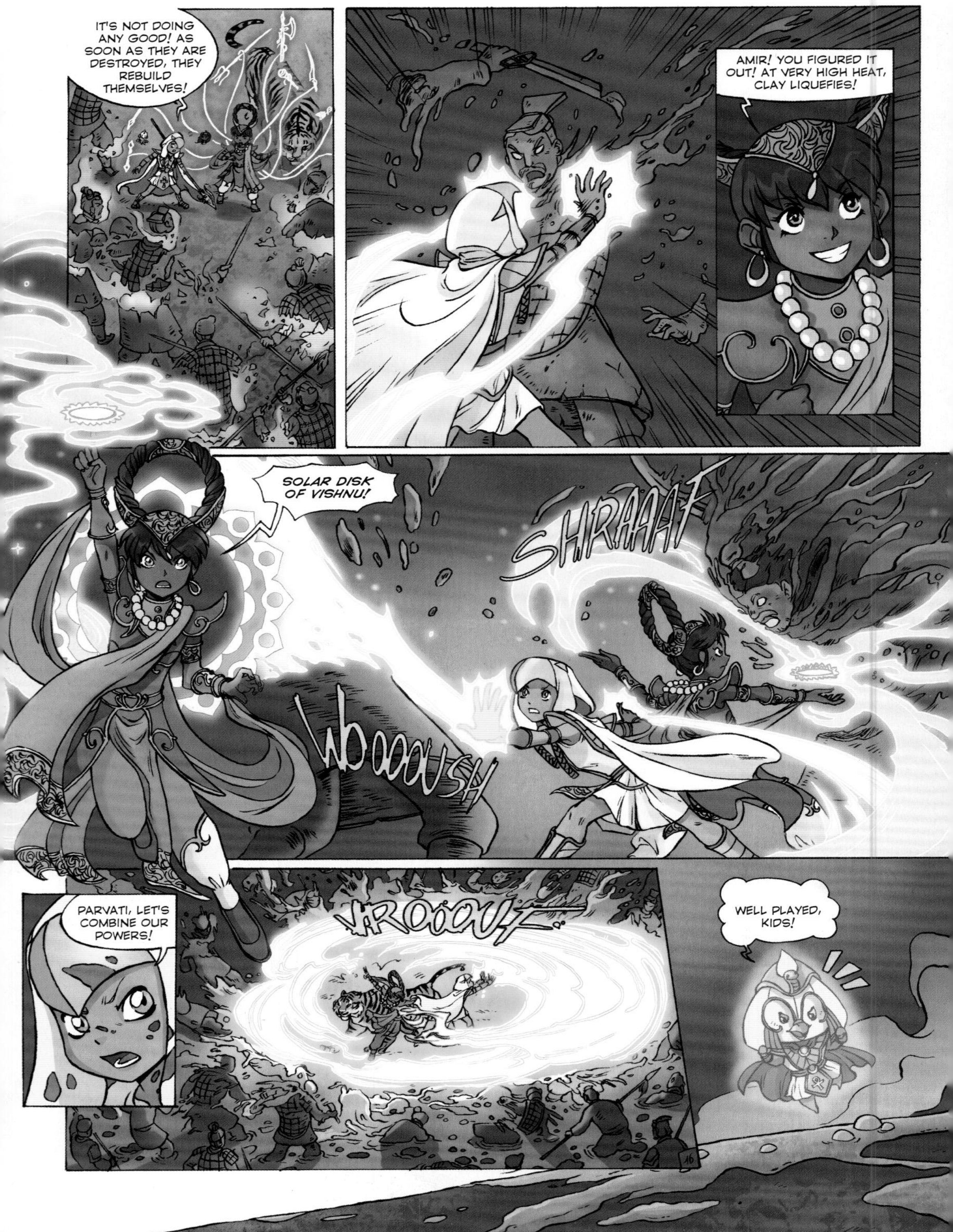
IT'S NOT DOING ANY GOOD! AS SOON AS THEY ARE DESTROYED, THEY REBUILD THEMSELVES!
AMIR! YOU FIGURED IT OUT! AT VERY HIGH HEAT, CLAY LIQUEFIES!
SOLAR DISK OF VISHNU!
SHRAAAF
WOOOOUSH
PARVATI, LET'S COMBINE OUR POWERS!
VROOOUF
WELL PLAYED, KIDS!
46

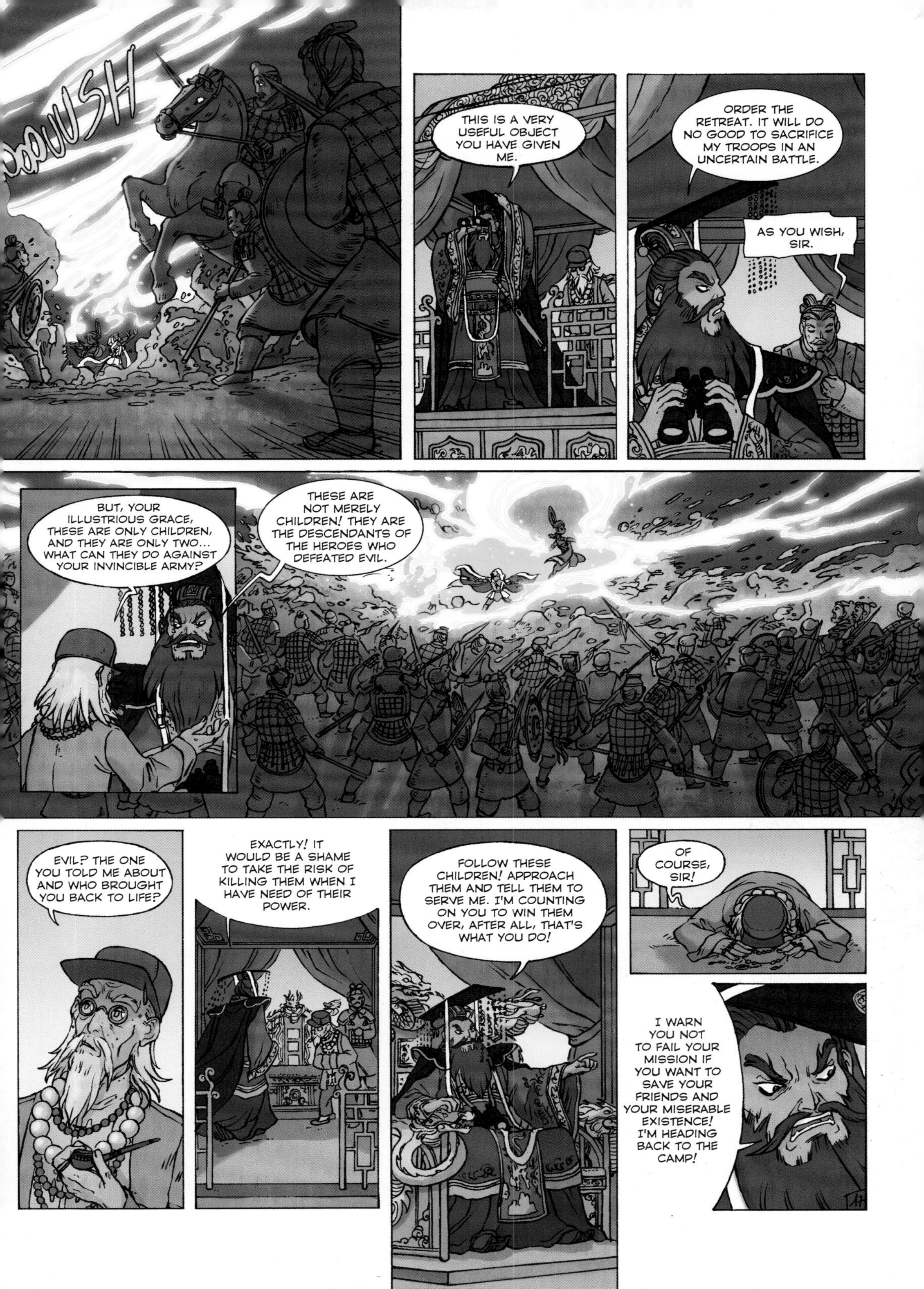
FOOOUUSH
THIS IS A VERY USEFUL OBJECT YOU HAVE GIVEN ME.
ORDER THE RETREAT. IT WILL DO NO GOOD TO SACRIFICE MY TROOPS IN AN UNCERTAIN BATTLE.
AS YOU WISH, SIR.
BUT, YOUR ILLUSTRIOUS GRACE, THESE ARE ONLY CHILDREN, AND THEY ARE ONLY TWO... WHAT CAN THEY DO AGAINST YOUR INVINCIBLE ARMY?
THESE ARE NOT MERELY CHILDREN! THEY ARE THE DESCENDANTS OF THE HEROES WHO DEFEATED EVIL.
EVIL? THE ONE YOU TOLD ME ABOUT AND WHO BROUGHT YOU BACK TO LIFE?
EXACTLY! IT WOULD BE A SHAME TO TAKE THE RISK OF KILLING THEM WHEN I HAVE NEED OF THEIR POWER.
FOLLOW THESE CHILDREN! APPROACH THEM AND TELL THEM TO SERVE ME. I'M COUNTING ON YOU TO WIN THEM OVER, AFTER ALL, THAT'S WHAT YOU DO!
OF COURSE, SIR!
I WARN YOU NOT TO FAIL YOUR MISSION IF YOU WANT TO SAVE YOUR FRIENDS AND YOUR MISERABLE EXISTENCE! I'M HEADING BACK TO THE CAMP!

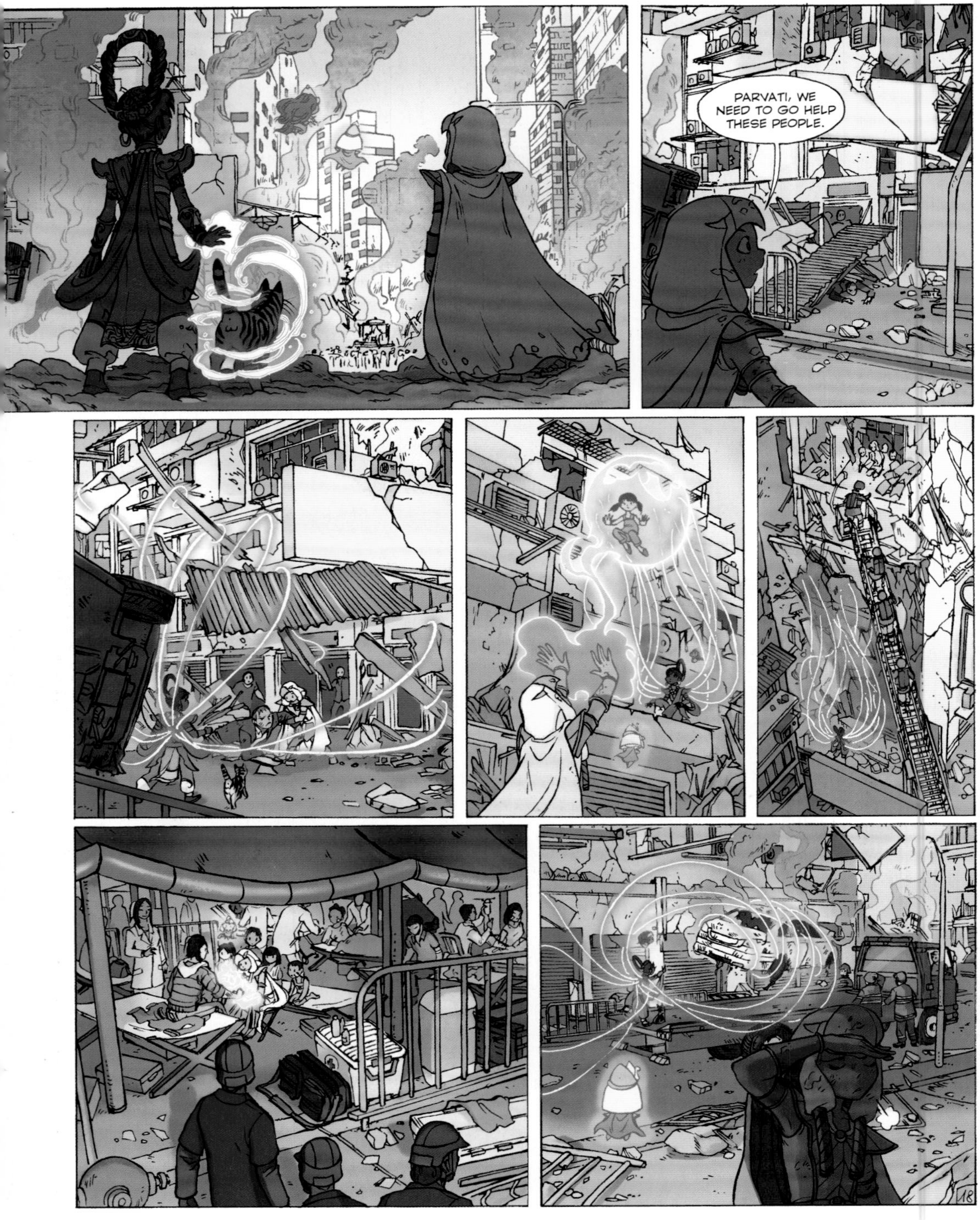
PARVATI, WE NEED TO GO HELP THESE PEOPLE.

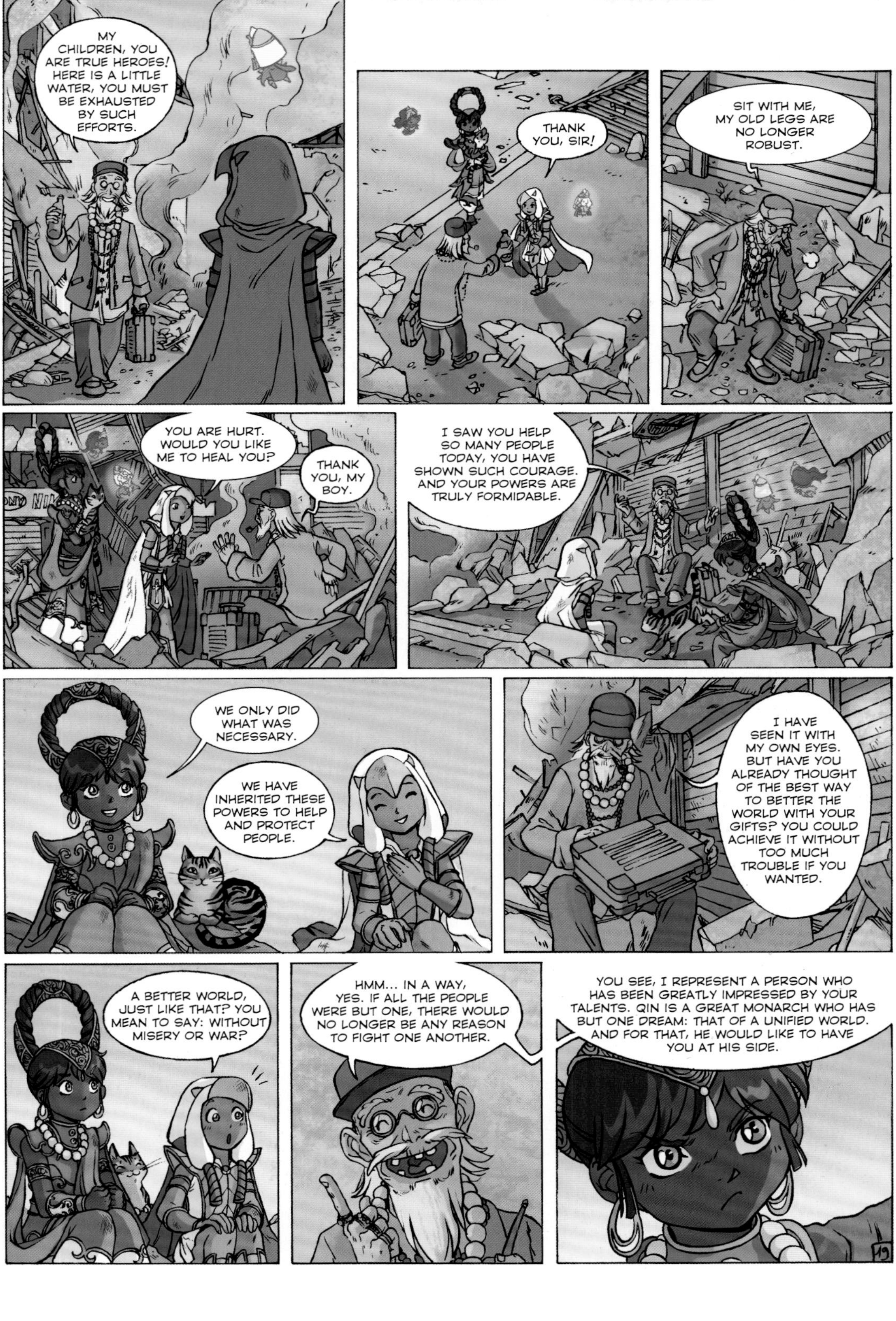
MY CHILDREN, YOU ARE TRUE HEROES! HERE IS A LITTLE WATER, YOU MUST BE EXHAUSTED BY SUCH EFFORTS.
THANK YOU, SIR!
SIT WITH ME, MY OLD LEGS ARE NO LONGER ROBUST.
YOU ARE HURT. WOULD YOU LIKE ME TO HEAL YOU?
THANK YOU, MY BOY.
I SAW YOU HELP SO MANY PEOPLE TODAY, YOU HAVE SHOWN SUCH COURAGE. AND YOUR POWERS ARE TRULY FORMIDABLE.
WE ONLY DID WHAT WAS NECESSARY.
WE HAVE INHERITED THESE POWERS TO HELP AND PROTECT PEOPLE.
I HAVE SEEN IT WITH MY OWN EYES. BUT HAVE YOU ALREADY THOUGHT OF THE BEST WAY TO BETTER THE WORLD WITH YOUR GIFTS? YOU COULD ACHIEVE IT WITHOUT TOO MUCH TROUBLE IF YOU WANTED.
A BETTER WORLD, JUST LIKE THAT? YOU MEAN TO SAY: WITHOUT MISERY OR WAR?
HMM... IN A WAY, YES. IF ALL THE PEOPLE WERE BUT ONE, THERE WOULD NO LONGER BE ANY REASON TO FIGHT ONE ANOTHER.
YOU SEE, I REPRESENT A PERSON WHO HAS BEEN GREATLY IMPRESSED BY YOUR TALENTS. QIN IS A GREAT MONARCH WHO HAS BUT ONE DREAM: THAT OF A UNIFIED WORLD. AND FOR THAT, HE WOULD LIKE TO HAVE YOU AT HIS SIDE.
19

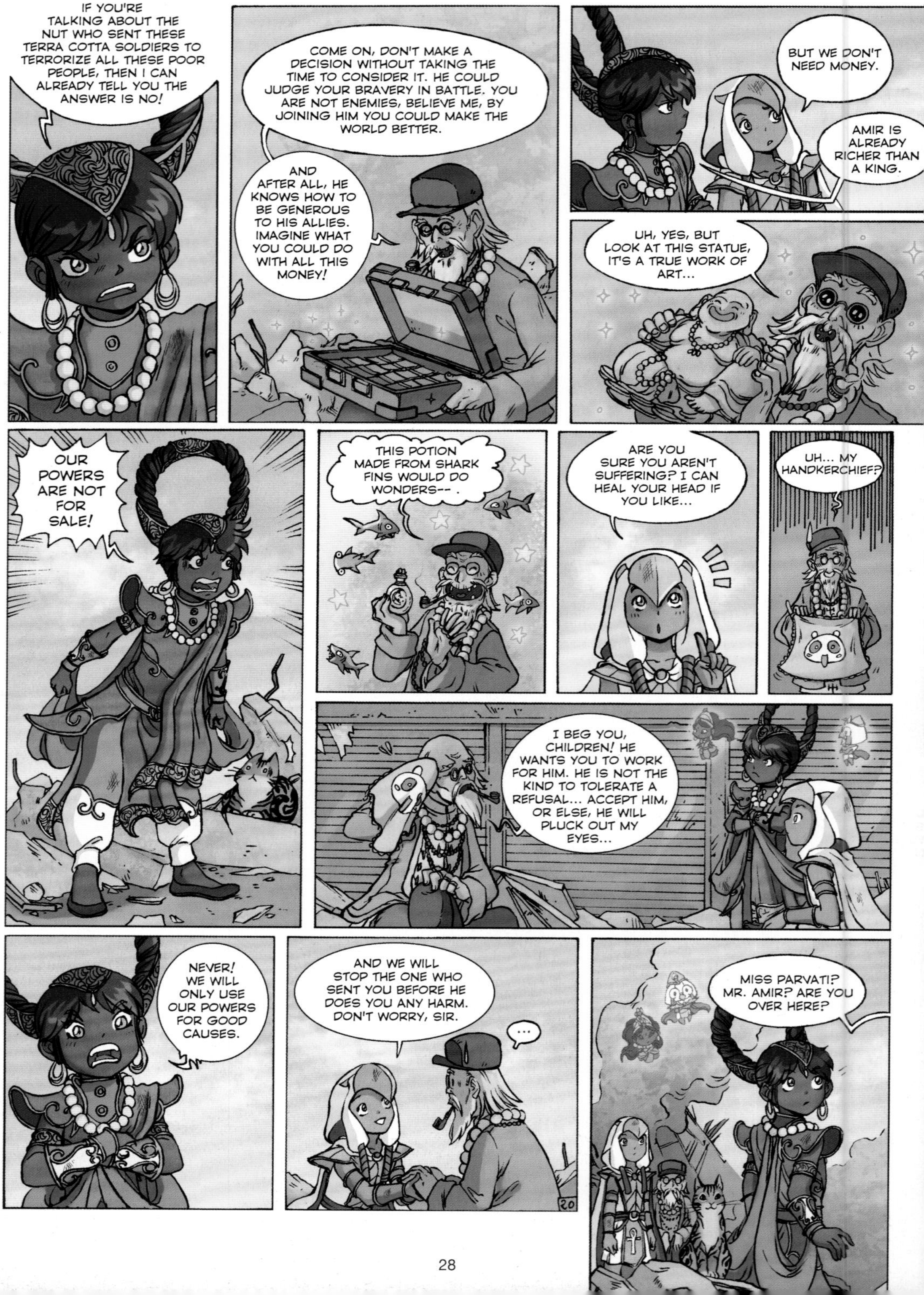
IF YOU'RE TALKING ABOUT THE NUT WHO SENT THESE TERRA COTTA SOLDIERS TO TERRORIZE ALL THESE POOR PEOPLE, THEN I CAN ALREADY TELL YOU THE ANSWER IS NO!
COME ON, DON'T MAKE A DECISION WITHOUT TAKING THE TIME TO CONSIDER IT. HE COULD JUDGE YOUR BRAVERY IN BATTLE. YOU ARE NOT ENEMIES, BELIEVE ME, BY JOINING HIM YOU COULD MAKE THE WORLD BETTER.
AND AFTER ALL, HE KNOWS HOW TO BE GENEROUS TO HIS ALLIES. IMAGINE WHAT YOU COULD DO WITH ALL THIS MONEY!
BUT WE DON'T NEED MONEY.
AMIR IS ALREADY RICHER THAN A KING.
UH, YES, BUT LOOK AT THIS STATUE, IT'S A TRUE WORK OF ART...
OUR POWERS ARE NOT FOR SALE!
THIS POTION MADE FROM SHARK FINS WOULD DO WONDERS-- .
ARE YOU SURE YOU AREN'T SUFFERING? I CAN HEAL YOUR HEAD IF YOU LIKE...
UH... MY HANDKERCHIEF?
I BEG YOU, CHILDREN! HE WANTS YOU TO WORK FOR HIM. HE IS NOT THE KIND TO TOLERATE A REFUSAL... ACCEPT HIM, OR ELSE, HE WILL PLUCK OUT MY EYES...
NEVER! WE WILL ONLY USE OUR POWERS FOR GOOD CAUSES.
AND WE WILL STOP THE ONE WHO SENT YOU BEFORE HE DOES YOU ANY HARM. DON'T WORRY, SIR.
...
20
MISS PARVATI? MR. AMIR? ARE YOU OVER HERE?

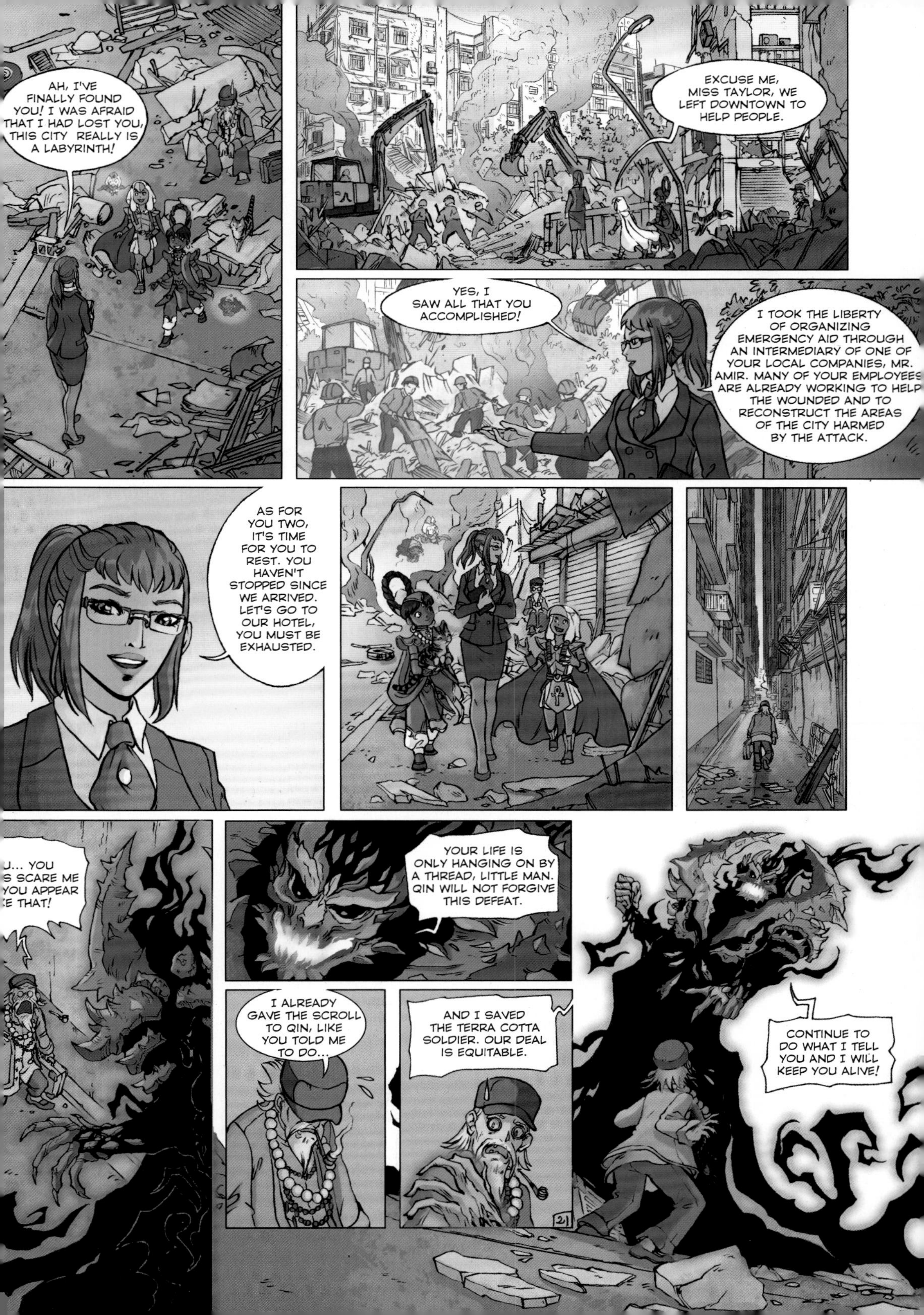
AH, I'VE FINALLY FOUND YOU! I WAS AFRAID THAT I HAD LOST YOU, THIS CITY REALLY IS A LABYRINTH!
EXCUSE ME, MISS TAYLOR, WE LEFT DOWNTOWN TO HELP PEOPLE.
YES, I SAW ALL THAT YOU ACCOMPLISHED!
I TOOK THE LIBERTY OF ORGANIZING EMERGENCY AID THROUGH AN INTERMEDIARY OF ONE OF YOUR LOCAL COMPANIES, MR. AMIR. MANY OF YOUR EMPLOYEES ARE ALREADY WORKING TO HELP THE WOUNDED AND TO RECONSTRUCT THE AREAS OF THE CITY HARMED BY THE ATTACK.
AS FOR YOU TWO, IT'S TIME FOR YOU TO REST. YOU HAVEN'T STOPPED SINCE WE ARRIVED. LET'S GO TO OUR HOTEL, YOU MUST BE EXHAUSTED.
U... YOU S SCARE ME YOU APPEAR E THAT!
YOUR LIFE IS ONLY HANGING ON BY A THREAD, LITTLE MAN. QIN WILL NOT FORGIVE THIS DEFEAT.
I ALREADY GAVE THE SCROLL TO QIN, LIKE YOU TOLD ME TO DO...
AND I SAVED THE TERRA COTTA SOLDIER. OUR DEAL IS EQUITABLE.
CONTINUE TO DO WHAT I TELL YOU AND I WILL KEEP YOU ALIVE!
21

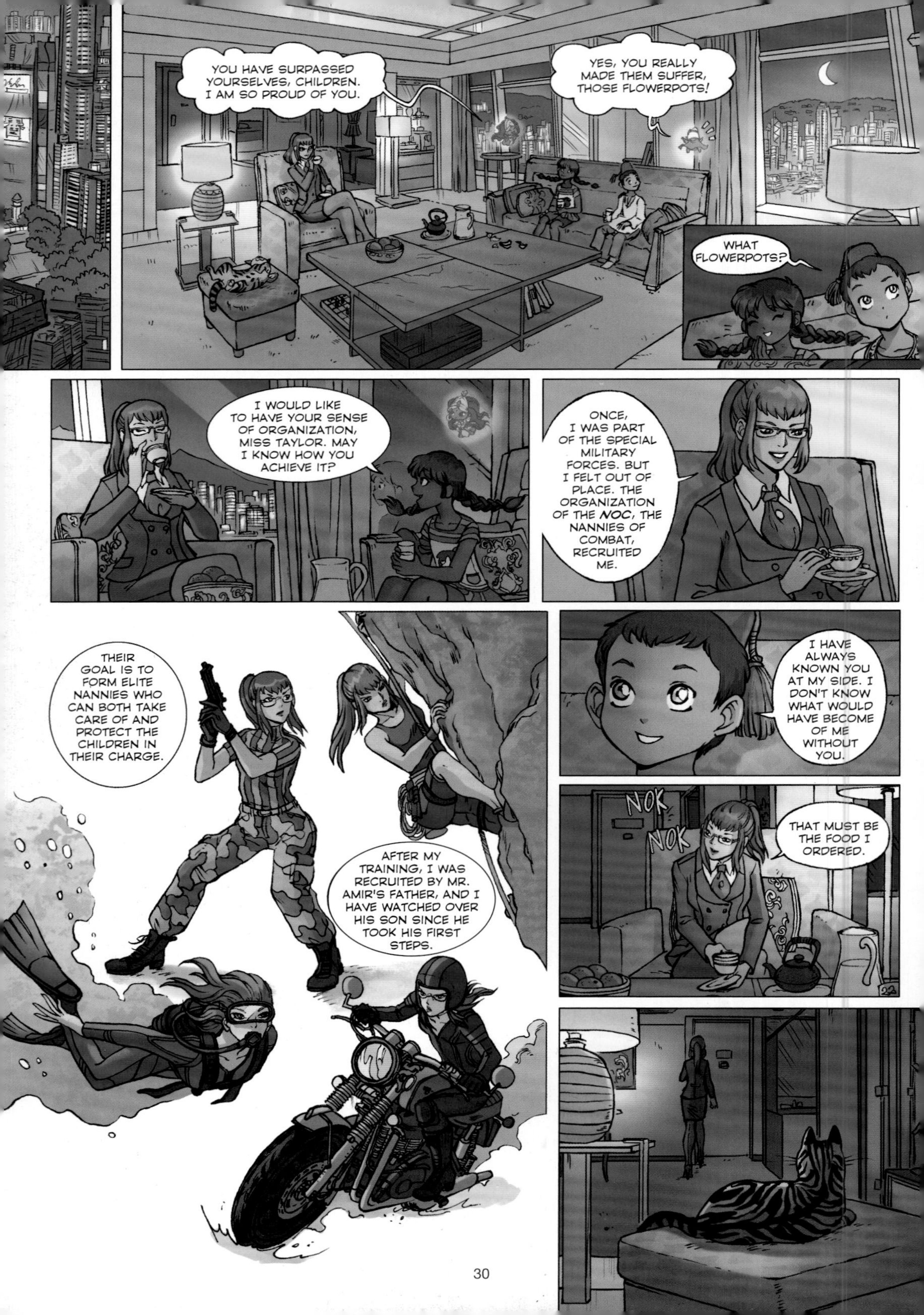
YOU HAVE SURPASSED YOURSELVES, CHILDREN. I AM SO PROUD OF YOU.
YES, YOU REALLY MADE THEM SUFFER, THOSE FLOWERPOTS!
WHAT FLOWERPOTS?
I WOULD LIKE TO HAVE YOUR SENSE OF ORGANIZATION, MISS TAYLOR. MAY I KNOW HOW YOU ACHIEVE IT?
ONCE, I WAS PART OF THE SPECIAL MILITARY FORCES. BUT I FELT OUT OF PLACE. THE ORGANIZATION OF THE NOC, THE NANNIES OF COMBAT, RECRUITED ME.
THEIR GOAL IS TO FORM ELITE NANNIES WHO CAN BOTH TAKE CARE OF AND PROTECT THE CHILDREN IN THEIR CHARGE.
AFTER MY TRAINING, I WAS RECRUITED BY MR. AMIR'S FATHER, AND I HAVE WATCHED OVER HIS SON SINCE HE TOOK HIS FIRST STEPS.
I HAVE ALWAYS KNOWN YOU AT MY SIDE. I DON'T KNOW WHAT WOULD HAVE BECOME OF ME WITHOUT YOU.
NOK
NOK
THAT MUST BE THE FOOD I ORDERED.

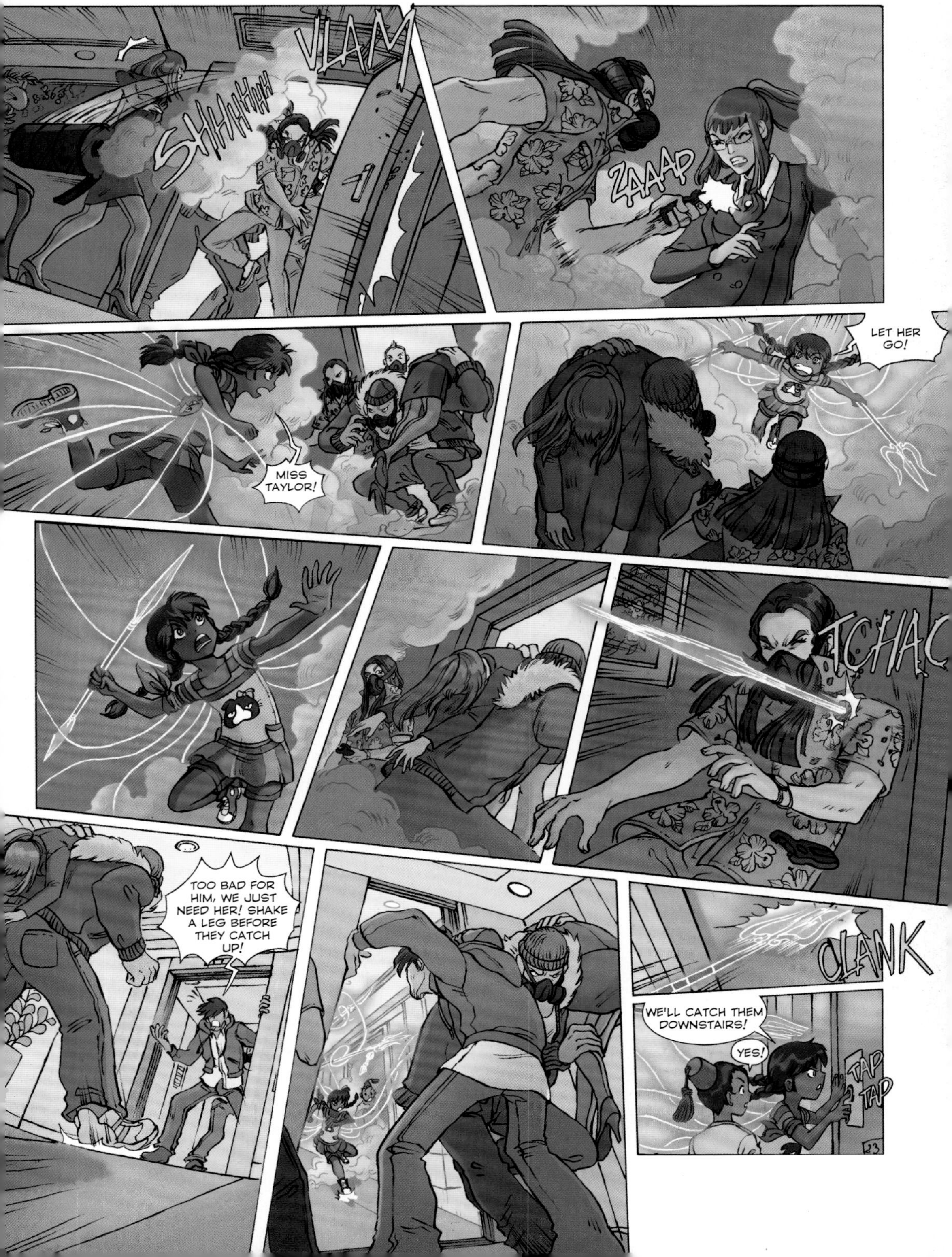
VLAM
SHHHHHH
ZAAAP
MISS TAYLOR!
LET HER GO!
TCHAC
TOO BAD FOR HIM, WE JUST NEED HER! SHAKE A LEG BEFORE THEY CATCH UP!
CLANK
WE'LL CATCH THEM DOWNSTAIRS!
YES!
TAP TAP

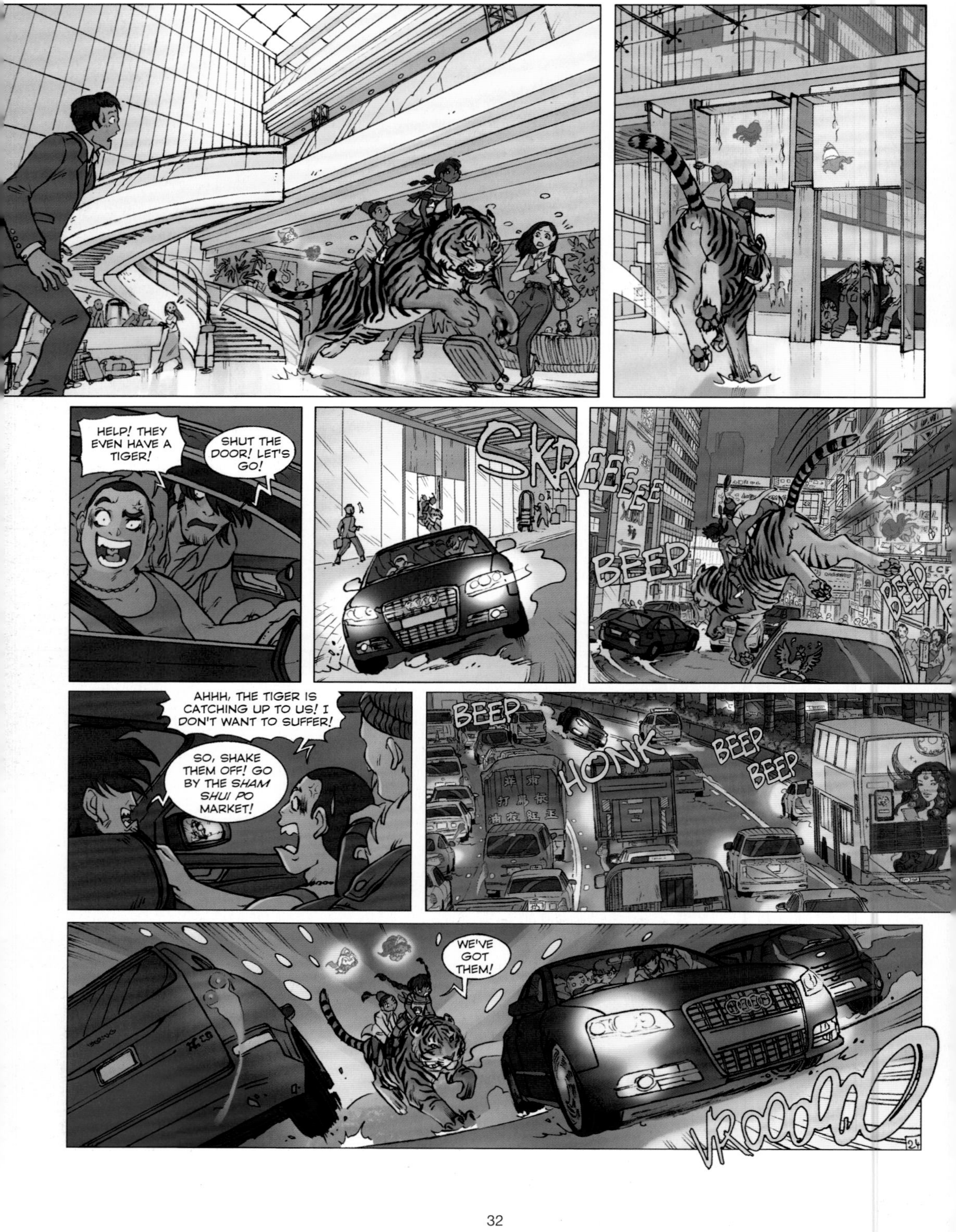
HELP! THEY EVEN HAVE A TIGER!
SHUT THE DOOR! LET'S GO!
SKREEEEEE
BEEP
AHHH, THE TIGER IS CATCHING UP TO US! I DON'T WANT TO SUFFER!
SO, SHAKE THEM OFF! GO BY THE *SHAM SHUI PO* MARKET!
BEEP
HONK
BEEP
BEEP
WE'VE GOT THEM!
VROOOOOO

BEE EEP

WATCH OUT!

BEEEEE EEEEEEP

SKREEEE

...?

!!!

CRASH

VROoooo

MISS TAYLOR!

I'VE LOST SIGHT OF THEM!

YOUR EYES AREN'T AS SHARP AS THEY USED TO BE!

WHEN I GET MY HANDS ON THEM, THEY--THEY ARE GOING TO GET IT!

PARVATI, LET'S GO BACK TO THE HOTEL, WITH A LITTLE LUCK, THEIR WOUNDED ACCOMPLICE IS STILL THERE.

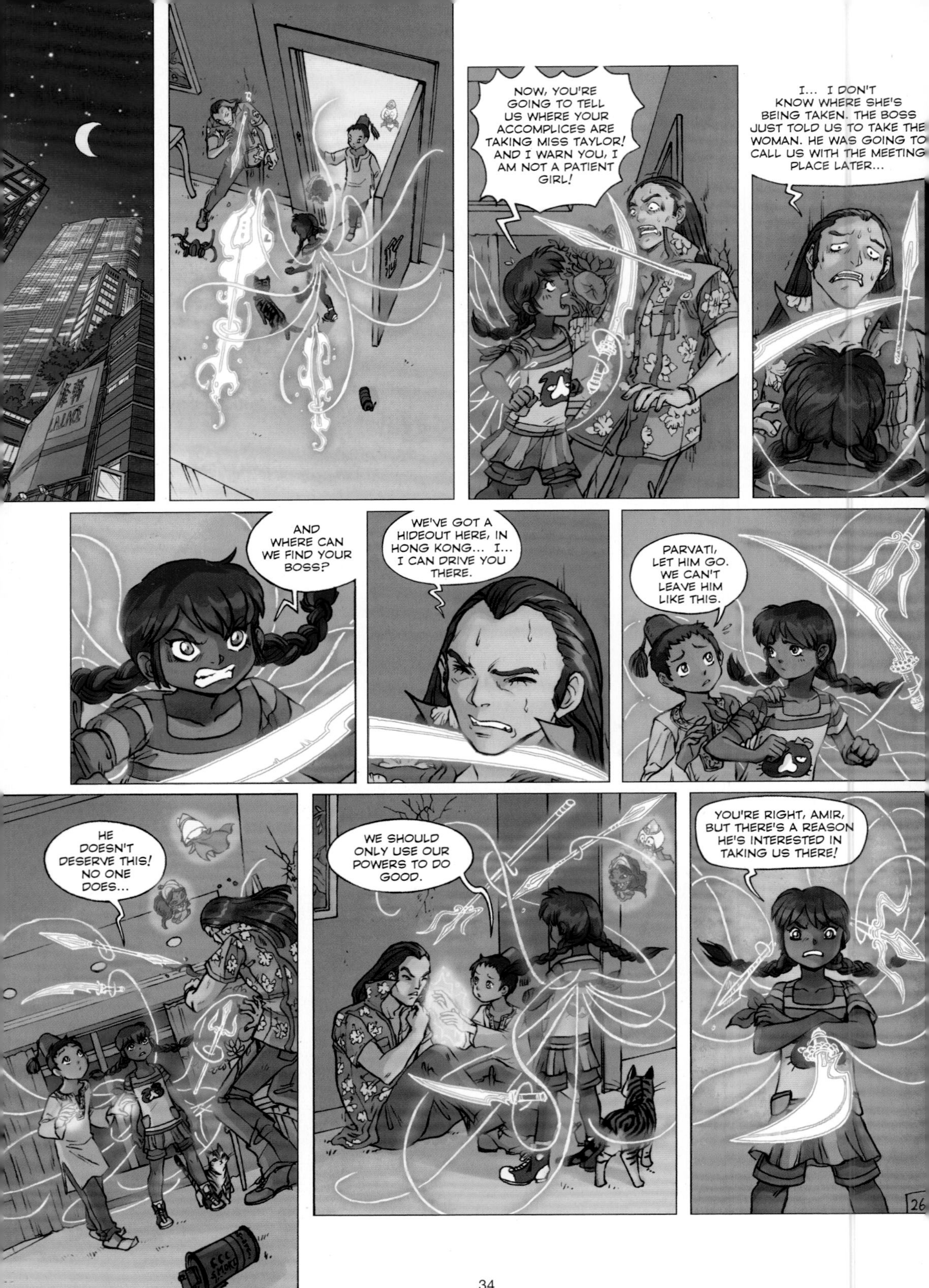
NOW, YOU'RE GOING TO TELL US WHERE YOUR ACCOMPLICES ARE TAKING MISS TAYLOR! AND I WARN YOU, I AM NOT A PATIENT GIRL!
I... I DON'T KNOW WHERE SHE'S BEING TAKEN. THE BOSS JUST TOLD US TO TAKE THE WOMAN. HE WAS GOING TO CALL US WITH THE MEETING PLACE LATER...
AND WHERE CAN WE FIND YOUR BOSS?
WE'VE GOT A HIDEOUT HERE, IN HONG KONG... I... I CAN DRIVE YOU THERE.
PARVATI, LET HIM GO. WE CAN'T LEAVE HIM LIKE THIS.
HE DOESN'T DESERVE THIS! NO ONE DOES...
WE SHOULD ONLY USE OUR POWERS TO DO GOOD.
YOU'RE RIGHT, AMIR, BUT THERE'S A REASON HE'S INTERESTED IN TAKING US THERE!
26

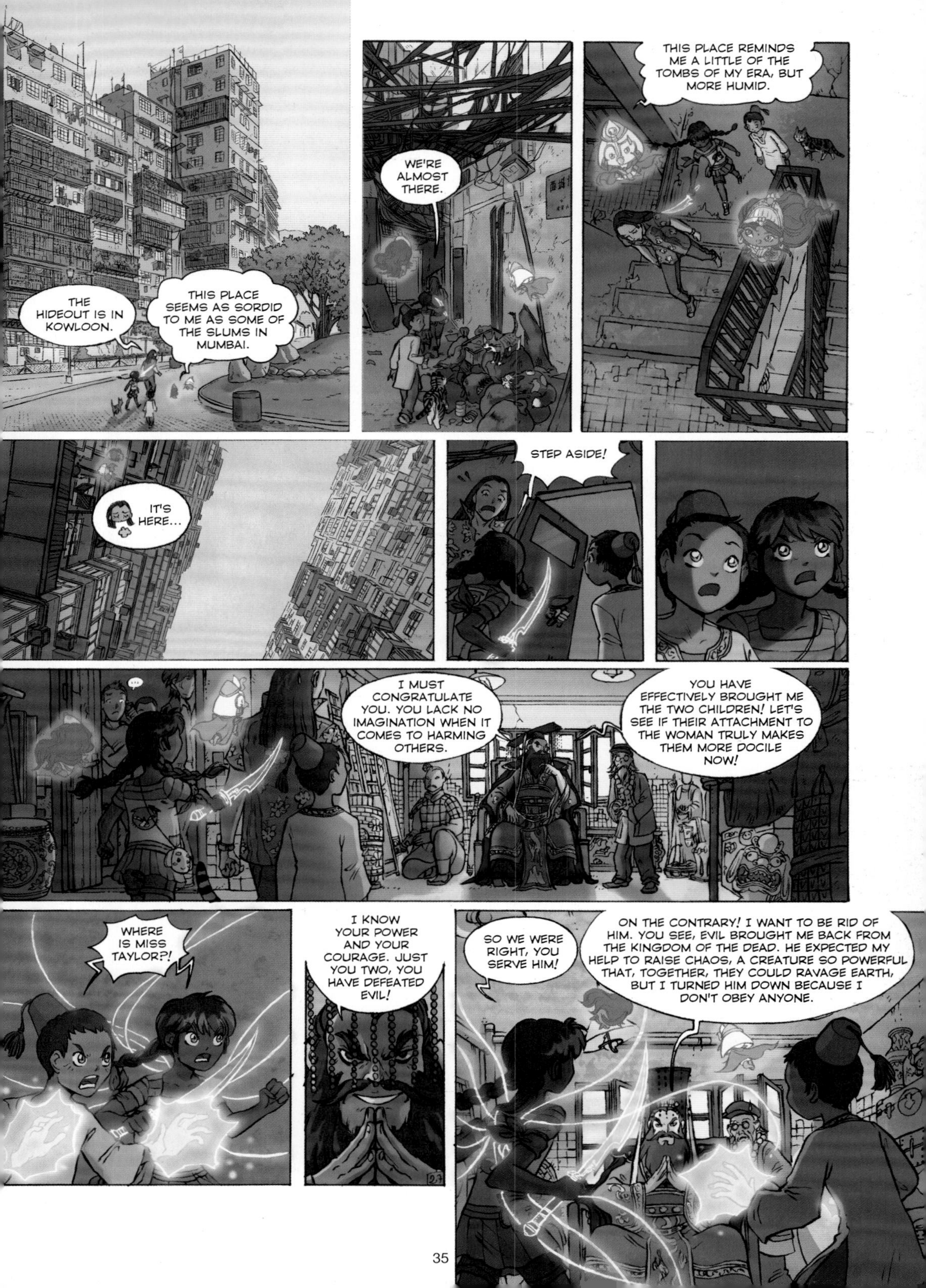
THE HIDEOUT IS IN KOWLOON.
THIS PLACE SEEMS AS SORDID TO ME AS SOME OF THE SLUMS IN MUMBAI.
WE'RE ALMOST THERE.
THIS PLACE REMINDS ME A LITTLE OF THE TOMBS OF MY ERA, BUT MORE HUMID.
IT'S HERE...
STEP ASIDE!
I MUST CONGRATULATE YOU. YOU LACK NO IMAGINATION WHEN IT COMES TO HARMING OTHERS.
YOU HAVE EFFECTIVELY BROUGHT ME THE TWO CHILDREN! LET'S SEE IF THEIR ATTACHMENT TO THE WOMAN TRULY MAKES THEM MORE DOCILE NOW!
WHERE IS MISS TAYLOR?!
I KNOW YOUR POWER AND YOUR COURAGE. JUST YOU TWO, YOU HAVE DEFEATED EVIL!
SO WE WERE RIGHT, YOU SERVE HIM!
ON THE CONTRARY! I WANT TO BE RID OF HIM. YOU SEE, EVIL BROUGHT ME BACK FROM THE KINGDOM OF THE DEAD. HE EXPECTED MY HELP TO RAISE CHAOS, A CREATURE SO POWERFUL THAT, TOGETHER, THEY COULD RAVAGE EARTH, BUT I TURNED HIM DOWN BECAUSE I DON'T OBEY ANYONE.

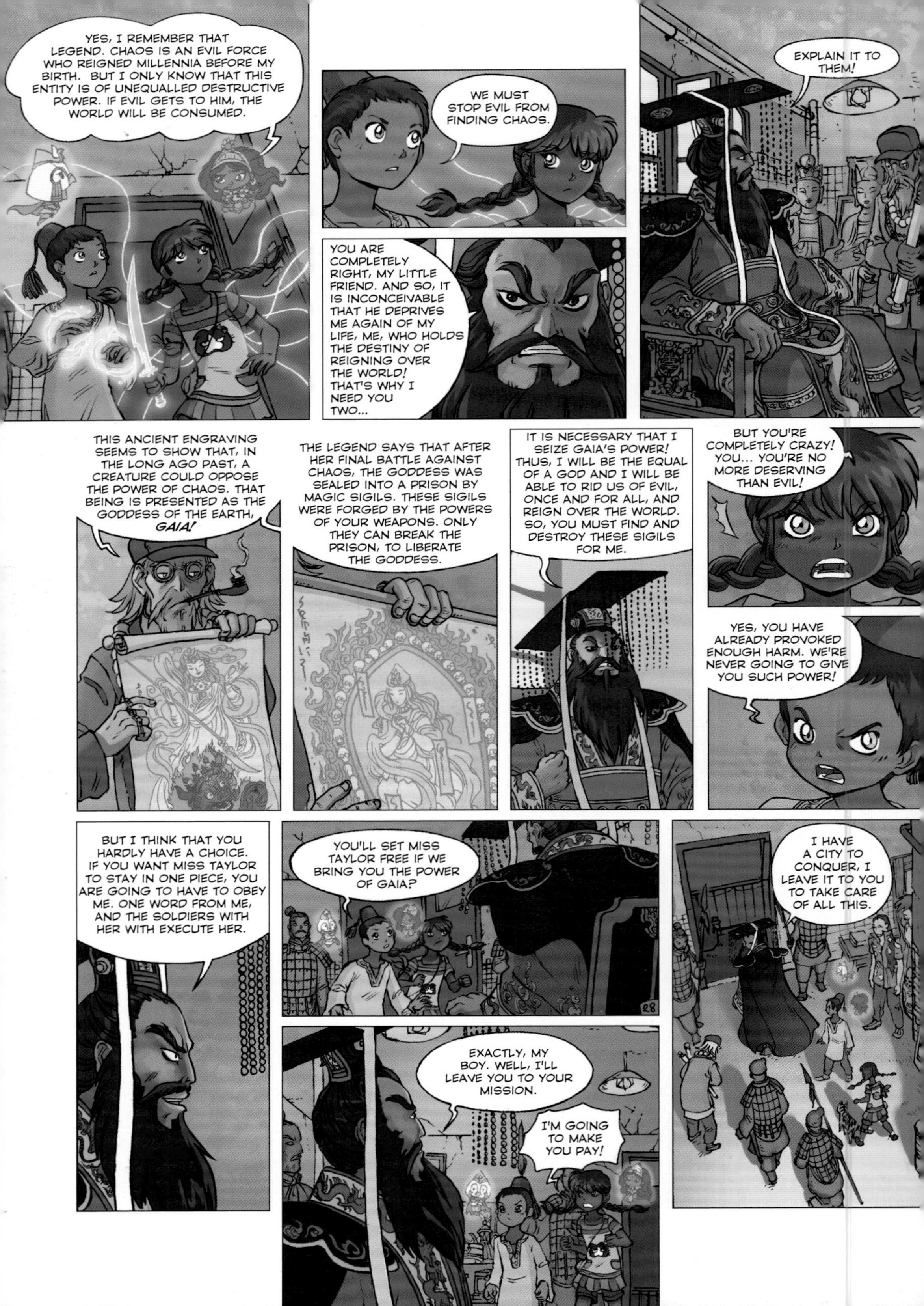
YES, I REMEMBER THAT LEGEND. CHAOS IS AN EVIL FORCE WHO REIGNED MILLENNIA BEFORE MY BIRTH. BUT I ONLY KNOW THAT THIS ENTITY IS OF UNEQUALLED DESTRUCTIVE POWER. IF EVIL GETS TO HIM, THE WORLD WILL BE CONSUMED.
WE MUST STOP EVIL FROM FINDING CHAOS.
YOU ARE COMPLETELY RIGHT, MY LITTLE FRIEND. AND SO, IT IS INCONCEIVABLE THAT HE DEPRIVES ME AGAIN OF MY LIFE, ME, WHO HOLDS THE DESTINY OF REIGNING OVER THE WORLD! THAT'S WHY I NEED YOU TWO...
EXPLAIN IT TO THEM!
THIS ANCIENT ENGRAVING SEEMS TO SHOW THAT, IN THE LONG AGO PAST, A CREATURE COULD OPPOSE THE POWER OF CHAOS. THAT BEING IS PRESENTED AS THE GODDESS OF THE EARTH, GAIA!
THE LEGEND SAYS THAT AFTER HER FINAL BATTLE AGAINST CHAOS, THE GODDESS WAS SEALED INTO A PRISON BY MAGIC SIGILS. THESE SIGILS WERE FORGED BY THE POWERS OF YOUR WEAPONS. ONLY THEY CAN BREAK THE PRISON, TO LIBERATE THE GODDESS.
IT IS NECESSARY THAT I SEIZE GAIA'S POWER! THUS, I WILL BE THE EQUAL OF A GOD AND I WILL BE ABLE TO RID US OF EVIL, ONCE AND FOR ALL, AND REIGN OVER THE WORLD. SO, YOU MUST FIND AND DESTROY THESE SIGILS FOR ME.
BUT YOU'RE COMPLETELY CRAZY! YOU... YOU'RE NO MORE DESERVING THAN EVIL!
YES, YOU HAVE ALREADY PROVOKED ENOUGH HARM. WE'RE NEVER GOING TO GIVE YOU SUCH POWER!
BUT I THINK THAT YOU HARDLY HAVE A CHOICE. IF YOU WANT MISS TAYLOR TO STAY IN ONE PIECE, YOU ARE GOING TO HAVE TO OBEY ME. ONE WORD FROM ME, AND THE SOLDIERS WITH HER WITH EXECUTE HER.
YOU'LL SET MISS TAYLOR FREE IF WE BRING YOU THE POWER OF GAIA?
EXACTLY, MY BOY. WELL, I'LL LEAVE YOU TO YOUR MISSION.
I'M GOING TO MAKE YOU PAY!
I HAVE A CITY TO CONQUER, I LEAVE IT TO YOU TO TAKE CARE OF ALL THIS.

YOU! YOU ARE TRULY WITHOUT HONOR!

I HAD NO CHOICE, I SWEAR TO YOU.

WHERE ARE THESE FAMOUS MAGICAL SIGILS THAT HOLD GAIA?

I DON'T REALLY KNOW... BUT WE HAVE... UH... *BORROWED* THIS SCROLL FROM A CITY TEMPLE... MAYBE ITS TRUE OWNER WOULD KNOW MORE?...

IT'S CRAZY, I HAD NEARLY FORGOTTEN THIS HISTORY WITH GAIA!

YES, ME TOO! I MUST SAY THAT IT WAS BARELY MORE THAN A LEGEND FOR ME.

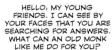

IT'S STRANGE THAT OUR WEAPONS WOULD BE A PART OF THE SIGILS. THAT MEANS THAT THEY HAVE EXISTED MILLENNIA BEFORE OUR BIRTH...

HELLO, MY YOUNG FRIENDS. I CAN SEE BY YOUR FACES THAT YOU ARE SEARCHING FOR ANSWERS. WHAT CAN AN OLD MONK LIKE ME DO FOR YOU?

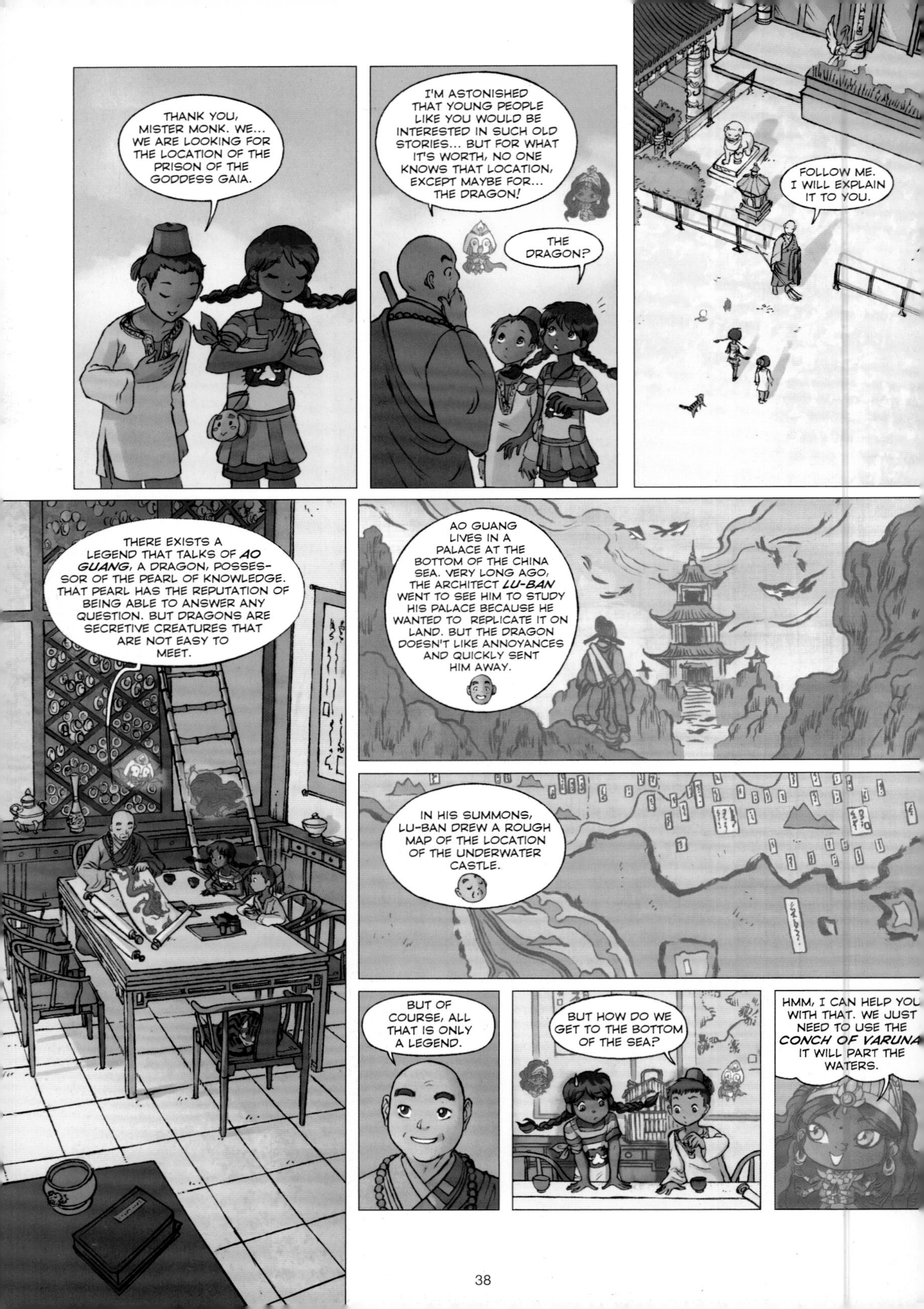
THANK YOU, MISTER MONK. WE... WE ARE LOOKING FOR THE LOCATION OF THE PRISON OF THE GODDESS GAIA.
I'M ASTONISHED THAT YOUNG PEOPLE LIKE YOU WOULD BE INTERESTED IN SUCH OLD STORIES... BUT FOR WHAT IT'S WORTH, NO ONE KNOWS THAT LOCATION, EXCEPT MAYBE FOR... THE DRAGON!
THE DRAGON?
FOLLOW ME. I WILL EXPLAIN IT TO YOU.
THERE EXISTS A LEGEND THAT TALKS OF *AO GUANG*, A DRAGON, POSSESSOR OF THE PEARL OF KNOWLEDGE. THAT PEARL HAS THE REPUTATION OF BEING ABLE TO ANSWER ANY QUESTION. BUT DRAGONS ARE SECRETIVE CREATURES THAT ARE NOT EASY TO MEET.
AO GUANG LIVES IN A PALACE AT THE BOTTOM OF THE CHINA SEA. VERY LONG AGO, THE ARCHITECT *LU-BAN* WENT TO SEE HIM TO STUDY HIS PALACE BECAUSE HE WANTED TO REPLICATE IT ON LAND. BUT THE DRAGON DOESN'T LIKE ANNOYANCES AND QUICKLY SENT HIM AWAY.
IN HIS SUMMONS, LU-BAN DREW A ROUGH MAP OF THE LOCATION OF THE UNDERWATER CASTLE.
BUT OF COURSE, ALL THAT IS ONLY A LEGEND.
BUT HOW DO WE GET TO THE BOTTOM OF THE SEA?
HMM, I CAN HELP YOU WITH THAT. WE JUST NEED TO USE THE ***CONCH OF VARUNA*** IT WILL PART THE WATERS.

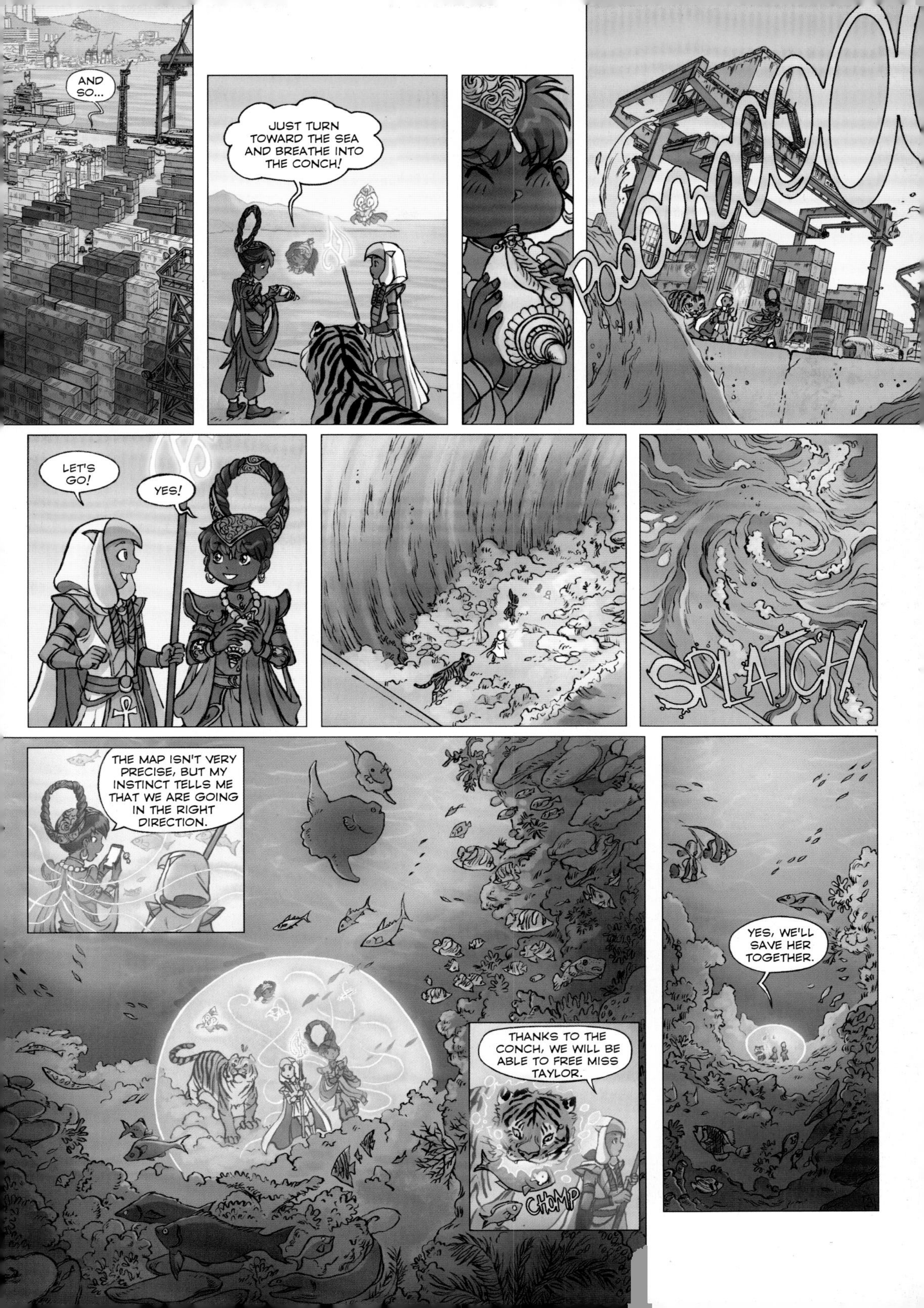

AND SO...
JUST TURN TOWARD THE SEA AND BREATHE INTO THE CONCH!
POOOOOOOOO
LET'S GO!
YES!
SPLATCH
THE MAP ISN'T VERY PRECISE, BUT MY INSTINCT TELLS ME THAT WE ARE GOING IN THE RIGHT DIRECTION.
THANKS TO THE CONCH, WE WILL BE ABLE TO FREE MISS TAYLOR.
CHOMP
YES, WE'LL SAVE HER TOGETHER.

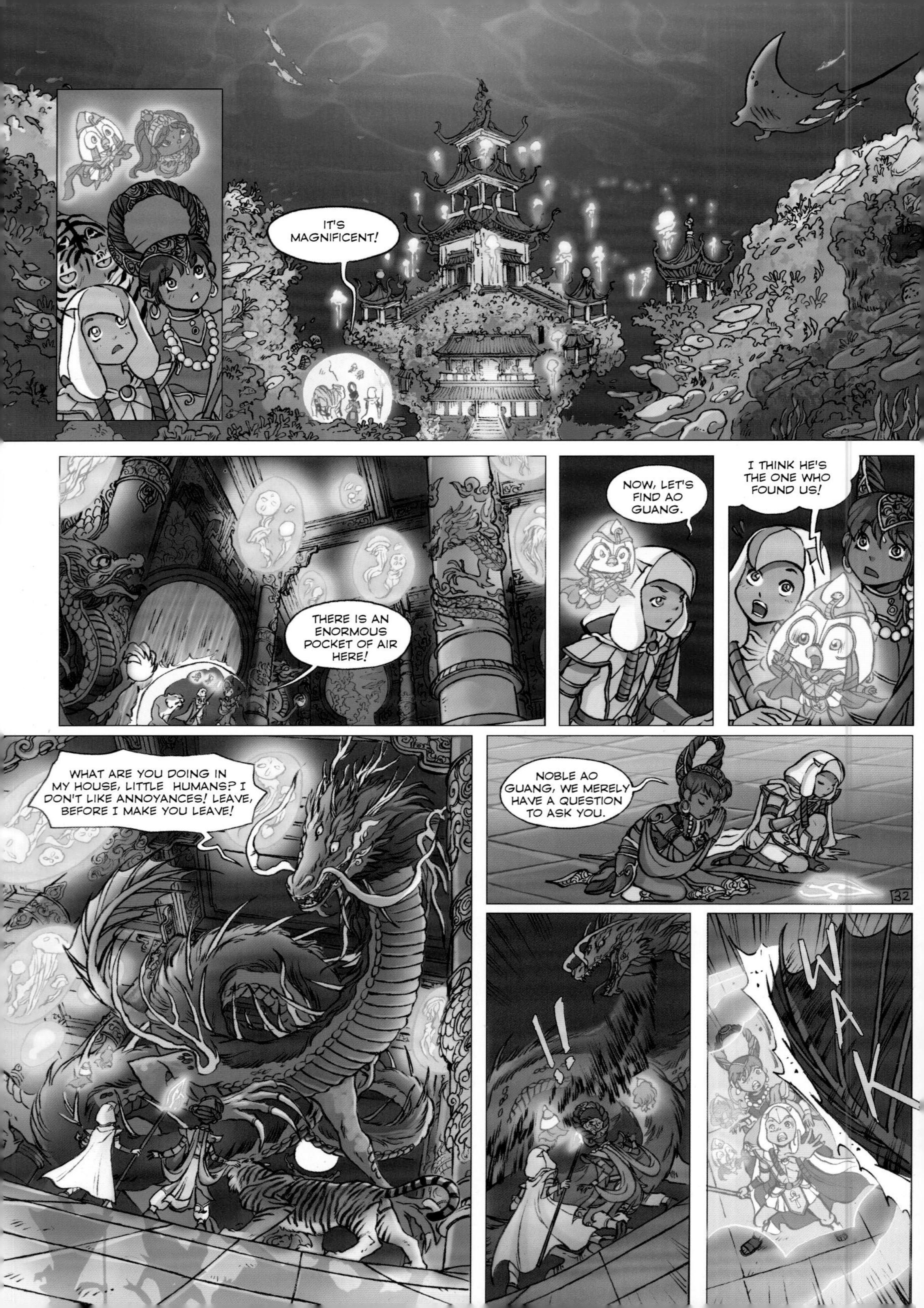
IT'S MAGNIFICENT!
THERE IS AN ENORMOUS POCKET OF AIR HERE!
NOW, LET'S FIND AO GUANG.
I THINK HE'S THE ONE WHO FOUND US!
WHAT ARE YOU DOING IN MY HOUSE, LITTLE HUMANS? I DON'T LIKE ANNOYANCES! LEAVE, BEFORE I MAKE YOU LEAVE!
NOBLE AO GUANG, WE MERELY HAVE A QUESTION TO ASK YOU.
!!
WAK

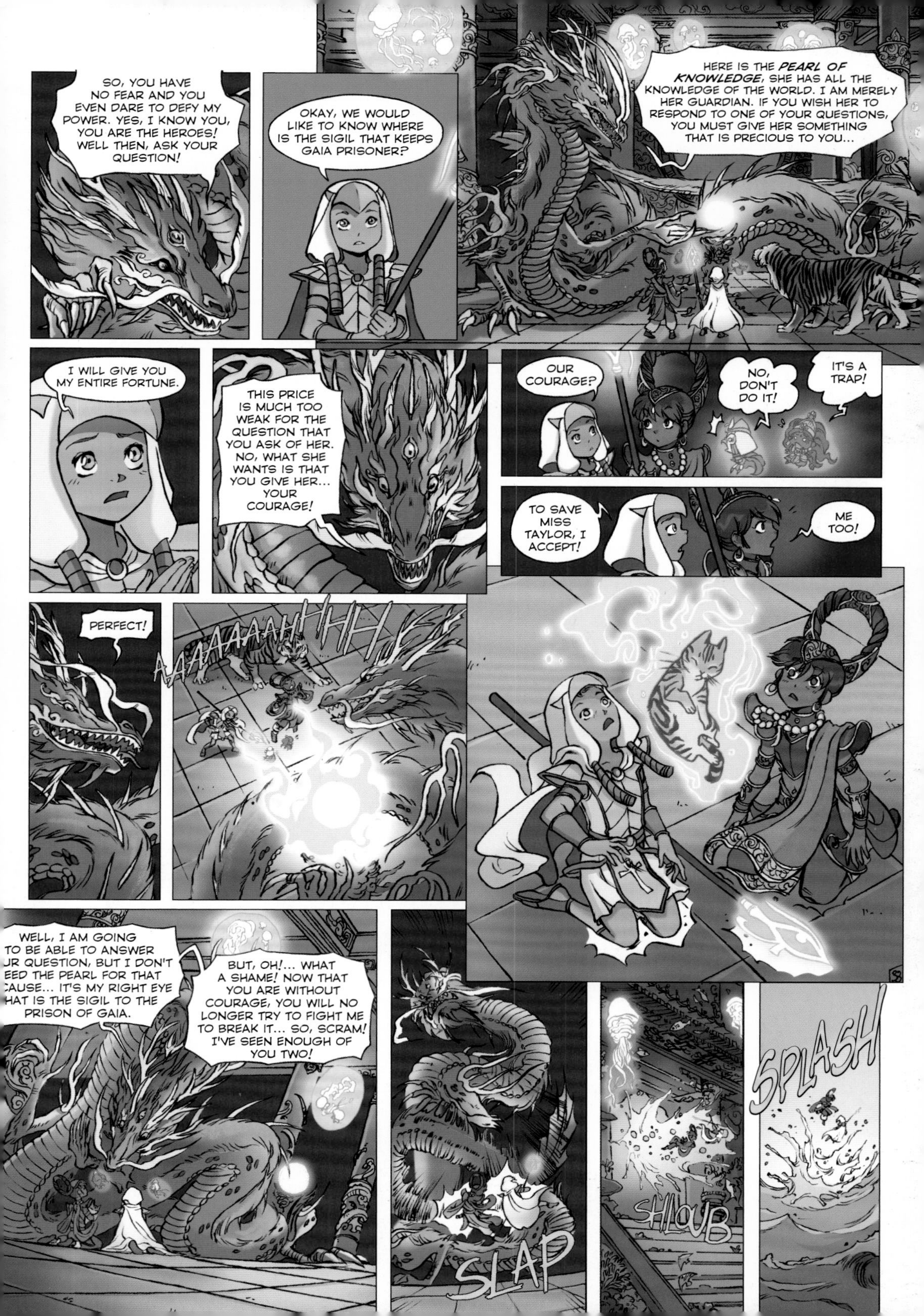

SO, YOU HAVE NO FEAR AND YOU EVEN DARE TO DEFY MY POWER. YES, I KNOW YOU, YOU ARE THE HEROES! WELL THEN, ASK YOUR QUESTION!
OKAY, WE WOULD LIKE TO KNOW WHERE IS THE SIGIL THAT KEEPS GAIA PRISONER?
HERE IS THE PEARL OF KNOWLEDGE, SHE HAS ALL THE KNOWLEDGE OF THE WORLD. I AM MERELY HER GUARDIAN. IF YOU WISH HER TO RESPOND TO ONE OF YOUR QUESTIONS, YOU MUST GIVE HER SOMETHING THAT IS PRECIOUS TO YOU...
I WILL GIVE YOU MY ENTIRE FORTUNE.
THIS PRICE IS MUCH TOO WEAK FOR THE QUESTION THAT YOU ASK OF HER. NO, WHAT SHE WANTS IS THAT YOU GIVE HER... YOUR COURAGE!
OUR COURAGE?
NO, DON'T DO IT!
IT'S A TRAP!
TO SAVE MISS TAYLOR, I ACCEPT!
ME TOO!
PERFECT!
AAAAAAAAHHHHH
WELL, I AM GOING TO BE ABLE TO ANSWER UR QUESTION, BUT I DON'T EED THE PEARL FOR THAT CAUSE... IT'S MY RIGHT EYE HAT IS THE SIGIL TO THE PRISON OF GAIA.
BUT, OH!... WHAT A SHAME! NOW THAT YOU ARE WITHOUT COURAGE, YOU WILL NO LONGER TRY TO FIGHT ME TO BREAK IT... SO, SCRAM! I'VE SEEN ENOUGH OF YOU TWO!
SLAP
SHLOUB
SPLASH

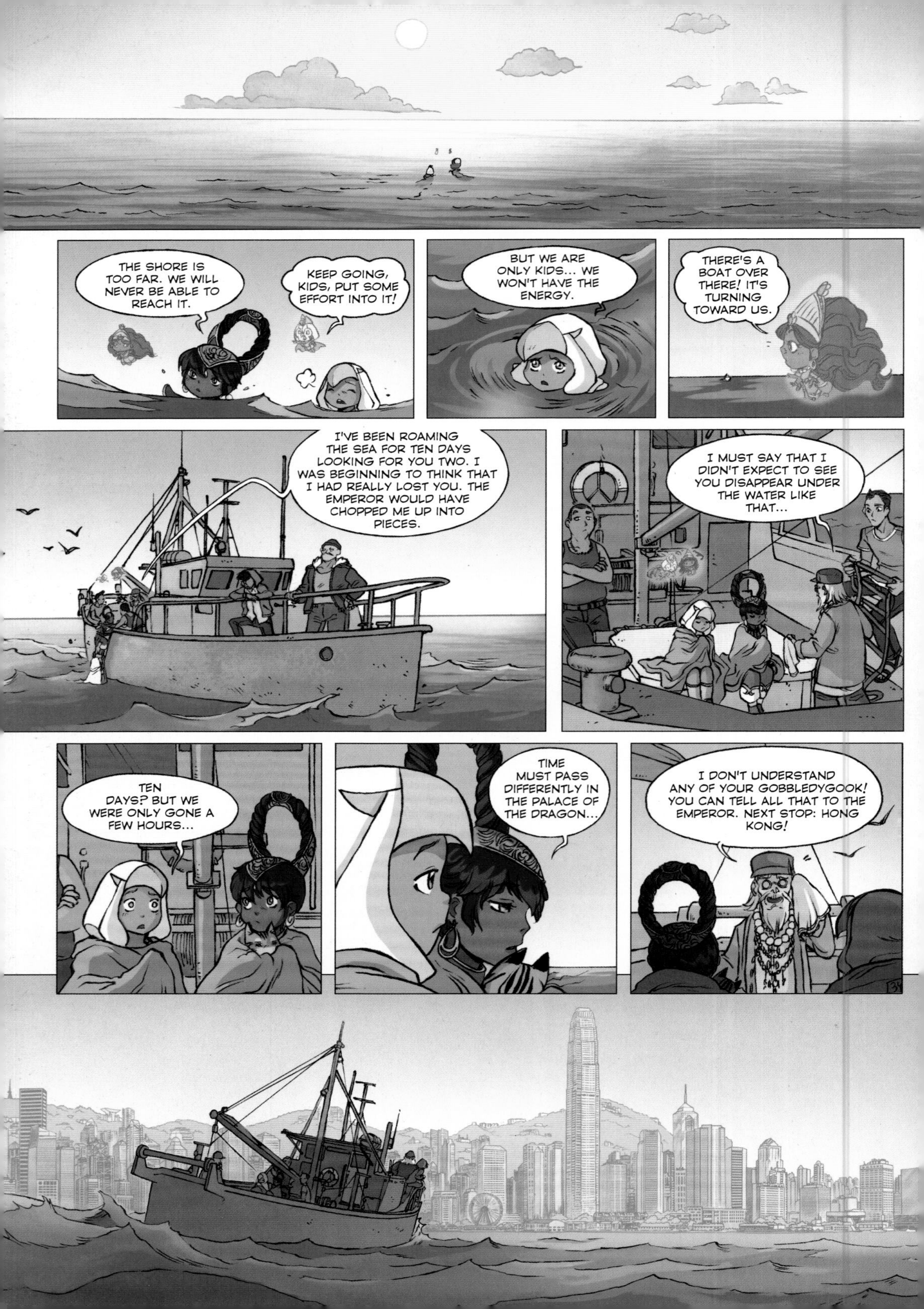
THE SHORE IS TOO FAR. WE WILL NEVER BE ABLE TO REACH IT.
KEEP GOING, KIDS, PUT SOME EFFORT INTO IT!
BUT WE ARE ONLY KIDS... WE WON'T HAVE THE ENERGY.
THERE'S A BOAT OVER THERE! IT'S TURNING TOWARD US.
I'VE BEEN ROAMING THE SEA FOR TEN DAYS LOOKING FOR YOU TWO. I WAS BEGINNING TO THINK THAT I HAD REALLY LOST YOU. THE EMPEROR WOULD HAVE CHOPPED ME UP INTO PIECES.
I MUST SAY THAT I DIDN'T EXPECT TO SEE YOU DISAPPEAR UNDER THE WATER LIKE THAT...
TEN DAYS? BUT WE WERE ONLY GONE A FEW HOURS...
TIME MUST PASS DIFFERENTLY IN THE PALACE OF THE DRAGON...
I DON'T UNDERSTAND ANY OF YOUR GOBBLEDYGOOK! YOU CAN TELL ALL THAT TO THE EMPEROR. NEXT STOP: HONG KONG!

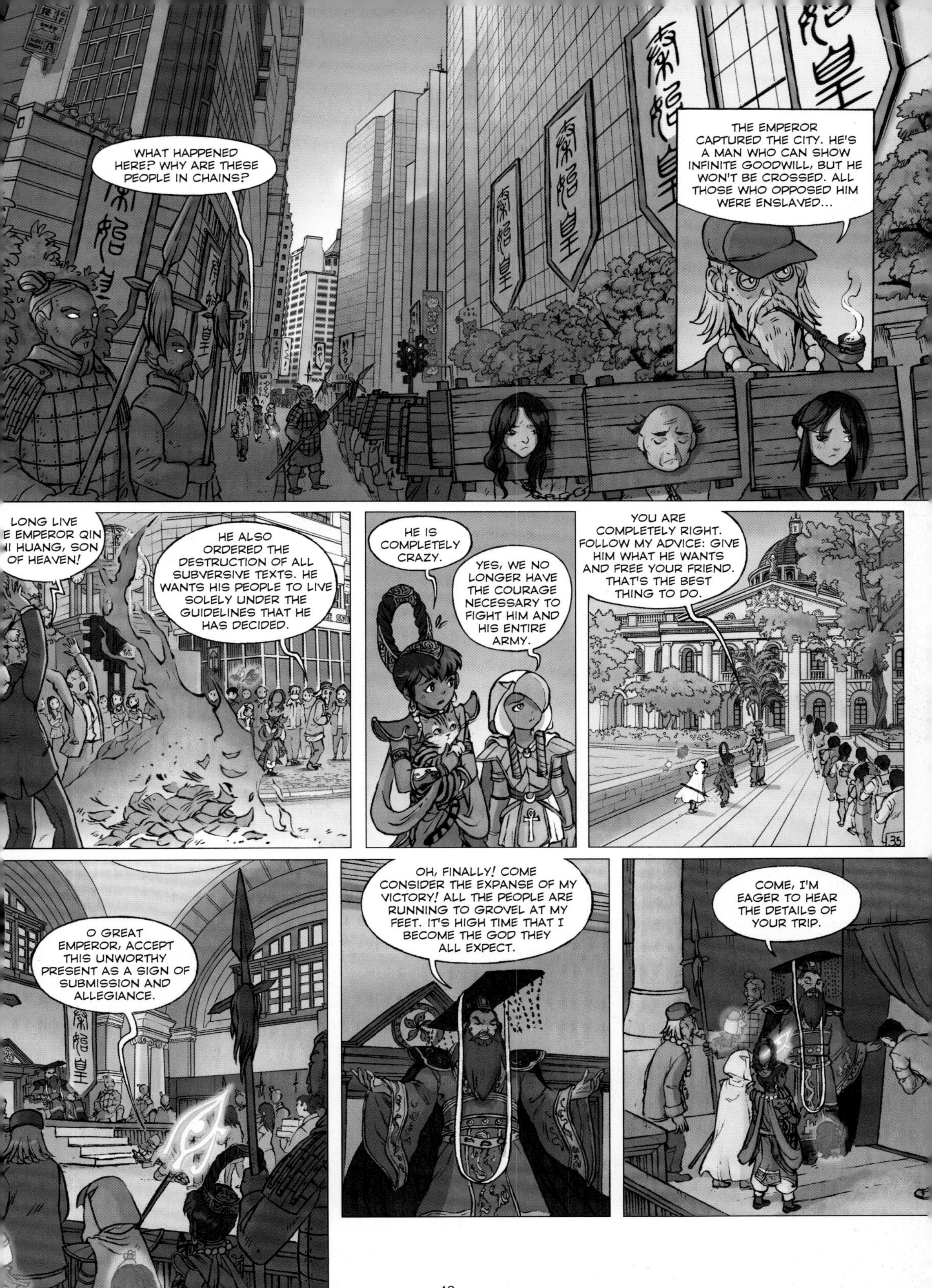
WHAT HAPPENED HERE? WHY ARE THESE PEOPLE IN CHAINS?
THE EMPEROR CAPTURED THE CITY. HE'S A MAN WHO CAN SHOW INFINITE GOODWILL, BUT HE WON'T BE CROSSED. ALL THOSE WHO OPPOSED HIM WERE ENSLAVED...
LONG LIVE E EMPEROR QIN I HUANG, SON OF HEAVEN!
HE ALSO ORDERED THE DESTRUCTION OF ALL SUBVERSIVE TEXTS. HE WANTS HIS PEOPLE TO LIVE SOLELY UNDER THE GUIDELINES THAT HE HAS DECIDED.
HE IS COMPLETELY CRAZY.
YES, WE NO LONGER HAVE THE COURAGE NECESSARY TO FIGHT HIM AND HIS ENTIRE ARMY.
YOU ARE COMPLETELY RIGHT. FOLLOW MY ADVICE: GIVE HIM WHAT HE WANTS AND FREE YOUR FRIEND. THAT'S THE BEST THING TO DO.
O GREAT EMPEROR, ACCEPT THIS UNWORTHY PRESENT AS A SIGN OF SUBMISSION AND ALLEGIANCE.
OH, FINALLY! COME CONSIDER THE EXPANSE OF MY VICTORY! ALL THE PEOPLE ARE RUNNING TO GROVEL AT MY FEET. IT'S HIGH TIME THAT I BECOME THE GOD THEY ALL EXPECT.
COME, I'M EAGER TO HEAR THE DETAILS OF YOUR TRIP.

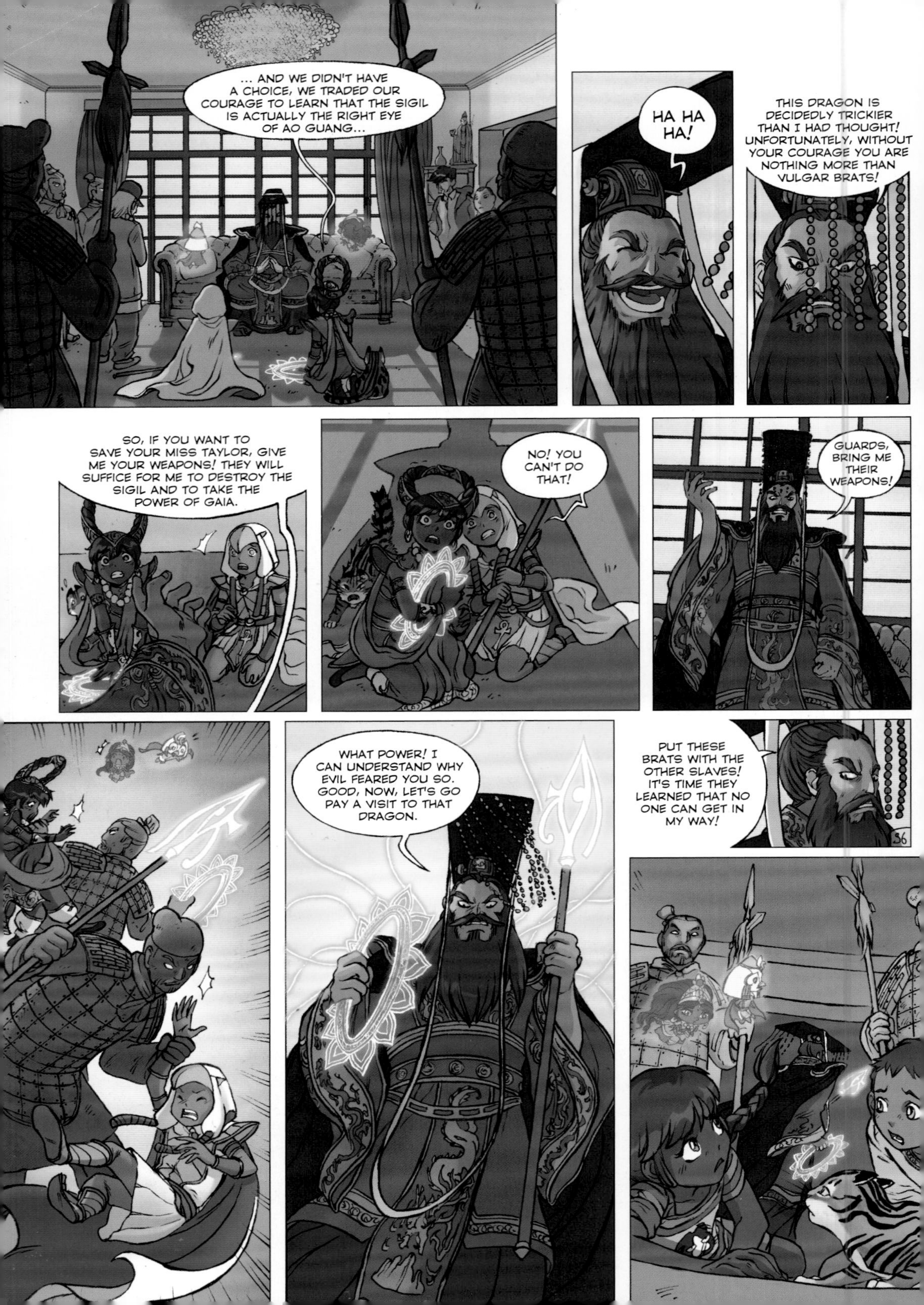
... AND WE DIDN'T HAVE A CHOICE, WE TRADED OUR COURAGE TO LEARN THAT THE SIGIL IS ACTUALLY THE RIGHT EYE OF AO GUANG...
HA HA HA!
THIS DRAGON IS DECIDEDLY TRICKIER THAN I HAD THOUGHT! UNFORTUNATELY, WITHOUT YOUR COURAGE YOU ARE NOTHING MORE THAN VULGAR BRATS!
SO, IF YOU WANT TO SAVE YOUR MISS TAYLOR, GIVE ME YOUR WEAPONS! THEY WILL SUFFICE FOR ME TO DESTROY THE SIGIL AND TO TAKE THE POWER OF GAIA.
NO! YOU CAN'T DO THAT!
GUARDS, BRING ME THEIR WEAPONS!
WHAT POWER! I CAN UNDERSTAND WHY EVIL FEARED YOU SO. GOOD, NOW, LET'S GO PAY A VISIT TO THAT DRAGON.
PUT THESE BRATS WITH THE OTHER SLAVES! IT'S TIME THEY LEARNED THAT NO ONE CAN GET IN MY WAY!
36

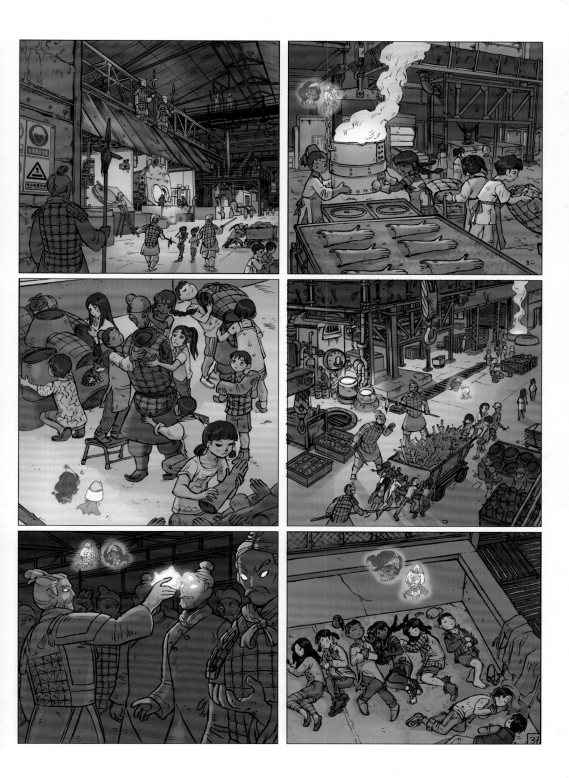

EVERYTHING IS DEFINITELY LOST... THE EMPEROR IS GOING TO WIN, AND EVEN IF HE MANAGES TO BEAT EVIL, HE WILL ENSLAVE THE ENTIRE WORLD.

SHHHHH

PARVATI, KEEP YOURSELF TOGETHER. YOU CAN DO THIS... I HAVE CONFIDENCE IN YOU!

IT'S TRUE! GET MOVING! WE DIDN'T DO ALL THIS JUST TO ABANDON OUR POWERS TO A PAIR OF WIMPS!

YOU REALLY HAVE NO FINESSE, NO TACT! THAT'S NOT HOW--

WATCH OUT!

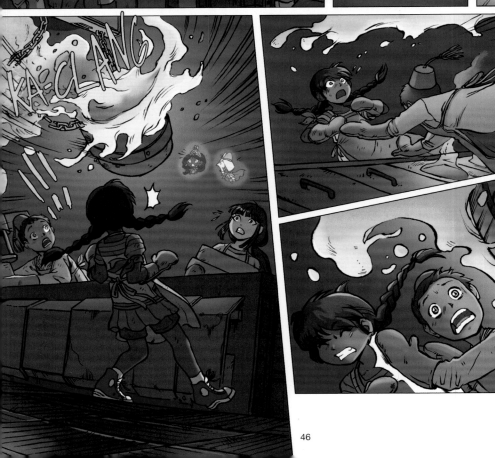

KA-CLANG

38

46

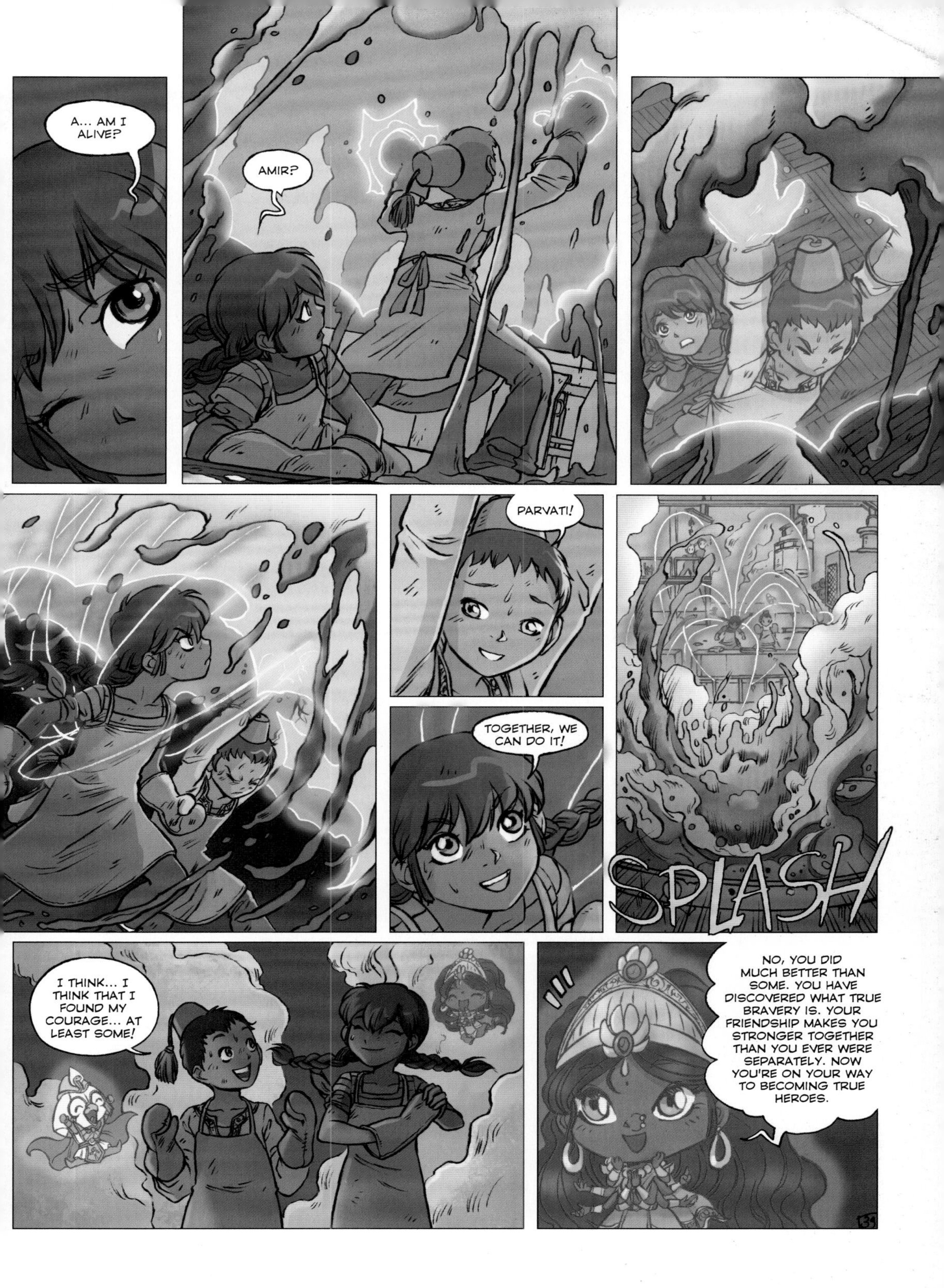
A... AM I ALIVE?
AMIR?
PARVATI!
TOGETHER, WE CAN DO IT!
SPLASH
I THINK... I THINK THAT I FOUND MY COURAGE... AT LEAST SOME!
!!!
NO, YOU DID MUCH BETTER THAN SOME. YOU HAVE DISCOVERED WHAT TRUE BRAVERY IS. YOUR FRIENDSHIP MAKES YOU STRONGER TOGETHER THAN YOU EVER WERE SEPARATELY. NOW YOU'RE ON YOUR WAY TO BECOMING TRUE HEROES.

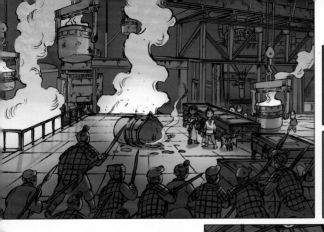

LET'S GO, HEROES! RID US OF ALL THESE FLOWERPOTS!

AFTER YOU, AMIR!

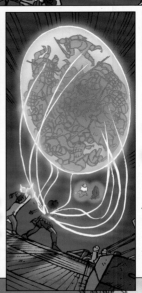

FLOUTC

IT'S STILL NOT TOO LATE TO THWART THE EMPEROR'S PLANS. IT HAS ONLY BEEN A COUPLE OF DAYS SINCE HE SEIZED YOUR WEAPONS. THAT MUST CORRESPOND TO MERE MINUTES IN THE PALACE OF THE DRAGON.

BEFORE THAT, LET'S GO FREE MISS TAYLOR.

WITH THEIR MASTER AT THE BOTTOM OF THE OCEAN, WE HAVE A CHANCE TO STOP THE GUARDS BEFORE THEY DO ANYTHING BAD TO HER.

40

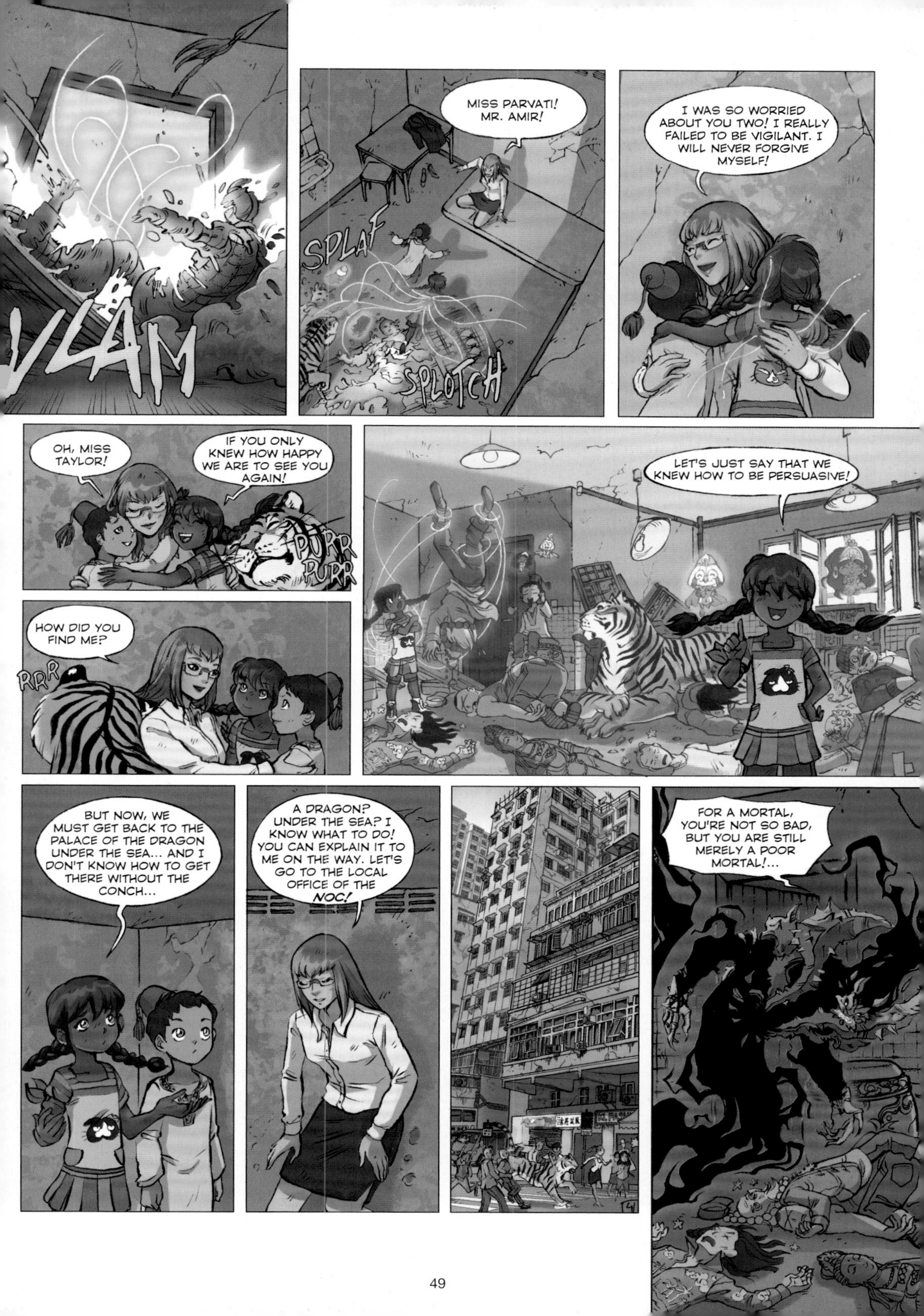
VLAM
MISS PARVATI! MR. AMIR!
SPLAF
SPLOTCH
I WAS SO WORRIED ABOUT YOU TWO! I REALLY FAILED TO BE VIGILANT. I WILL NEVER FORGIVE MYSELF!
OH, MISS TAYLOR!
IF YOU ONLY KNEW HOW HAPPY WE ARE TO SEE YOU AGAIN!
PURR PURR
HOW DID YOU FIND ME?
RRR
LET'S JUST SAY THAT WE KNEW HOW TO BE PERSUASIVE!
BUT NOW, WE MUST GET BACK TO THE PALACE OF THE DRAGON UNDER THE SEA... AND I DON'T KNOW HOW TO GET THERE WITHOUT THE CONCH...
A DRAGON? UNDER THE SEA? I KNOW WHAT TO DO! YOU CAN EXPLAIN IT TO ME ON THE WAY. LET'S GO TO THE LOCAL OFFICE OF THE NOC!
FOR A MORTAL, YOU'RE NOT SO BAD, BUT YOU ARE STILL MERELY A POOR MORTAL!...

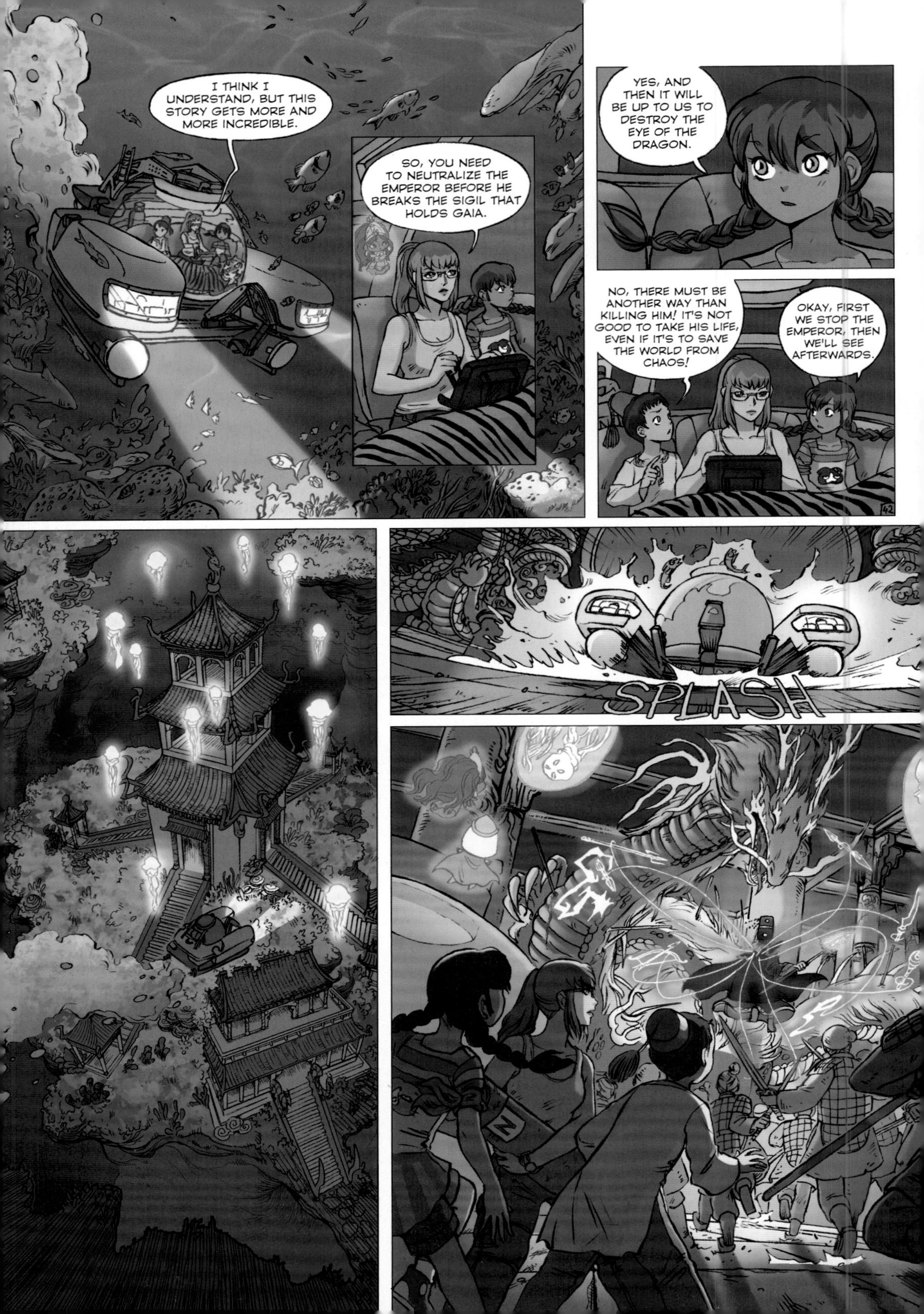
I THINK I UNDERSTAND, BUT THIS STORY GETS MORE AND MORE INCREDIBLE.
SO, YOU NEED TO NEUTRALIZE THE EMPEROR BEFORE HE BREAKS THE SIGIL THAT HOLDS GAIA.
YES, AND THEN IT WILL BE UP TO US TO DESTROY THE EYE OF THE DRAGON.
NO, THERE MUST BE ANOTHER WAY THAN KILLING HIM! IT'S NOT GOOD TO TAKE HIS LIFE, EVEN IF IT'S TO SAVE THE WORLD FROM CHAOS!
OKAY, FIRST WE STOP THE EMPEROR, THEN WE'LL SEE AFTERWARDS.
42
SPLASH

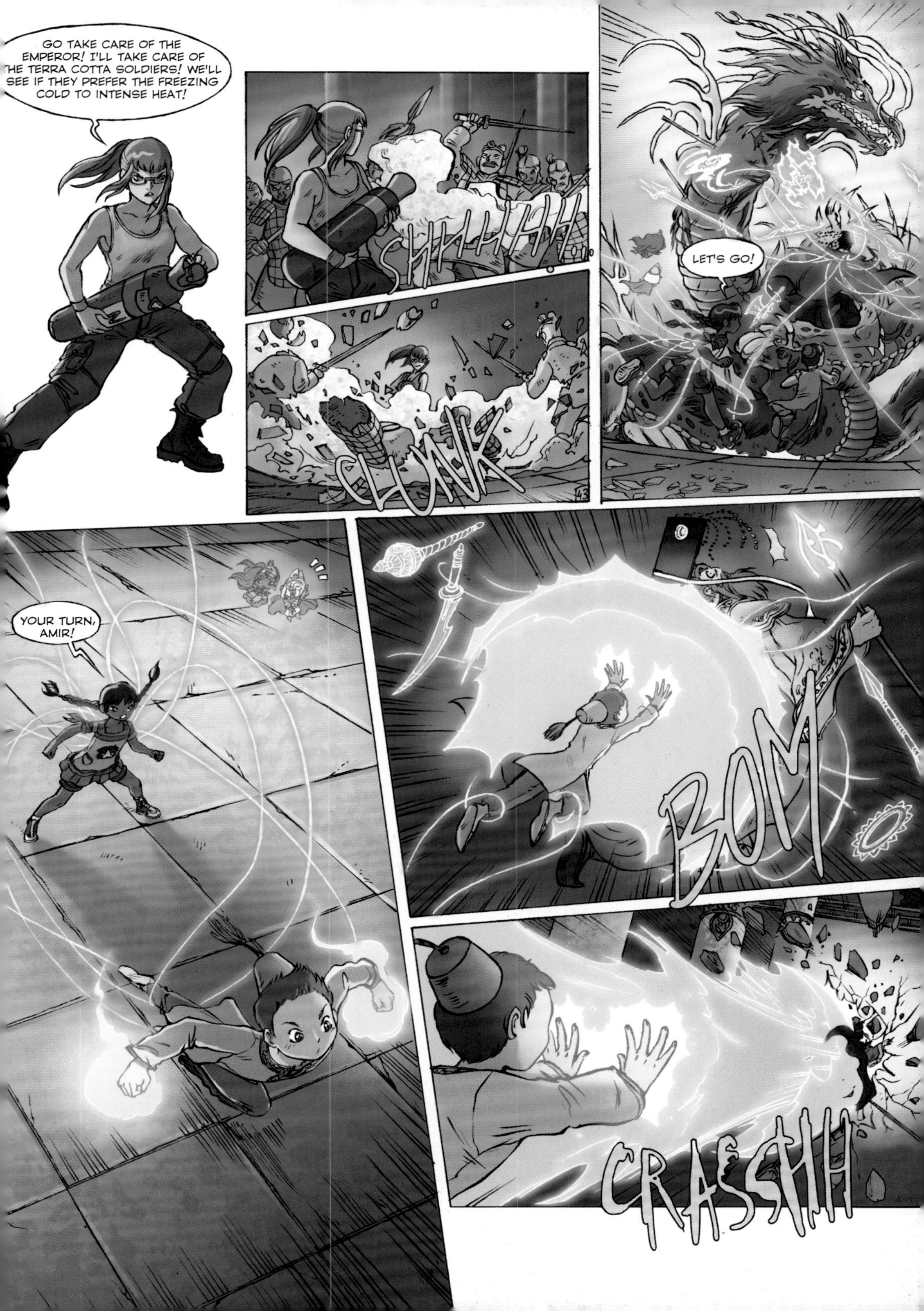
GO TAKE CARE OF THE EMPEROR! I'LL TAKE CARE OF THE TERRA COTTA SOLDIERS! WE'LL SEE IF THEY PREFER THE FREEZING COLD TO INTENSE HEAT!
SHHHHHH...
CLUNK
LET'S GO!
YOUR TURN, AMIR!
BOM
CRASSHH

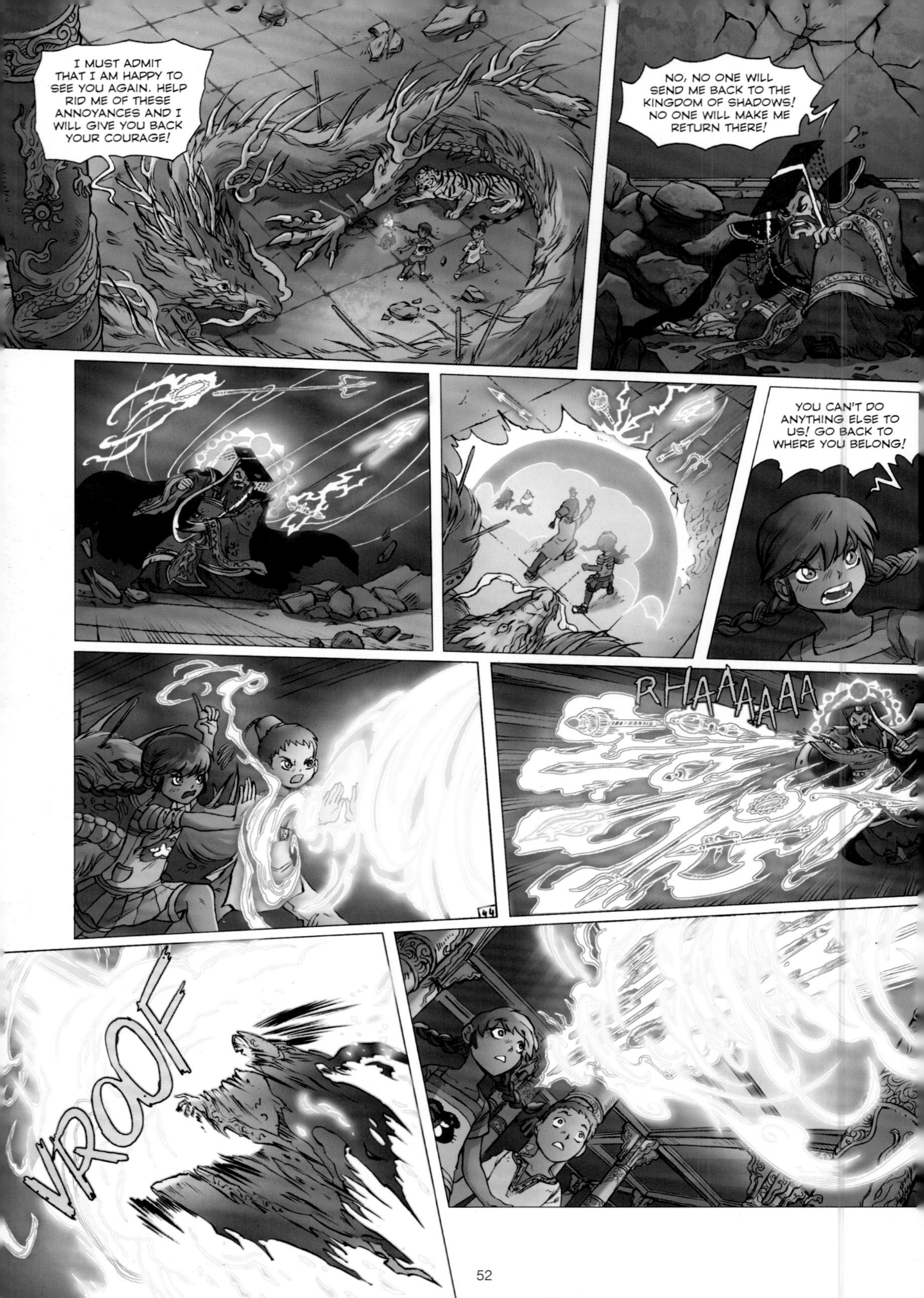
I MUST ADMIT THAT I AM HAPPY TO SEE YOU AGAIN. HELP RID ME OF THESE ANNOYANCES AND I WILL GIVE YOU BACK YOUR COURAGE!
NO, NO ONE WILL SEND ME BACK TO THE KINGDOM OF SHADOWS! NO ONE WILL MAKE ME RETURN THERE!
YOU CAN'T DO ANYTHING ELSE TO US! GO BACK TO WHERE YOU BELONG!
RHAAAAAAA
VROOF

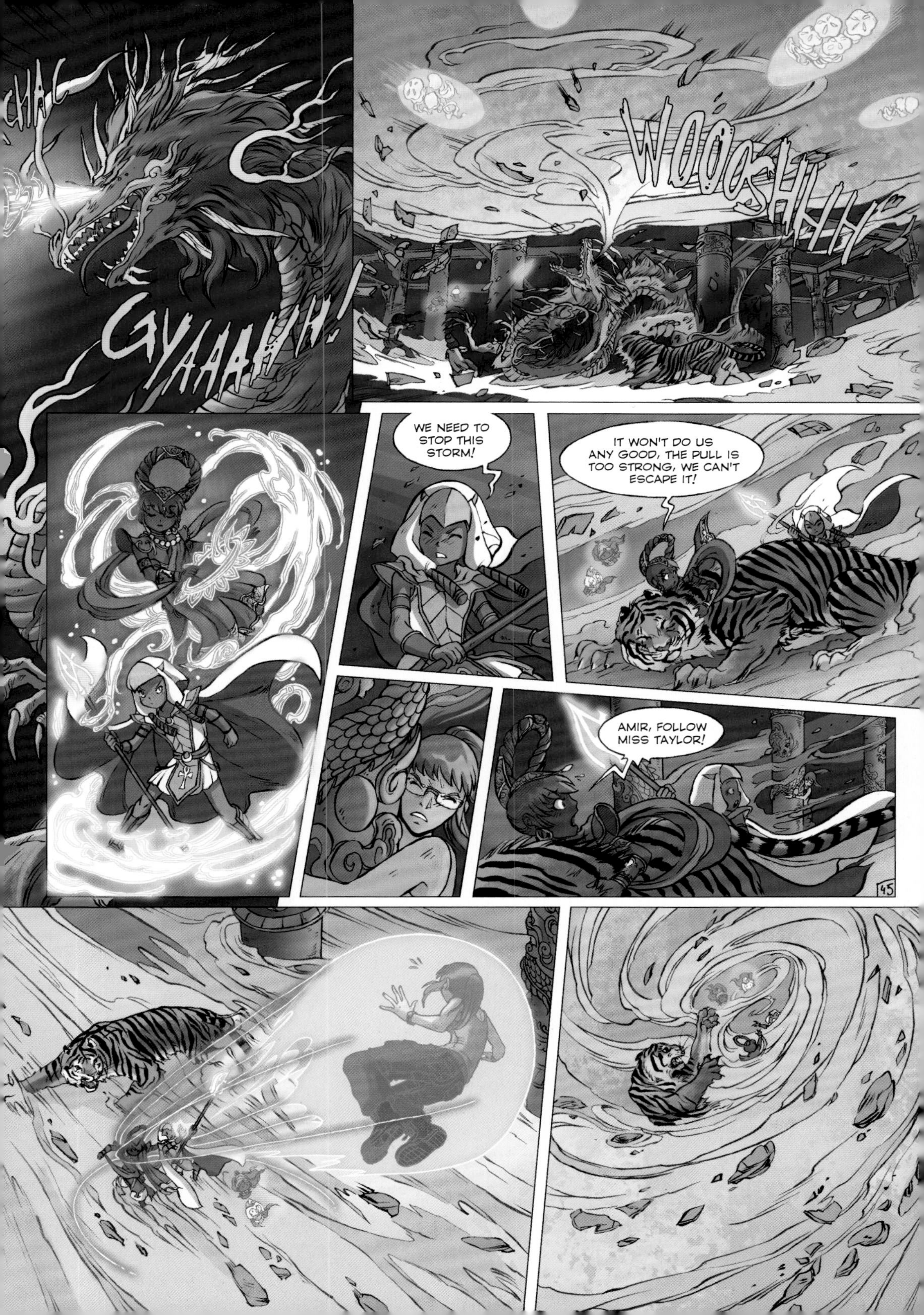
CHAC
GYAAAHH!
WOOOSHHH!
WE NEED TO STOP THIS STORM!
IT WON'T DO US ANY GOOD, THE PULL IS TOO STRONG, WE CAN'T ESCAPE IT!
AMIR, FOLLOW MISS TAYLOR!
45

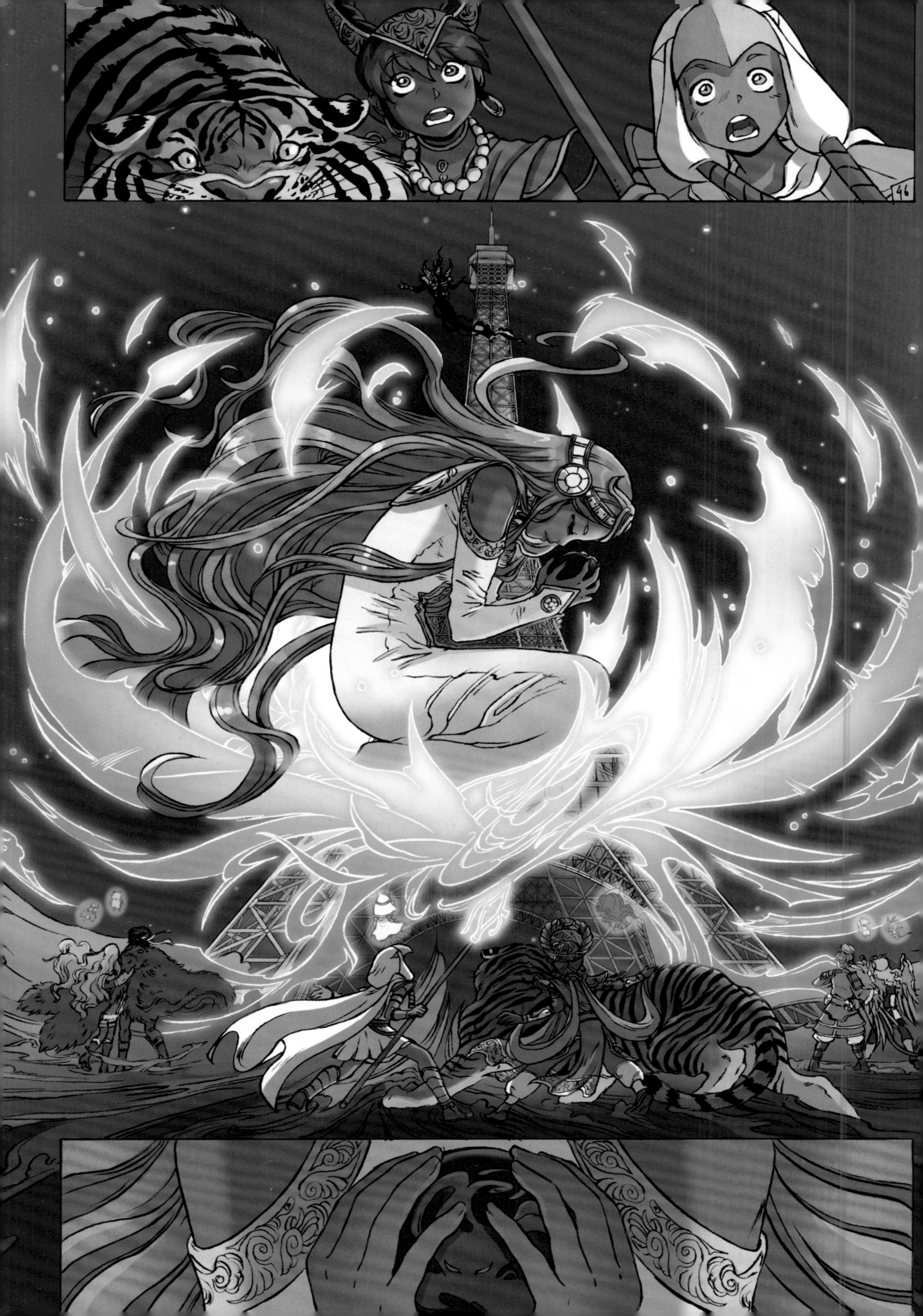
46

# PART 8 : SAINT PETERSBURG

*Story*
**PATRICIA LYFOUNG**

*Art*
**ZIMRA**

*Color*
**MAGALI PAILLAT**

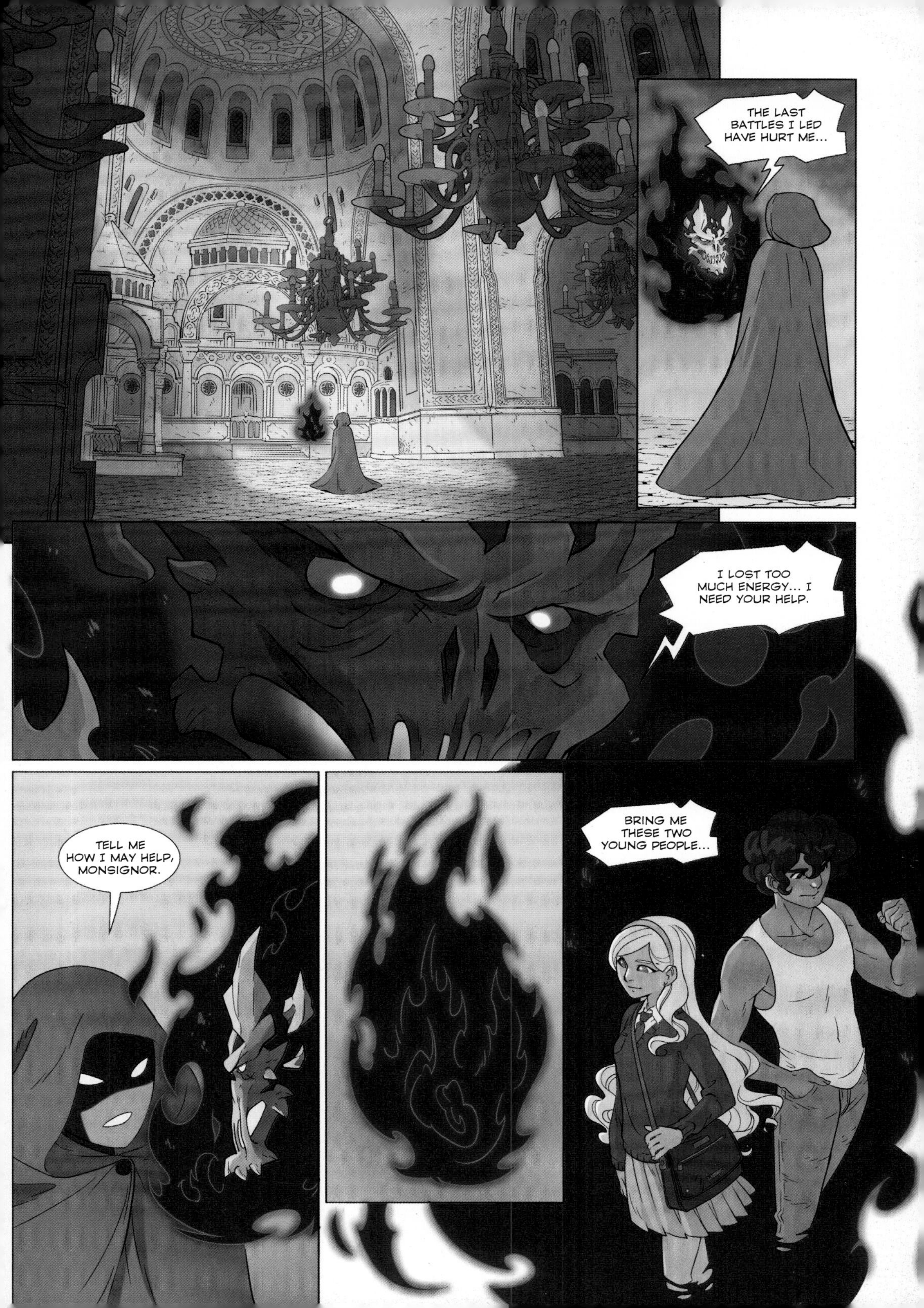
THE LAST BATTLES I LED HAVE HURT ME...
I LOST TOO MUCH ENERGY... I NEED YOUR HELP.
TELL ME HOW I MAY HELP, MONSIGNOR.
BRING ME THESE TWO YOUNG PEOPLE...

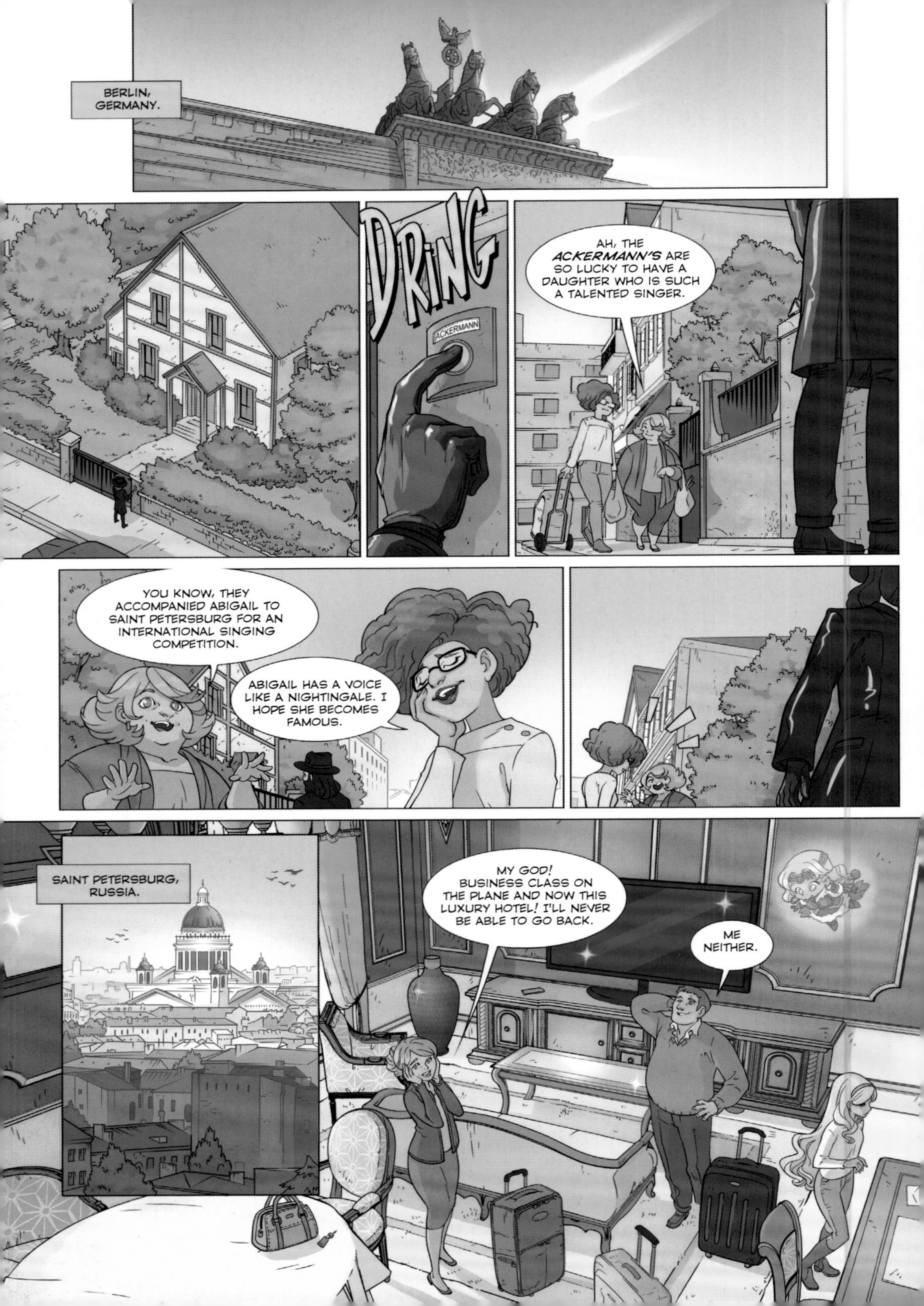
BERLIN, GERMANY.
DRING
ACKERMANN
AH, THE ACKERMANN'S ARE SO LUCKY TO HAVE A DAUGHTER WHO IS SUCH A TALENTED SINGER.
YOU KNOW, THEY ACCOMPANIED ABIGAIL TO SAINT PETERSBURG FOR AN INTERNATIONAL SINGING COMPETITION.
ABIGAIL HAS A VOICE LIKE A NIGHTINGALE. I HOPE SHE BECOMES FAMOUS.
SAINT PETERSBURG, RUSSIA.
MY GOD! BUSINESS CLASS ON THE PLANE AND NOW THIS LUXURY HOTEL! I'LL NEVER BE ABLE TO GO BACK.
ME NEITHER.

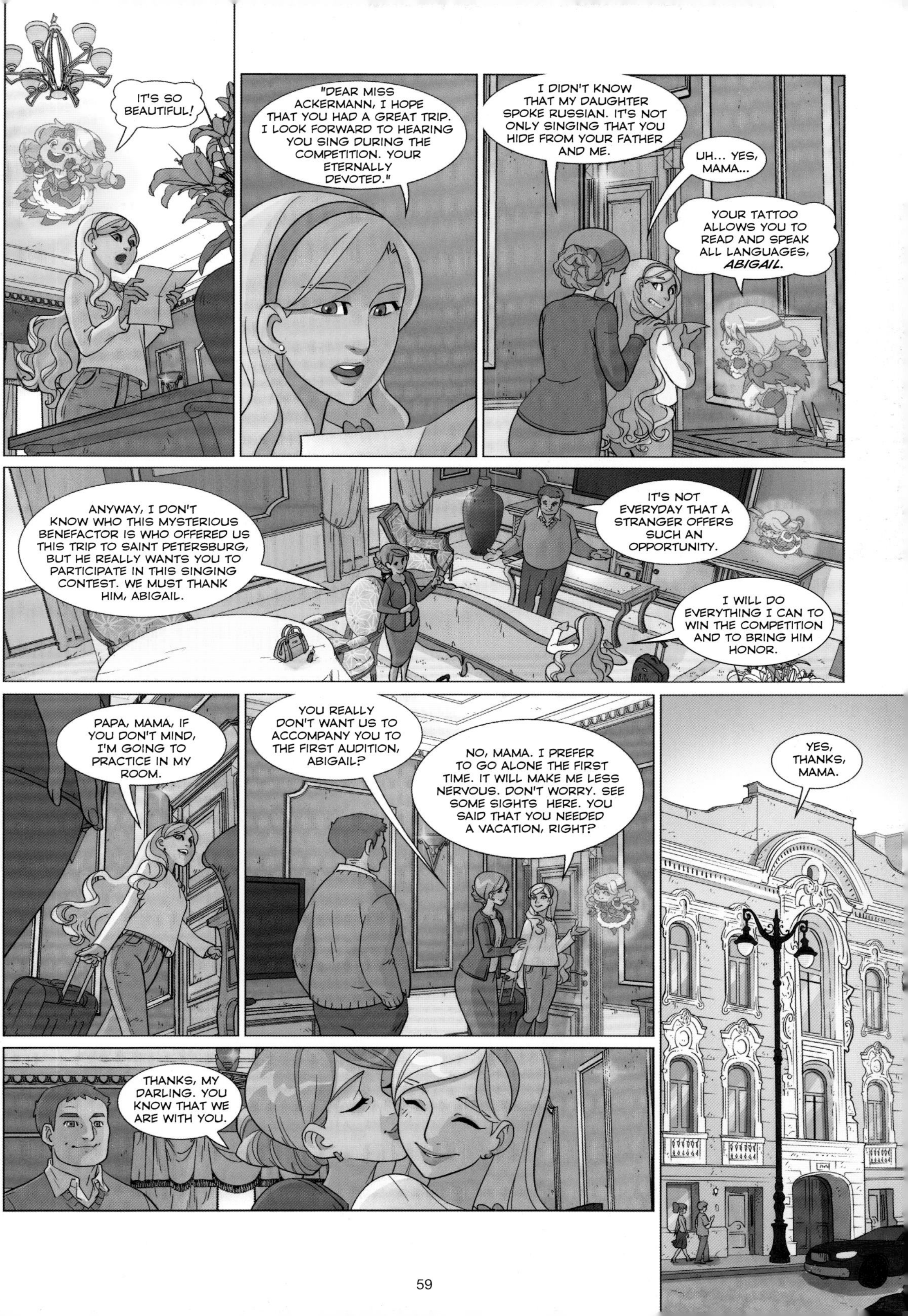
IT'S SO BEAUTIFUL!
"DEAR MISS ACKERMANN, I HOPE THAT YOU HAD A GREAT TRIP. I LOOK FORWARD TO HEARING YOU SING DURING THE COMPETITION. YOUR ETERNALLY DEVOTED."
I DIDN'T KNOW THAT MY DAUGHTER SPOKE RUSSIAN. IT'S NOT ONLY SINGING THAT YOU HIDE FROM YOUR FATHER AND ME.
UH... YES, MAMA...
YOUR TATTOO ALLOWS YOU TO READ AND SPEAK ALL LANGUAGES, ABIGAIL.
ANYWAY, I DON'T KNOW WHO THIS MYSTERIOUS BENEFACTOR IS WHO OFFERED US THIS TRIP TO SAINT PETERSBURG, BUT HE REALLY WANTS YOU TO PARTICIPATE IN THIS SINGING CONTEST. WE MUST THANK HIM, ABIGAIL.
IT'S NOT EVERYDAY THAT A STRANGER OFFERS SUCH AN OPPORTUNITY.
I WILL DO EVERYTHING I CAN TO WIN THE COMPETITION AND TO BRING HIM HONOR.
PAPA, MAMA, IF YOU DON'T MIND, I'M GOING TO PRACTICE IN MY ROOM.
YOU REALLY DON'T WANT US TO ACCOMPANY YOU TO THE FIRST AUDITION, ABIGAIL?
NO, MAMA. I PREFER TO GO ALONE THE FIRST TIME. IT WILL MAKE ME LESS NERVOUS. DON'T WORRY. SEE SOME SIGHTS HERE. YOU SAID THAT YOU NEEDED A VACATION, RIGHT?
YES, THANKS, MAMA.
THANKS, MY DARLING. YOU KNOW THAT WE ARE WITH YOU.

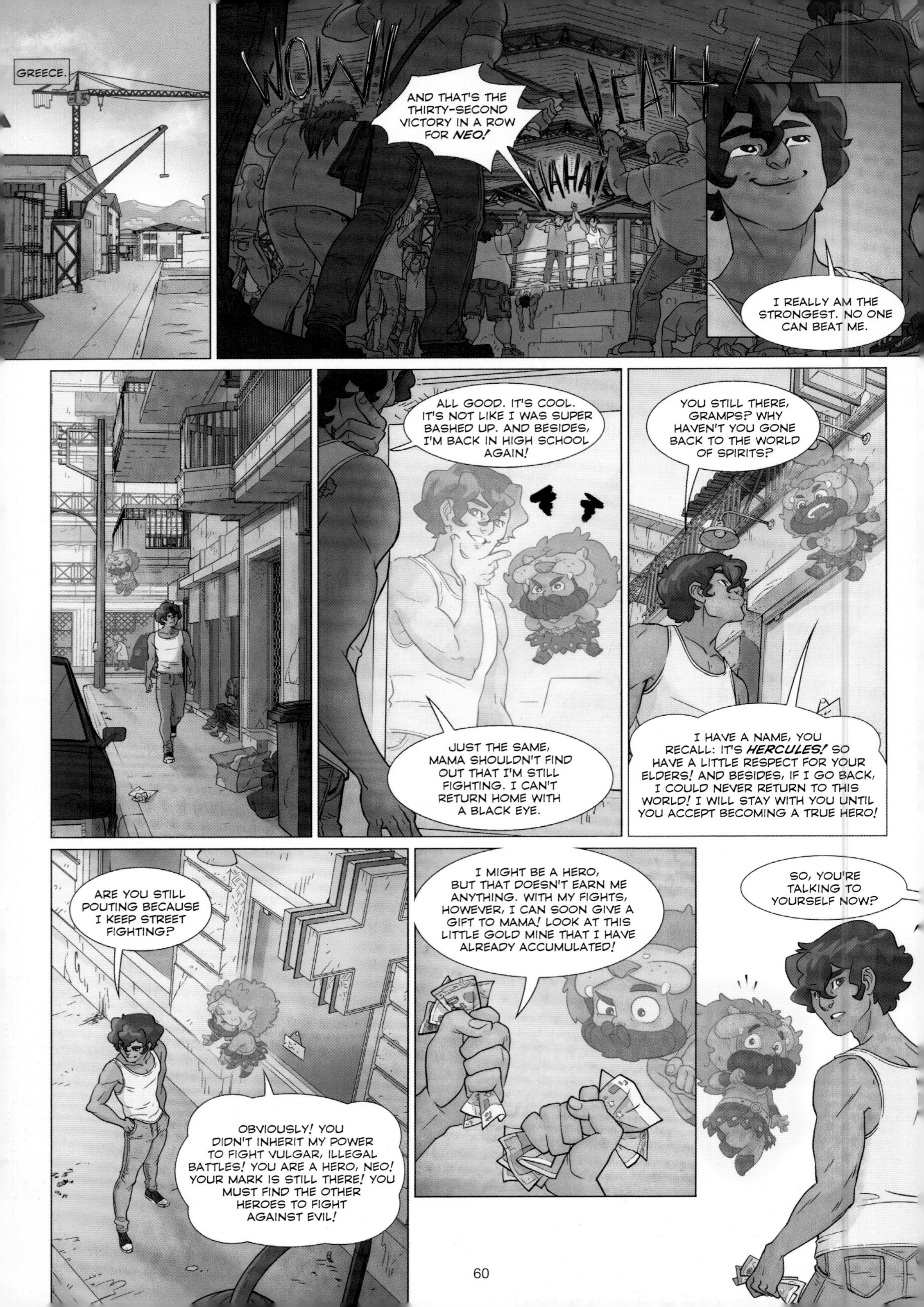
GREECE.
WOW!!
AND THAT'S THE THIRTY-SECOND VICTORY IN A ROW FOR NEO!
YEAH!!
HAHA!
I REALLY AM THE STRONGEST. NO ONE CAN BEAT ME.
ALL GOOD. IT'S COOL. IT'S NOT LIKE I WAS SUPER BASHED UP. AND BESIDES, I'M BACK IN HIGH SCHOOL AGAIN!
JUST THE SAME, MAMA SHOULDN'T FIND OUT THAT I'M STILL FIGHTING. I CAN'T RETURN HOME WITH A BLACK EYE.
YOU STILL THERE, GRAMPS? WHY HAVEN'T YOU GONE BACK TO THE WORLD OF SPIRITS?
I HAVE A NAME, YOU RECALL: IT'S HERCULES! SO HAVE A LITTLE RESPECT FOR YOUR ELDERS! AND BESIDES, IF I GO BACK, I COULD NEVER RETURN TO THIS WORLD! I WILL STAY WITH YOU UNTIL YOU ACCEPT BECOMING A TRUE HERO!
ARE YOU STILL POUTING BECAUSE I KEEP STREET FIGHTING?
OBVIOUSLY! YOU DIDN'T INHERIT MY POWER TO FIGHT VULGAR, ILLEGAL BATTLES! YOU ARE A HERO, NEO! YOUR MARK IS STILL THERE! YOU MUST FIND THE OTHER HEROES TO FIGHT AGAINST EVIL!
I MIGHT BE A HERO, BUT THAT DOESN'T EARN ME ANYTHING. WITH MY FIGHTS, HOWEVER, I CAN SOON GIVE A GIFT TO MAMA! LOOK AT THIS LITTLE GOLD MINE THAT I HAVE ALREADY ACCUMULATED!
SO, YOU'RE TALKING TO YOURSELF NOW?

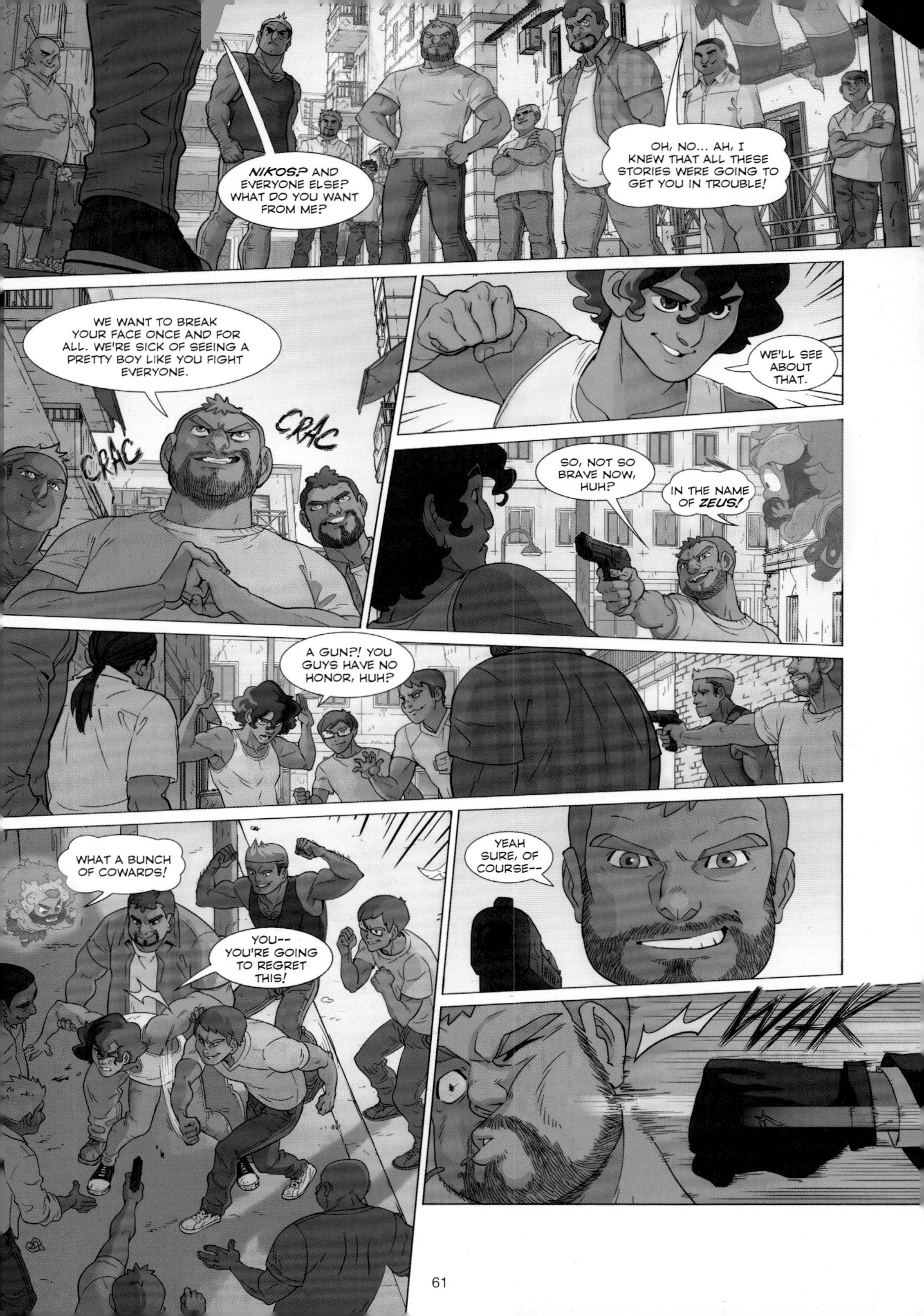
NIKOS? AND EVERYONE ELSE? WHAT DO YOU WANT FROM ME?
OH, NO... AH, I KNEW THAT ALL THESE STORIES WERE GOING TO GET YOU IN TROUBLE!
WE WANT TO BREAK YOUR FACE ONCE AND FOR ALL. WE'RE SICK OF SEEING A PRETTY BOY LIKE YOU FIGHT EVERYONE.
CRAC
CRAC
WE'LL SEE ABOUT THAT.
SO, NOT SO BRAVE NOW, HUH?
IN THE NAME OF ZEUS!
A GUN?! YOU GUYS HAVE NO HONOR, HUH?
WHAT A BUNCH OF COWARDS!
YOU-- YOU'RE GOING TO REGRET THIS!
YEAH SURE, OF COURSE--
WAK

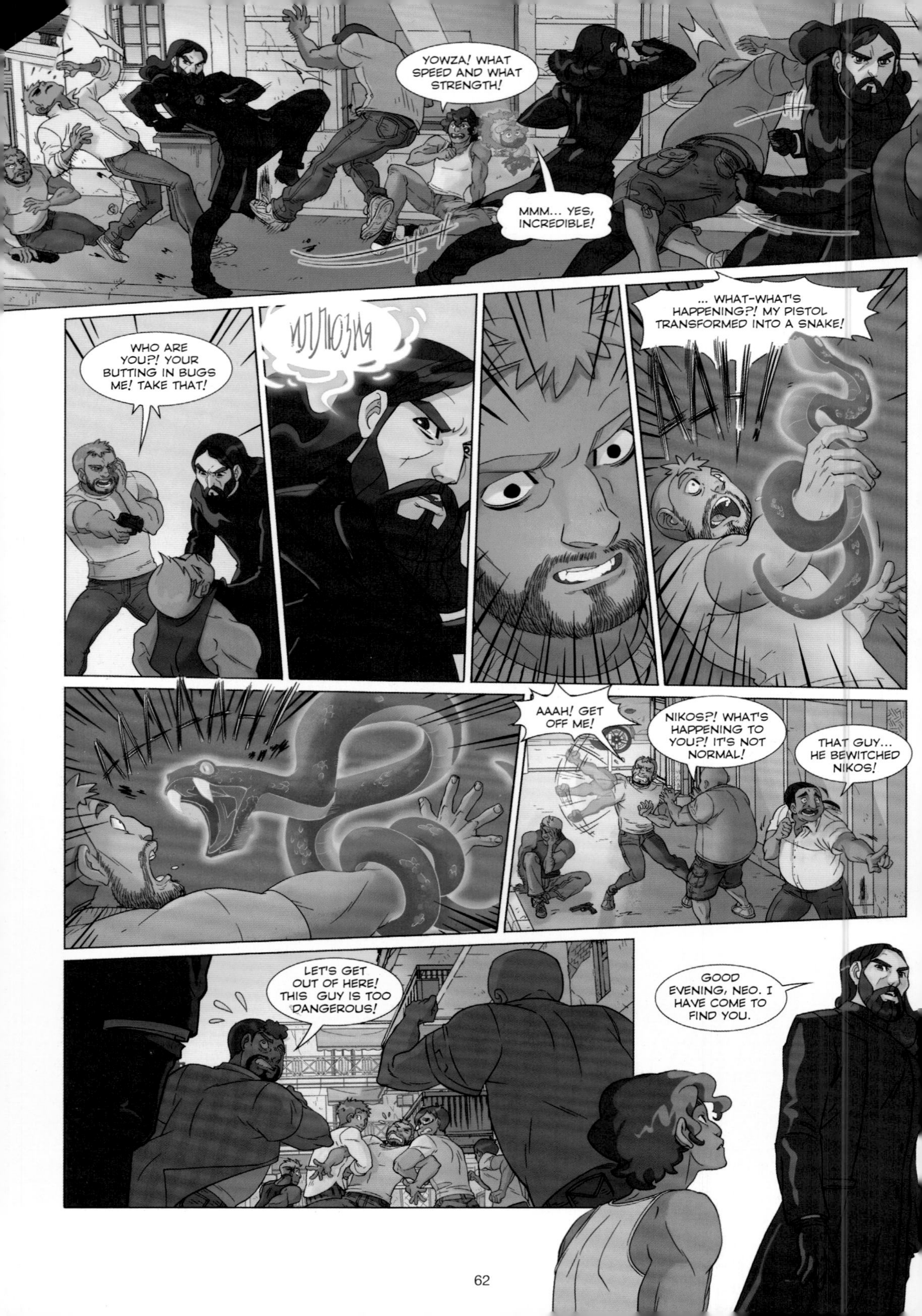

YOWZA! WHAT SPEED AND WHAT STRENGTH!
MMM... YES, INCREDIBLE!
WHO ARE YOU?! YOUR BUTTING IN BUGS ME! TAKE THAT!
ИЛЛЮЗИЯ
... WHAT-WHAT'S HAPPENING?! MY PISTOL TRANSFORMED INTO A SNAKE!
AAH!
AAAAAH!
AAAH! GET OFF ME!
NIKOS?! WHAT'S HAPPENING TO YOU?! IT'S NOT NORMAL!
THAT GUY... HE BEWITCHED NIKOS!
LET'S GET OUT OF HERE! THIS GUY IS TOO DANGEROUS!
GOOD EVENING, NEO. I HAVE COME TO FIND YOU.

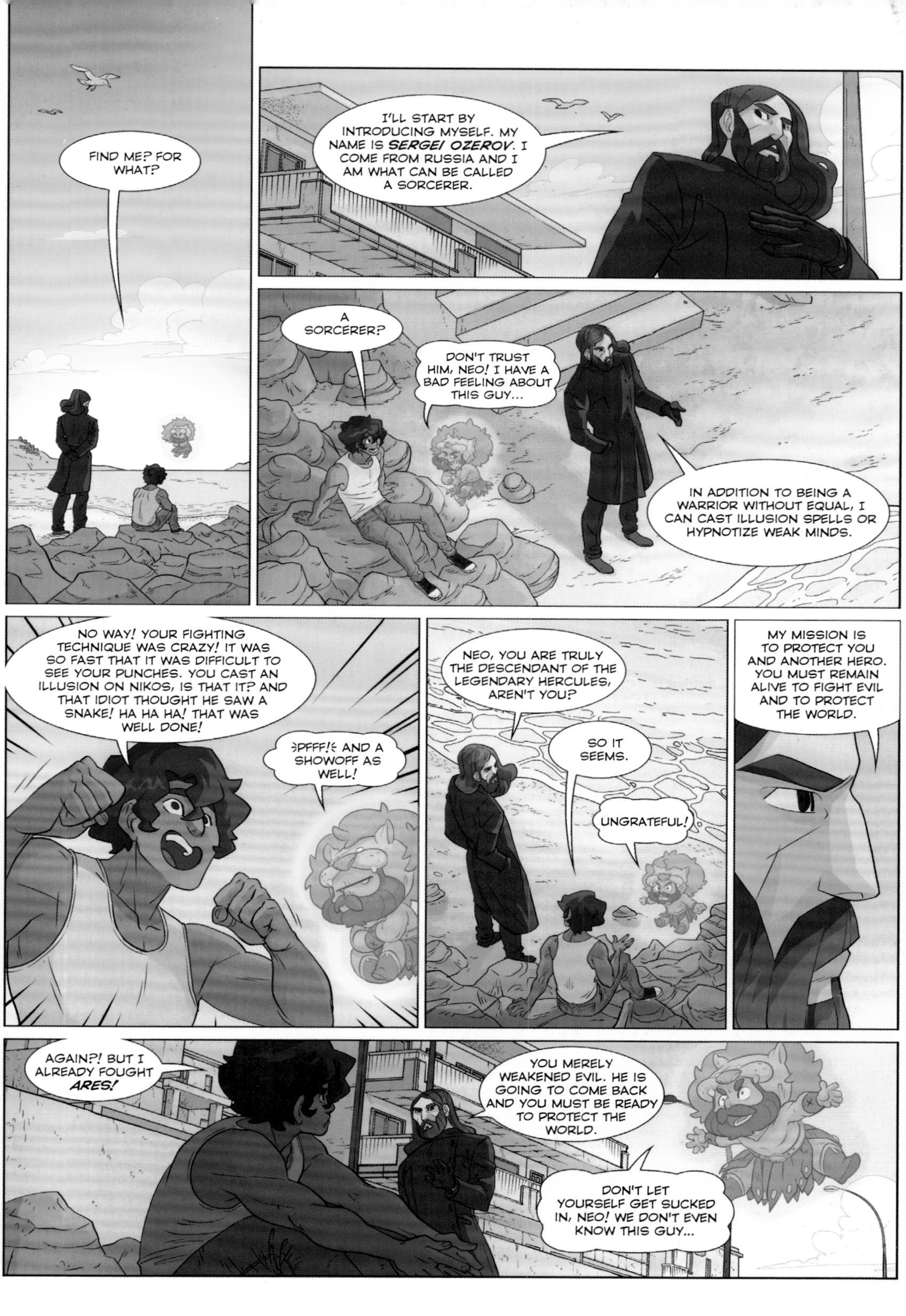
FIND ME? FOR WHAT?
I'LL START BY INTRODUCING MYSELF. MY NAME IS SERGEI OZEROV. I COME FROM RUSSIA AND I AM WHAT CAN BE CALLED A SORCERER.
A SORCERER?
DON'T TRUST HIM, NEO! I HAVE A BAD FEELING ABOUT THIS GUY...
IN ADDITION TO BEING A WARRIOR WITHOUT EQUAL, I CAN CAST ILLUSION SPELLS OR HYPNOTIZE WEAK MINDS.
NO WAY! YOUR FIGHTING TECHNIQUE WAS CRAZY! IT WAS SO FAST THAT IT WAS DIFFICULT TO SEE YOUR PUNCHES. YOU CAST AN ILLUSION ON NIKOS, IS THAT IT? AND THAT IDIOT THOUGHT HE SAW A SNAKE! HA HA HA! THAT WAS WELL DONE!
PFFF! AND A SHOWOFF AS WELL!
NEO, YOU ARE TRULY THE DESCENDANT OF THE LEGENDARY HERCULES, AREN'T YOU?
SO IT SEEMS.
UNGRATEFUL!
MY MISSION IS TO PROTECT YOU AND ANOTHER HERO. YOU MUST REMAIN ALIVE TO FIGHT EVIL AND TO PROTECT THE WORLD.
AGAIN?! BUT I ALREADY FOUGHT ARES!
YOU MERELY WEAKENED EVIL. HE IS GOING TO COME BACK AND YOU MUST BE READY TO PROTECT THE WORLD.
DON'T LET YOURSELF GET SUCKED IN, NEO! WE DON'T EVEN KNOW THIS GUY...

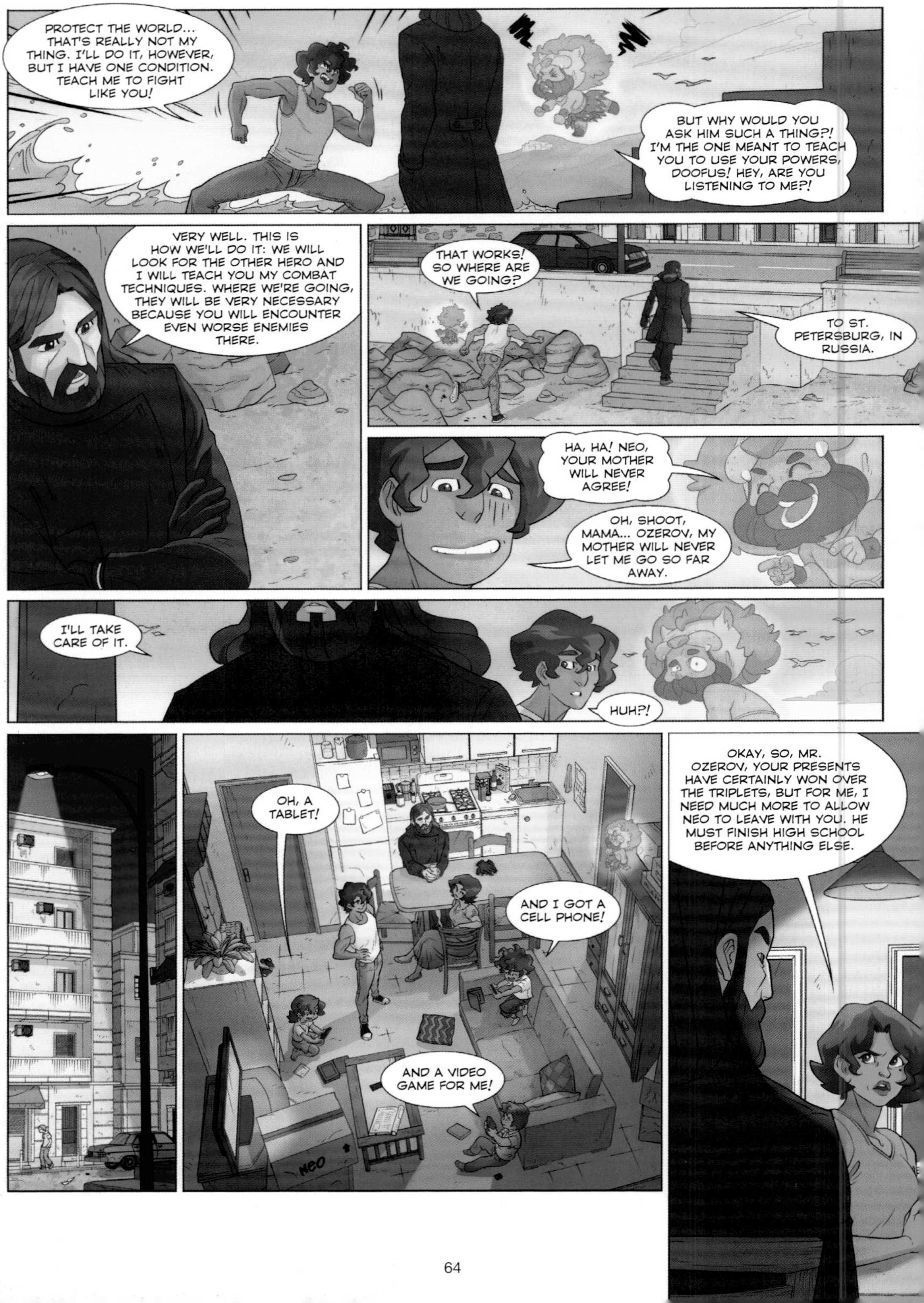
PROTECT THE WORLD... THAT'S REALLY NOT MY THING. I'LL DO IT, HOWEVER, BUT I HAVE ONE CONDITION. TEACH ME TO FIGHT LIKE YOU!
BUT WHY WOULD YOU ASK HIM SUCH A THING?! I'M THE ONE MEANT TO TEACH YOU TO USE YOUR POWERS, DOOFUS! HEY, ARE YOU LISTENING TO ME?!
VERY WELL. THIS IS HOW WE'LL DO IT: WE WILL LOOK FOR THE OTHER HERO AND I WILL TEACH YOU MY COMBAT TECHNIQUES. WHERE WE'RE GOING, THEY WILL BE VERY NECESSARY BECAUSE YOU WILL ENCOUNTER EVEN WORSE ENEMIES THERE.
THAT WORKS! SO WHERE ARE WE GOING?
TO ST. PETERSBURG, IN RUSSIA.
HA, HA! NEO, YOUR MOTHER WILL NEVER AGREE!
OH, SHOOT, MAMA... OZEROV, MY MOTHER WILL NEVER LET ME GO SO FAR AWAY.
I'LL TAKE CARE OF IT.
HUH?!
OH, A TABLET!
AND I GOT A CELL PHONE!
AND A VIDEO GAME FOR ME!
NEO
OKAY, SO, MR. OZEROV, YOUR PRESENTS HAVE CERTAINLY WON OVER THE TRIPLETS, BUT FOR ME, I NEED MUCH MORE TO ALLOW NEO TO LEAVE WITH YOU. HE MUST FINISH HIGH SCHOOL BEFORE ANYTHING ELSE.

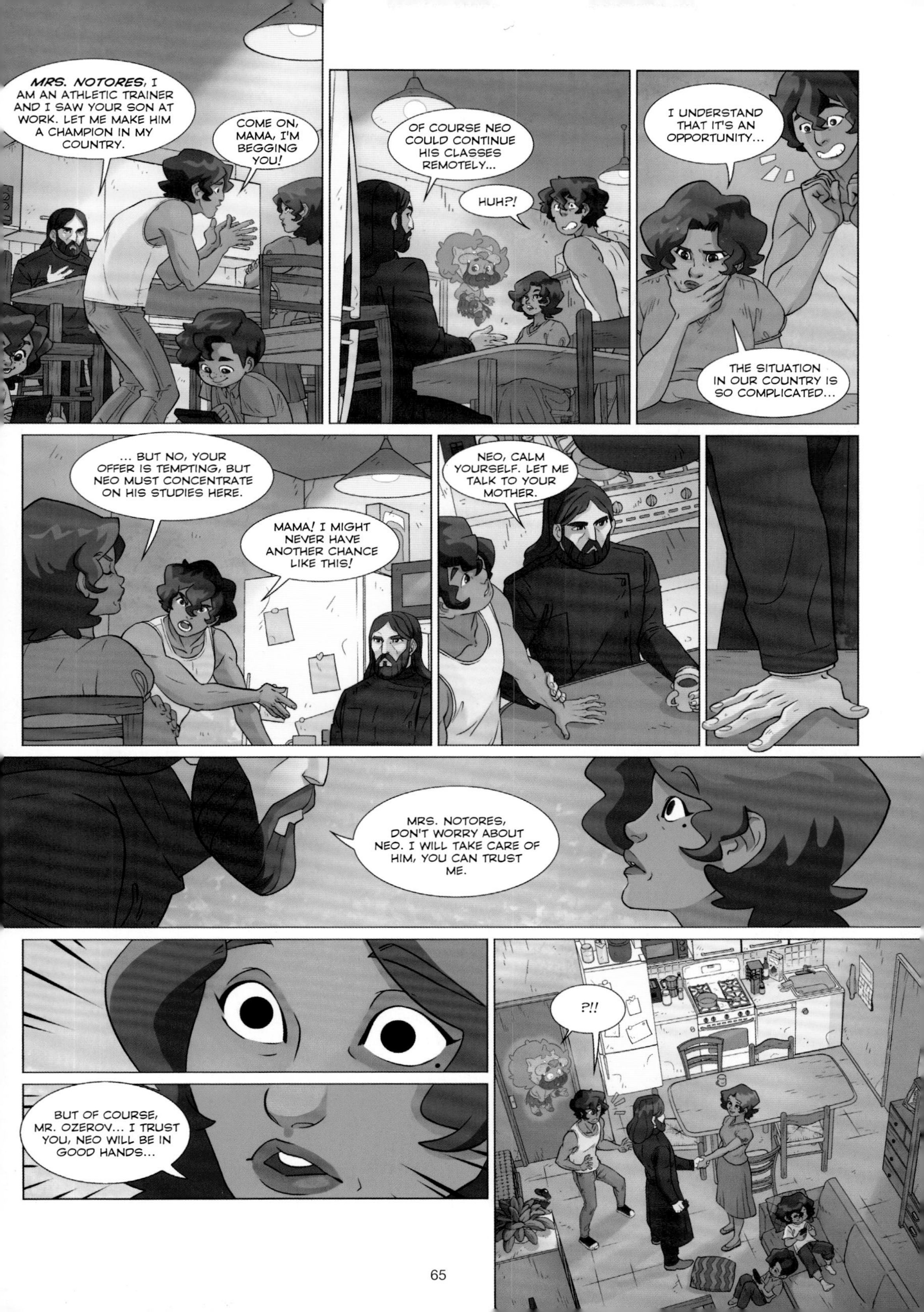

MRS. NOTORES, I AM AN ATHLETIC TRAINER AND I SAW YOUR SON AT WORK. LET ME MAKE HIM A CHAMPION IN MY COUNTRY.
COME ON, MAMA, I'M BEGGING YOU!
OF COURSE NEO COULD CONTINUE HIS CLASSES REMOTELY...
HUH?!
I UNDERSTAND THAT IT'S AN OPPORTUNITY...
THE SITUATION IN OUR COUNTRY IS SO COMPLICATED...
... BUT NO, YOUR OFFER IS TEMPTING, BUT NEO MUST CONCENTRATE ON HIS STUDIES HERE.
MAMA! I MIGHT NEVER HAVE ANOTHER CHANCE LIKE THIS!
NEO, CALM YOURSELF. LET ME TALK TO YOUR MOTHER.
MRS. NOTORES, DON'T WORRY ABOUT NEO. I WILL TAKE CARE OF HIM, YOU CAN TRUST ME.
BUT OF COURSE, MR. OZEROV... I TRUST YOU, NEO WILL BE IN GOOD HANDS...
?!!

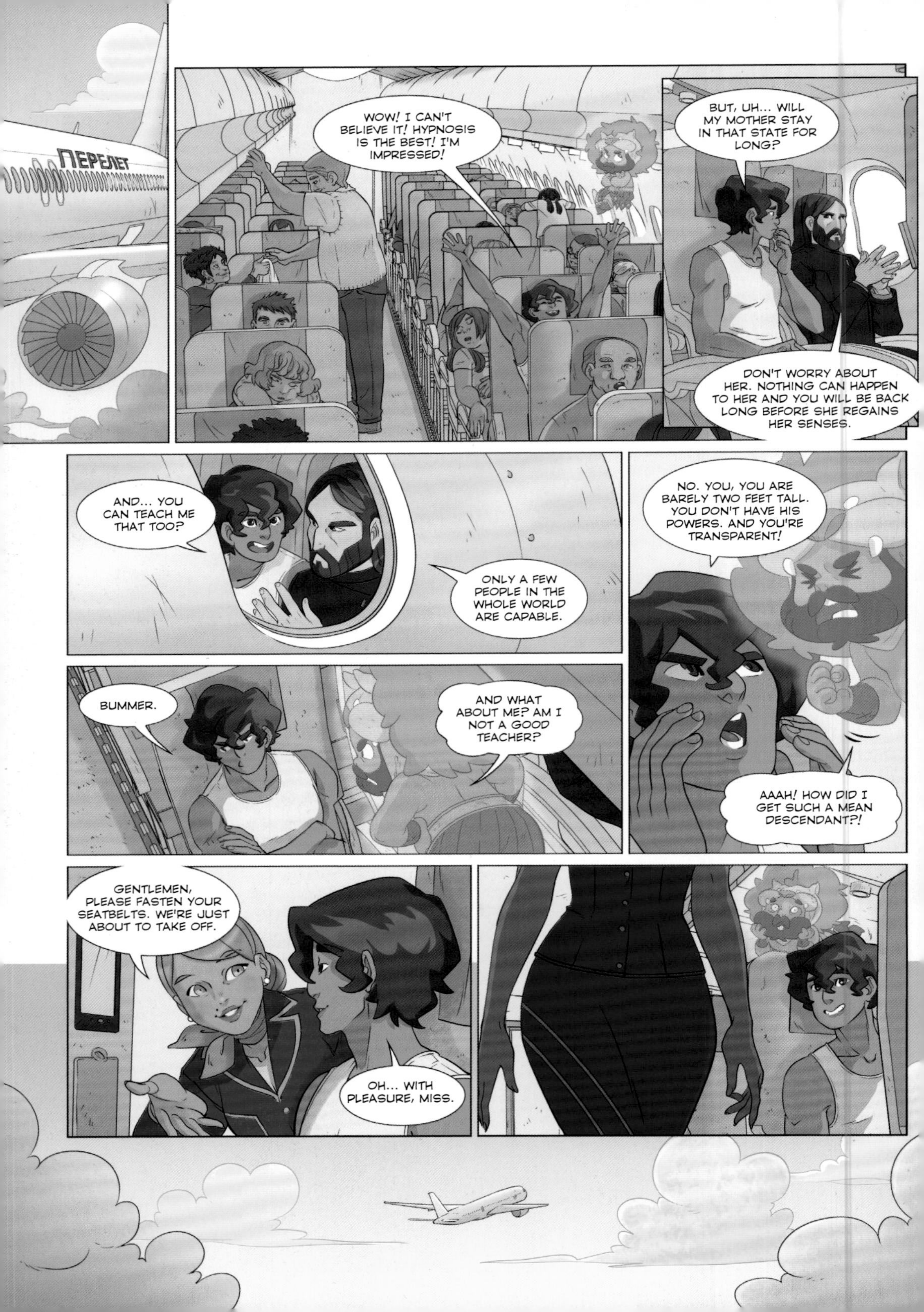
ПЕРЕЛЕТ
WOW! I CAN'T BELIEVE IT! HYPNOSIS IS THE BEST! I'M IMPRESSED!
BUT, UH... WILL MY MOTHER STAY IN THAT STATE FOR LONG?
DON'T WORRY ABOUT HER. NOTHING CAN HAPPEN TO HER AND YOU WILL BE BACK LONG BEFORE SHE REGAINS HER SENSES.
AND... YOU CAN TEACH ME THAT TOO?
ONLY A FEW PEOPLE IN THE WHOLE WORLD ARE CAPABLE.
BUMMER.
AND WHAT ABOUT ME? AM I NOT A GOOD TEACHER?
NO. YOU, YOU ARE BARELY TWO FEET TALL. YOU DON'T HAVE HIS POWERS. AND YOU'RE TRANSPARENT!
AAAH! HOW DID I GET SUCH A MEAN DESCENDANT?!
GENTLEMEN, PLEASE FASTEN YOUR SEATBELTS. WE'RE JUST ABOUT TO TAKE OFF.
OH... WITH PLEASURE, MISS.

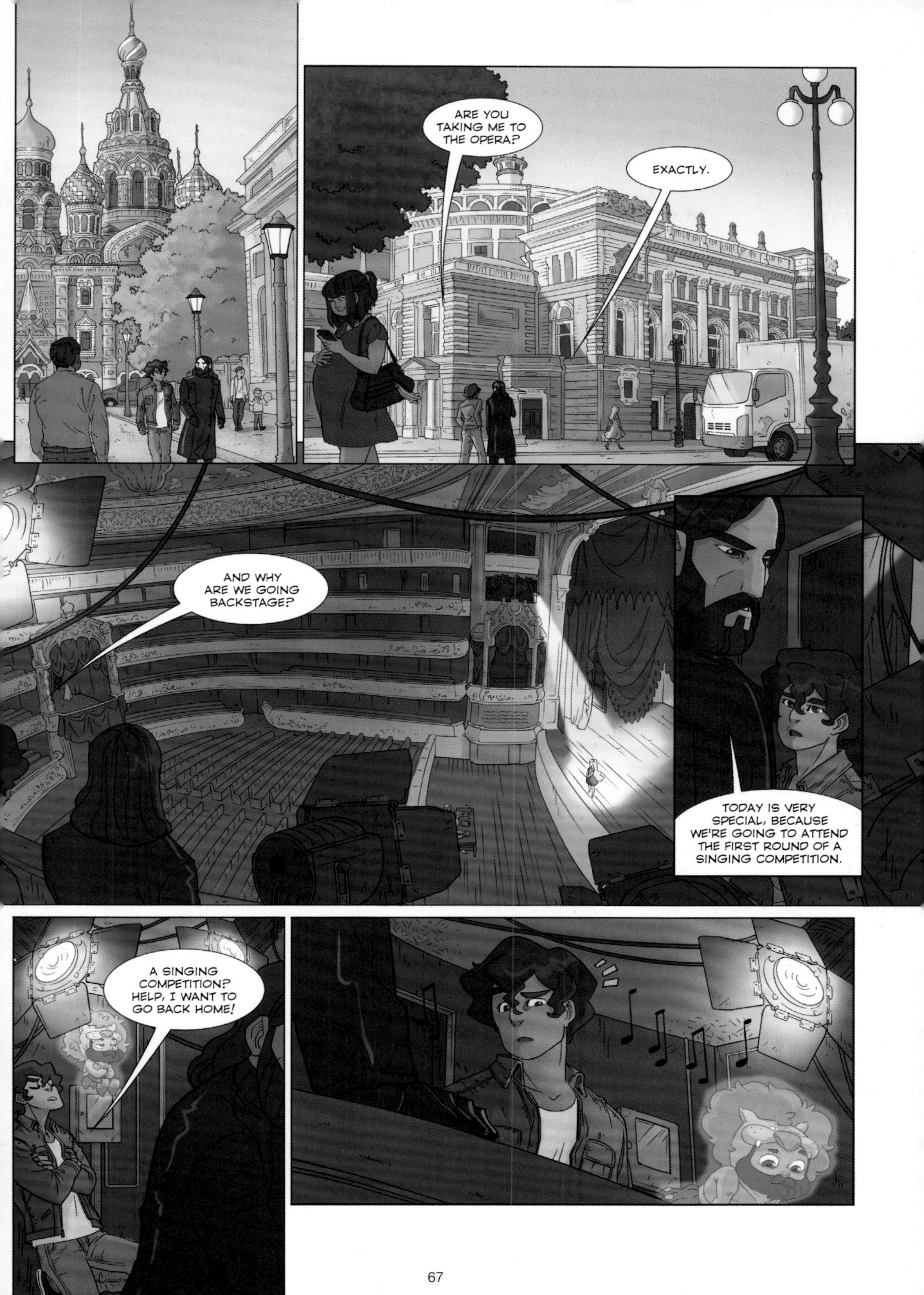
ARE YOU TAKING ME TO THE OPERA?
EXACTLY.
AND WHY ARE WE GOING BACKSTAGE?
TODAY IS VERY SPECIAL, BECAUSE WE'RE GOING TO ATTEND THE FIRST ROUND OF A SINGING COMPETITION.
A SINGING COMPETITION? HELP, I WANT TO GO BACK HOME!

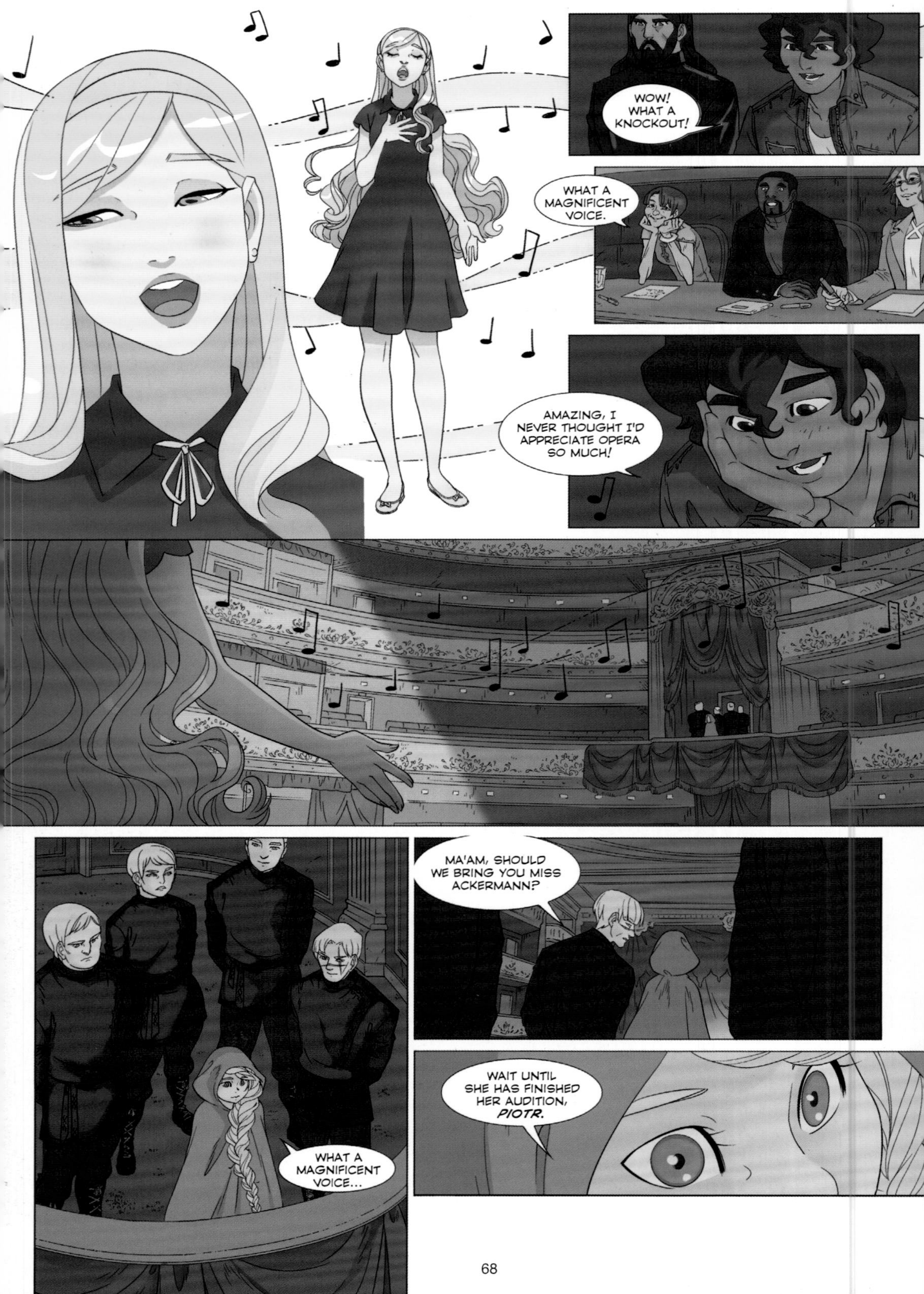
WOW! WHAT A KNOCKOUT!
WHAT A MAGNIFICENT VOICE.
AMAZING, I NEVER THOUGHT I'D APPRECIATE OPERA SO MUCH!
WHAT A MAGNIFICENT VOICE...
MA'AM, SHOULD WE BRING YOU MISS ACKERMANN?
WAIT UNTIL SHE HAS FINISHED HER AUDITION, *PIOTR.*

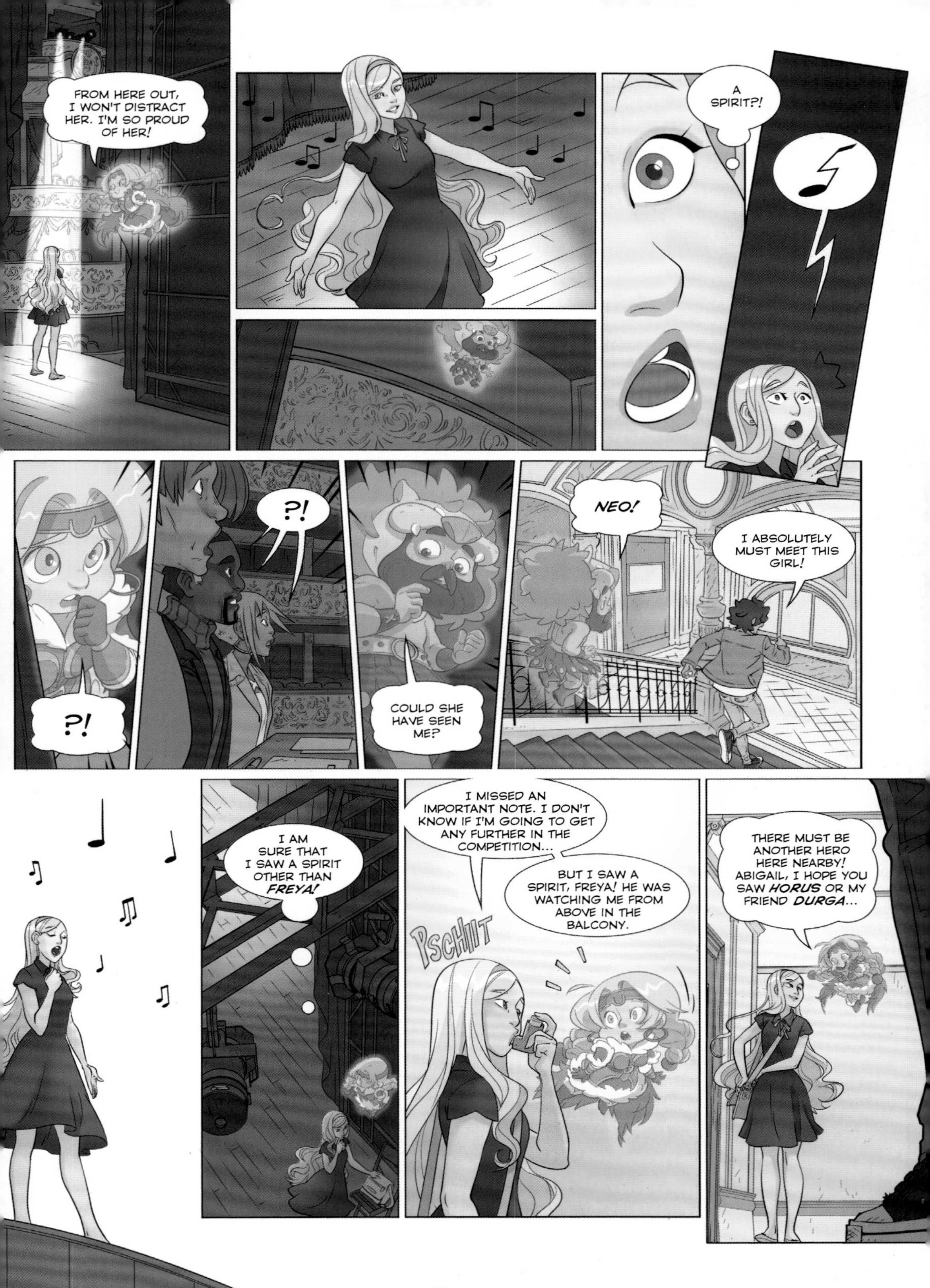
FROM HERE OUT, I WON'T DISTRACT HER. I'M SO PROUD OF HER!
A SPIRIT?!
?!
?!
COULD SHE HAVE SEEN ME?
NEO!
I ABSOLUTELY MUST MEET THIS GIRL!
I AM SURE THAT I SAW A SPIRIT OTHER THAN FREYA!
I MISSED AN IMPORTANT NOTE. I DON'T KNOW IF I'M GOING TO GET ANY FURTHER IN THE COMPETITION...
BUT I SAW A SPIRIT, FREYA! HE WAS WATCHING ME FROM ABOVE IN THE BALCONY.
PSCHIIT
THERE MUST BE ANOTHER HERO HERE NEARBY! ABIGAIL, I HOPE YOU SAW HORUS OR MY FRIEND DURGA...

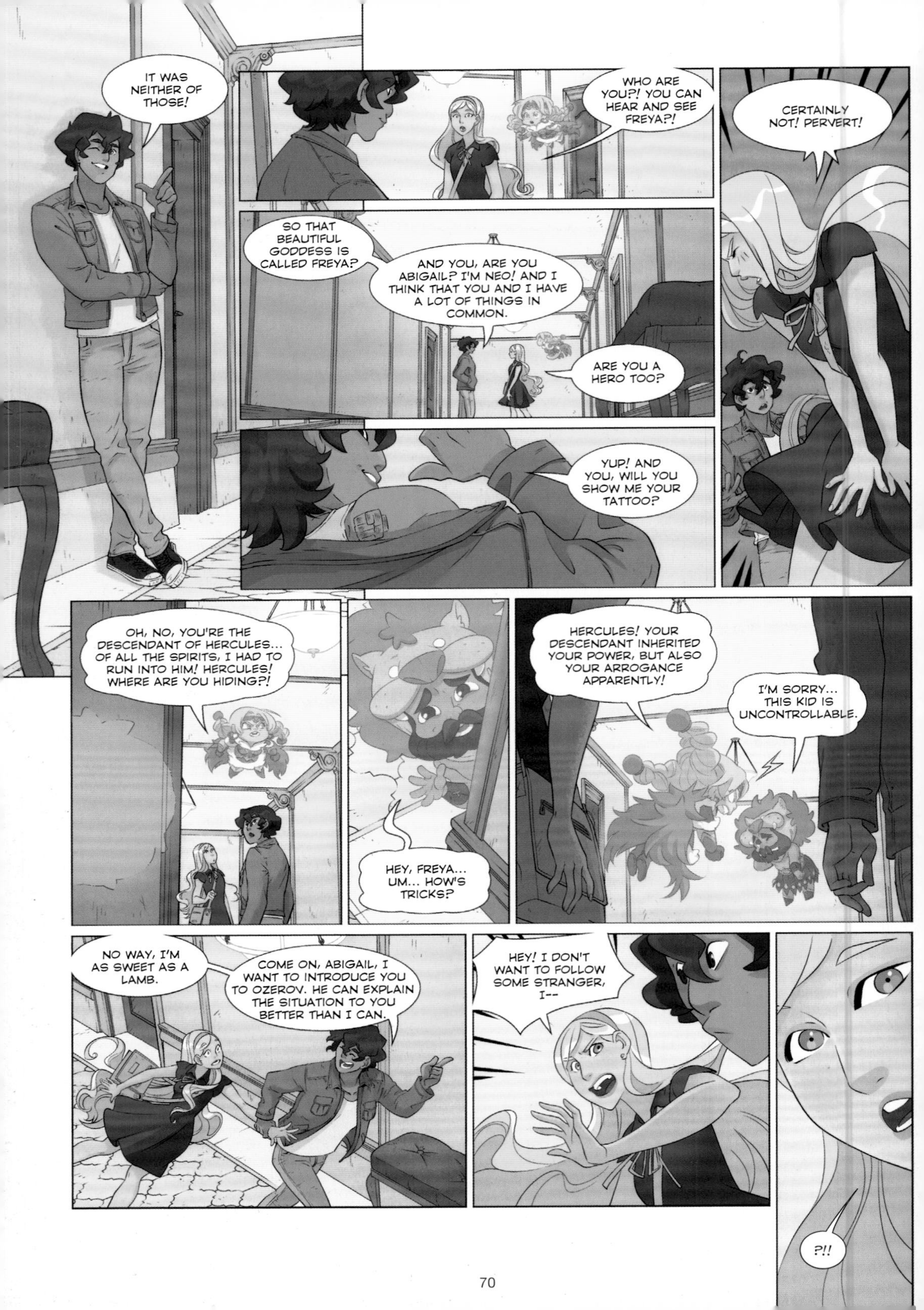
IT WAS NEITHER OF THOSE!
WHO ARE YOU?! YOU CAN HEAR AND SEE FREYA?!
SO THAT BEAUTIFUL GODDESS IS CALLED FREYA?
AND YOU, ARE YOU ABIGAIL? I'M NEO! AND I THINK THAT YOU AND I HAVE A LOT OF THINGS IN COMMON.
ARE YOU A HERO TOO?
YUP! AND YOU, WILL YOU SHOW ME YOUR TATTOO?
CERTAINLY NOT! PERVERT!
OH, NO, YOU'RE THE DESCENDANT OF HERCULES... OF ALL THE SPIRITS, I HAD TO RUN INTO HIM! HERCULES! WHERE ARE YOU HIDING?!
HEY, FREYA... UM... HOW'S TRICKS?
HERCULES! YOUR DESCENDANT INHERITED YOUR POWER, BUT ALSO YOUR ARROGANCE APPARENTLY!
I'M SORRY... THIS KID IS UNCONTROLLABLE.
NO WAY, I'M AS SWEET AS A LAMB.
COME ON, ABIGAIL, I WANT TO INTRODUCE YOU TO OZEROV. HE CAN EXPLAIN THE SITUATION TO YOU BETTER THAN I CAN.
HEY! I DON'T WANT TO FOLLOW SOME STRANGER, I--
?!!

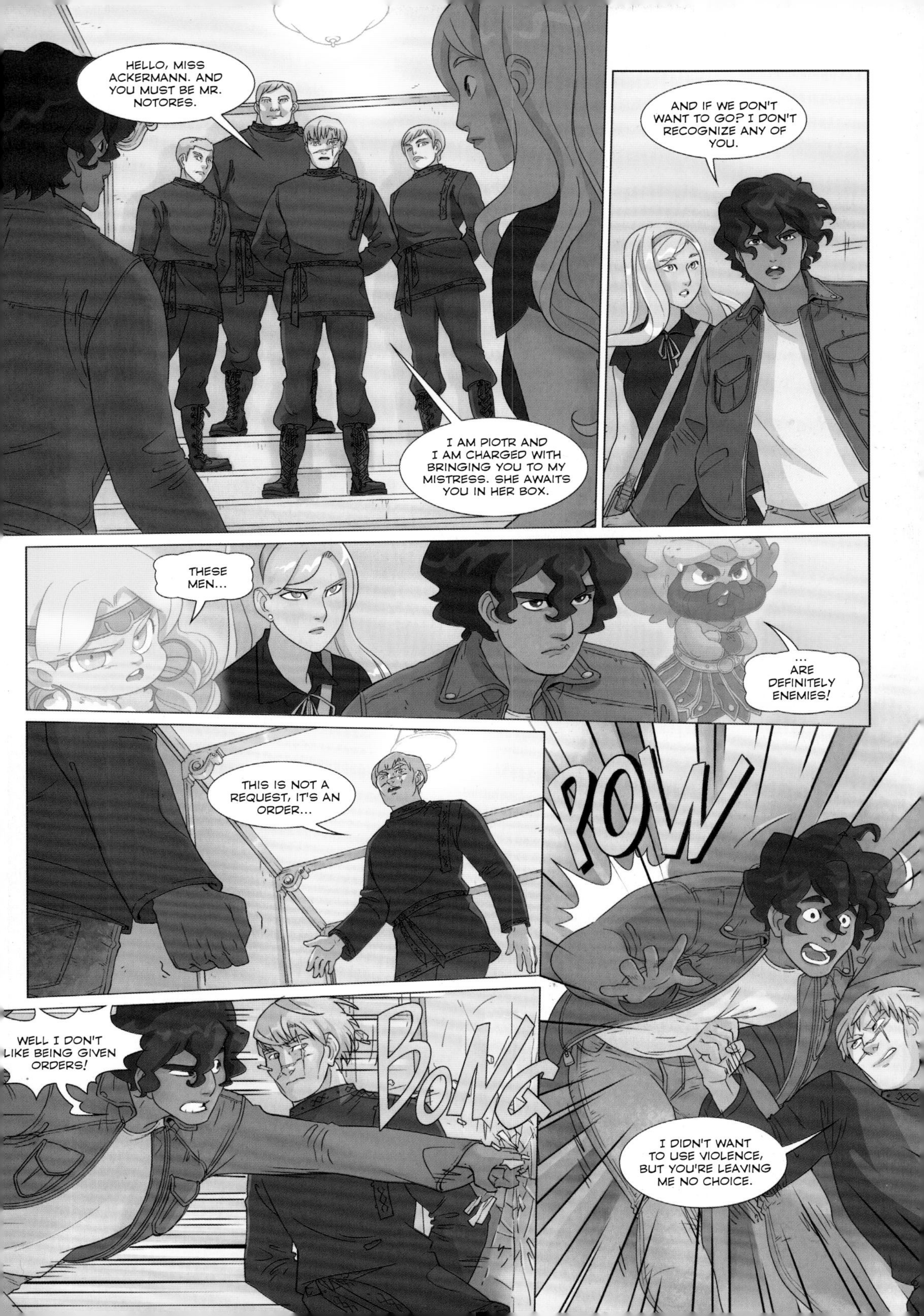
HELLO, MISS ACKERMANN. AND YOU MUST BE MR. NOTORES.
I AM PIOTR AND I AM CHARGED WITH BRINGING YOU TO MY MISTRESS. SHE AWAITS YOU IN HER BOX.
AND IF WE DON'T WANT TO GO? I DON'T RECOGNIZE ANY OF YOU.
THESE MEN...
... ARE DEFINITELY ENEMIES!
THIS IS NOT A REQUEST, IT'S AN ORDER...
POW
WELL I DON'T LIKE BEING GIVEN ORDERS!
BONG
I DIDN'T WANT TO USE VIOLENCE, BUT YOU'RE LEAVING ME NO CHOICE.

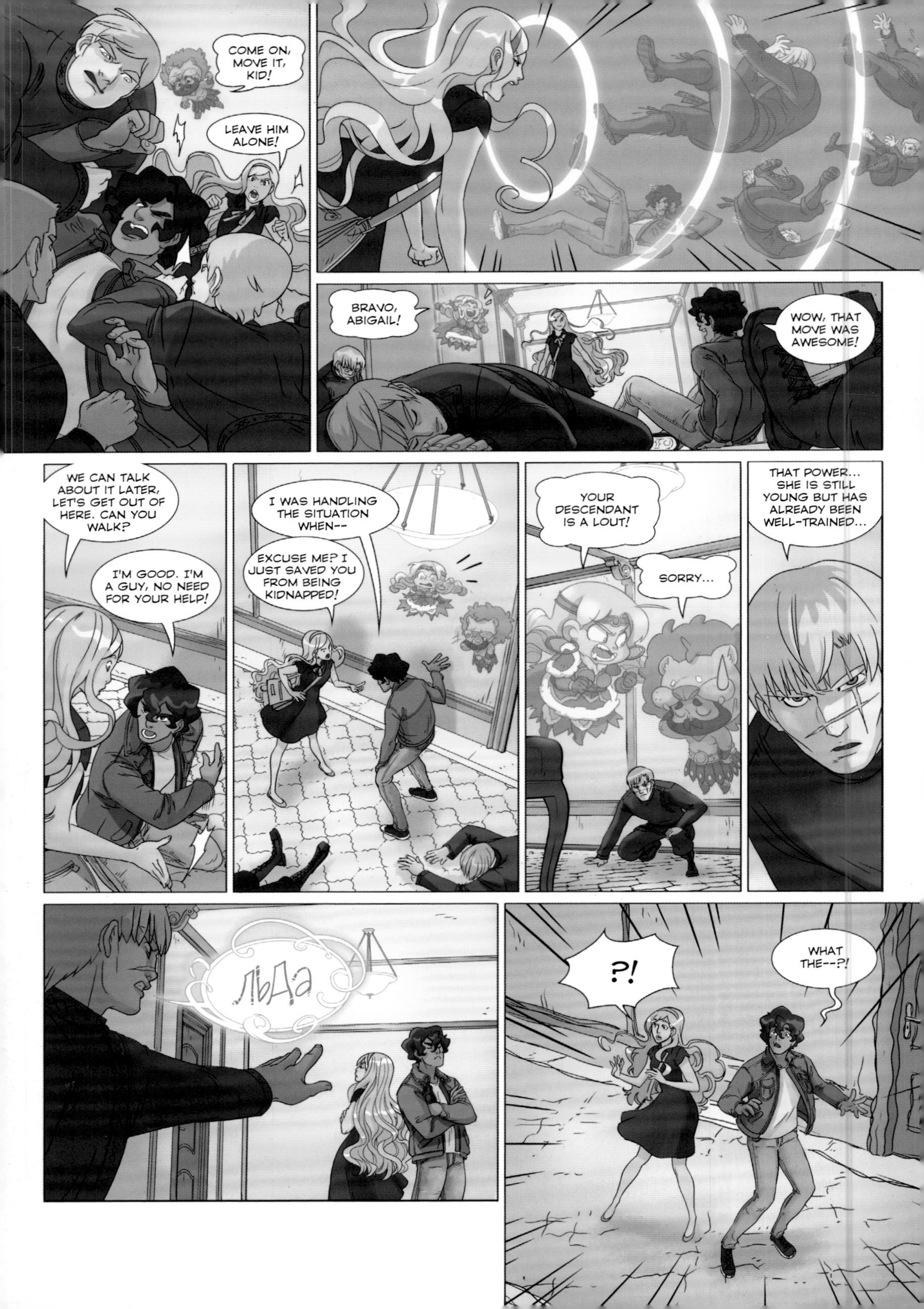
COME ON, MOVE IT, KID!
LEAVE HIM ALONE!
BRAVO, ABIGAIL!
WOW, THAT MOVE WAS AWESOME!
WE CAN TALK ABOUT IT LATER, LET'S GET OUT OF HERE. CAN YOU WALK?
I'M GOOD. I'M A GUY, NO NEED FOR YOUR HELP!
I WAS HANDLING THE SITUATION WHEN--
EXCUSE ME? I JUST SAVED YOU FROM BEING KIDNAPPED!
YOUR DESCENDANT IS A LOUT!
SORRY...
THAT POWER... SHE IS STILL YOUNG BUT HAS ALREADY BEEN WELL-TRAINED...
льда
?!
WHAT THE--?!

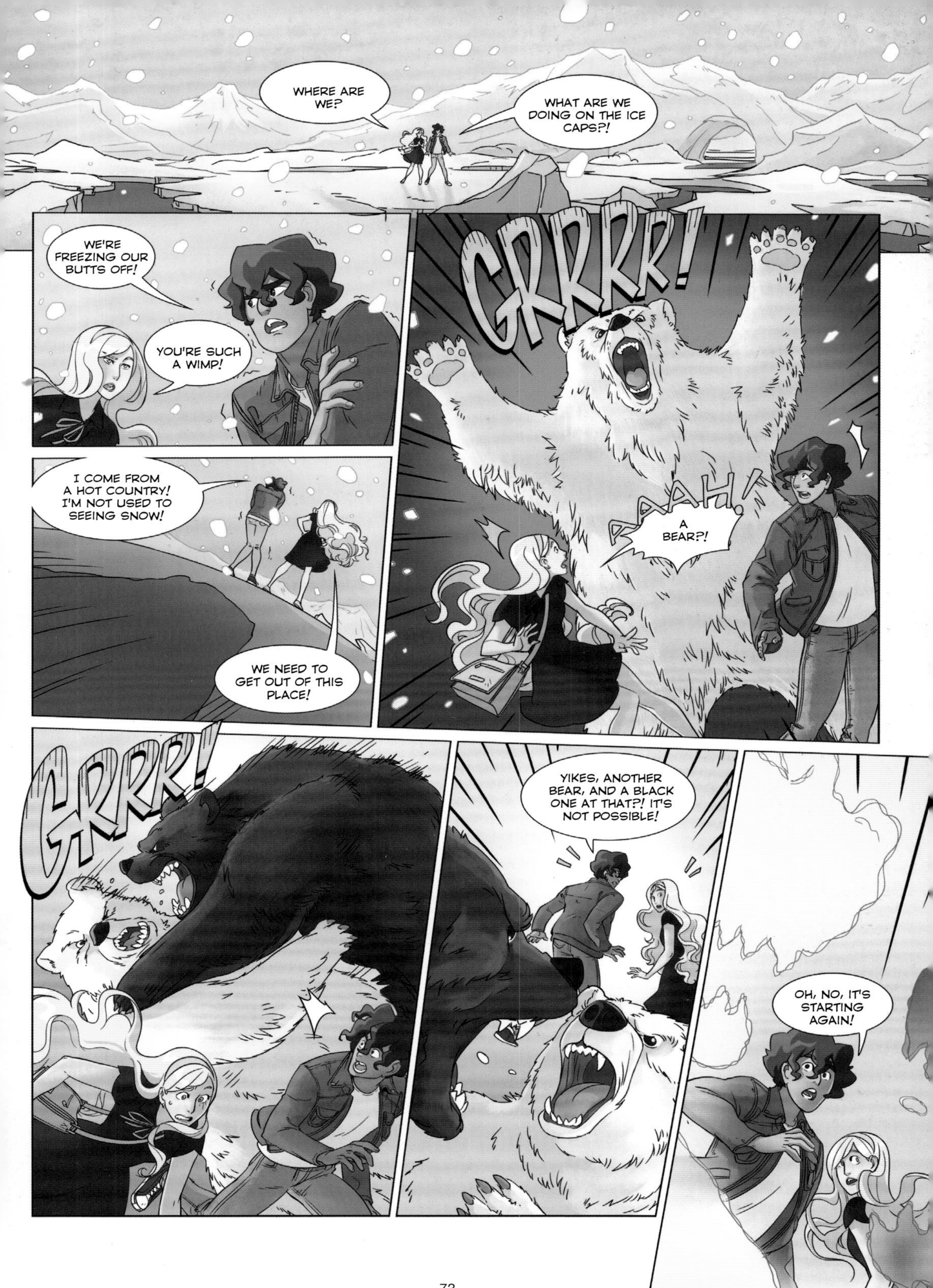

WHERE ARE WE?
WHAT ARE WE DOING ON THE ICE CAPS?!
WE'RE FREEZING OUR BUTTS OFF!
YOU'RE SUCH A WIMP!
GRRRR!
I COME FROM A HOT COUNTRY! I'M NOT USED TO SEEING SNOW!
WE NEED TO GET OUT OF THIS PLACE!
AAAH!
A BEAR?!
GRRR!
YIKES, ANOTHER BEAR, AND A BLACK ONE AT THAT?! IT'S NOT POSSIBLE!
OH, NO, IT'S STARTING AGAIN!

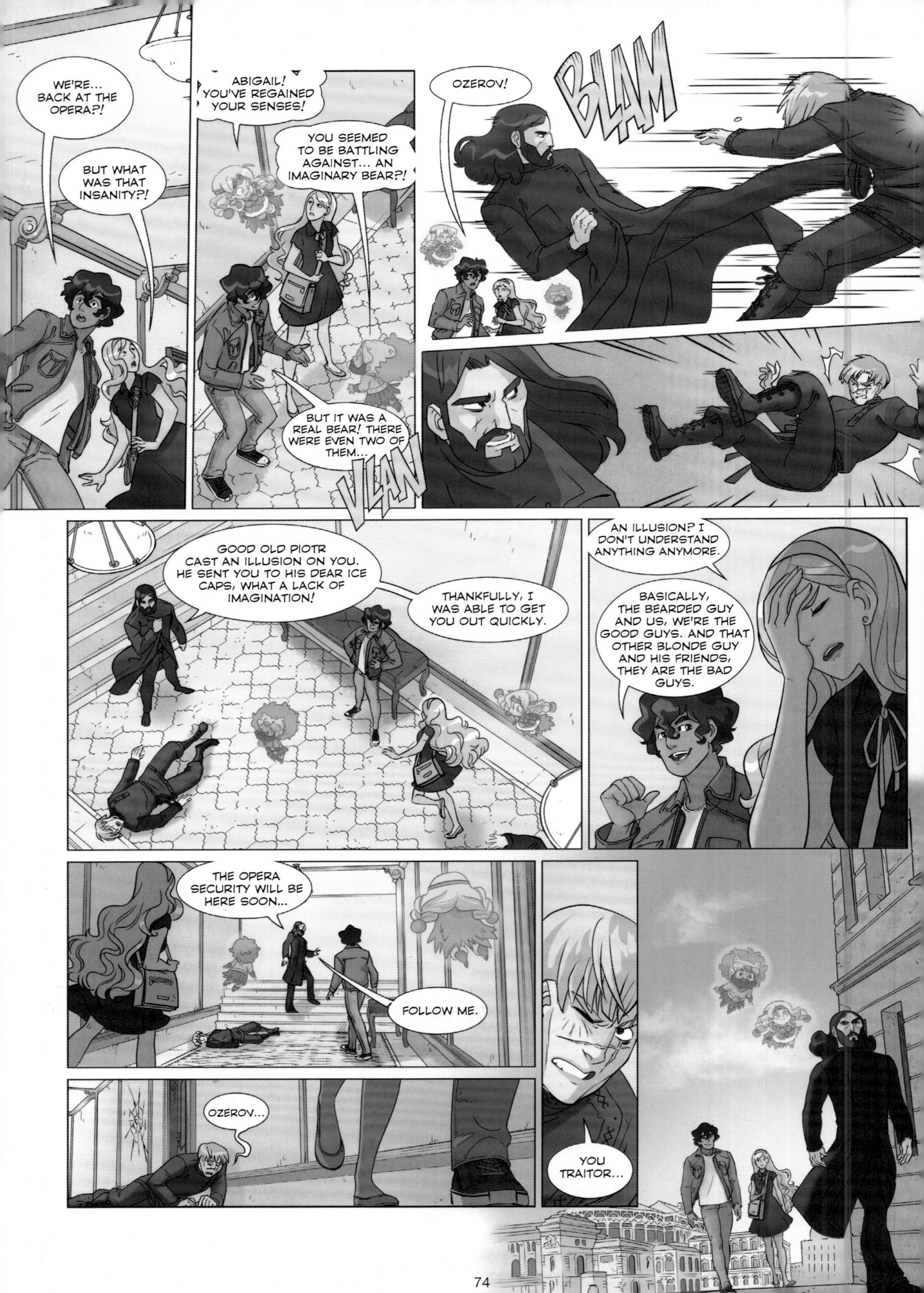
WE'RE... BACK AT THE OPERA?!
BUT WHAT WAS THAT INSANITY?!
ABIGAIL! YOU'VE REGAINED YOUR SENSES!
YOU SEEMED TO BE BATTLING AGAINST... AN IMAGINARY BEAR?!
BUT IT WAS A REAL BEAR! THERE WERE EVEN TWO OF THEM...
VLAN
OZEROV!
BLAM
GOOD OLD PIOTR CAST AN ILLUSION ON YOU. HE SENT YOU TO HIS DEAR ICE CAPS, WHAT A LACK OF IMAGINATION!
THANKFULLY, I WAS ABLE TO GET YOU OUT QUICKLY.
AN ILLUSION? I DON'T UNDERSTAND ANYTHING ANYMORE.
BASICALLY, THE BEARDED GUY AND US, WE'RE THE GOOD GUYS. AND THAT OTHER BLONDE GUY AND HIS FRIENDS, THEY ARE THE BAD GUYS.
THE OPERA SECURITY WILL BE HERE SOON...
FOLLOW ME.
OZEROV...
YOU TRAITOR...

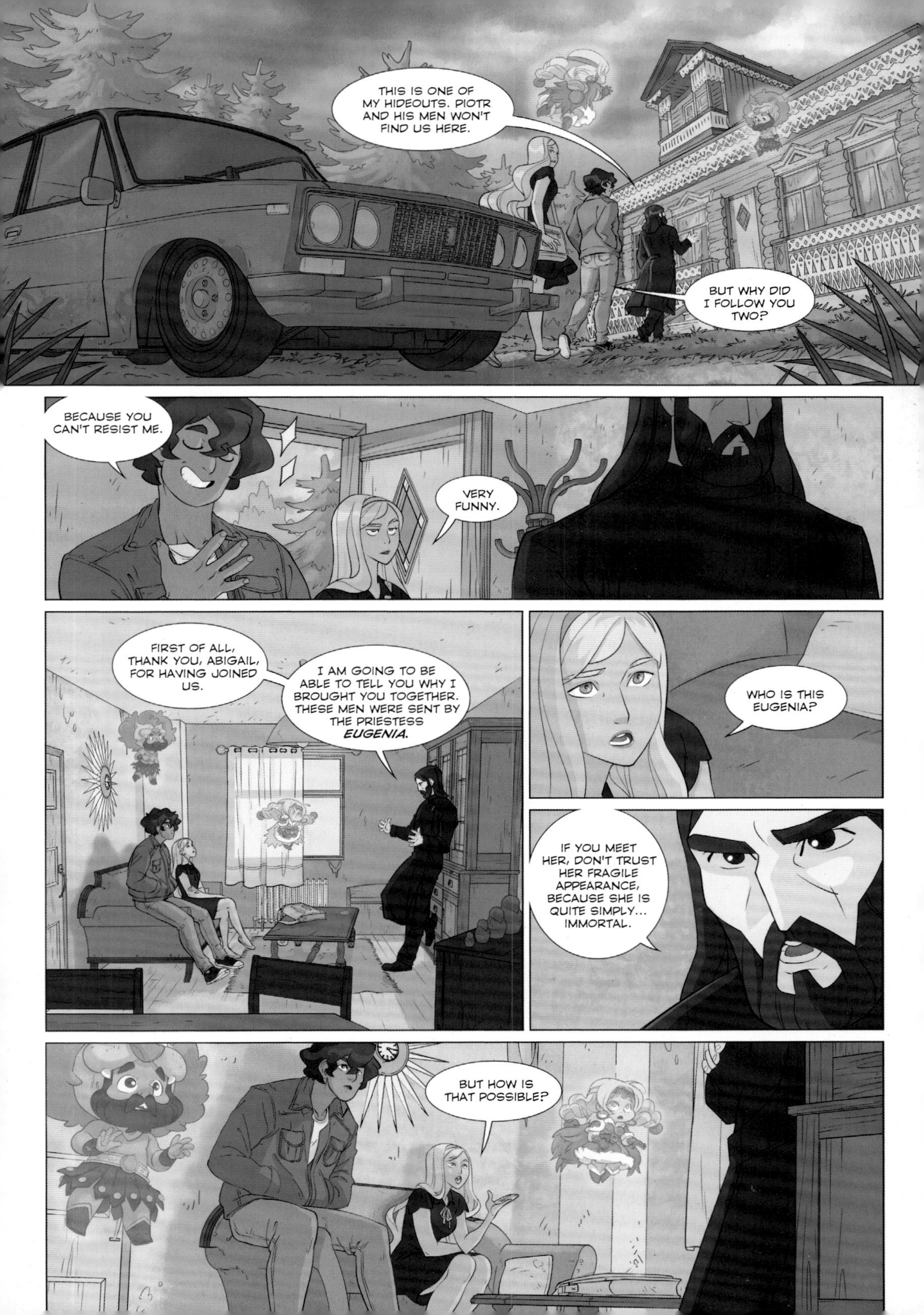
THIS IS ONE OF MY HIDEOUTS. PIOTR AND HIS MEN WON'T FIND US HERE.
BUT WHY DID I FOLLOW YOU TWO?
BECAUSE YOU CAN'T RESIST ME.
VERY FUNNY.
FIRST OF ALL, THANK YOU, ABIGAIL, FOR HAVING JOINED US.
I AM GOING TO BE ABLE TO TELL YOU WHY I BROUGHT YOU TOGETHER. THESE MEN WERE SENT BY THE PRIESTESS ***EUGENIA***.
WHO IS THIS EUGENIA?
IF YOU MEET HER, DON'T TRUST HER FRAGILE APPEARANCE, BECAUSE SHE IS QUITE SIMPLY... IMMORTAL.
BUT HOW IS THAT POSSIBLE?

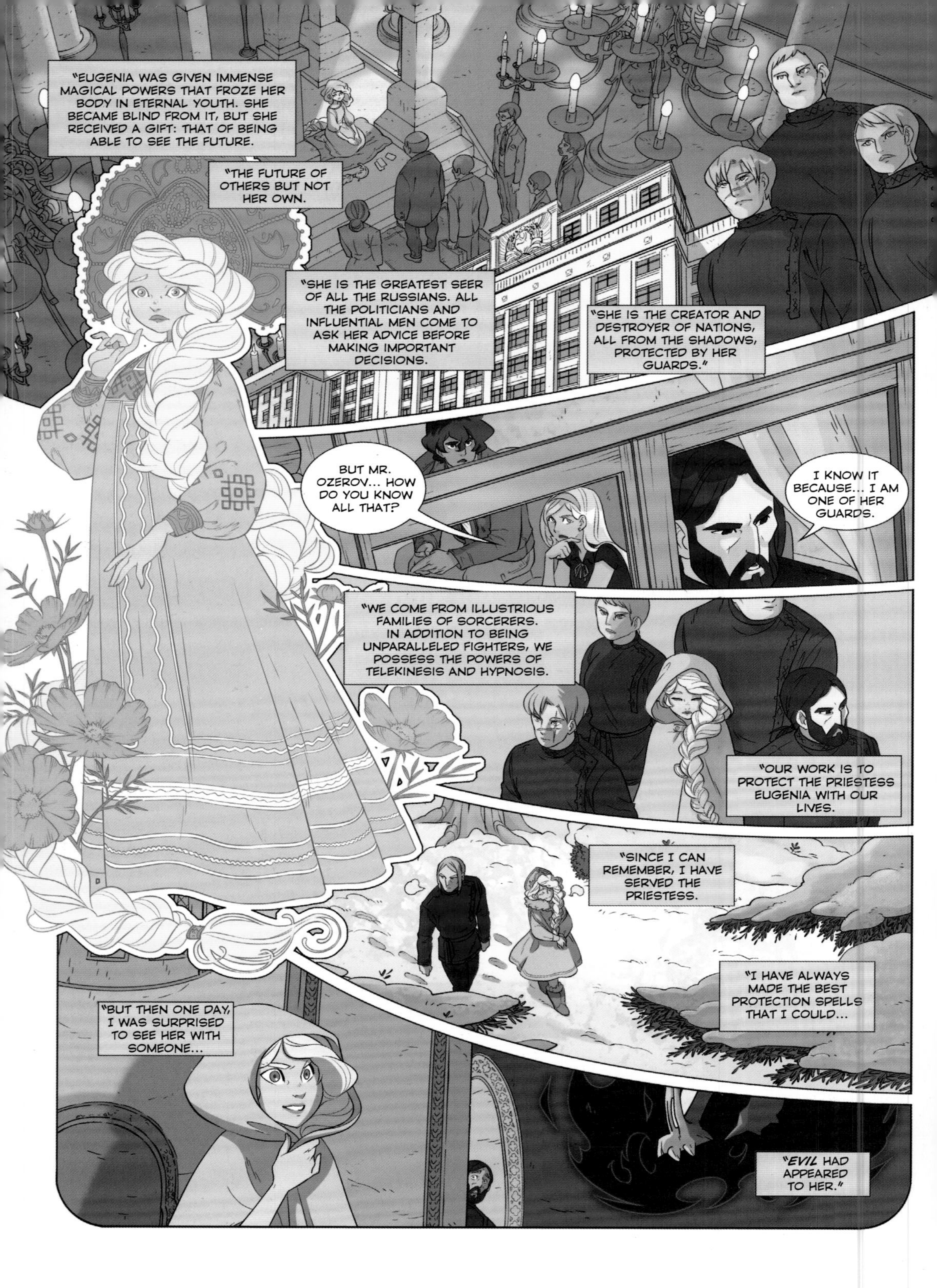
"EUGENIA WAS GIVEN IMMENSE MAGICAL POWERS THAT FROZE HER BODY IN ETERNAL YOUTH. SHE BECAME BLIND FROM IT, BUT SHE RECEIVED A GIFT: THAT OF BEING ABLE TO SEE THE FUTURE.
"THE FUTURE OF OTHERS BUT NOT HER OWN.
"SHE IS THE GREATEST SEER OF ALL THE RUSSIANS. ALL THE POLITICIANS AND INFLUENTIAL MEN COME TO ASK HER ADVICE BEFORE MAKING IMPORTANT DECISIONS.
"SHE IS THE CREATOR AND DESTROYER OF NATIONS, ALL FROM THE SHADOWS, PROTECTED BY HER GUARDS."
BUT MR. OZEROV... HOW DO YOU KNOW ALL THAT?
I KNOW IT BECAUSE... I AM ONE OF HER GUARDS.
"WE COME FROM ILLUSTRIOUS FAMILIES OF SORCERERS. IN ADDITION TO BEING UNPARALLELED FIGHTERS, WE POSSESS THE POWERS OF TELEKINESIS AND HYPNOSIS.
"OUR WORK IS TO PROTECT THE PRIESTESS EUGENIA WITH OUR LIVES.
"SINCE I CAN REMEMBER, I HAVE SERVED THE PRIESTESS.
"I HAVE ALWAYS MADE THE BEST PROTECTION SPELLS THAT I COULD...
"BUT THEN ONE DAY, I WAS SURPRISED TO SEE HER WITH SOMEONE...
"*EVIL* HAD APPEARED TO HER."

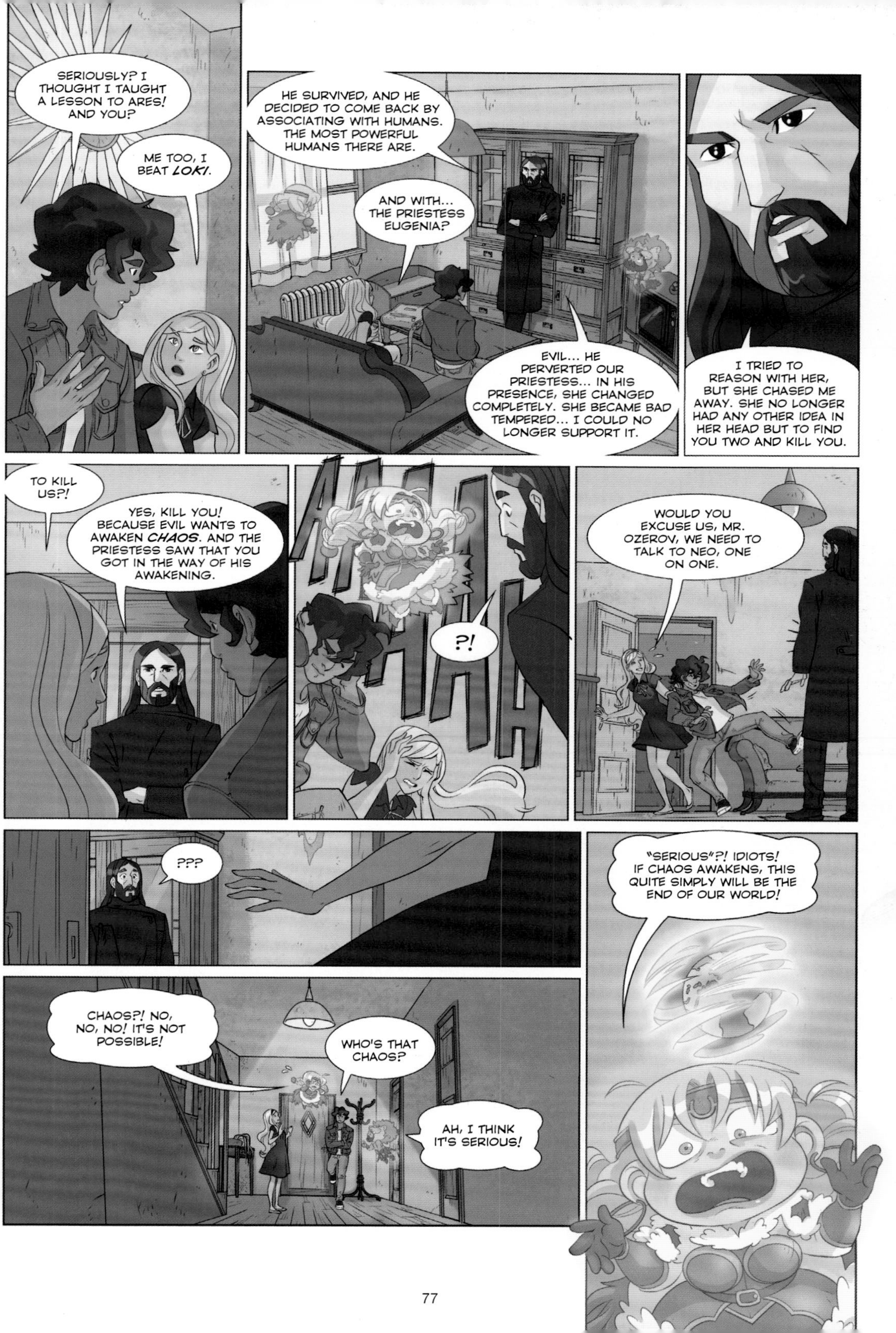
SERIOUSLY? I THOUGHT I TAUGHT A LESSON TO ARES! AND YOU?
ME TOO, I BEAT LOKI.
HE SURVIVED, AND HE DECIDED TO COME BACK BY ASSOCIATING WITH HUMANS. THE MOST POWERFUL HUMANS THERE ARE.
AND WITH... THE PRIESTESS EUGENIA?
EVIL... HE PERVERTED OUR PRIESTESS... IN HIS PRESENCE, SHE CHANGED COMPLETELY. SHE BECAME BAD TEMPERED... I COULD NO LONGER SUPPORT IT.
I TRIED TO REASON WITH HER, BUT SHE CHASED ME AWAY. SHE NO LONGER HAD ANY OTHER IDEA IN HER HEAD BUT TO FIND YOU TWO AND KILL YOU.
TO KILL US?!
YES, KILL YOU! BECAUSE EVIL WANTS TO AWAKEN CHAOS. AND THE PRIESTESS SAW THAT YOU GOT IN THE WAY OF HIS AWAKENING.
AAAHHH
?!
WOULD YOU EXCUSE US, MR. OZEROV, WE NEED TO TALK TO NEO, ONE ON ONE.
???
CHAOS?! NO, NO, NO! IT'S NOT POSSIBLE!
WHO'S THAT CHAOS?
AH, I THINK IT'S SERIOUS!
"SERIOUS"?! IDIOTS! IF CHAOS AWAKENS, THIS QUITE SIMPLY WILL BE THE END OF OUR WORLD!

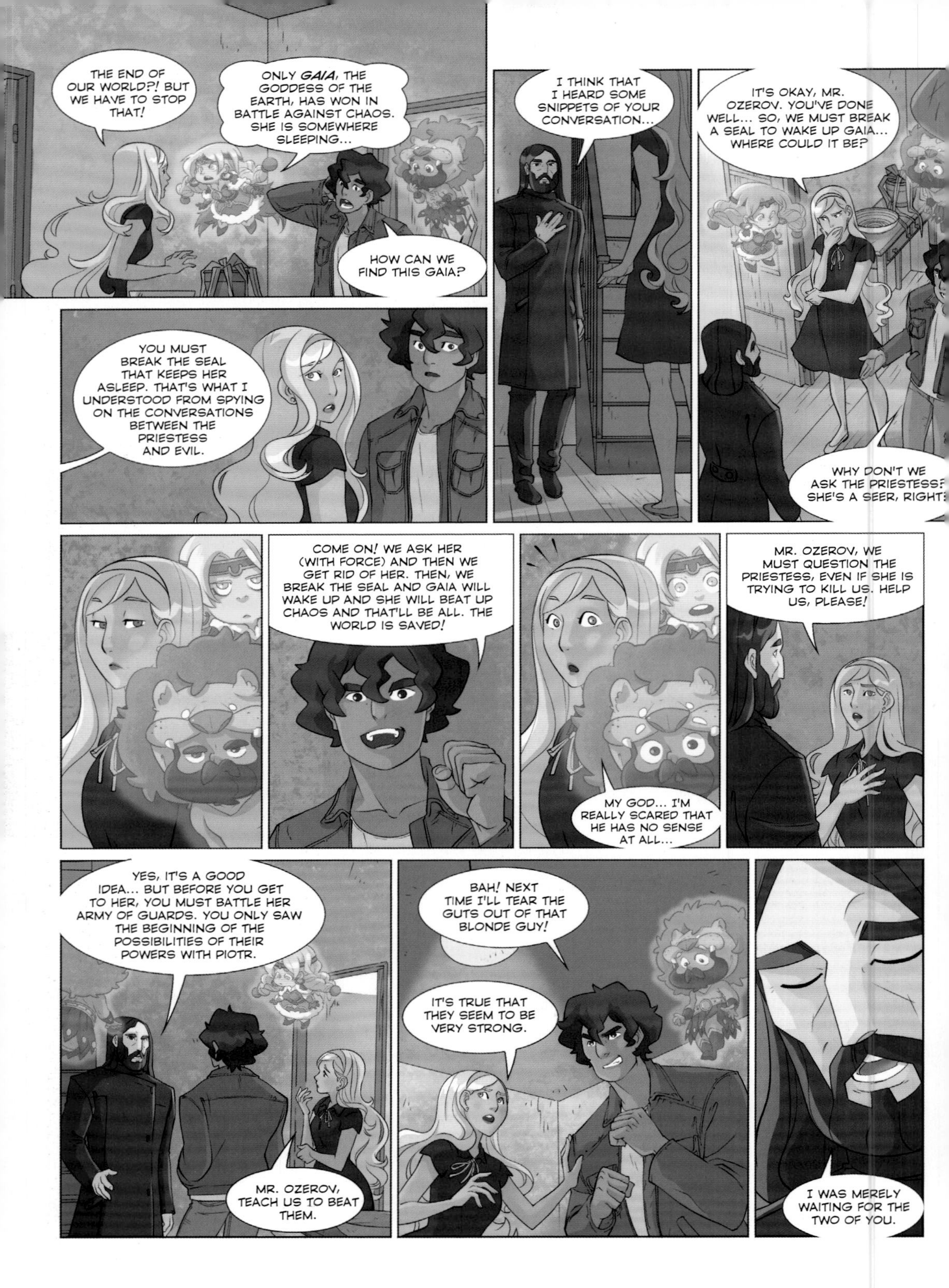
THE END OF OUR WORLD?! BUT WE HAVE TO STOP THAT!
ONLY GAIA, THE GODDESS OF THE EARTH, HAS WON IN BATTLE AGAINST CHAOS. SHE IS SOMEWHERE SLEEPING...
HOW CAN WE FIND THIS GAIA?
I THINK THAT I HEARD SOME SNIPPETS OF YOUR CONVERSATION...
IT'S OKAY, MR. OZEROV. YOU'VE DONE WELL... SO, WE MUST BREAK A SEAL TO WAKE UP GAIA... WHERE COULD IT BE?
YOU MUST BREAK THE SEAL THAT KEEPS HER ASLEEP. THAT'S WHAT I UNDERSTOOD FROM SPYING ON THE CONVERSATIONS BETWEEN THE PRIESTESS AND EVIL.
WHY DON'T WE ASK THE PRIESTESS? SHE'S A SEER, RIGHT?
COME ON! WE ASK HER (WITH FORCE) AND THEN WE GET RID OF HER. THEN, WE BREAK THE SEAL AND GAIA WILL WAKE UP AND SHE WILL BEAT UP CHAOS AND THAT'LL BE ALL. THE WORLD IS SAVED!
MY GOD... I'M REALLY SCARED THAT HE HAS NO SENSE AT ALL...
MR. OZEROV, WE MUST QUESTION THE PRIESTESS, EVEN IF SHE IS TRYING TO KILL US. HELP US, PLEASE!
YES, IT'S A GOOD IDEA... BUT BEFORE YOU GET TO HER, YOU MUST BATTLE HER ARMY OF GUARDS. YOU ONLY SAW THE BEGINNING OF THE POSSIBILITIES OF THEIR POWERS WITH PIOTR.
MR. OZEROV, TEACH US TO BEAT THEM.
BAH! NEXT TIME I'LL TEAR THE GUTS OUT OF THAT BLONDE GUY!
IT'S TRUE THAT THEY SEEM TO BE VERY STRONG.
I WAS MERELY WAITING FOR THE TWO OF YOU.

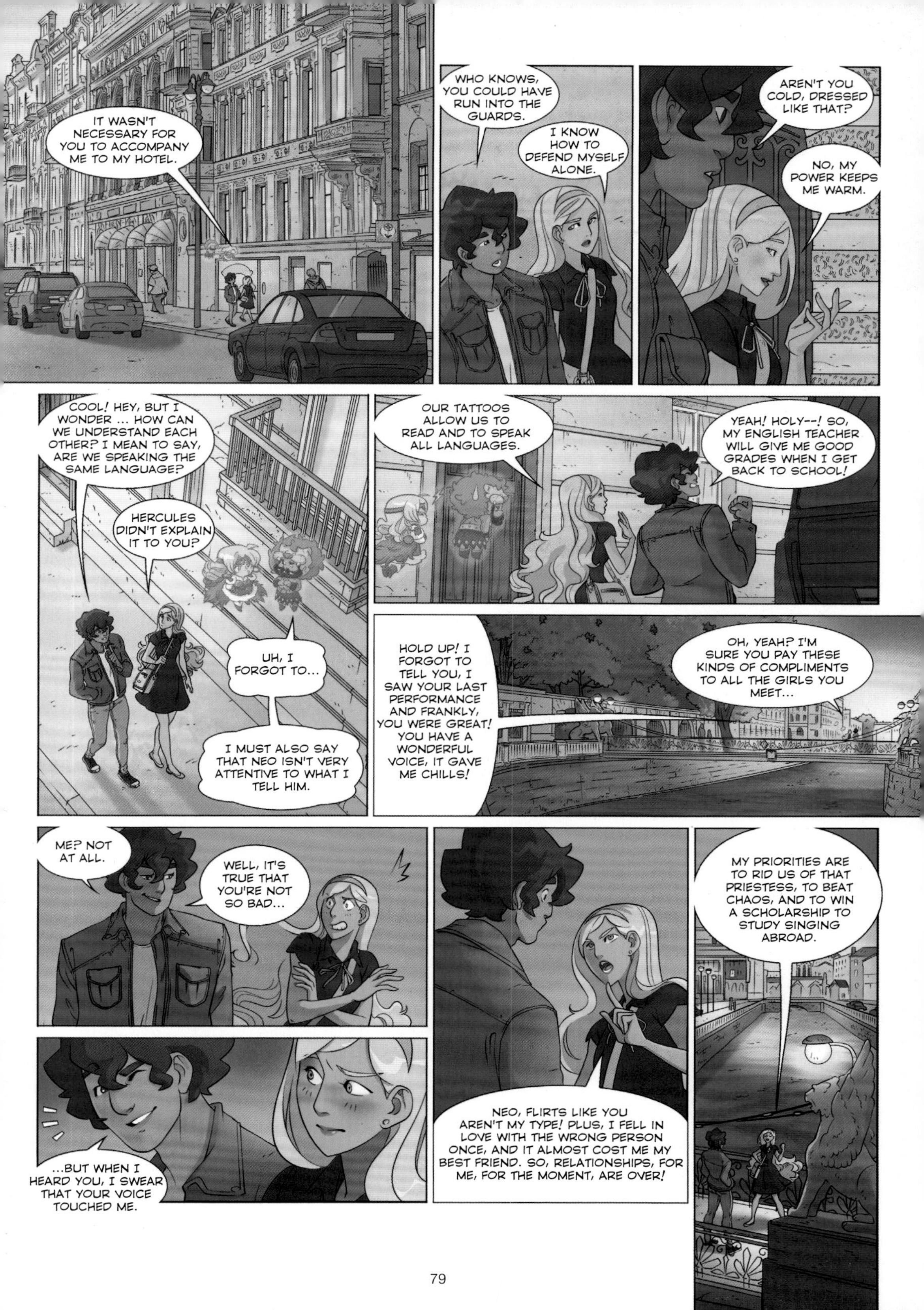
IT WASN'T NECESSARY FOR YOU TO ACCOMPANY ME TO MY HOTEL.
WHO KNOWS, YOU COULD HAVE RUN INTO THE GUARDS.
I KNOW HOW TO DEFEND MYSELF ALONE.
AREN'T YOU COLD, DRESSED LIKE THAT?
NO, MY POWER KEEPS ME WARM.
COOL! HEY, BUT I WONDER ... HOW CAN WE UNDERSTAND EACH OTHER? I MEAN TO SAY, ARE WE SPEAKING THE SAME LANGUAGE?
HERCULES DIDN'T EXPLAIN IT TO YOU?
UH, I FORGOT TO...
I MUST ALSO SAY THAT NEO ISN'T VERY ATTENTIVE TO WHAT I TELL HIM.
OUR TATTOOS ALLOW US TO READ AND TO SPEAK ALL LANGUAGES.
YEAH! HOLY--! SO, MY ENGLISH TEACHER WILL GIVE ME GOOD GRADES WHEN I GET BACK TO SCHOOL!
HOLD UP! I FORGOT TO TELL YOU, I SAW YOUR LAST PERFORMANCE AND FRANKLY, YOU WERE GREAT! YOU HAVE A WONDERFUL VOICE, IT GAVE ME CHILLS!
OH, YEAH? I'M SURE YOU PAY THESE KINDS OF COMPLIMENTS TO ALL THE GIRLS YOU MEET...
ME? NOT AT ALL.
WELL, IT'S TRUE THAT YOU'RE NOT SO BAD...
...BUT WHEN I HEARD YOU, I SWEAR THAT YOUR VOICE TOUCHED ME.
NEO, FLIRTS LIKE YOU AREN'T MY TYPE! PLUS, I FELL IN LOVE WITH THE WRONG PERSON ONCE, AND IT ALMOST COST ME MY BEST FRIEND. SO, RELATIONSHIPS, FOR ME, FOR THE MOMENT, ARE OVER!
MY PRIORITIES ARE TO RID US OF THAT PRIESTESS, TO BEAT CHAOS, AND TO WIN A SCHOLARSHIP TO STUDY SINGING ABROAD.

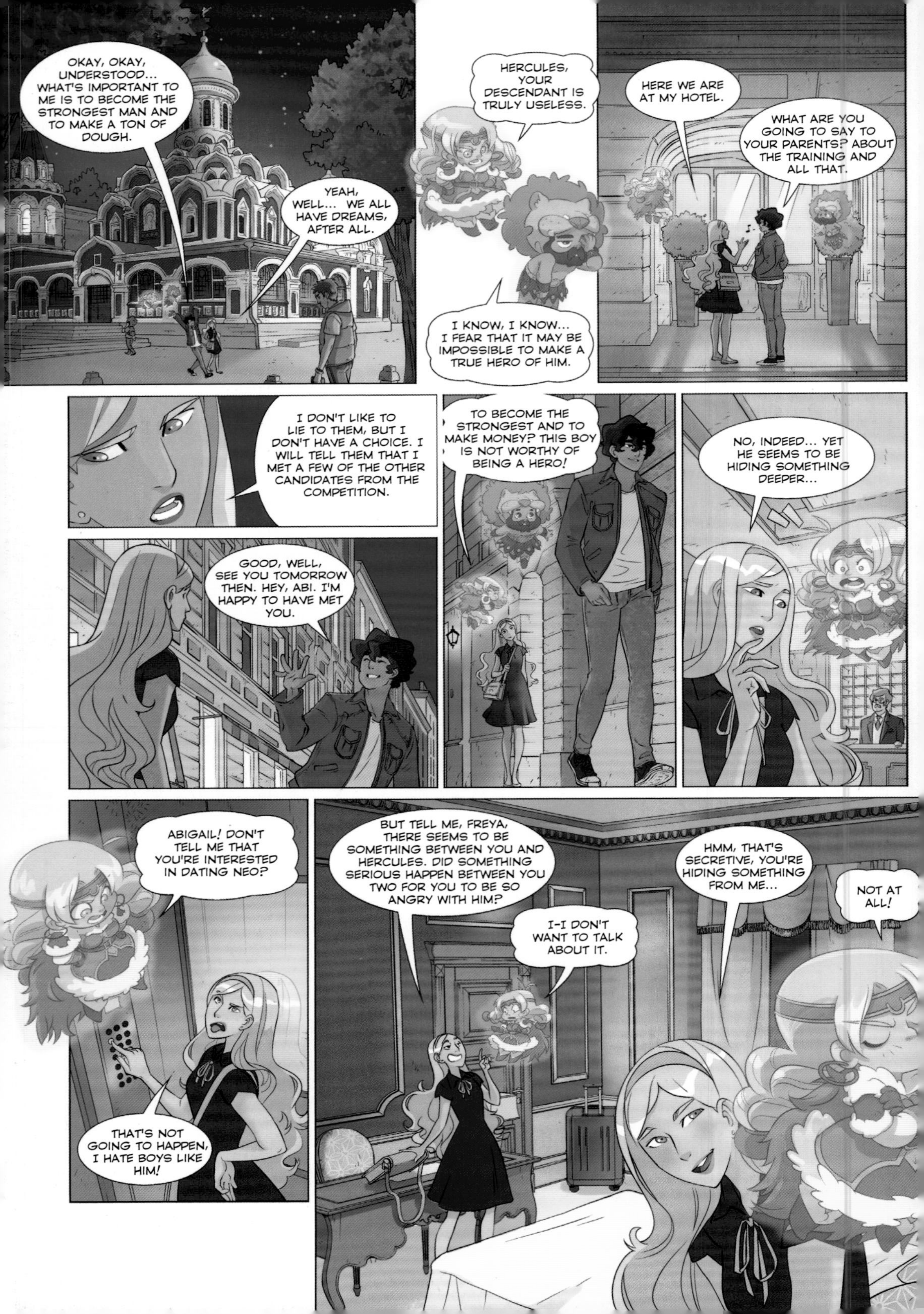

OKAY, OKAY, UNDERSTOOD... WHAT'S IMPORTANT TO ME IS TO BECOME THE STRONGEST MAN AND TO MAKE A TON OF DOUGH.
YEAH, WELL... WE ALL HAVE DREAMS, AFTER ALL.
HERCULES, YOUR DESCENDANT IS TRULY USELESS.
I KNOW, I KNOW... I FEAR THAT IT MAY BE IMPOSSIBLE TO MAKE A TRUE HERO OF HIM.
HERE WE ARE AT MY HOTEL.
WHAT ARE YOU GOING TO SAY TO YOUR PARENTS? ABOUT THE TRAINING AND ALL THAT.
I DON'T LIKE TO LIE TO THEM, BUT I DON'T HAVE A CHOICE. I WILL TELL THEM THAT I MET A FEW OF THE OTHER CANDIDATES FROM THE COMPETITION.
GOOD, WELL, SEE YOU TOMORROW THEN. HEY, ABI. I'M HAPPY TO HAVE MET YOU.
TO BECOME THE STRONGEST AND TO MAKE MONEY? THIS BOY IS NOT WORTHY OF BEING A HERO!
NO, INDEED... YET HE SEEMS TO BE HIDING SOMETHING DEEPER...
ABIGAIL! DON'T TELL ME THAT YOU'RE INTERESTED IN DATING NEO?
THAT'S NOT GOING TO HAPPEN, I HATE BOYS LIKE HIM!
BUT TELL ME, FREYA, THERE SEEMS TO BE SOMETHING BETWEEN YOU AND HERCULES. DID SOMETHING SERIOUS HAPPEN BETWEEN YOU TWO FOR YOU TO BE SO ANGRY WITH HIM?
I-I DON'T WANT TO TALK ABOUT IT.
HMM, THAT'S SECRETIVE, YOU'RE HIDING SOMETHING FROM ME...
NOT AT ALL!

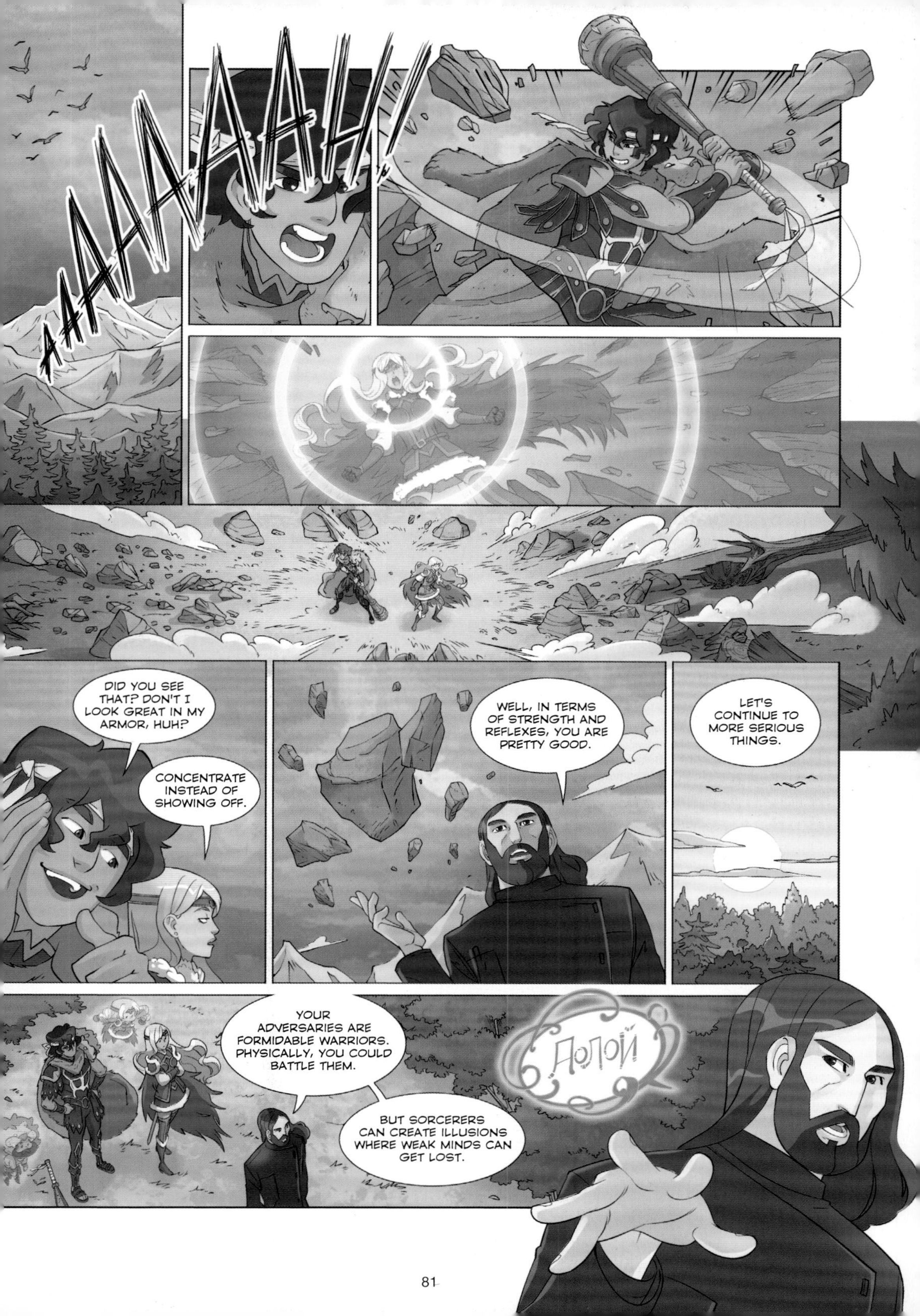
AAAAAAAAH!
DID YOU SEE THAT? DON'T I LOOK GREAT IN MY ARMOR, HUH?
CONCENTRATE INSTEAD OF SHOWING OFF.
WELL, IN TERMS OF STRENGTH AND REFLEXES, YOU ARE PRETTY GOOD.
LET'S CONTINUE TO MORE SERIOUS THINGS.
YOUR ADVERSARIES ARE FORMIDABLE WARRIORS. PHYSICALLY, YOU COULD BATTLE THEM.
BUT SORCERERS CAN CREATE ILLUSIONS WHERE WEAK MINDS CAN GET LOST.
ДОЛОЙ

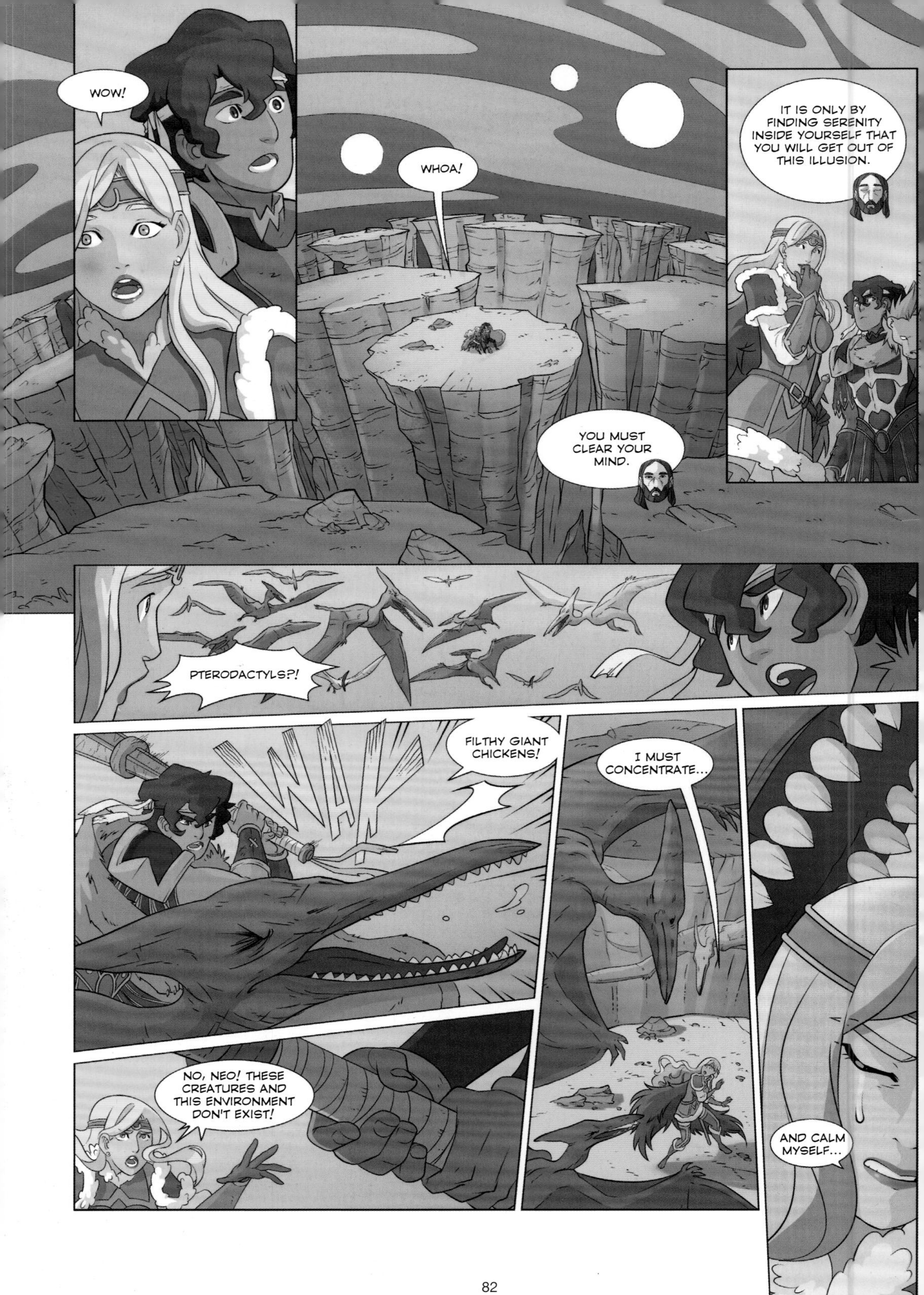
WOW!
WHOA!
IT IS ONLY BY FINDING SERENITY INSIDE YOURSELF THAT YOU WILL GET OUT OF THIS ILLUSION.
YOU MUST CLEAR YOUR MIND.
PTERODACTYLS?!
WAK
FILTHY GIANT CHICKENS!
NO, NEO! THESE CREATURES AND THIS ENVIRONMENT DON'T EXIST!
I MUST CONCENTRATE...
AND CALM MYSELF...

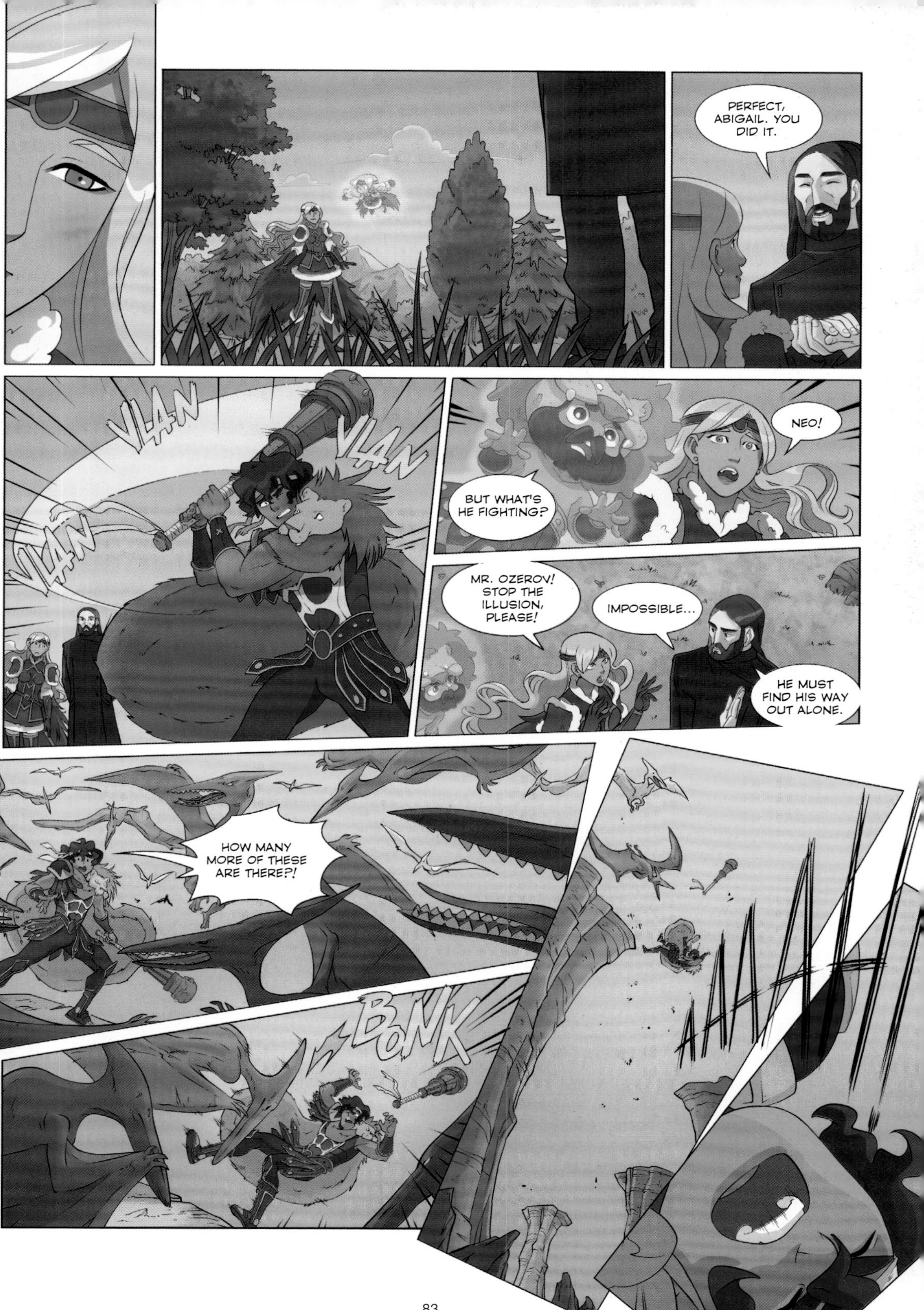
PERFECT, ABIGAIL. YOU DID IT.
VLAN
VLAN
VLAN
NEO!
BUT WHAT'S HE FIGHTING?
MR. OZEROV! STOP THE ILLUSION, PLEASE!
IMPOSSIBLE...
HE MUST FIND HIS WAY OUT ALONE.
HOW MANY MORE OF THESE ARE THERE?!
BONK
AAAAHHH

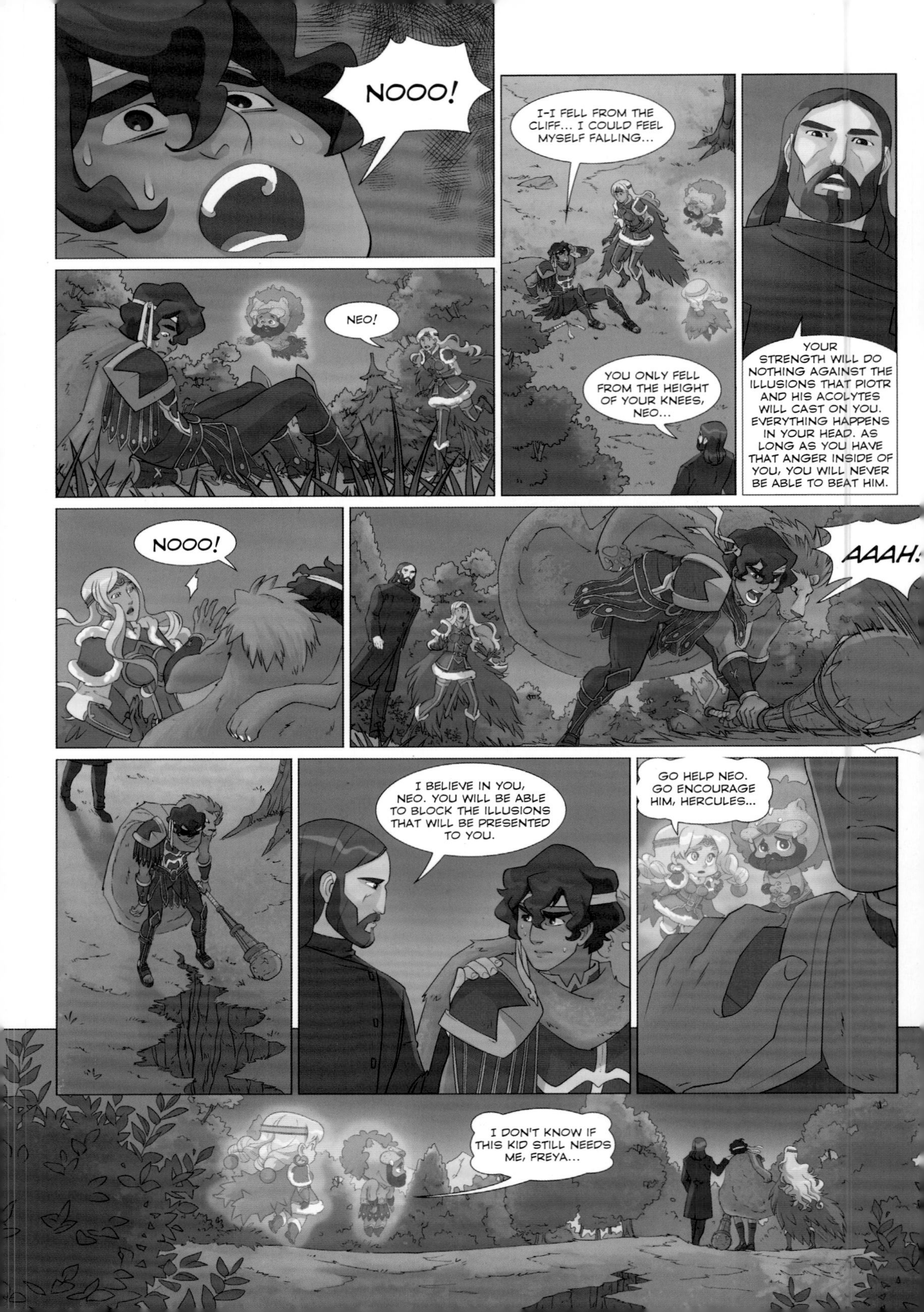
NOOO!
I-I FELL FROM THE CLIFF... I COULD FEEL MYSELF FALLING...
YOUR STRENGTH WILL DO NOTHING AGAINST THE ILLUSIONS THAT PIOTR AND HIS ACOLYTES WILL CAST ON YOU. EVERYTHING HAPPENS IN YOUR HEAD. AS LONG AS YOU HAVE THAT ANGER INSIDE OF YOU, YOU WILL NEVER BE ABLE TO BEAT HIM.
NEO!
YOU ONLY FELL FROM THE HEIGHT OF YOUR KNEES, NEO...
NOOO!
AAAH!
I BELIEVE IN YOU, NEO. YOU WILL BE ABLE TO BLOCK THE ILLUSIONS THAT WILL BE PRESENTED TO YOU.
GO HELP NEO. GO ENCOURAGE HIM, HERCULES...
I DON'T KNOW IF THIS KID STILL NEEDS ME, FREYA...

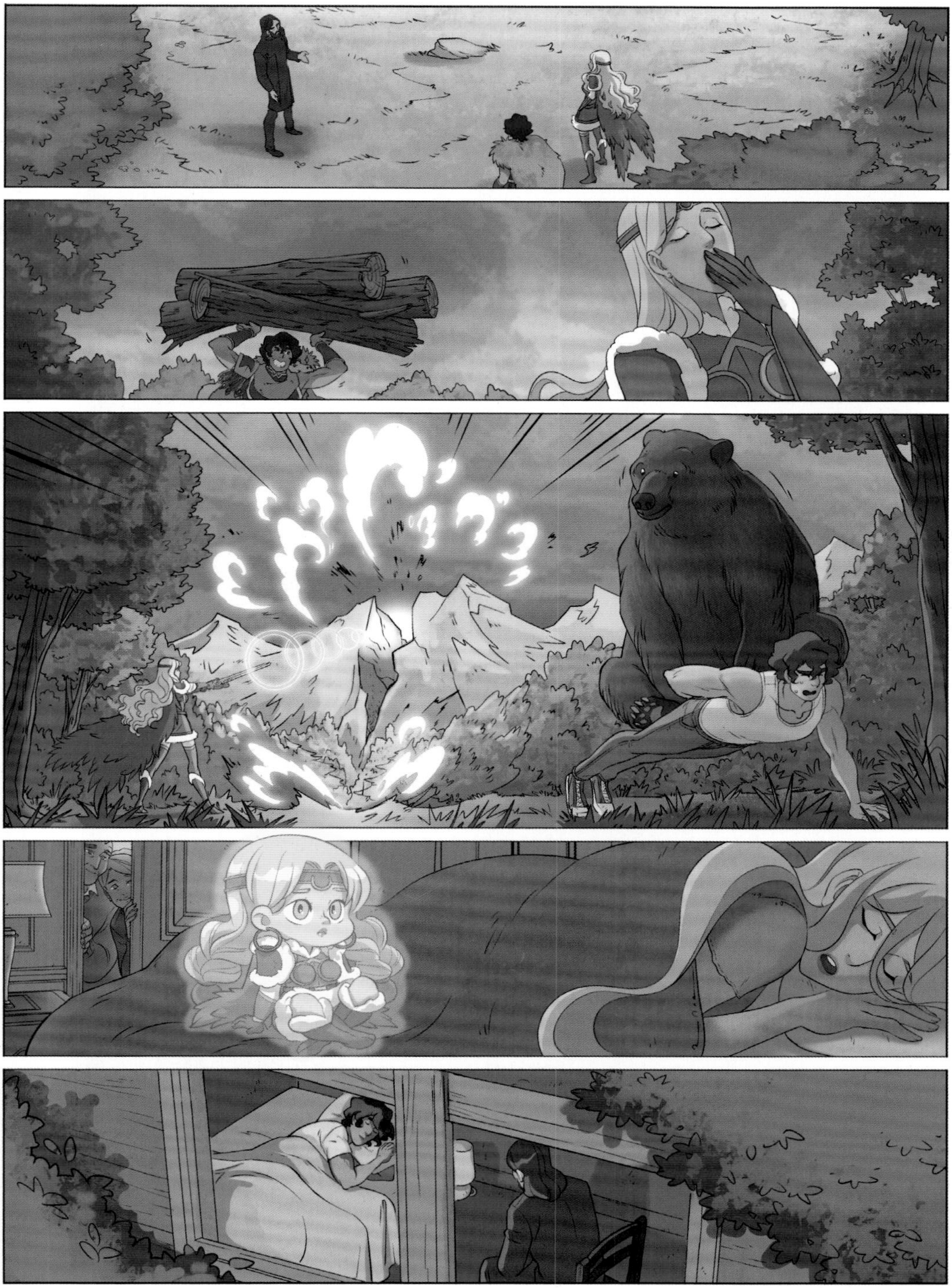

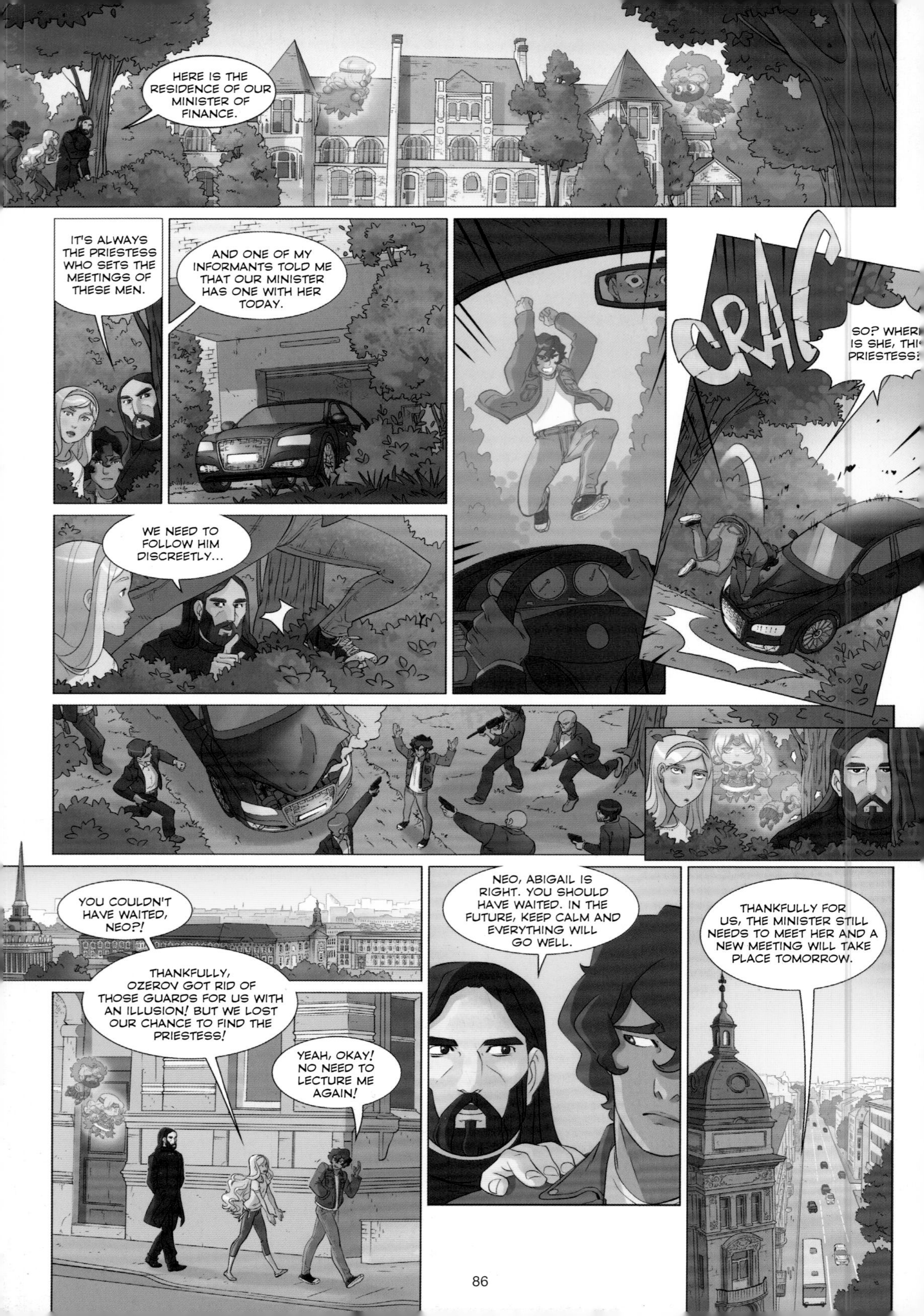
HERE IS THE RESIDENCE OF OUR MINISTER OF FINANCE.
IT'S ALWAYS THE PRIESTESS WHO SETS THE MEETINGS OF THESE MEN.
AND ONE OF MY INFORMANTS TOLD ME THAT OUR MINISTER HAS ONE WITH HER TODAY.
WE NEED TO FOLLOW HIM DISCREETLY...
CRAC
SO? WHER IS SHE, THI PRIESTESS?
YOU COULDN'T HAVE WAITED, NEO?!
THANKFULLY, OZEROV GOT RID OF THOSE GUARDS FOR US WITH AN ILLUSION! BUT WE LOST OUR CHANCE TO FIND THE PRIESTESS!
YEAH, OKAY! NO NEED TO LECTURE ME AGAIN!
NEO, ABIGAIL IS RIGHT. YOU SHOULD HAVE WAITED. IN THE FUTURE, KEEP CALM AND EVERYTHING WILL GO WELL.
THANKFULLY FOR US, THE MINISTER STILL NEEDS TO MEET HER AND A NEW MEETING WILL TAKE PLACE TOMORROW.

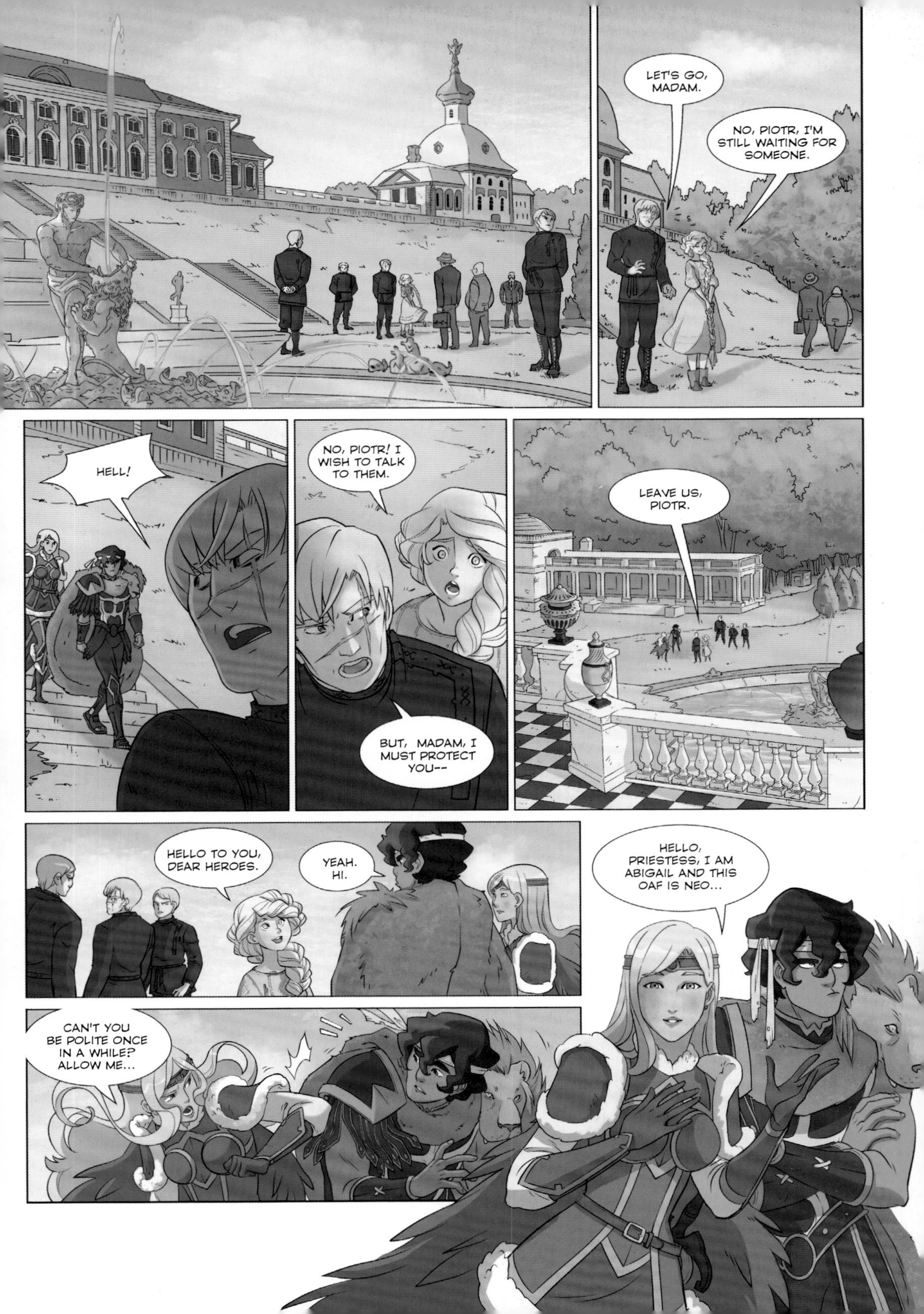
LET'S GO, MADAM.
NO, PIOTR, I'M STILL WAITING FOR SOMEONE.
HELL!
NO, PIOTR! I WISH TO TALK TO THEM.
BUT, MADAM, I MUST PROTECT YOU--
LEAVE US, PIOTR.
HELLO TO YOU, DEAR HEROES.
YEAH. HI.
HELLO, PRIESTESS, I AM ABIGAIL AND THIS OAF IS NEO...
CAN'T YOU BE POLITE ONCE IN A WHILE? ALLOW ME...

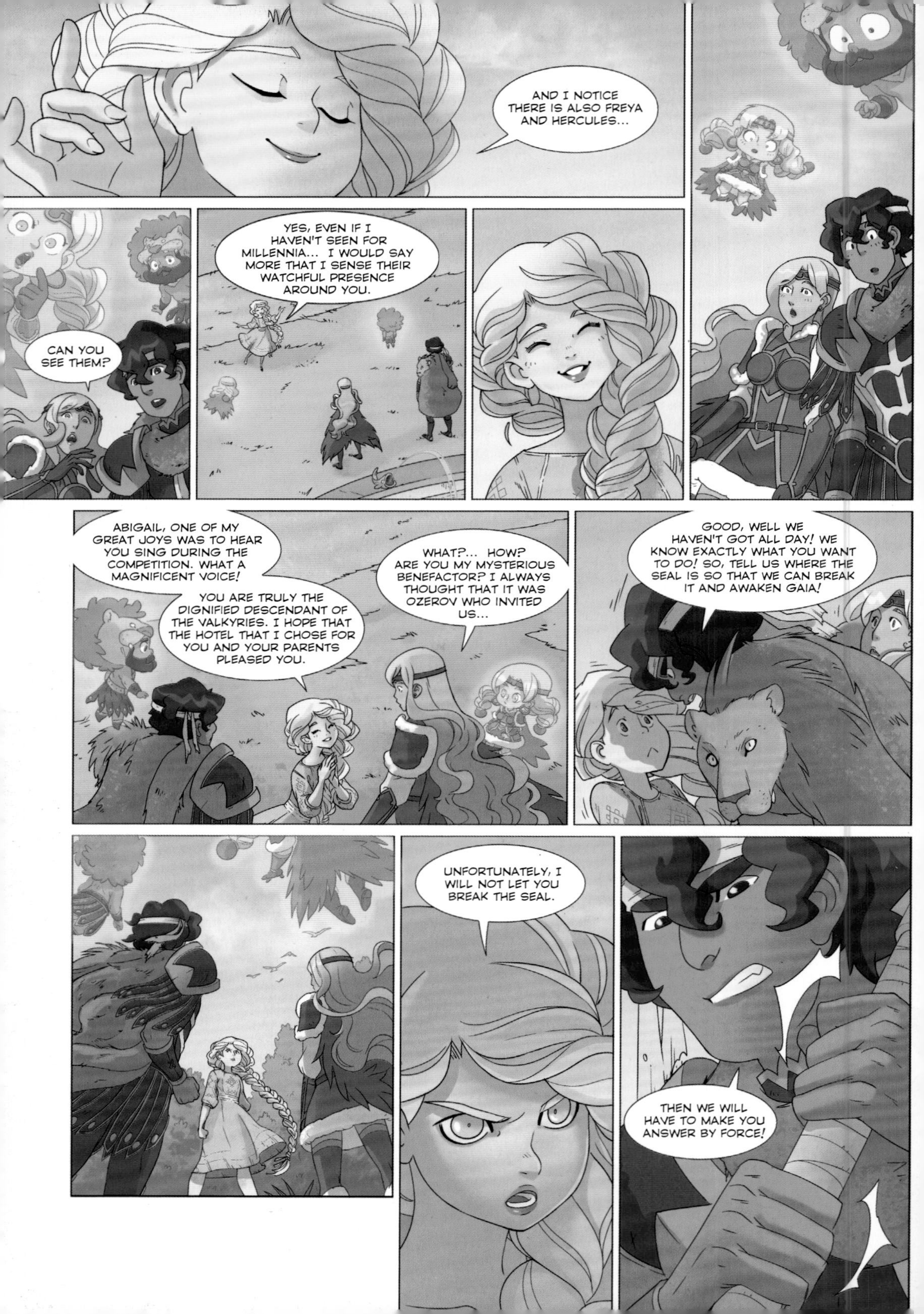

AND I NOTICE THERE IS ALSO FREYA AND HERCULES...
CAN YOU SEE THEM?
YES, EVEN IF I HAVEN'T SEEN FOR MILLENNIA... I WOULD SAY MORE THAT I SENSE THEIR WATCHFUL PRESENCE AROUND YOU.
ABIGAIL, ONE OF MY GREAT JOYS WAS TO HEAR YOU SING DURING THE COMPETITION. WHAT A MAGNIFICENT VOICE!
YOU ARE TRULY THE DIGNIFIED DESCENDANT OF THE VALKYRIES. I HOPE THAT THE HOTEL THAT I CHOSE FOR YOU AND YOUR PARENTS PLEASED YOU.
WHAT?... HOW? ARE YOU MY MYSTERIOUS BENEFACTOR? I ALWAYS THOUGHT THAT IT WAS OZEROV WHO INVITED US...
GOOD, WELL WE HAVEN'T GOT ALL DAY! WE KNOW EXACTLY WHAT YOU WANT TO DO! SO, TELL US WHERE THE SEAL IS SO THAT WE CAN BREAK IT AND AWAKEN GAIA!
UNFORTUNATELY, I WILL NOT LET YOU BREAK THE SEAL.
THEN WE WILL HAVE TO MAKE YOU ANSWER BY FORCE!

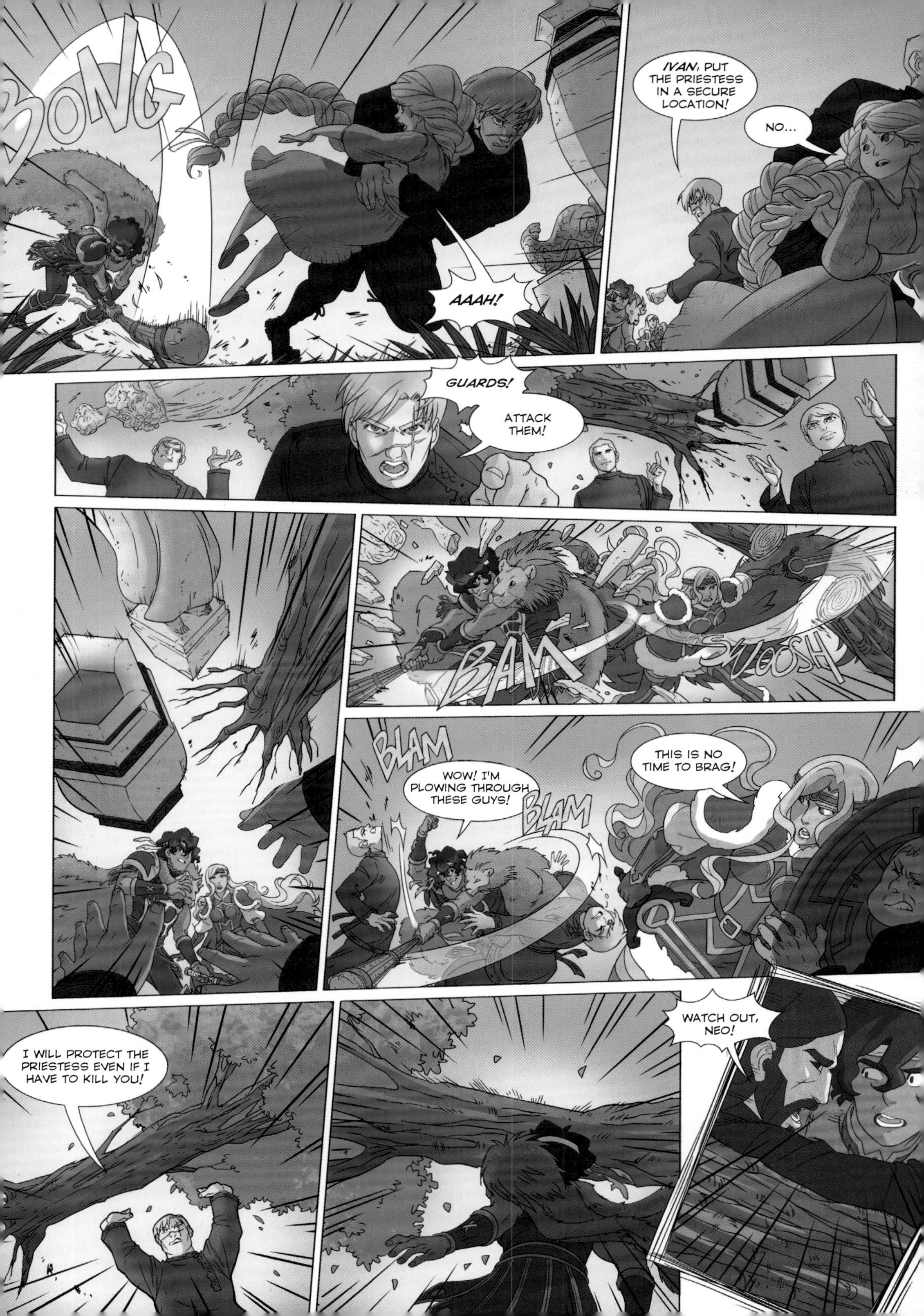
BONG
AAAH!
IVAN, PUT THE PRIESTESS IN A SECURE LOCATION!
NO...
GUARDS!
ATTACK THEM!
BAM
SWOOSH
BLAM
WOW! I'M PLOWING THROUGH THESE GUYS!
BLAM
THIS IS NO TIME TO BRAG!
I WILL PROTECT THE PRIESTESS EVEN IF I HAVE TO KILL YOU!
WATCH OUT, NEO!

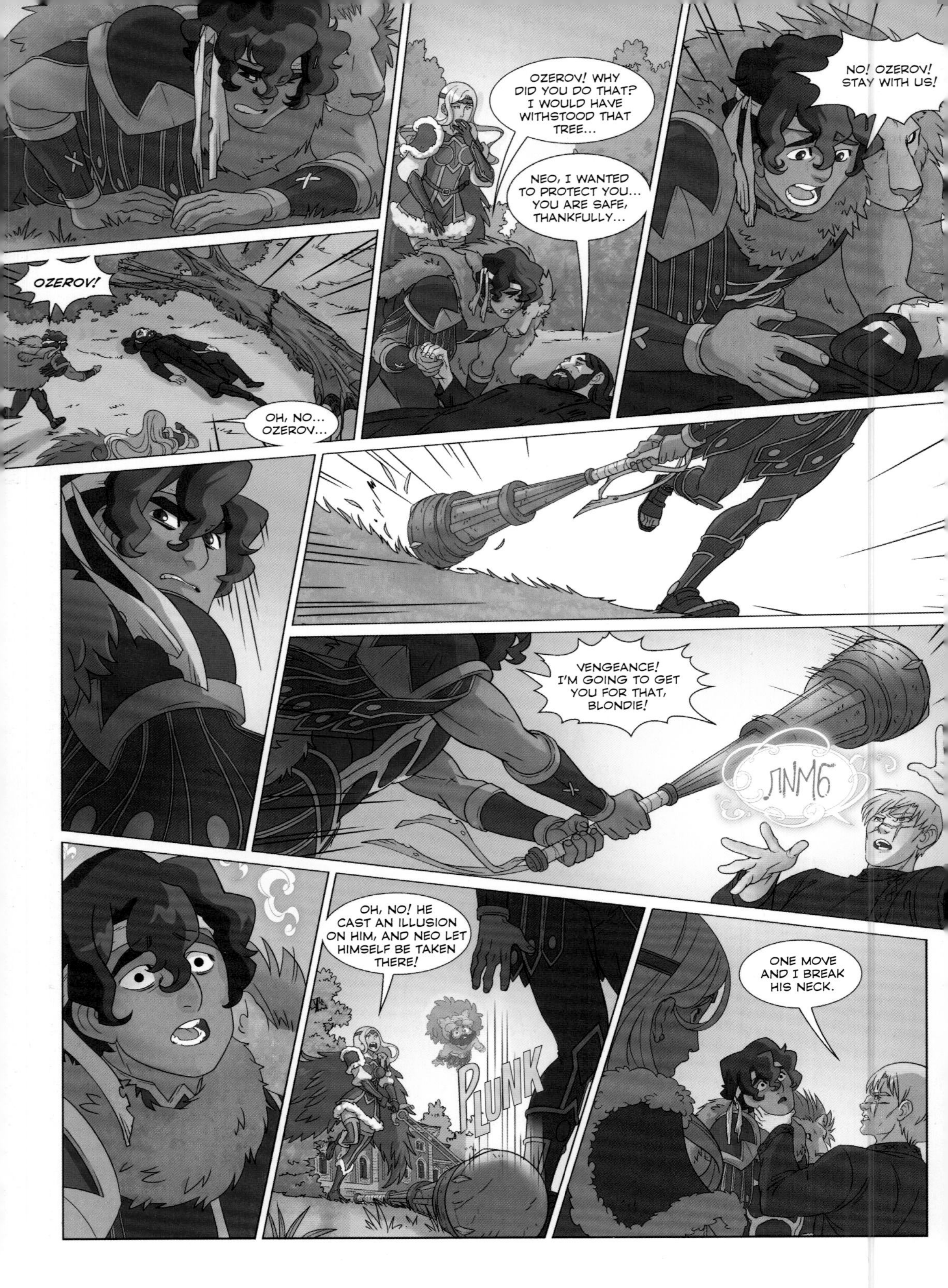
OZEROV! WHY DID YOU DO THAT? I WOULD HAVE WITHSTOOD THAT TREE...
NEO, I WANTED TO PROTECT YOU... YOU ARE SAFE, THANKFULLY...
NO! OZEROV! STAY WITH US!
OZEROV!
OH, NO... OZEROV...
VENGEANCE! I'M GOING TO GET YOU FOR THAT, BLONDIE!
OH, NO! HE CAST AN ILLUSION ON HIM, AND NEO LET HIMSELF BE TAKEN THERE!
PLUNK
ONE MOVE AND I BREAK HIS NECK.

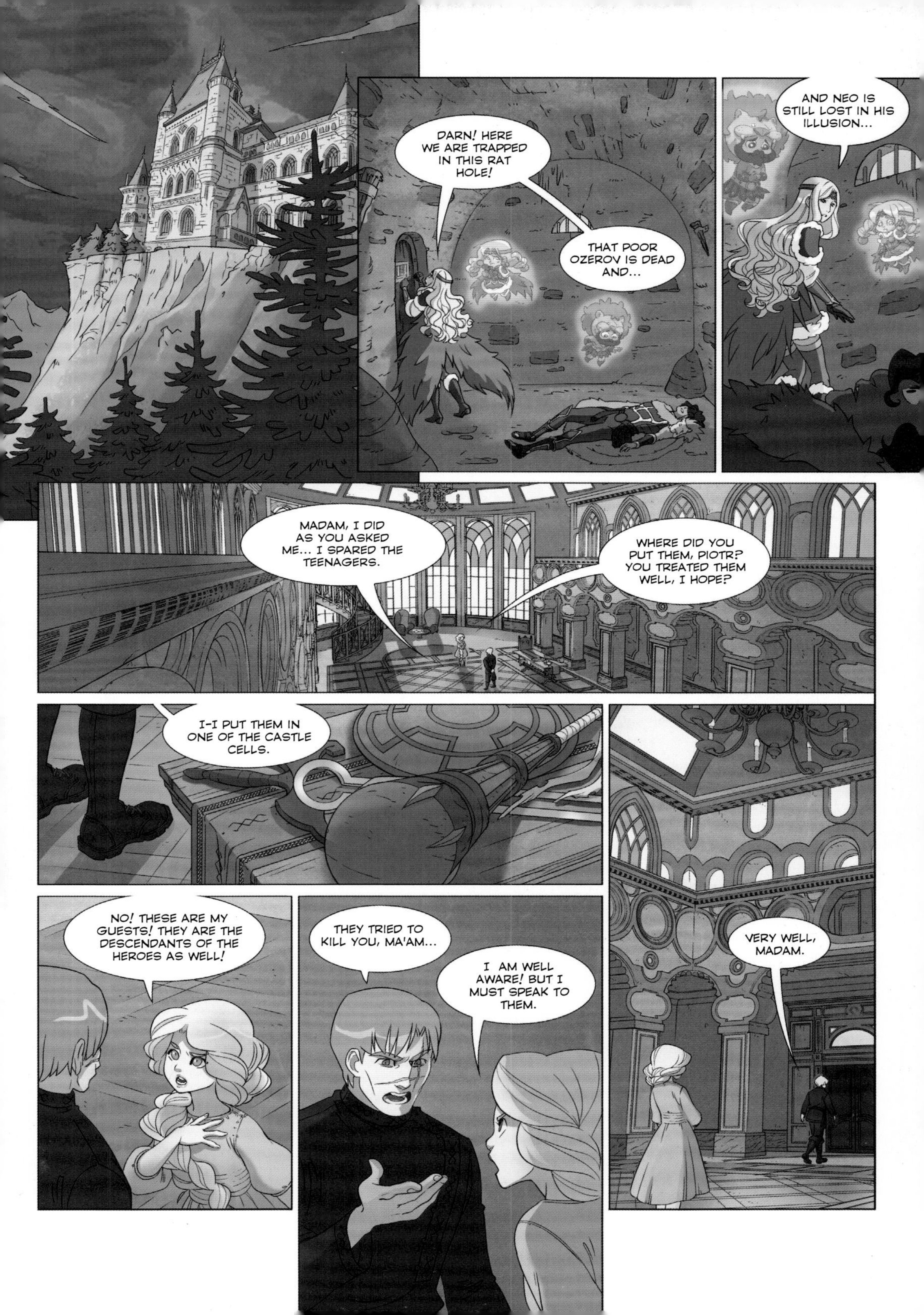
DARN! HERE WE ARE TRAPPED IN THIS RAT HOLE!
THAT POOR OZEROV IS DEAD AND...
AND NEO IS STILL LOST IN HIS ILLUSION...
MADAM, I DID AS YOU ASKED ME... I SPARED THE TEENAGERS.
WHERE DID YOU PUT THEM, PIOTR? YOU TREATED THEM WELL, I HOPE?
I-I PUT THEM IN ONE OF THE CASTLE CELLS.
NO! THESE ARE MY GUESTS! THEY ARE THE DESCENDANTS OF THE HEROES AS WELL!
THEY TRIED TO KILL YOU, MA'AM...
I AM WELL AWARE! BUT I MUST SPEAK TO THEM.
VERY WELL, MADAM.

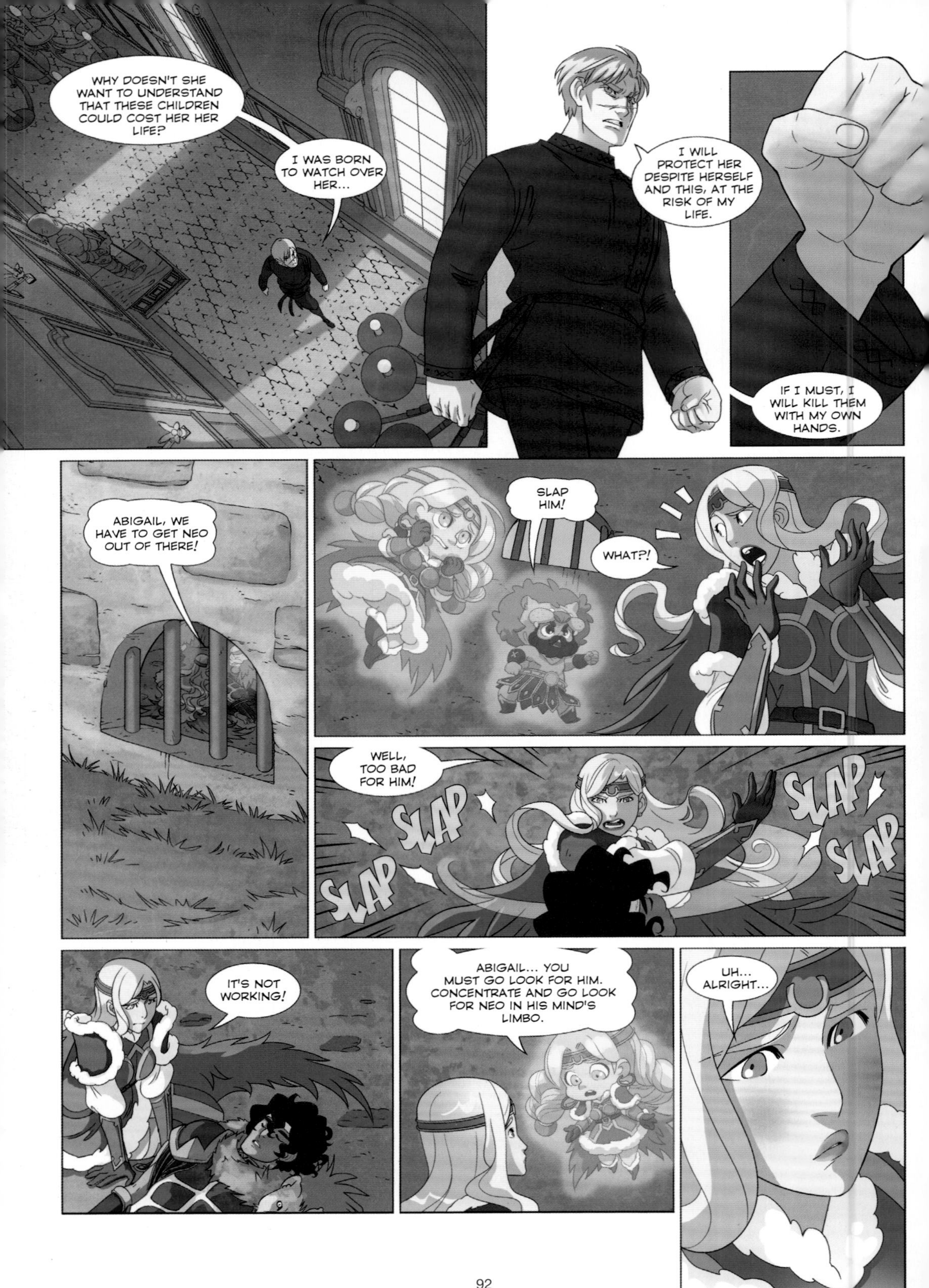
WHY DOESN'T SHE WANT TO UNDERSTAND THAT THESE CHILDREN COULD COST HER HER LIFE?
I WAS BORN TO WATCH OVER HER...
I WILL PROTECT HER DESPITE HERSELF AND THIS, AT THE RISK OF MY LIFE.
IF I MUST, I WILL KILL THEM WITH MY OWN HANDS.
ABIGAIL, WE HAVE TO GET NEO OUT OF THERE!
SLAP HIM!
WHAT?!
WELL, TOO BAD FOR HIM!
SLAP
SLAP
SLAP
SLAP
SLAP
IT'S NOT WORKING!
ABIGAIL... YOU MUST GO LOOK FOR HIM. CONCENTRATE AND GO LOOK FOR NEO IN HIS MIND'S LIMBO.
UH... ALRIGHT...

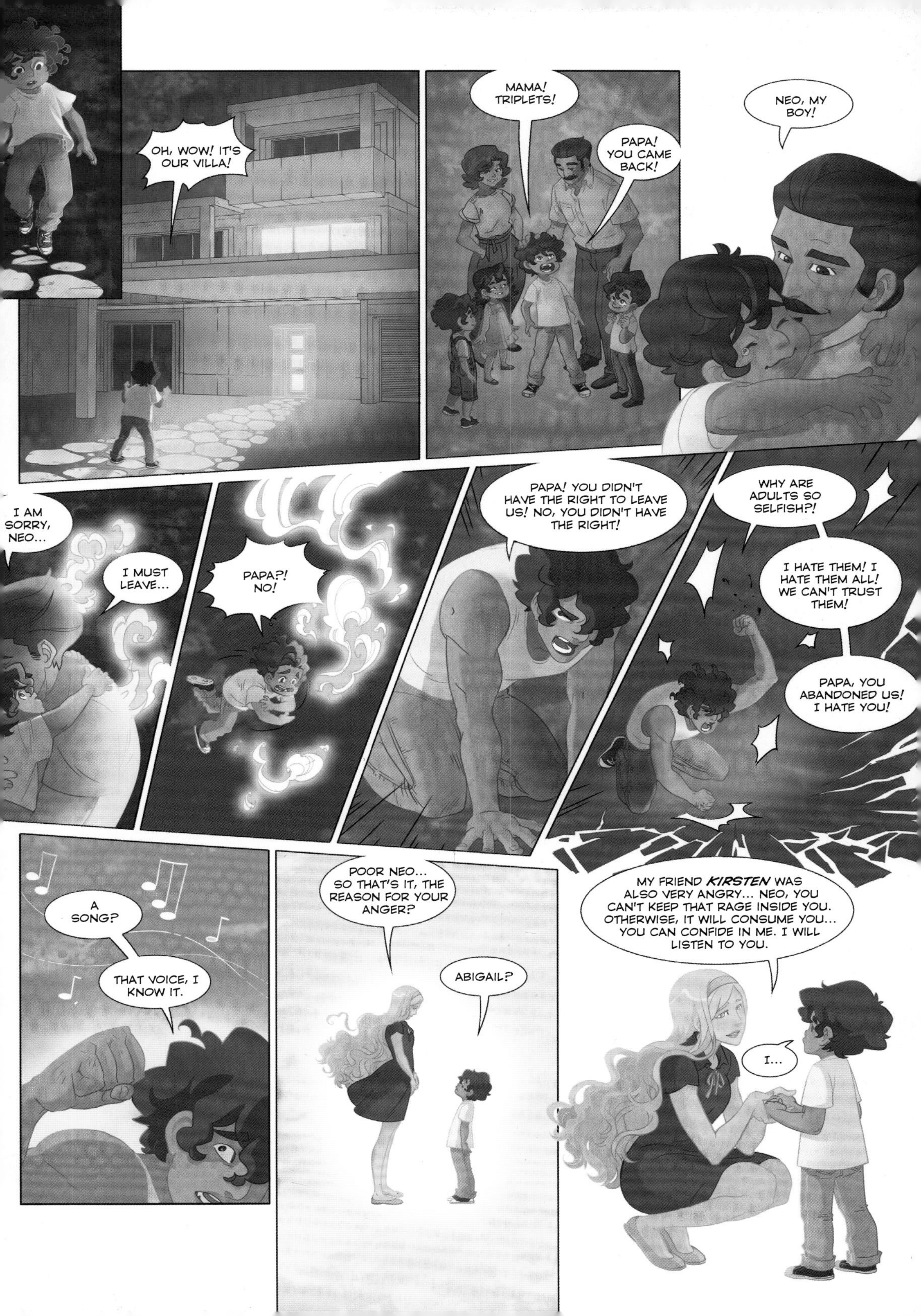
OH, WOW! IT'S OUR VILLA!
MAMA! TRIPLETS!
PAPA! YOU CAME BACK!
NEO, MY BOY!
I AM SORRY, NEO...
I MUST LEAVE...
PAPA?! NO!
PAPA! YOU DIDN'T HAVE THE RIGHT TO LEAVE US! NO, YOU DIDN'T HAVE THE RIGHT!
WHY ARE ADULTS SO SELFISH?!
I HATE THEM! I HATE THEM ALL! WE CAN'T TRUST THEM!
PAPA, YOU ABANDONED US! I HATE YOU!
A SONG?
THAT VOICE, I KNOW IT.
POOR NEO... SO THAT'S IT, THE REASON FOR YOUR ANGER?
ABIGAIL?
MY FRIEND KIRSTEN WAS ALSO VERY ANGRY... NEO, YOU CAN'T KEEP THAT RAGE INSIDE YOU. OTHERWISE, IT WILL CONSUME YOU... YOU CAN CONFIDE IN ME. I WILL LISTEN TO YOU.
I...

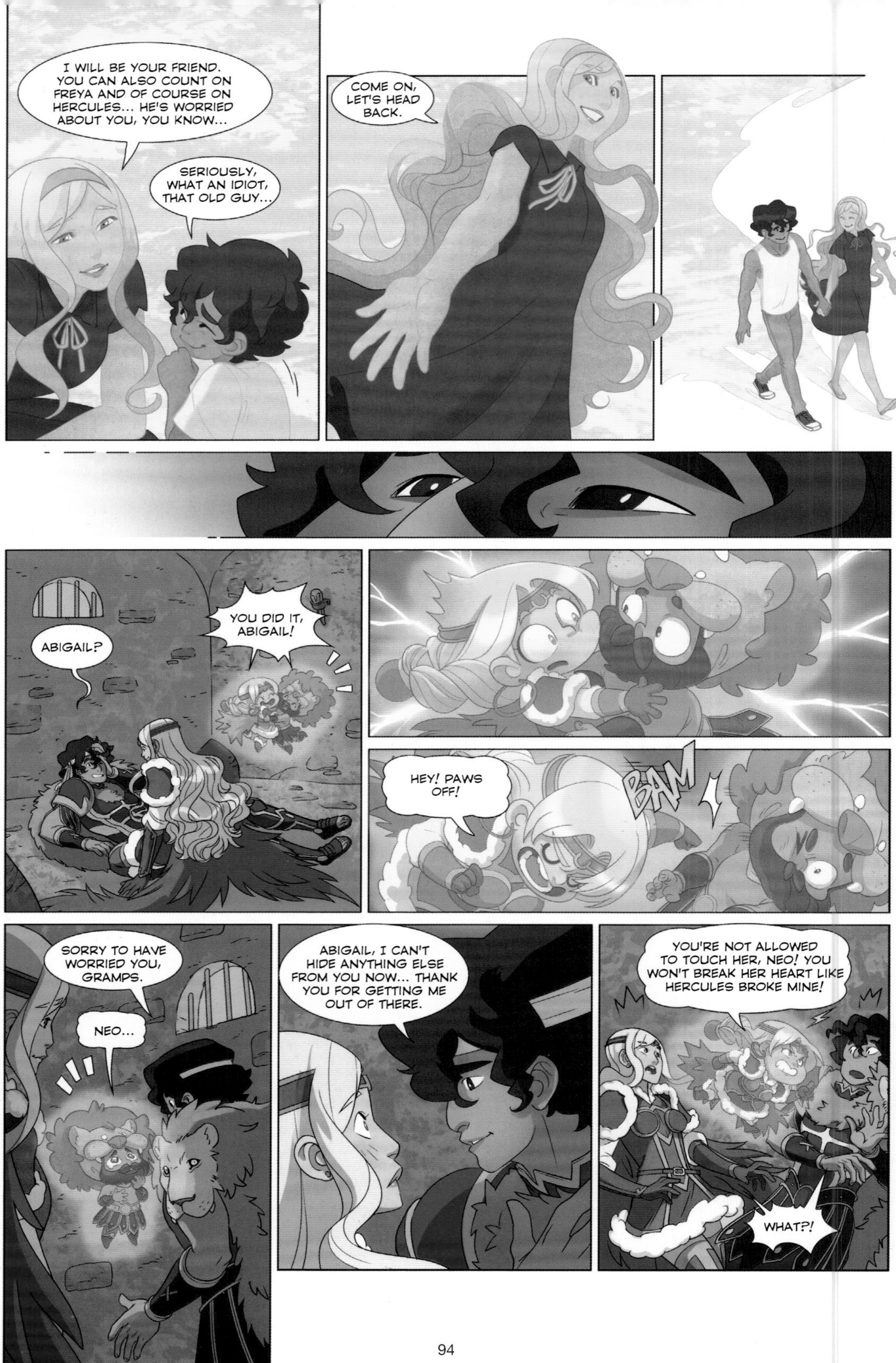
I WILL BE YOUR FRIEND. YOU CAN ALSO COUNT ON FREYA AND OF COURSE ON HERCULES... HE'S WORRIED ABOUT YOU, YOU KNOW...
SERIOUSLY, WHAT AN IDIOT, THAT OLD GUY...
COME ON, LET'S HEAD BACK.
ABIGAIL?
YOU DID IT, ABIGAIL!
HEY! PAWS OFF!
BAM
SORRY TO HAVE WORRIED YOU, GRAMPS.
NEO...
ABIGAIL, I CAN'T HIDE ANYTHING ELSE FROM YOU NOW... THANK YOU FOR GETTING ME OUT OF THERE.
YOU'RE NOT ALLOWED TO TOUCH HER, NEO! YOU WON'T BREAK HER HEART LIKE HERCULES BROKE MINE!
WHAT?!

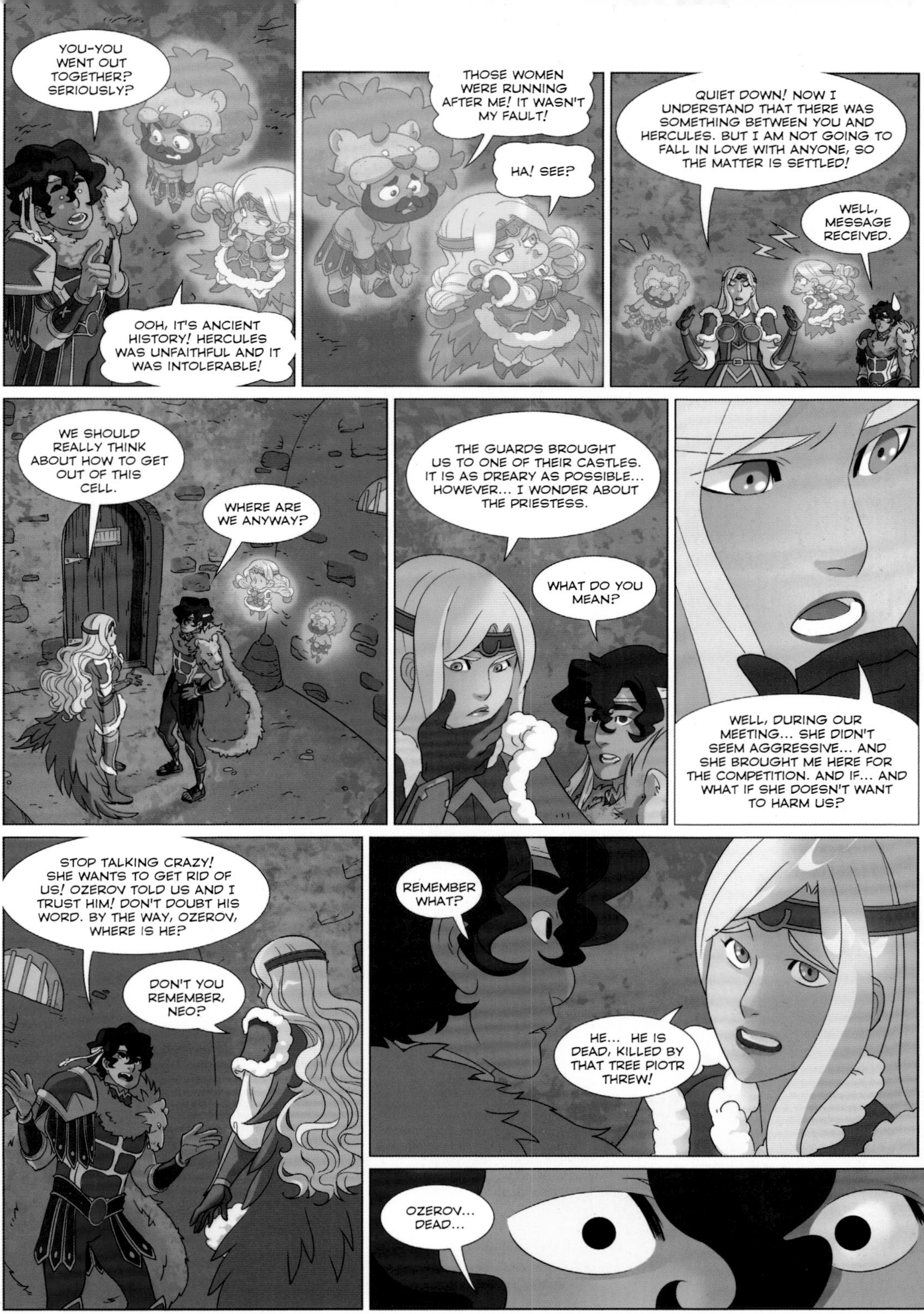

YOU-YOU WENT OUT TOGETHER? SERIOUSLY?
OOH, IT'S ANCIENT HISTORY! HERCULES WAS UNFAITHFUL AND IT WAS INTOLERABLE!
THOSE WOMEN WERE RUNNING AFTER ME! IT WASN'T MY FAULT!
HA! SEE?
QUIET DOWN! NOW I UNDERSTAND THAT THERE WAS SOMETHING BETWEEN YOU AND HERCULES. BUT I AM NOT GOING TO FALL IN LOVE WITH ANYONE, SO THE MATTER IS SETTLED!
WELL, MESSAGE RECEIVED.
WE SHOULD REALLY THINK ABOUT HOW TO GET OUT OF THIS CELL.
WHERE ARE WE ANYWAY?
THE GUARDS BROUGHT US TO ONE OF THEIR CASTLES. IT IS AS DREARY AS POSSIBLE... HOWEVER... I WONDER ABOUT THE PRIESTESS.
WHAT DO YOU MEAN?
WELL, DURING OUR MEETING... SHE DIDN'T SEEM AGGRESSIVE... AND SHE BROUGHT ME HERE FOR THE COMPETITION. AND IF... AND WHAT IF SHE DOESN'T WANT TO HARM US?
STOP TALKING CRAZY! SHE WANTS TO GET RID OF US! OZEROV TOLD US AND I TRUST HIM! DON'T DOUBT HIS WORD. BY THE WAY, OZEROV, WHERE IS HE?
DON'T YOU REMEMBER, NEO?
REMEMBER WHAT?
HE... HE IS DEAD, KILLED BY THAT TREE PIOTR THREW!
OZEROV... DEAD...

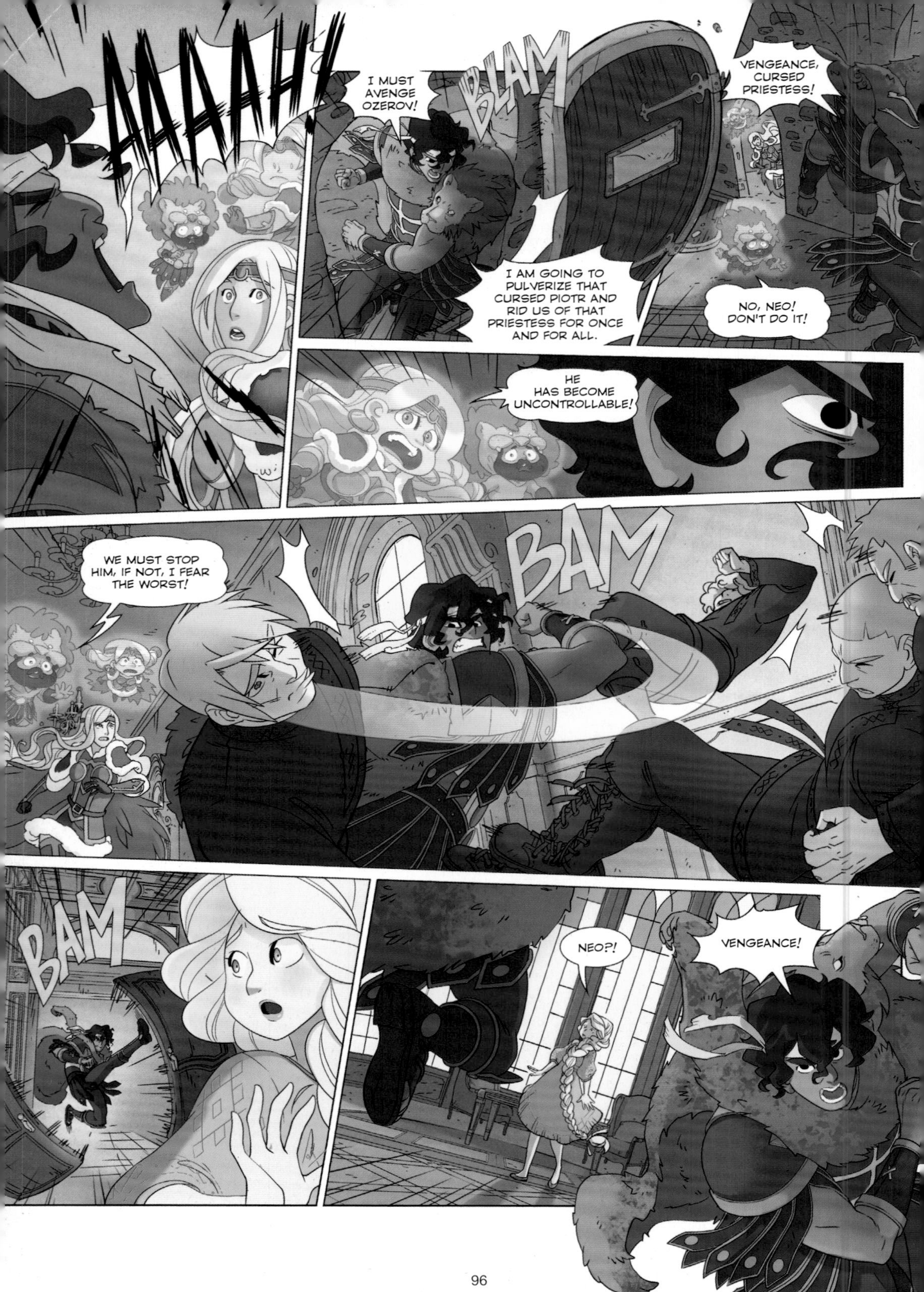
AAAAH!
I MUST AVENGE OZEROV!
BLAM
I AM GOING TO PULVERIZE THAT CURSED PIOTR AND RID US OF THAT PRIESTESS FOR ONCE AND FOR ALL.
VENGEANCE, CURSED PRIESTESS!
NO, NEO! DON'T DO IT!
HE HAS BECOME UNCONTROLLABLE!
WE MUST STOP HIM, IF NOT, I FEAR THE WORST!
BAM
BAM
NEO?!
VENGEANCE!

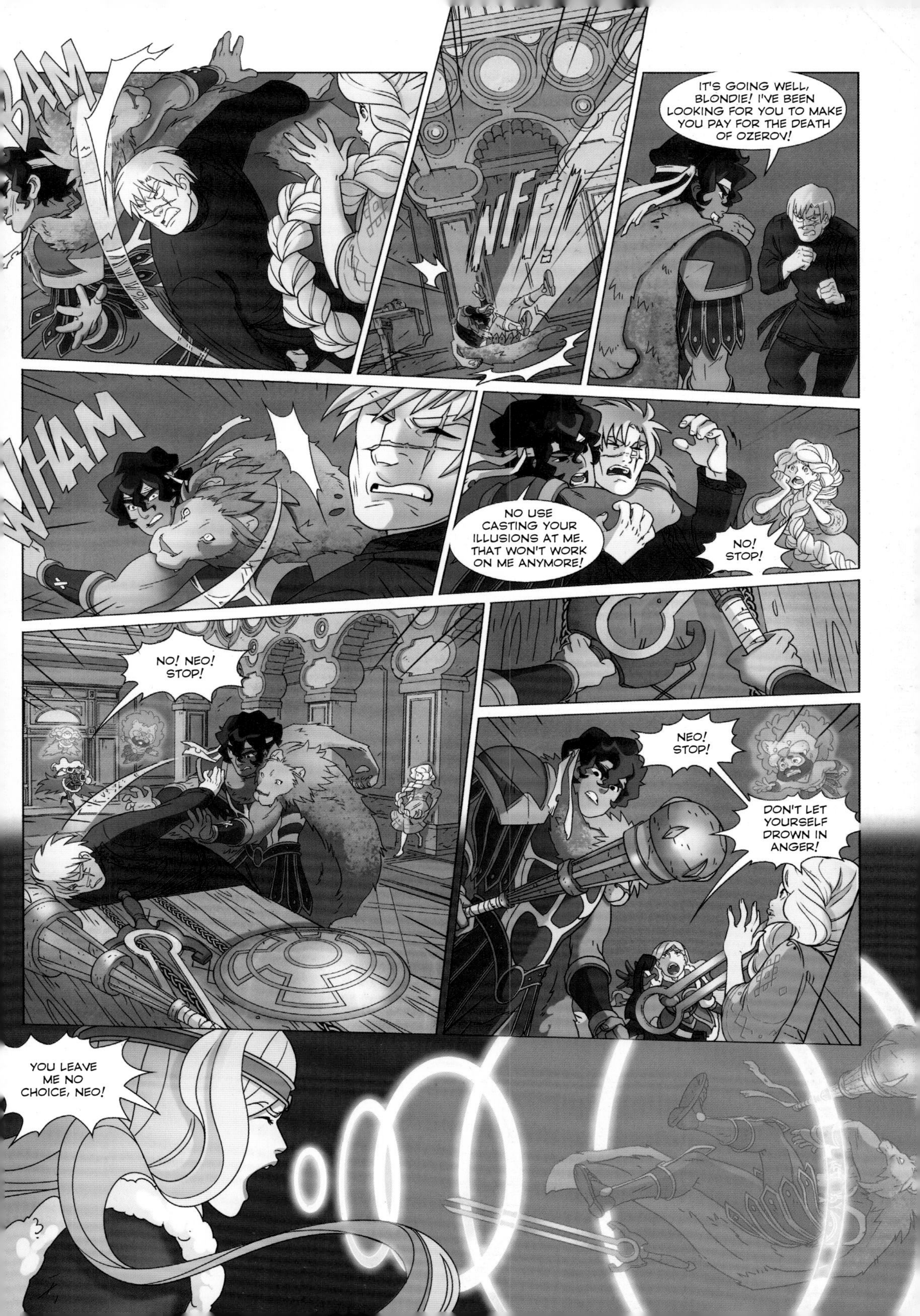
BAM
WNFF
IT'S GOING WELL, BLONDIE! I'VE BEEN LOOKING FOR YOU TO MAKE YOU PAY FOR THE DEATH OF OZEROV!
WHAM
NO USE CASTING YOUR ILLUSIONS AT ME. THAT WON'T WORK ON ME ANYMORE!
NO! STOP!
NO! NEO! STOP!
NEO! STOP!
DON'T LET YOURSELF DROWN IN ANGER!
YOU LEAVE ME NO CHOICE, NEO!

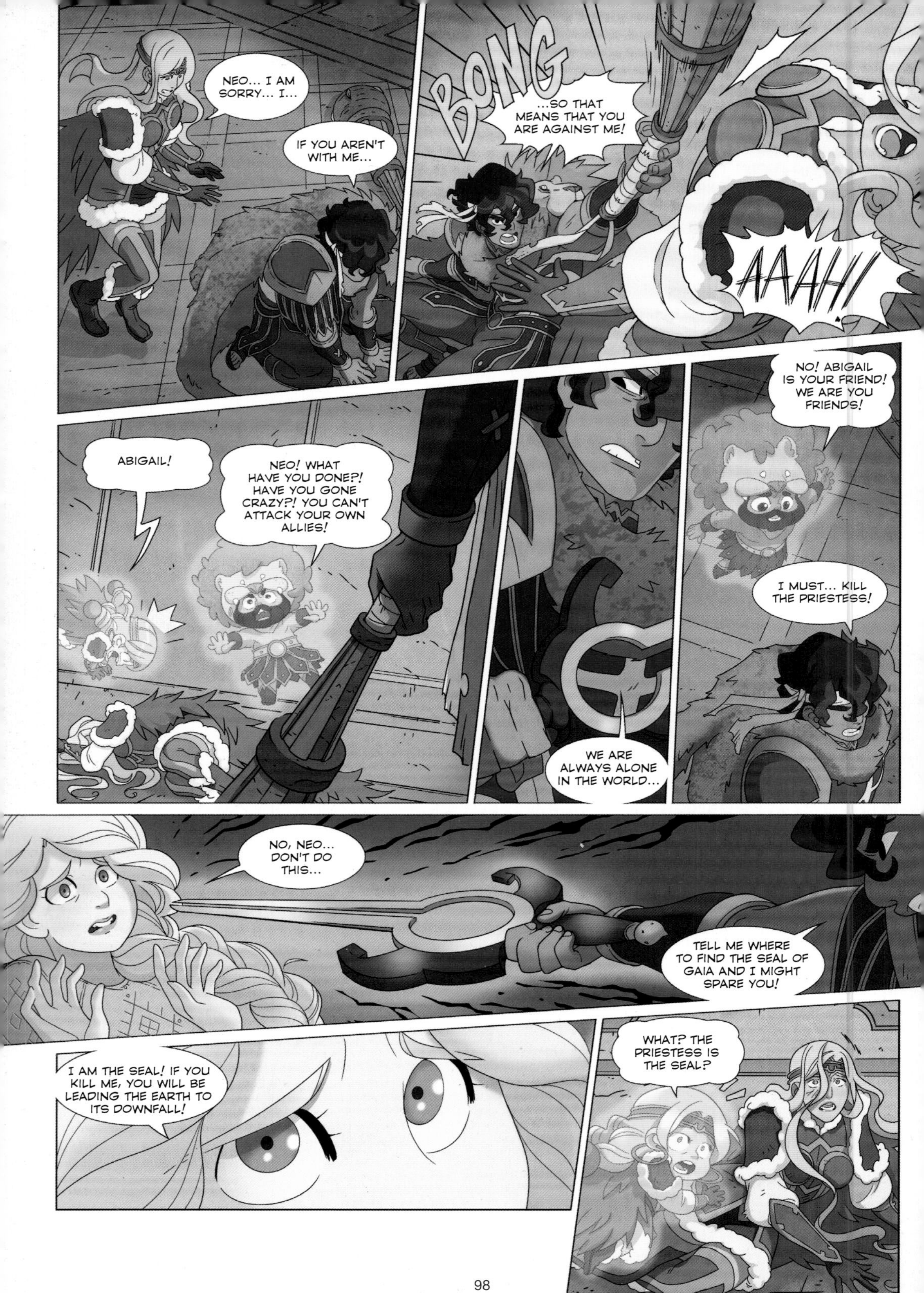
NEO... I AM SORRY... I...
IF YOU AREN'T WITH ME...
BONG
...SO THAT MEANS THAT YOU ARE AGAINST ME!
AAAH!
ABIGAIL!
NEO! WHAT HAVE YOU DONE?! HAVE YOU GONE CRAZY?! YOU CAN'T ATTACK YOUR OWN ALLIES!
WE ARE ALWAYS ALONE IN THE WORLD...
NO! ABIGAIL IS YOUR FRIEND! WE ARE YOU FRIENDS!
I MUST... KILL THE PRIESTESS!
NO, NEO... DON'T DO THIS...
TELL ME WHERE TO FIND THE SEAL OF GAIA AND I MIGHT SPARE YOU!
I AM THE SEAL! IF YOU KILL ME, YOU WILL BE LEADING THE EARTH TO ITS DOWNFALL!
WHAT? THE PRIESTESS IS THE SEAL?

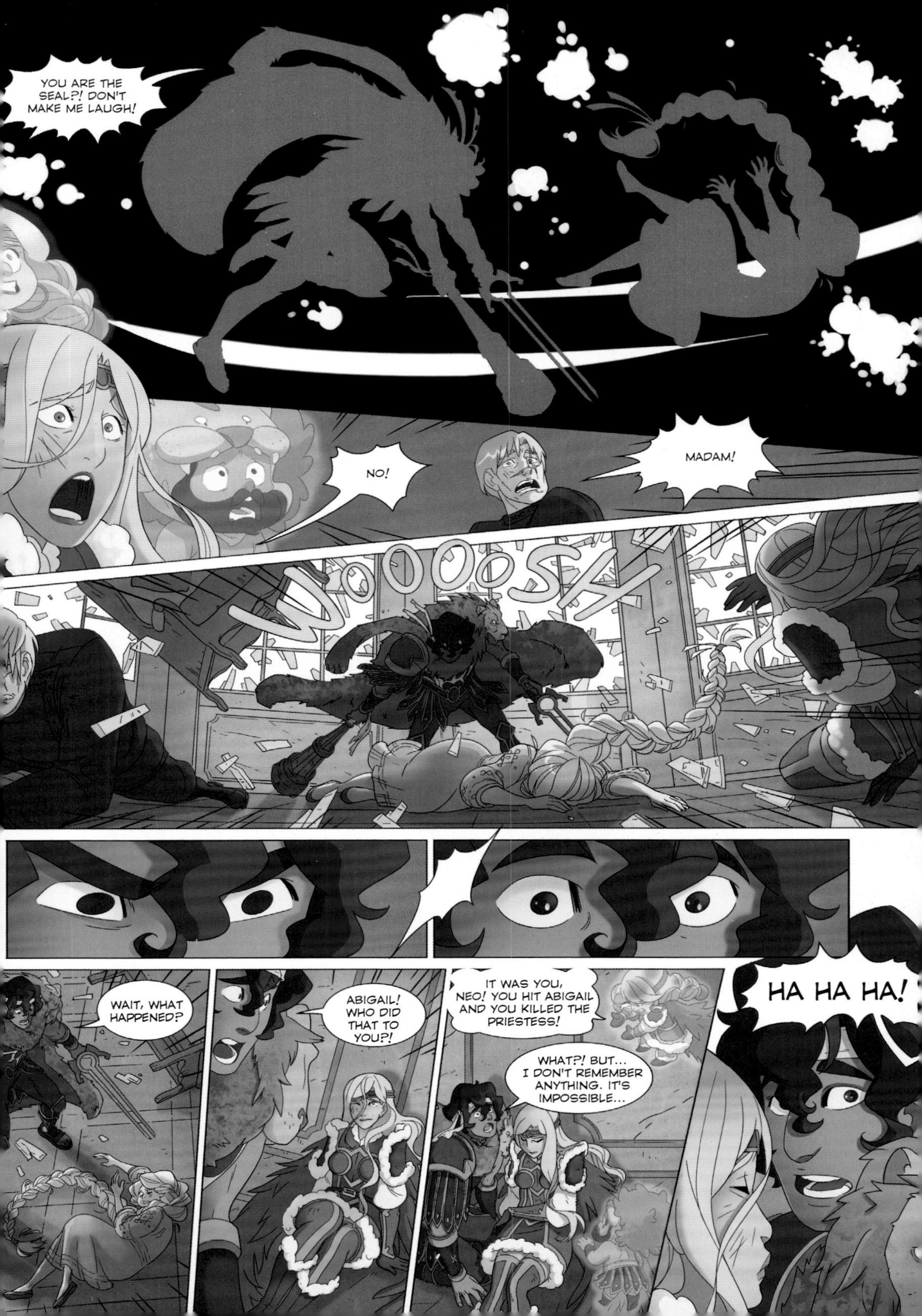
YOU ARE THE SEAL?! DON'T MAKE ME LAUGH!
NO!
MADAM!
WOOOOOSH
WAIT, WHAT HAPPENED?
ABIGAIL! WHO DID THAT TO YOU?!
IT WAS YOU, NEO! YOU HIT ABIGAIL AND YOU KILLED THE PRIESTESS!
WHAT?! BUT... I DON'T REMEMBER ANYTHING. IT'S IMPOSSIBLE...
HA HA HA!

OZEROV?! YOU'RE ALIVE?!

IN FLESH AND BLOOD, NEO. I'M DOING MUCH BETTER THAN ABIGAIL, PIOTR, OR THE PRIESTESS. IT SEEMS I MANAGED TO DODGE THAT TREE.

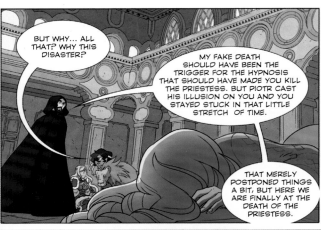

BUT WHY... ALL THAT? WHY THIS DISASTER?

MY FAKE DEATH SHOULD HAVE BEEN THE TRIGGER FOR THE HYPNOSIS THAT SHOULD HAVE MADE YOU KILL THE PRIESTESS. BUT PIOTR CAST HIS ILLUSION ON YOU AND YOU STAYED STUCK IN THAT LITTLE STRETCH OF TIME.

THAT MERELY POSTPONED THINGS A BIT, BUT HERE WE ARE FINALLY AT THE DEATH OF THE PRIESTESS.

YOU HYPNOTIZED ME SO THAT I WOULD KILL THE PRIESTESS?!

SINCE ALWAYS, I HAVE BEEN RAISED TO PROTECT THE PRIESTESS. BUT, YEAR AFTER YEAR, MY BODY WITHERED WHILE HERS STAYED EVER YOUNG AND BEAUTIFUL. JEALOUSY GNAWED AT ME...

EVIL CONTACTED ME. HE OFFERED ME ETERNAL YOUTH IN EXCHANGE FOR THE LIFE OF THE PRIESTESS. BUT ONLY THE WEAPONS OF THE MYTHIC HEROES COULD KILL HER! SO I HAD TO TRICK YOU TO GAIN YOUR CONFIDENCE AND TRAIN YOU SO THAT I COULD HONOR MY CONTRACT.

YOU... YOU WERE ACTING THIS WHOLE TIME?!

YES, NEO. THE DAYS SPENT WITH YOU WERE THE LONGEST THAT I HAVE EVER KNOWN. WHAT IRONY JUST THE SAME! THE DESCENDANT OF HERCULES, LIKE YOUR FAMOUS ANCESTOR, KILLS HIS FAMILY OUT OF ANGER! HOW FUNNY!

YOU PIECE OF GARBAGE ! BECAUSE OF YOU, I HIT ABIGAIL AND KILLED THE PRIESTESS!

NEO, CALM DOWN, IT'S NOT YOUR FAULT...

ABIGAIL, I WILL NEVER FORGIVE MYSELF FOR THAT STRIKE...

PIOTR... PERHAPS IT'S NOT TOO LATE... FORGIVE THE CHILDREN, AND HELP THEM FIGHT EVIL.

WHAT IRONY FOR A SEER TO BE ABLE TO SEE EVERYONE'S FUTURE EXCEPT HER OWN...

I PROMISE YOU, MADAM.

OZEROV! THIS IS GOING TO COST YOU DEARLY!

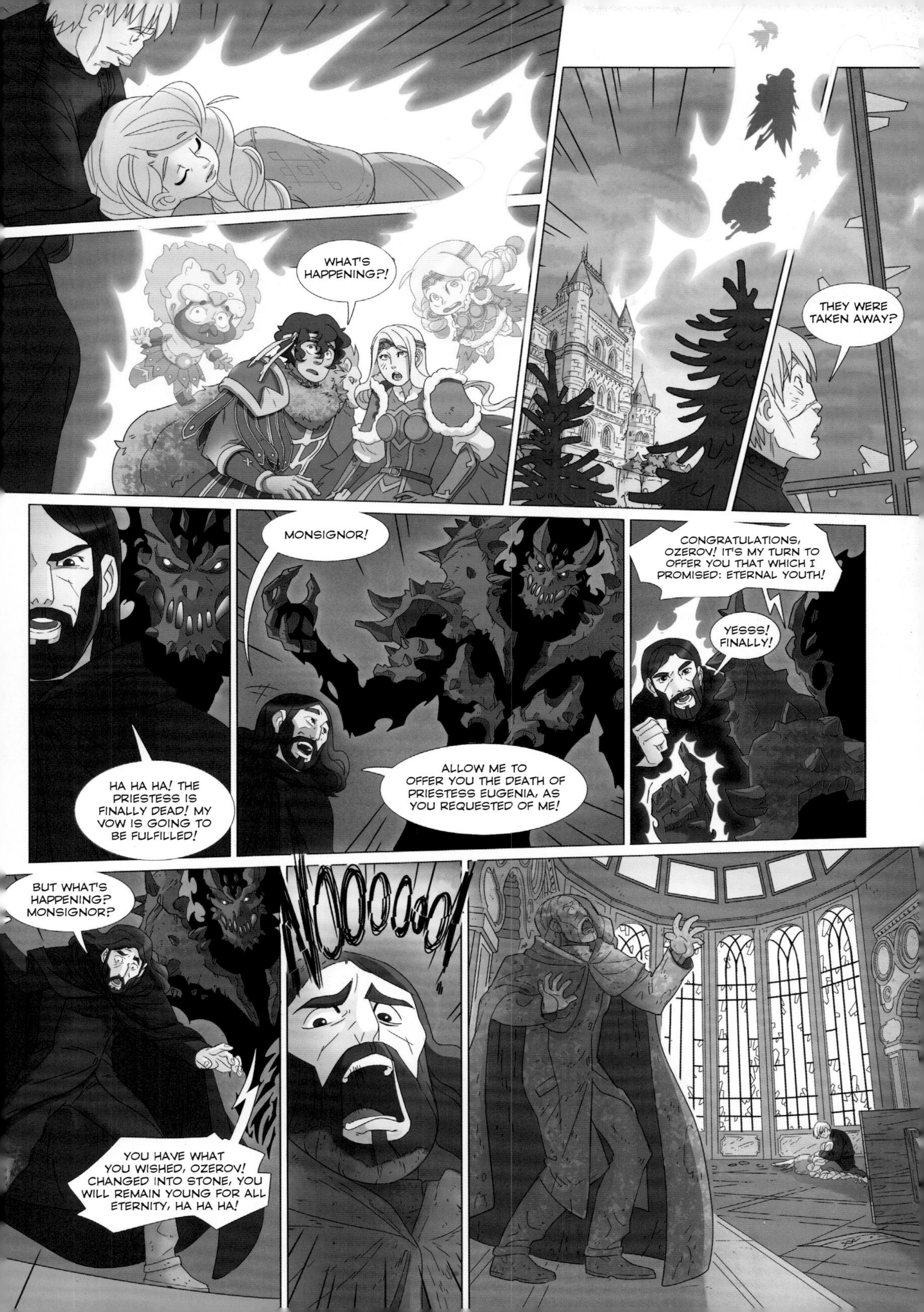
WHAT'S HAPPENING?!
THEY WERE TAKEN AWAY?
HA HA HA! THE PRIESTESS IS FINALLY DEAD! MY VOW IS GOING TO BE FULFILLED!
MONSIGNOR!
ALLOW ME TO OFFER YOU THE DEATH OF PRIESTESS EUGENIA, AS YOU REQUESTED OF ME!
CONGRATULATIONS, OZEROV! IT'S MY TURN TO OFFER YOU THAT WHICH I PROMISED: ETERNAL YOUTH!
YESSS! FINALLY!
BUT WHAT'S HAPPENING? MONSIGNOR?
YOU HAVE WHAT YOU WISHED, OZEROV! CHANGED INTO STONE, YOU WILL REMAIN YOUNG FOR ALL ETERNITY, HA HA HA!
NOOOOO!

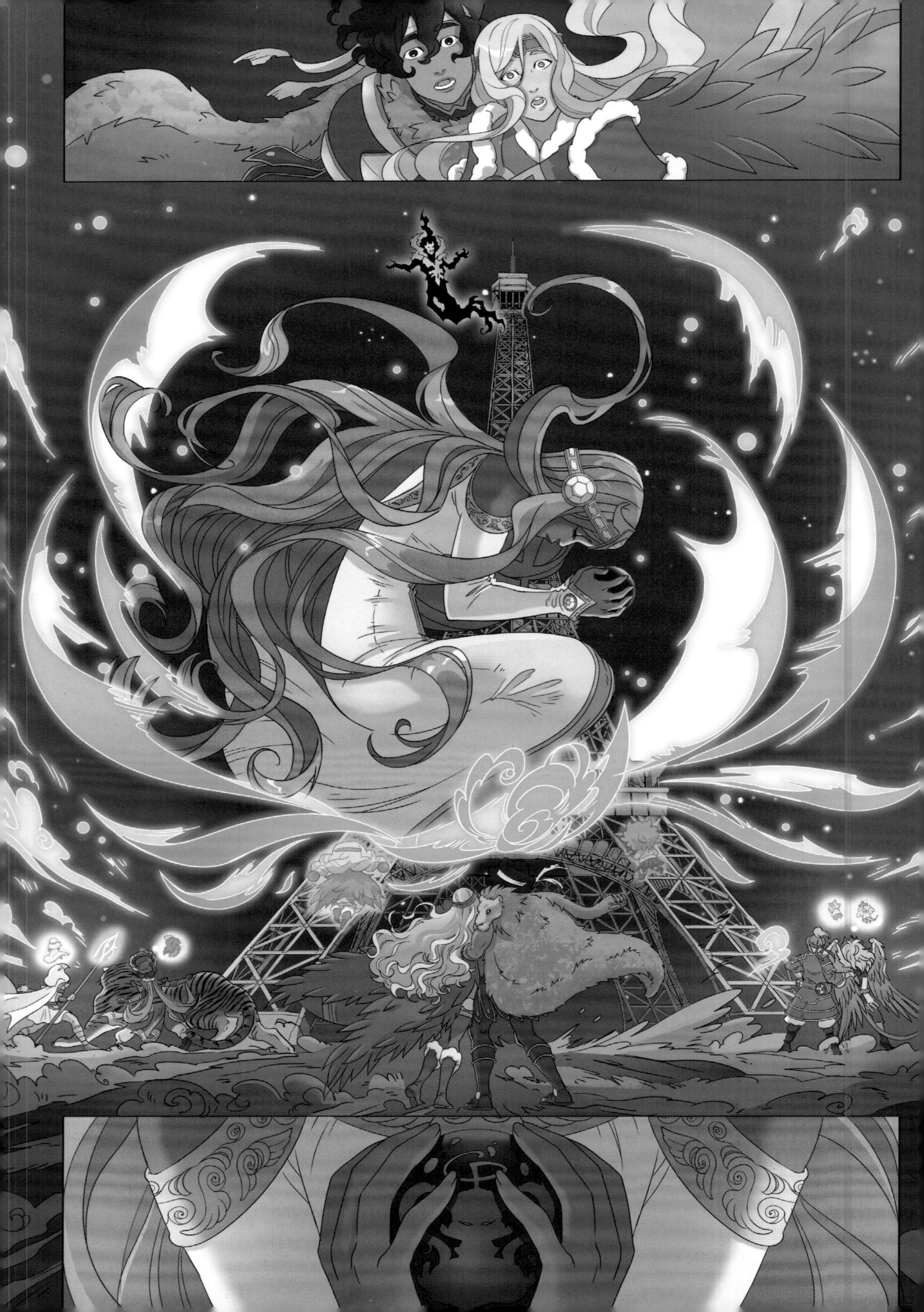

# PART 9 : STONEHENGE

Story by
**PATRICK SOBRAL**
with help from **NICOLAS JARRY**

Art and Color
**JÉRÔME ALQUIÉ**

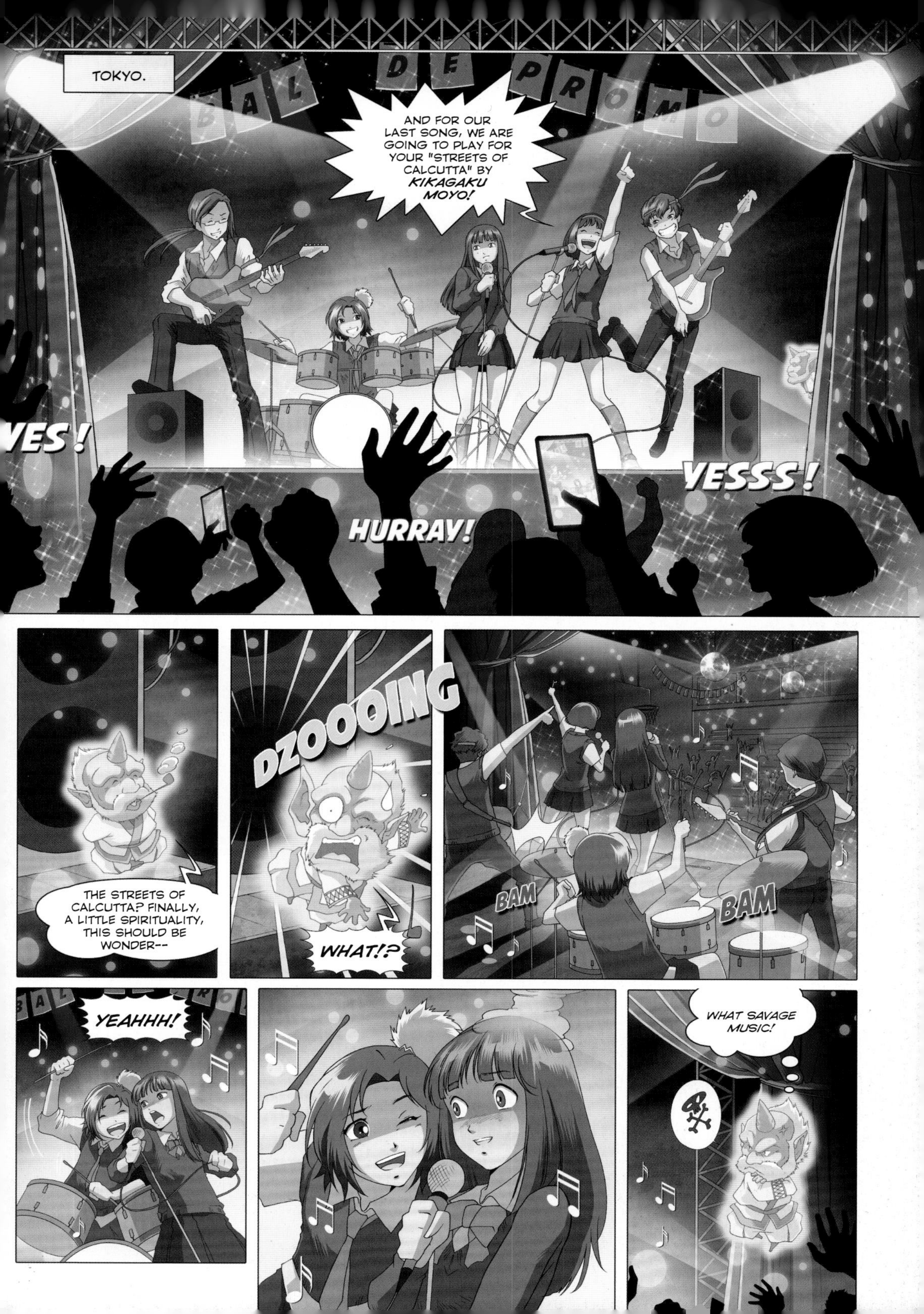
TOKYO.
BAL DE PROMO
AND FOR OUR LAST SONG, WE ARE GOING TO PLAY FOR YOUR "STREETS OF CALCUTTA" BY KIKAGAKU MOYO!
YES!
YESSS!
HURRAY!
THE STREETS OF CALCUTTA? FINALLY, A LITTLE SPIRITUALITY, THIS SHOULD BE WONDER--
DZOOOOING
WHAT!?
BAM
BAM
YEAHHH!
WHAT SAVAGE MUSIC!

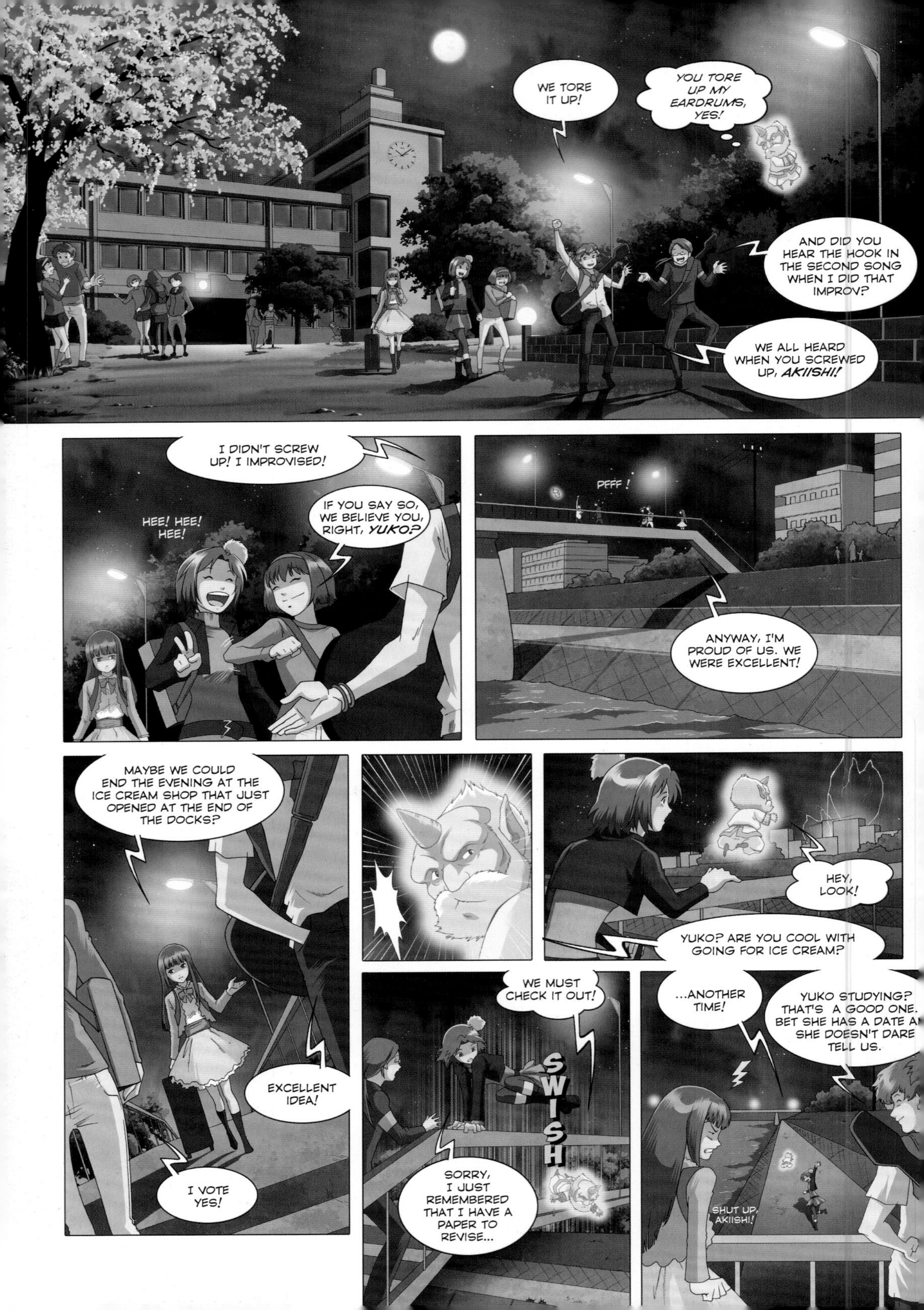

WE TORE IT UP!
YOU TORE UP MY EARDRUMS, YES!
AND DID YOU HEAR THE HOOK IN THE SECOND SONG WHEN I DID THAT IMPROV?
WE ALL HEARD WHEN YOU SCREWED UP, AKIISHI!
I DIDN'T SCREW UP! I IMPROVISED!
HEE! HEE! HEE!
IF YOU SAY SO, WE BELIEVE YOU, RIGHT, YUKO?
PFFF!
ANYWAY, I'M PROUD OF US. WE WERE EXCELLENT!
MAYBE WE COULD END THE EVENING AT THE ICE CREAM SHOP THAT JUST OPENED AT THE END OF THE DOCKS?
EXCELLENT IDEA!
I VOTE YES!
HEY, LOOK!
YUKO? ARE YOU COOL WITH GOING FOR ICE CREAM?
WE MUST CHECK IT OUT!
SWISH
SORRY, I JUST REMEMBERED THAT I HAVE A PAPER TO REVISE...
...ANOTHER TIME!
YUKO STUDYING? THAT'S A GOOD ONE. BET SHE HAS A DATE A SHE DOESN'T DARE TELL US.
SHUT UP, AKIISHI!

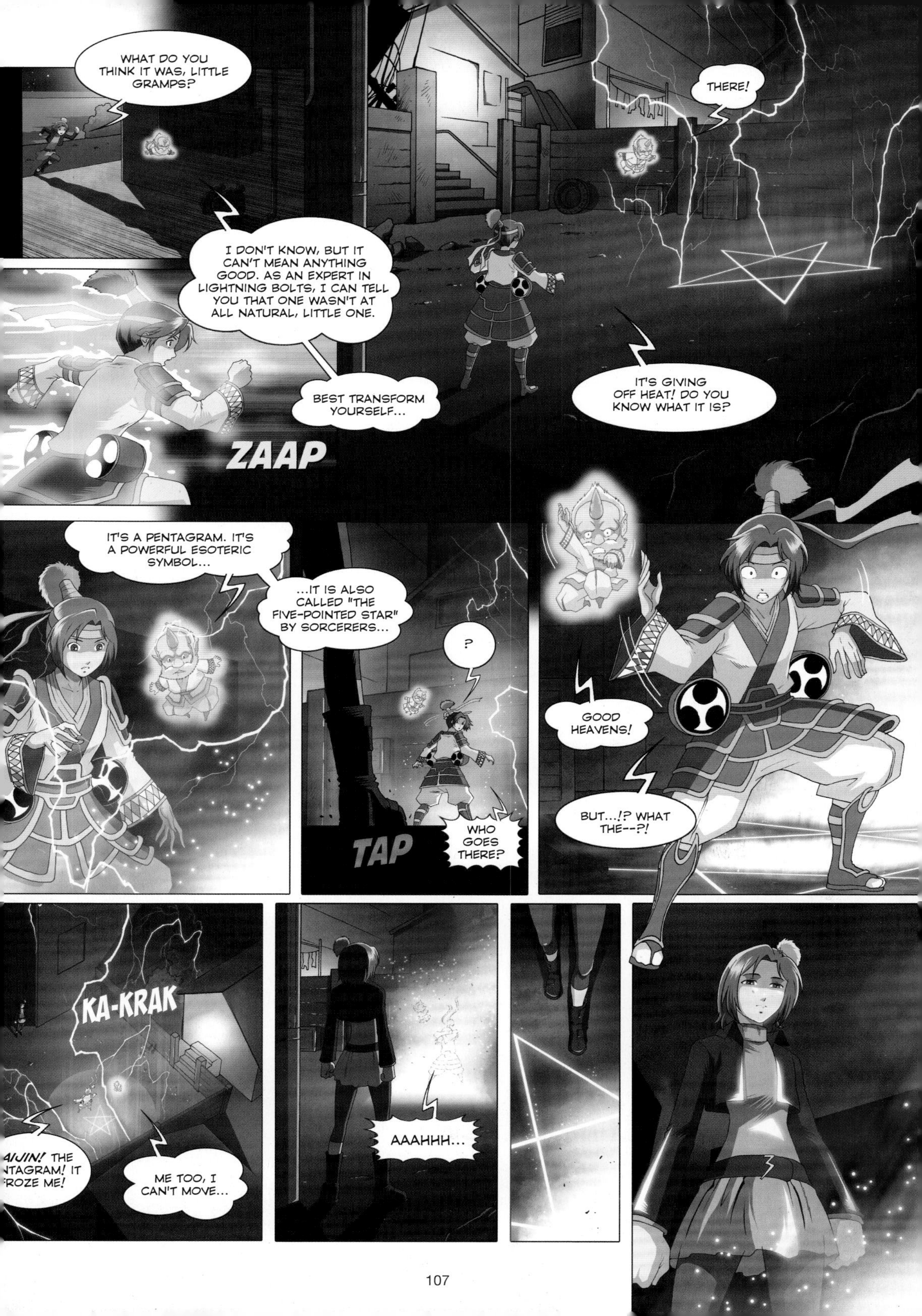
WHAT DO YOU THINK IT WAS, LITTLE GRAMPS?
I DON'T KNOW, BUT IT CAN'T MEAN ANYTHING GOOD. AS AN EXPERT IN LIGHTNING BOLTS, I CAN TELL YOU THAT ONE WASN'T AT ALL NATURAL, LITTLE ONE.
BEST TRANSFORM YOURSELF...
ZAAP
THERE!
IT'S GIVING OFF HEAT! DO YOU KNOW WHAT IT IS?
IT'S A PENTAGRAM. IT'S A POWERFUL ESOTERIC SYMBOL...
...IT IS ALSO CALLED "THE FIVE-POINTED STAR" BY SORCERERS...
?
TAP
WHO GOES THERE?
GOOD HEAVENS!
BUT...!? WHAT THE--?!
KA-KRAK
AIJIN! THE NTAGRAM! IT FROZE ME!
ME TOO, I CAN'T MOVE...
AAAHHH...

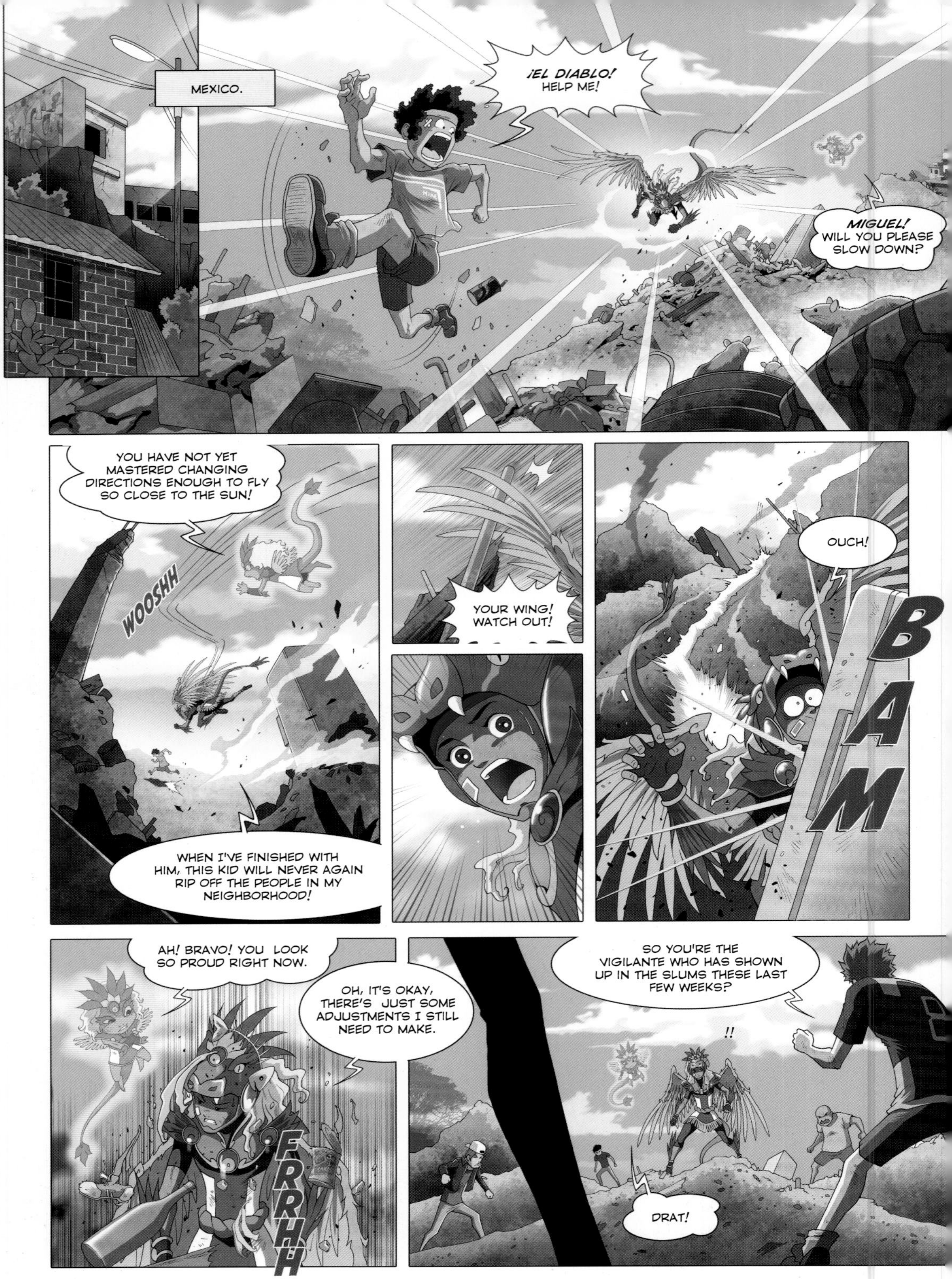
MEXICO.
¡EL DIABLO! HELP ME!
MIGUEL! WILL YOU PLEASE SLOW DOWN?
YOU HAVE NOT YET MASTERED CHANGING DIRECTIONS ENOUGH TO FLY SO CLOSE TO THE SUN!
WOOSHH
WHEN I'VE FINISHED WITH HIM, THIS KID WILL NEVER AGAIN RIP OFF THE PEOPLE IN MY NEIGHBORHOOD!
YOUR WING! WATCH OUT!
OUCH!
BAM
AH! BRAVO! YOU LOOK SO PROUD RIGHT NOW.
OH, IT'S OKAY, THERE'S JUST SOME ADJUSTMENTS I STILL NEED TO MAKE.
FRRHH
SO YOU'RE THE VIGILANTE WHO HAS SHOWN UP IN THE SLUMS THESE LAST FEW WEEKS?
!!
DRAT!

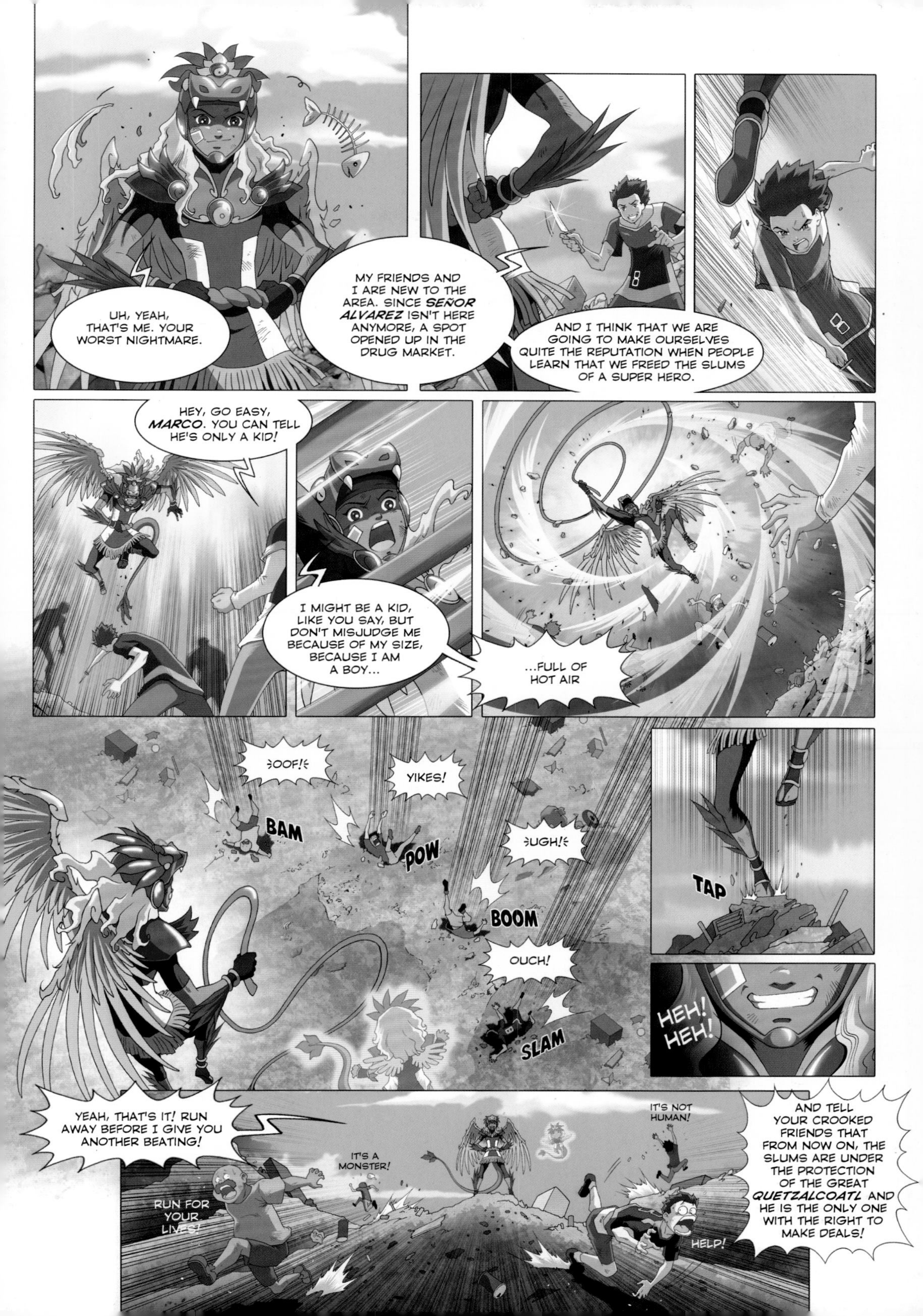
UH, YEAH, THAT'S ME. YOUR WORST NIGHTMARE.
MY FRIENDS AND I ARE NEW TO THE AREA. SINCE SEÑOR ALVAREZ ISN'T HERE ANYMORE, A SPOT OPENED UP IN THE DRUG MARKET.
AND I THINK THAT WE ARE GOING TO MAKE OURSELVES QUITE THE REPUTATION WHEN PEOPLE LEARN THAT WE FREED THE SLUMS OF A SUPER HERO.
HEY, GO EASY, MARCO. YOU CAN TELL HE'S ONLY A KID!
I MIGHT BE A KID, LIKE YOU SAY, BUT DON'T MISJUDGE ME BECAUSE OF MY SIZE, BECAUSE I AM A BOY...
...FULL OF HOT AIR
OOF!
BAM
YIKES!
POW
UGH!
BOOM
OUCH!
SLAM
TAP
HEH! HEH!
YEAH, THAT'S IT! RUN AWAY BEFORE I GIVE YOU ANOTHER BEATING!
RUN FOR YOUR LIVES!
IT'S A MONSTER!
IT'S NOT HUMAN!
HELP!
AND TELL YOUR CROOKED FRIENDS THAT FROM NOW ON, THE SLUMS ARE UNDER THE PROTECTION OF THE GREAT QUETZALCOATL AND HE IS THE ONLY ONE WITH THE RIGHT TO MAKE DEALS!

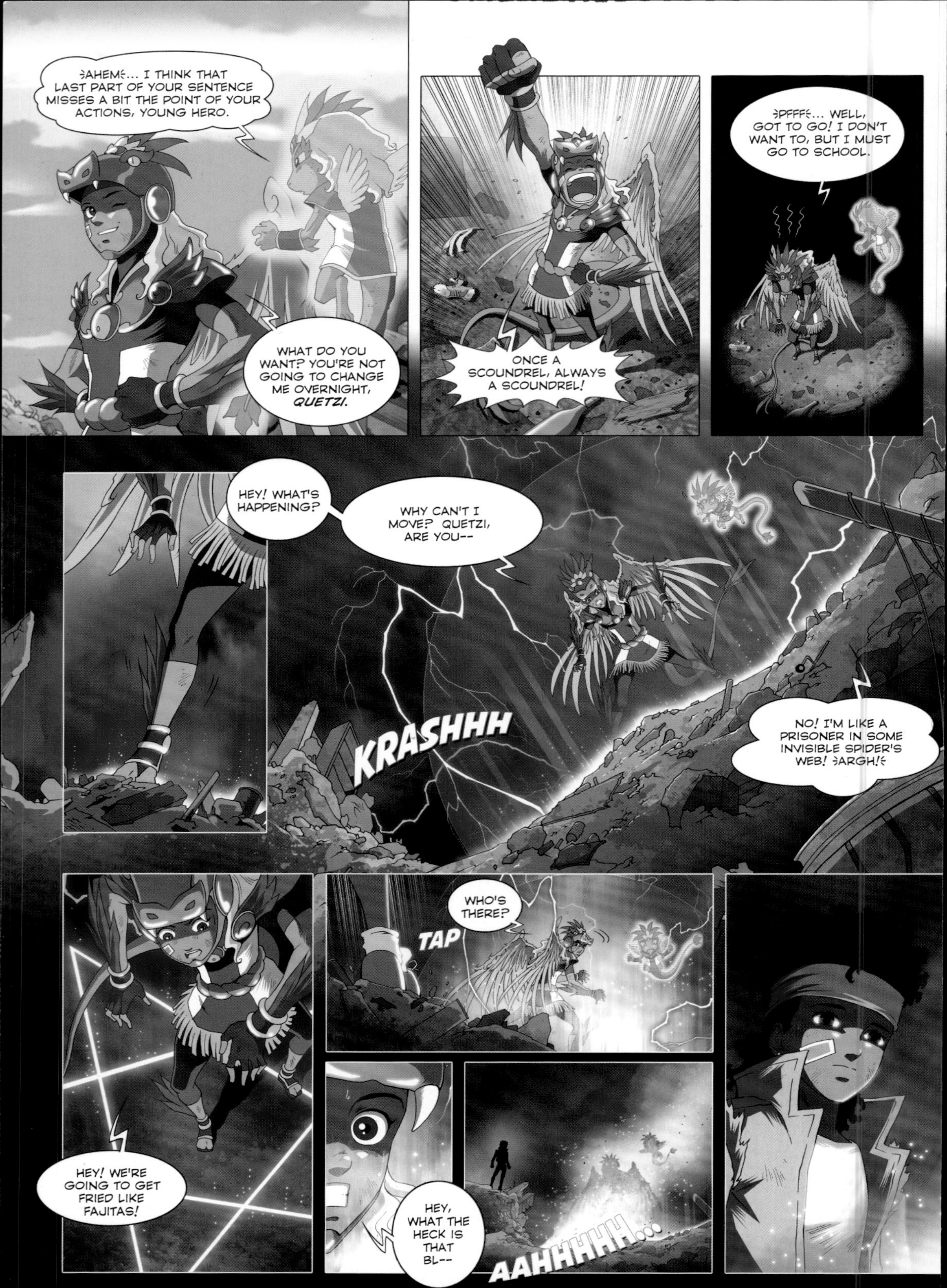

ϡAHEMϟ... I THINK THAT LAST PART OF YOUR SENTENCE MISSES A BIT THE POINT OF YOUR ACTIONS, YOUNG HERO.
WHAT DO YOU WANT? YOU'RE NOT GOING TO CHANGE ME OVERNIGHT, QUETZI.
ONCE A SCOUNDREL, ALWAYS A SCOUNDREL!
ϡPFFFϟ... WELL, GOT TO GO! I DON'T WANT TO, BUT I MUST GO TO SCHOOL.
HEY! WHAT'S HAPPENING?
WHY CAN'T I MOVE? QUETZI, ARE YOU--
KRASHHH
NO! I'M LIKE A PRISONER IN SOME INVISIBLE SPIDER'S WEB! ϡARGH!ϟ
HEY! WE'RE GOING TO GET FRIED LIKE FAJITAS!
WHO'S THERE?
TAP
HEY, WHAT THE HECK IS THAT BL--
AAHHHHH...

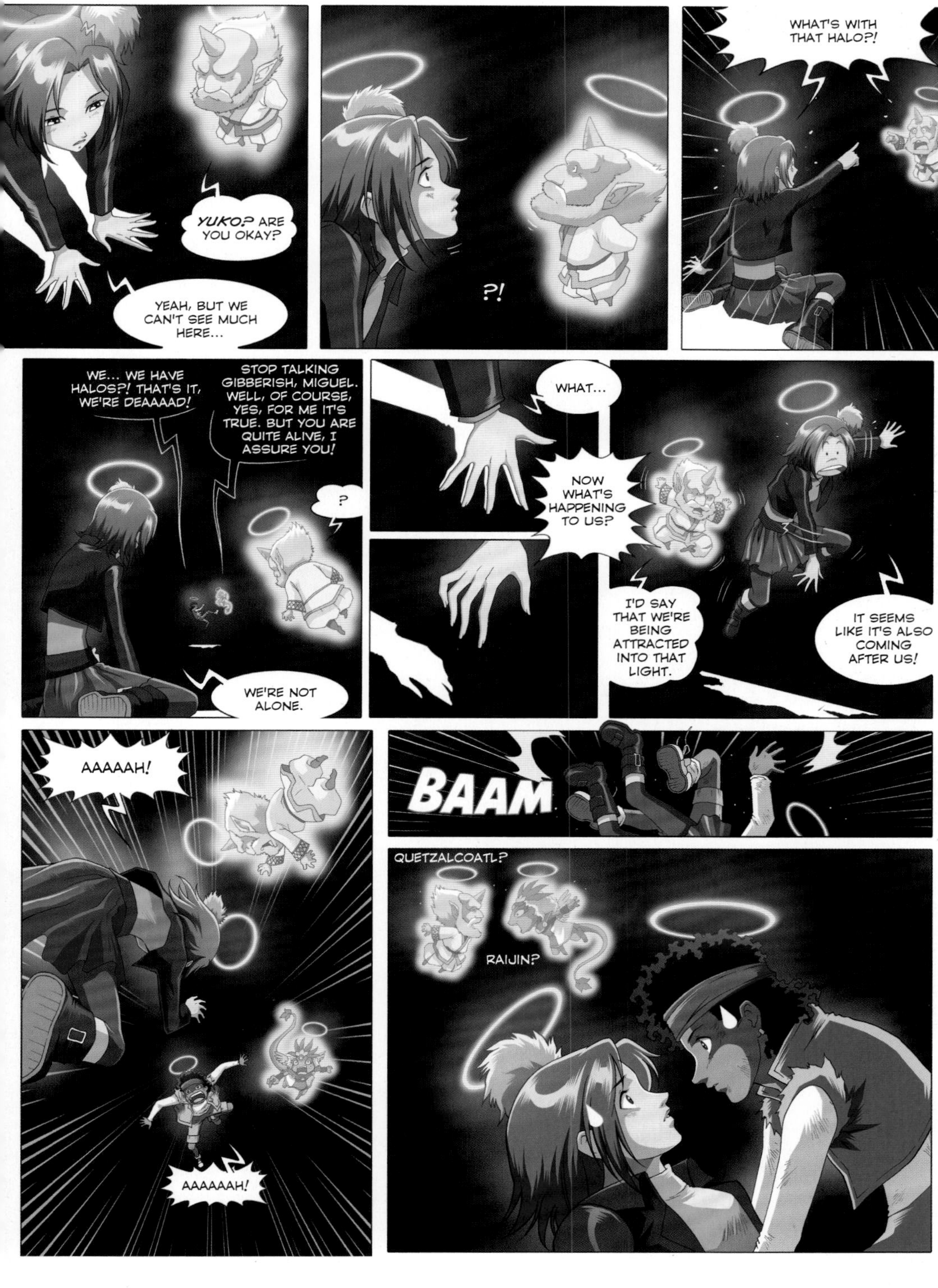
YUKO? ARE YOU OKAY?
YEAH, BUT WE CAN'T SEE MUCH HERE...
?!
WHAT'S WITH THAT HALO?!
WE... WE HAVE HALOS?! THAT'S IT, WE'RE DEAAAAD!
STOP TALKING GIBBERISH, MIGUEL. WELL, OF COURSE, YES, FOR ME IT'S TRUE. BUT YOU ARE QUITE ALIVE, I ASSURE YOU!
?
WE'RE NOT ALONE.
WHAT...
NOW WHAT'S HAPPENING TO US?
I'D SAY THAT WE'RE BEING ATTRACTED INTO THAT LIGHT.
IT SEEMS LIKE IT'S ALSO COMING AFTER US!
AAAAAH!
AAAAAAH!
BAAM
QUETZALCOATL?
RAIJIN?

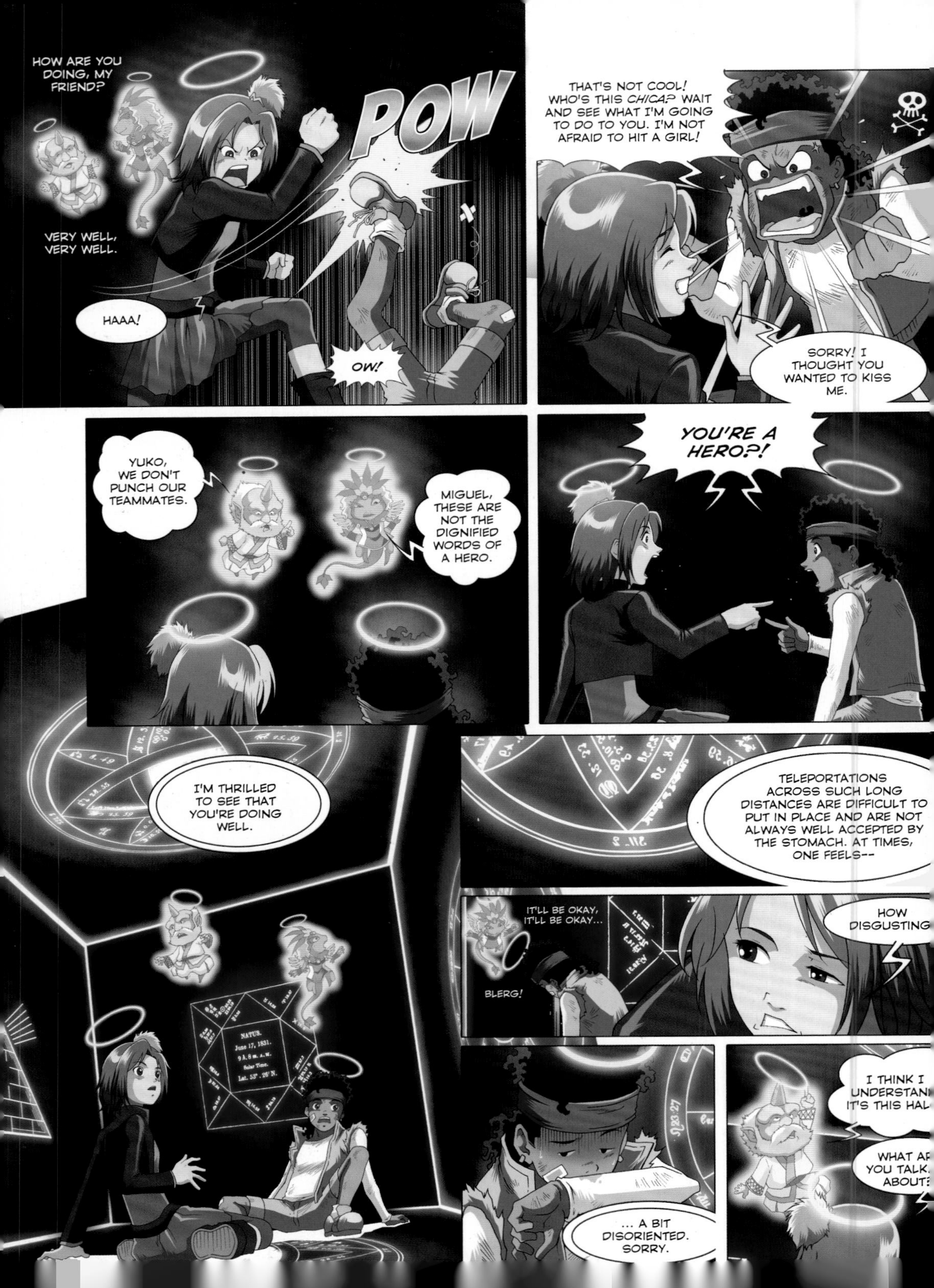
HOW ARE YOU DOING, MY FRIEND?
VERY WELL, VERY WELL.
POW
HAAA!
OW!
THAT'S NOT COOL! WHO'S THIS *CHICA*? WAIT AND SEE WHAT I'M GOING TO DO TO YOU. I'M NOT AFRAID TO HIT A GIRL!
SORRY! I THOUGHT YOU WANTED TO KISS ME.
YUKO, WE DON'T PUNCH OUR TEAMMATES.
MIGUEL, THESE ARE NOT THE DIGNIFIED WORDS OF A HERO.
YOU'RE A HERO?!
I'M THRILLED TO SEE THAT YOU'RE DOING WELL.
NATUS. June 17, 1831. 9 h. 8 m. a.m. Solar Time. Lat. 53°. 25' N.
TELEPORTATIONS ACROSS SUCH LONG DISTANCES ARE DIFFICULT TO PUT IN PLACE AND ARE NOT ALWAYS WELL ACCEPTED BY THE STOMACH. AT TIMES, ONE FEELS--
IT'LL BE OKAY, IT'LL BE OKAY...
BLERG!
HOW DISGUSTING
... A BIT DISORIENTED. SORRY.
I THINK I UNDERSTAN IT'S THIS HAL
WHAT AR YOU TALK ABOUT?

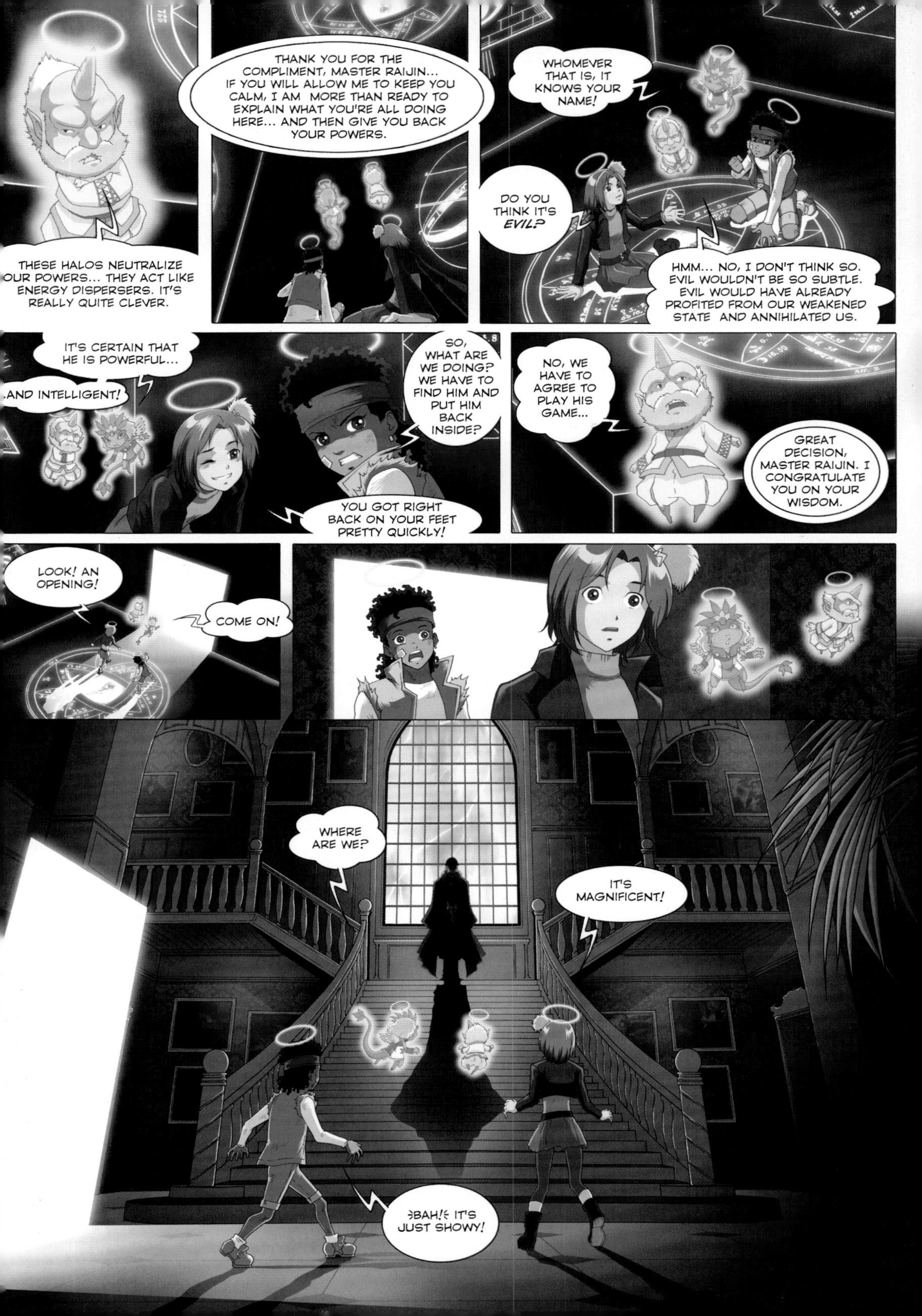
THESE HALOS NEUTRALIZE OUR POWERS... THEY ACT LIKE ENERGY DISPERSERS. IT'S REALLY QUITE CLEVER.
THANK YOU FOR THE COMPLIMENT, MASTER RAIJIN... IF YOU WILL ALLOW ME TO KEEP YOU CALM, I AM MORE THAN READY TO EXPLAIN WHAT YOU'RE ALL DOING HERE... AND THEN GIVE YOU BACK YOUR POWERS.
WHOMEVER THAT IS, IT KNOWS YOUR NAME!
DO YOU THINK IT'S *EVIL?*
HMM... NO, I DON'T THINK SO. EVIL WOULDN'T BE SO SUBTLE. EVIL WOULD HAVE ALREADY PROFITED FROM OUR WEAKENED STATE AND ANNIHILATED US.
IT'S CERTAIN THAT HE IS POWERFUL...
...AND INTELLIGENT!
SO, WHAT ARE WE DOING? WE HAVE TO FIND HIM AND PUT HIM BACK INSIDE?
YOU GOT RIGHT BACK ON YOUR FEET PRETTY QUICKLY!
NO, WE HAVE TO AGREE TO PLAY HIS GAME...
GREAT DECISION, MASTER RAIJIN. I CONGRATULATE YOU ON YOUR WISDOM.
LOOK! AN OPENING!
COME ON!
WHERE ARE WE?
IT'S MAGNIFICENT!
BAH! IT'S JUST SHOWY!

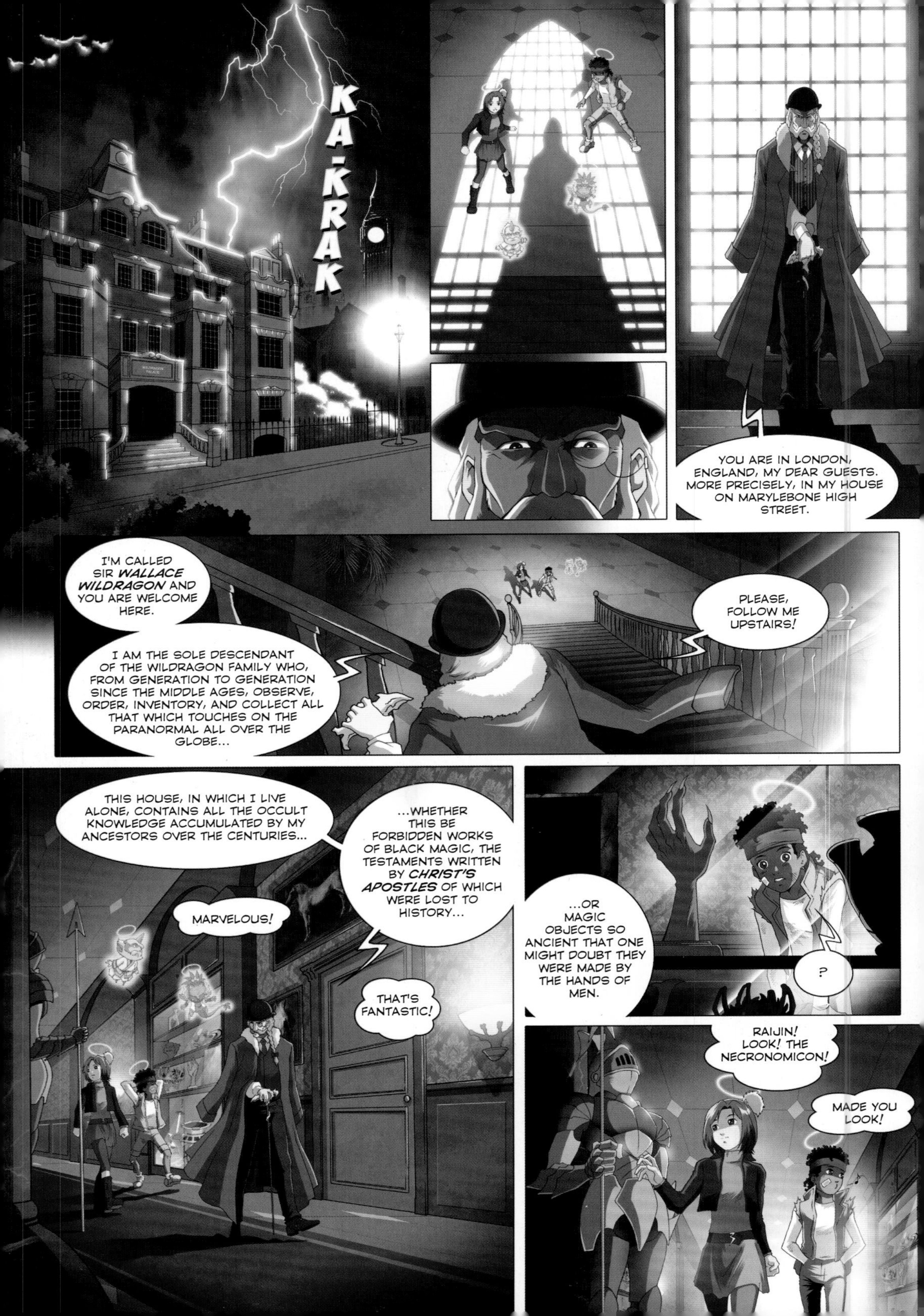
KA-KRAK
YOU ARE IN LONDON, ENGLAND, MY DEAR GUESTS. MORE PRECISELY, IN MY HOUSE ON MARYLEBONE HIGH STREET.
I'M CALLED SIR WALLACE WILDRAGON AND YOU ARE WELCOME HERE.
I AM THE SOLE DESCENDANT OF THE WILDRAGON FAMILY WHO, FROM GENERATION TO GENERATION SINCE THE MIDDLE AGES, OBSERVE, ORDER, INVENTORY, AND COLLECT ALL THAT WHICH TOUCHES ON THE PARANORMAL ALL OVER THE GLOBE...
PLEASE, FOLLOW ME UPSTAIRS!
THIS HOUSE, IN WHICH I LIVE ALONE, CONTAINS ALL THE OCCULT KNOWLEDGE ACCUMULATED BY MY ANCESTORS OVER THE CENTURIES...
...WHETHER THIS BE FORBIDDEN WORKS OF BLACK MAGIC, THE TESTAMENTS WRITTEN BY CHRIST'S APOSTLES OF WHICH WERE LOST TO HISTORY...
MARVELOUS!
THAT'S FANTASTIC!
...OR MAGIC OBJECTS SO ANCIENT THAT ONE MIGHT DOUBT THEY WERE MADE BY THE HANDS OF MEN.
?
RAIJIN! LOOK! THE NECRONOMICON!
MADE YOU LOOK!

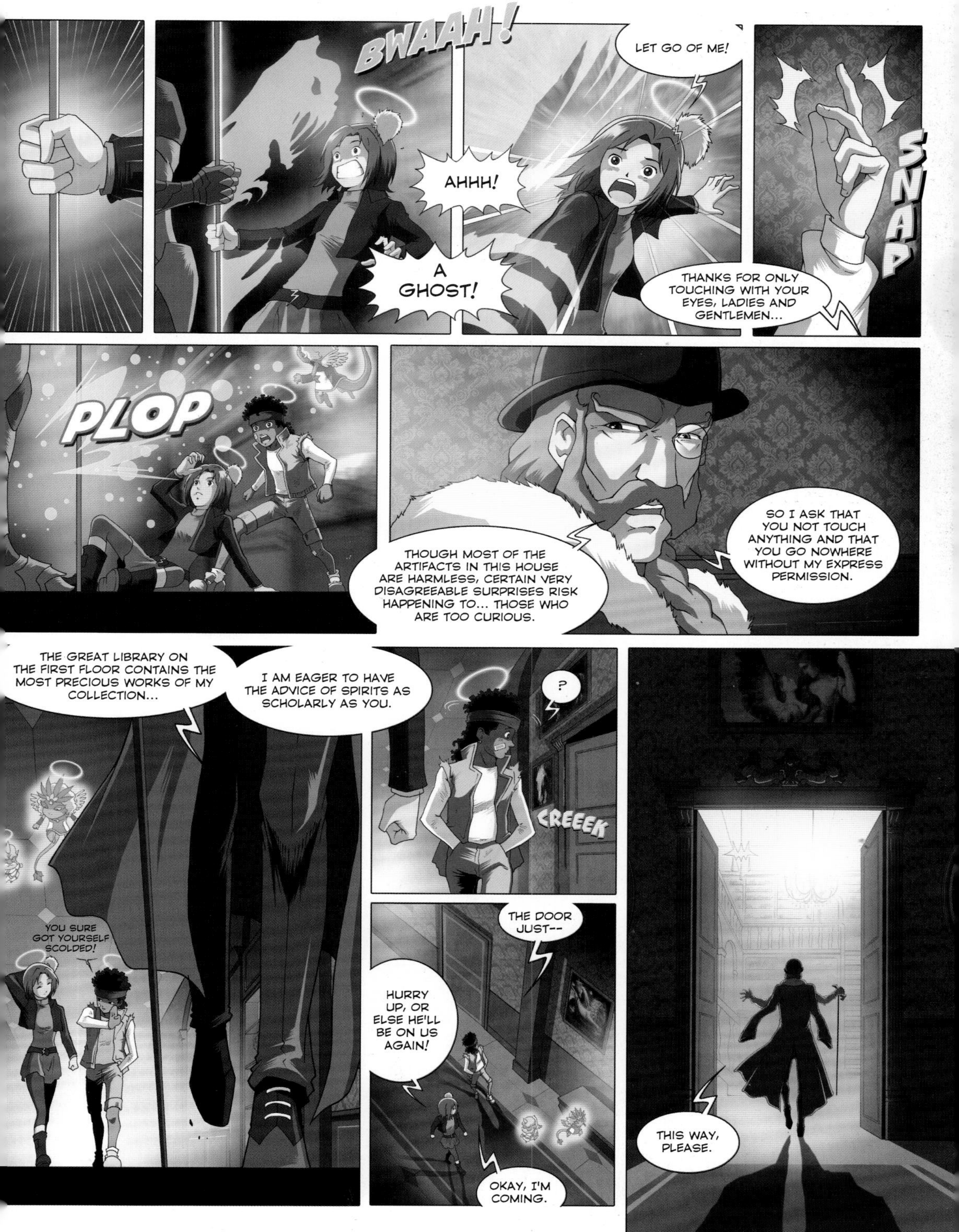
BWAAH!
AHHH!
A GHOST!
LET GO OF ME!
SNAP
THANKS FOR ONLY TOUCHING WITH YOUR EYES, LADIES AND GENTLEMEN...
PLOP
THOUGH MOST OF THE ARTIFACTS IN THIS HOUSE ARE HARMLESS, CERTAIN VERY DISAGREEABLE SURPRISES RISK HAPPENING TO... THOSE WHO ARE TOO CURIOUS.
SO I ASK THAT YOU NOT TOUCH ANYTHING AND THAT YOU GO NOWHERE WITHOUT MY EXPRESS PERMISSION.
THE GREAT LIBRARY ON THE FIRST FLOOR CONTAINS THE MOST PRECIOUS WORKS OF MY COLLECTION...
I AM EAGER TO HAVE THE ADVICE OF SPIRITS AS SCHOLARLY AS YOU.
YOU SURE GOT YOURSELF SCOLDED!
?
CREEEK
THE DOOR JUST--
HURRY UP, OR ELSE HE'LL BE ON US AGAIN!
OKAY, I'M COMING.
THIS WAY, PLEASE.

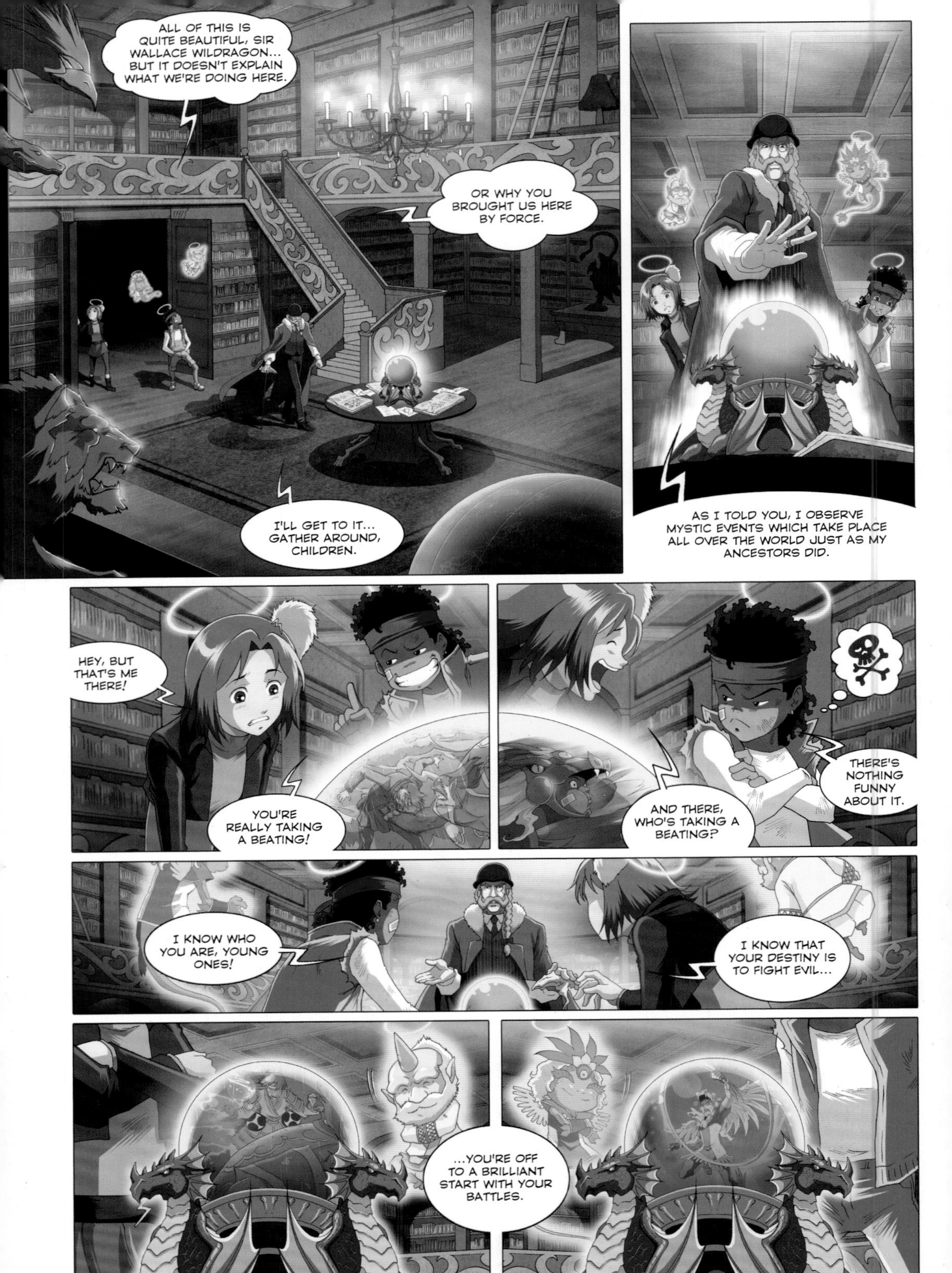
ALL OF THIS IS QUITE BEAUTIFUL, SIR WALLACE WILDRAGON... BUT IT DOESN'T EXPLAIN WHAT WE'RE DOING HERE.
OR WHY YOU BROUGHT US HERE BY FORCE.
I'LL GET TO IT... GATHER AROUND, CHILDREN.
AS I TOLD YOU, I OBSERVE MYSTIC EVENTS WHICH TAKE PLACE ALL OVER THE WORLD JUST AS MY ANCESTORS DID.
HEY, BUT THAT'S ME THERE!
YOU'RE REALLY TAKING A BEATING!
AND THERE, WHO'S TAKING A BEATING?
THERE'S NOTHING FUNNY ABOUT IT.
I KNOW WHO YOU ARE, YOUNG ONES!
I KNOW THAT YOUR DESTINY IS TO FIGHT EVIL...
...YOU'RE OFF TO A BRILLIANT START WITH YOUR BATTLES.

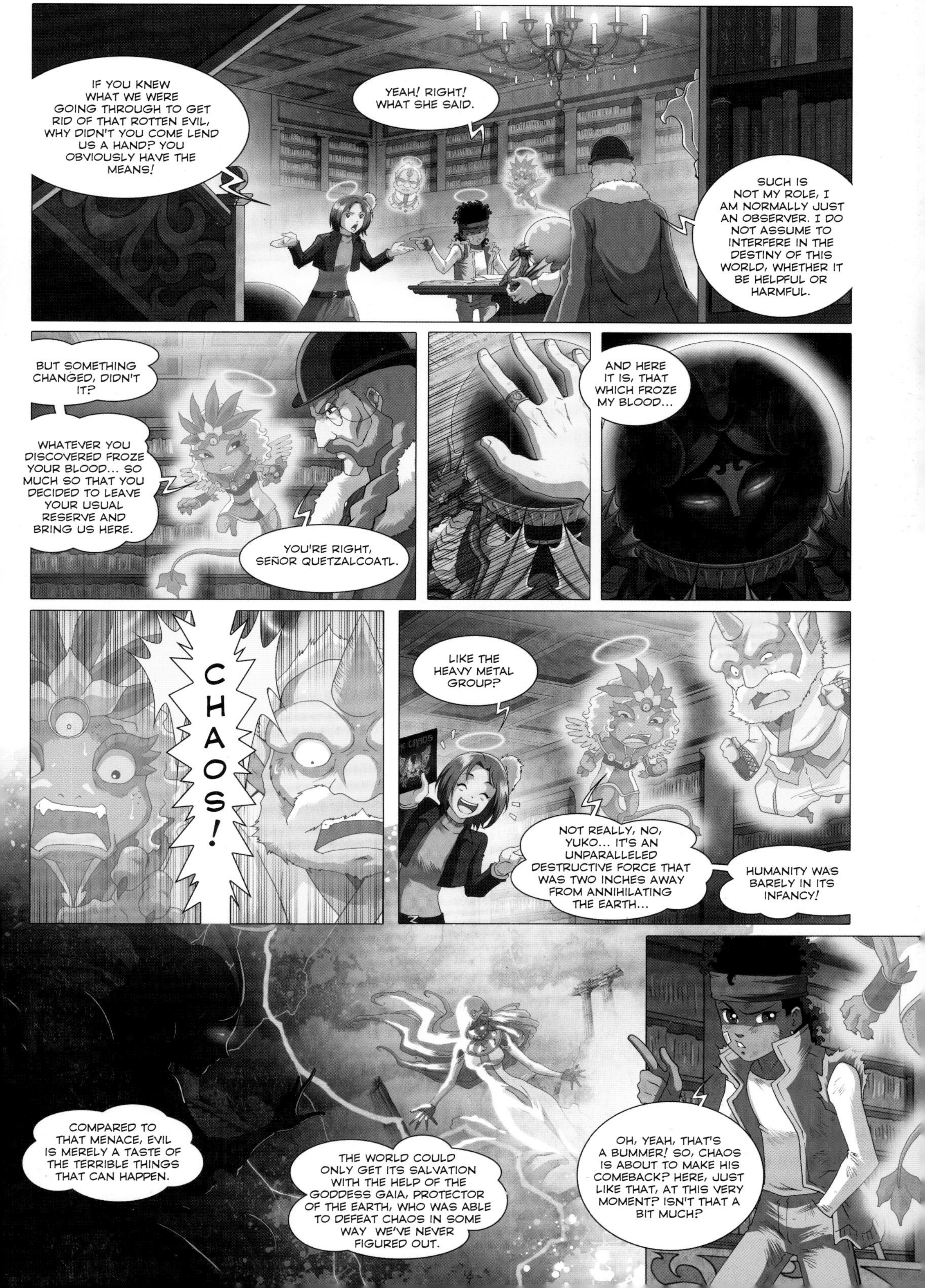
IF YOU KNEW WHAT WE WERE GOING THROUGH TO GET RID OF THAT ROTTEN EVIL, WHY DIDN'T YOU COME LEND US A HAND? YOU OBVIOUSLY HAVE THE MEANS!
YEAH! RIGHT! WHAT SHE SAID.
SUCH IS NOT MY ROLE, I AM NORMALLY JUST AN OBSERVER. I DO NOT ASSUME TO INTERFERE IN THE DESTINY OF THIS WORLD, WHETHER IT BE HELPFUL OR HARMFUL.
BUT SOMETHING CHANGED, DIDN'T IT?
WHATEVER YOU DISCOVERED FROZE YOUR BLOOD... SO MUCH SO THAT YOU DECIDED TO LEAVE YOUR USUAL RESERVE AND BRING US HERE.
YOU'RE RIGHT, SEÑOR QUETZALCOATL.
AND HERE IT IS, THAT WHICH FROZE MY BLOOD...
CHAOS!
LIKE THE HEAVY METAL GROUP?
NOT REALLY, NO, YUKO... IT'S AN UNPARALLELED DESTRUCTIVE FORCE THAT WAS TWO INCHES AWAY FROM ANNIHILATING THE EARTH...
HUMANITY WAS BARELY IN ITS INFANCY!
COMPARED TO THAT MENACE, EVIL IS MERELY A TASTE OF THE TERRIBLE THINGS THAT CAN HAPPEN.
THE WORLD COULD ONLY GET ITS SALVATION WITH THE HELP OF THE GODDESS GAIA, PROTECTOR OF THE EARTH, WHO WAS ABLE TO DEFEAT CHAOS IN SOME WAY WE'VE NEVER FIGURED OUT.
OH, YEAH, THAT'S A BUMMER! SO, CHAOS IS ABOUT TO MAKE HIS COMEBACK? HERE, JUST LIKE THAT, AT THIS VERY MOMENT? ISN'T THAT A BIT MUCH?

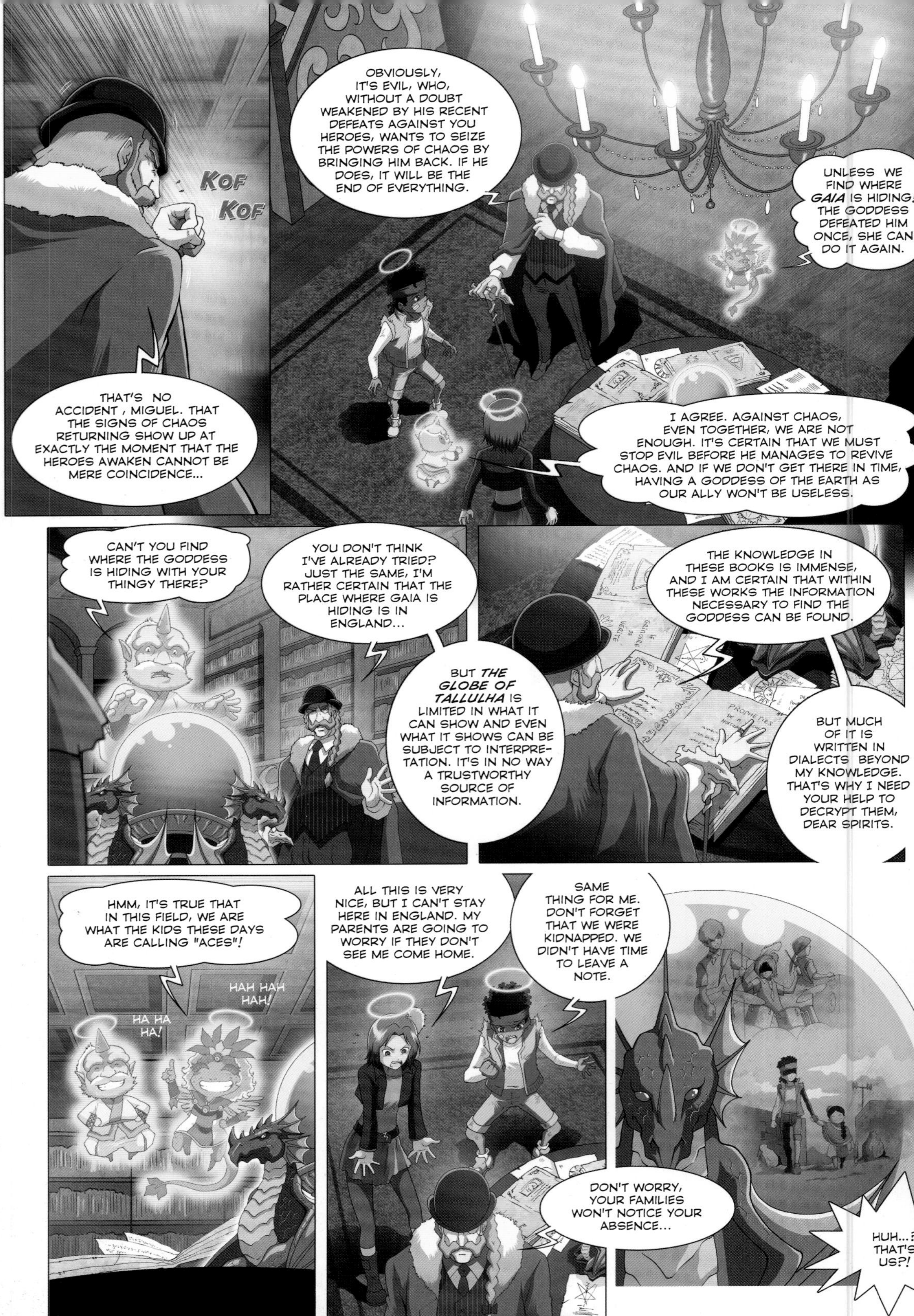

KOF
KOF
OBVIOUSLY, IT'S EVIL, WHO, WITHOUT A DOUBT WEAKENED BY HIS RECENT DEFEATS AGAINST YOU HEROES, WANTS TO SEIZE THE POWERS OF CHAOS BY BRINGING HIM BACK. IF HE DOES, IT WILL BE THE END OF EVERYTHING.
UNLESS WE FIND WHERE GAIA IS HIDING! THE GODDESS DEFEATED HIM ONCE, SHE CAN DO IT AGAIN.
THAT'S NO ACCIDENT , MIGUEL. THAT THE SIGNS OF CHAOS RETURNING SHOW UP AT EXACTLY THE MOMENT THAT THE HEROES AWAKEN CANNOT BE MERE COINCIDENCE...
I AGREE. AGAINST CHAOS, EVEN TOGETHER, WE ARE NOT ENOUGH. IT'S CERTAIN THAT WE MUST STOP EVIL BEFORE HE MANAGES TO REVIVE CHAOS. AND IF WE DON'T GET THERE IN TIME, HAVING A GODDESS OF THE EARTH AS OUR ALLY WON'T BE USELESS.
CAN'T YOU FIND WHERE THE GODDESS IS HIDING WITH YOUR THINGY THERE?
YOU DON'T THINK I'VE ALREADY TRIED? JUST THE SAME, I'M RATHER CERTAIN THAT THE PLACE WHERE GAIA IS HIDING IS IN ENGLAND...
BUT THE GLOBE OF TALLULHA IS LIMITED IN WHAT IT CAN SHOW AND EVEN WHAT IT SHOWS CAN BE SUBJECT TO INTERPRE-TATION. IT'S IN NO WAY A TRUSTWORTHY SOURCE OF INFORMATION.
THE KNOWLEDGE IN THESE BOOKS IS IMMENSE, AND I AM CERTAIN THAT WITHIN THESE WORKS THE INFORMATION NECESSARY TO FIND THE GODDESS CAN BE FOUND.
BUT MUCH OF IT IS WRITTEN IN DIALECTS BEYOND MY KNOWLEDGE. THAT'S WHY I NEED YOUR HELP TO DECRYPT THEM, DEAR SPIRITS.
HMM, IT'S TRUE THAT IN THIS FIELD, WE ARE WHAT THE KIDS THESE DAYS ARE CALLING "ACES"!
HA HA HA!
HAH HAH HAH!
ALL THIS IS VERY NICE, BUT I CAN'T STAY HERE IN ENGLAND. MY PARENTS ARE GOING TO WORRY IF THEY DON'T SEE ME COME HOME.
SAME THING FOR ME. DON'T FORGET THAT WE WERE KIDNAPPED. WE DIDN'T HAVE TIME TO LEAVE A NOTE.
DON'T WORRY, YOUR FAMILIES WON'T NOTICE YOUR ABSENCE...
HUH...? THAT'S US?!

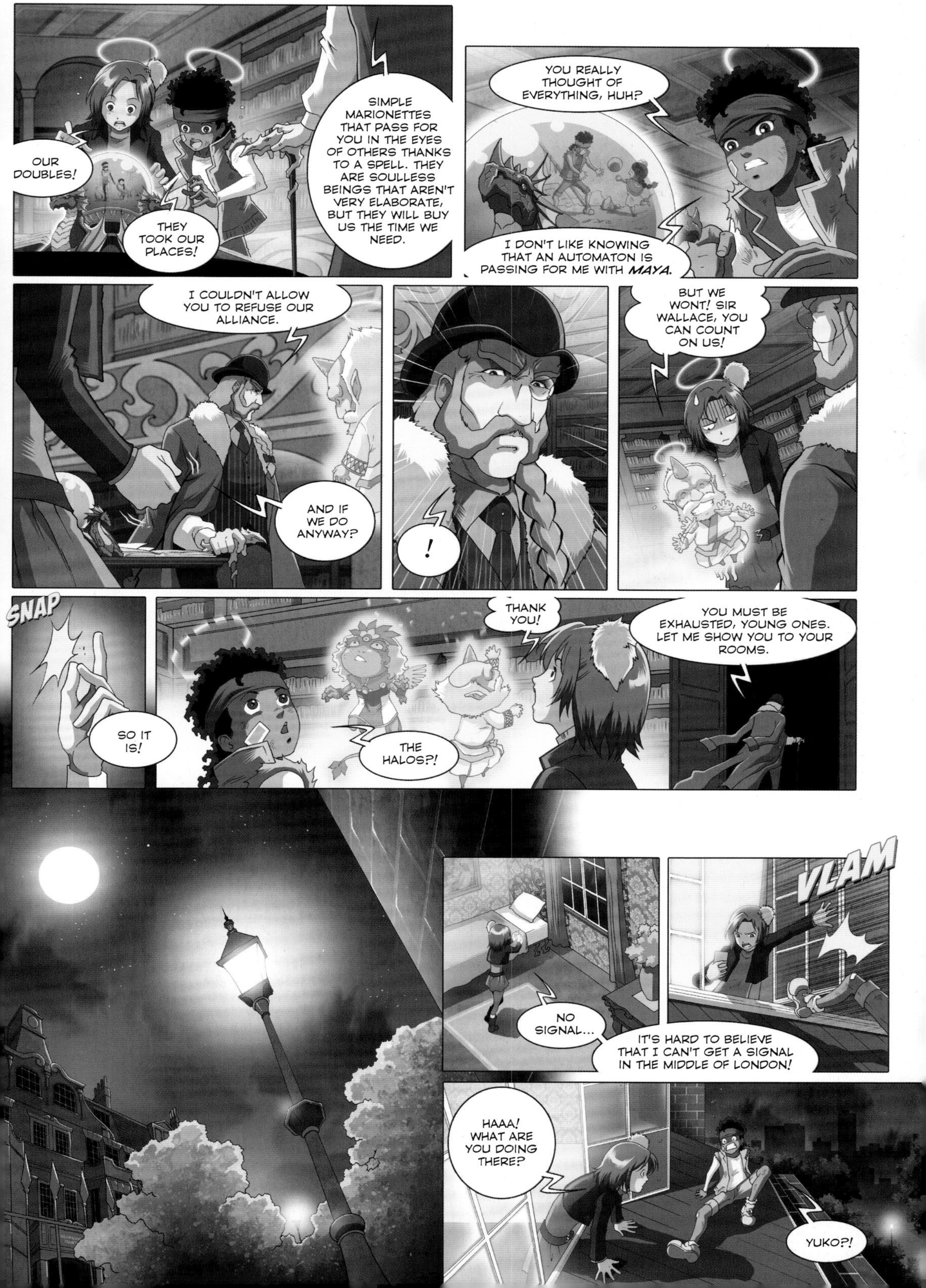
OUR DOUBLES!
THEY TOOK OUR PLACES!
SIMPLE MARIONETTES THAT PASS FOR YOU IN THE EYES OF OTHERS THANKS TO A SPELL. THEY ARE SOULLESS BEINGS THAT AREN'T VERY ELABORATE, BUT THEY WILL BUY US THE TIME WE NEED.
YOU REALLY THOUGHT OF EVERYTHING, HUH?
I DON'T LIKE KNOWING THAT AN AUTOMATON IS PASSING FOR ME WITH MAYA.
I COULDN'T ALLOW YOU TO REFUSE OUR ALLIANCE.
AND IF WE DO ANYWAY?
!
BUT WE WONT! SIR WALLACE, YOU CAN COUNT ON US!
SNAP
SO IT IS!
THE HALOS?!
THANK YOU!
YOU MUST BE EXHAUSTED, YOUNG ONES. LET ME SHOW YOU TO YOUR ROOMS.
NO SIGNAL...
IT'S HARD TO BELIEVE THAT I CAN'T GET A SIGNAL IN THE MIDDLE OF LONDON!
VLAM
HAAA! WHAT ARE YOU DOING THERE?
YUKO?!

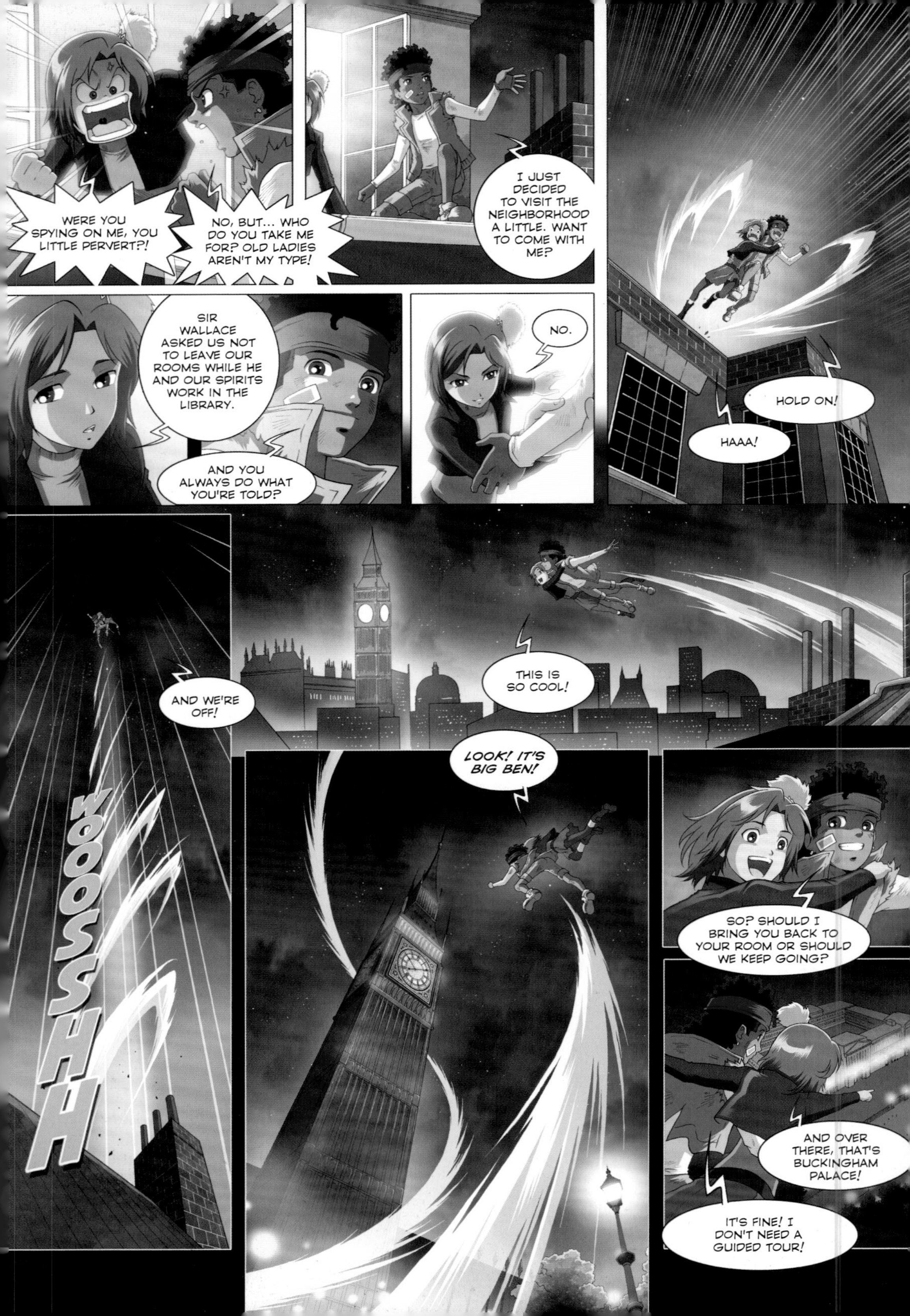
WERE YOU SPYING ON ME, YOU LITTLE PERVERT?!
NO, BUT... WHO DO YOU TAKE ME FOR? OLD LADIES AREN'T MY TYPE!
I JUST DECIDED TO VISIT THE NEIGHBORHOOD A LITTLE. WANT TO COME WITH ME?
SIR WALLACE ASKED US NOT TO LEAVE OUR ROOMS WHILE HE AND OUR SPIRITS WORK IN THE LIBRARY.
AND YOU ALWAYS DO WHAT YOU'RE TOLD?
NO.
HOLD ON!
HAAA!
AND WE'RE OFF!
WOOOSSHHH
THIS IS SO COOL!
LOOK! IT'S BIG BEN!
SO? SHOULD I BRING YOU BACK TO YOUR ROOM OR SHOULD WE KEEP GOING?
AND OVER THERE, THAT'S BUCKINGHAM PALACE!
IT'S FINE! I DON'T NEED A GUIDED TOUR!

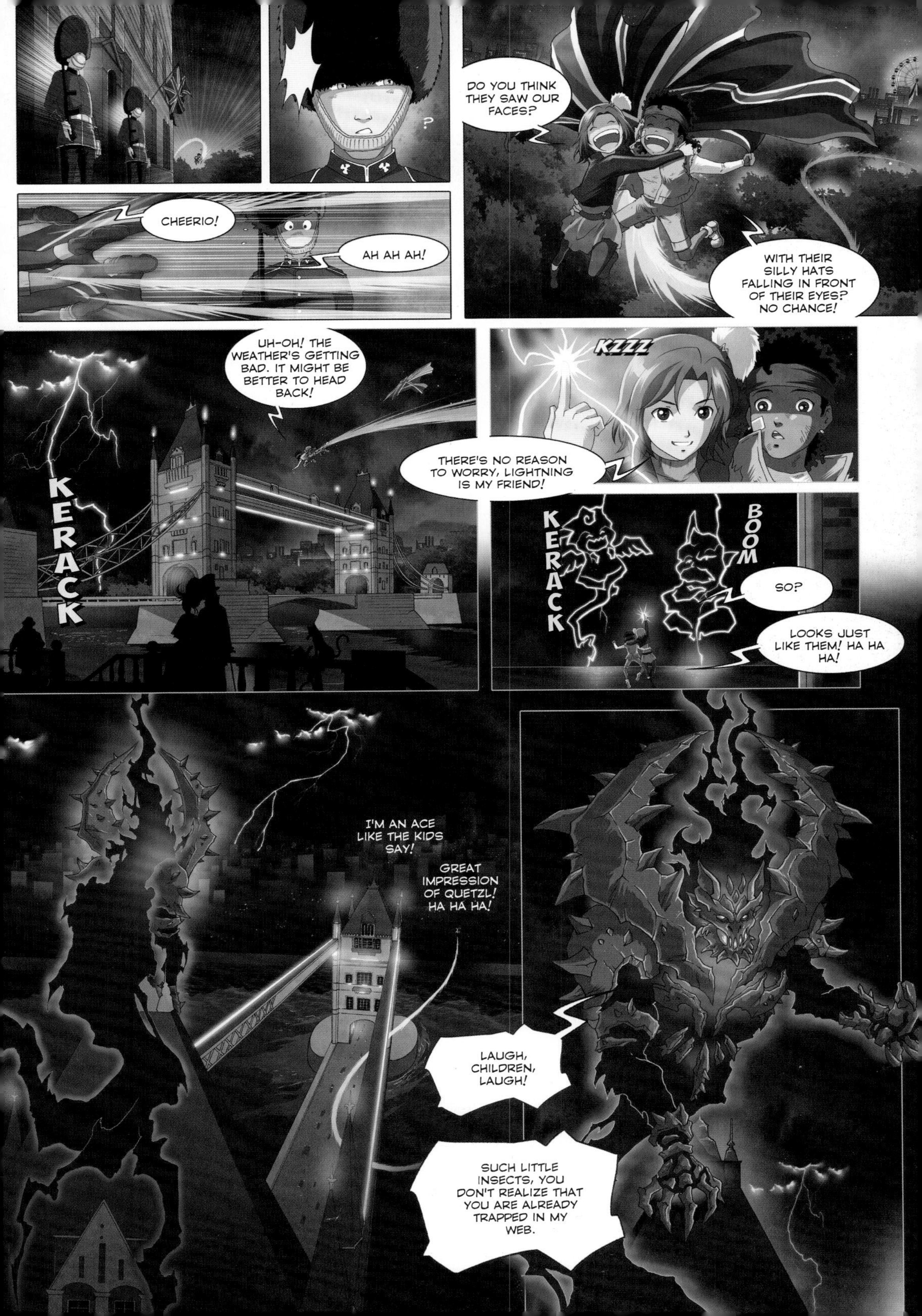
?
CHEERIO!
AH AH AH!
DO YOU THINK THEY SAW OUR FACES?
WITH THEIR SILLY HATS FALLING IN FRONT OF THEIR EYES? NO CHANCE!
UH-OH! THE WEATHER'S GETTING BAD. IT MIGHT BE BETTER TO HEAD BACK!
KERACK
KZZZ
THERE'S NO REASON TO WORRY, LIGHTNING IS MY FRIEND!
KERACK
BOOM
SO?
LOOKS JUST LIKE THEM! HA HA HA!
I'M AN ACE LIKE THE KIDS SAY!
GREAT IMPRESSION OF QUETZL! HA HA HA!
LAUGH, CHILDREN, LAUGH!
SUCH LITTLE INSECTS, YOU DON'T REALIZE THAT YOU ARE ALREADY TRAPPED IN MY WEB.

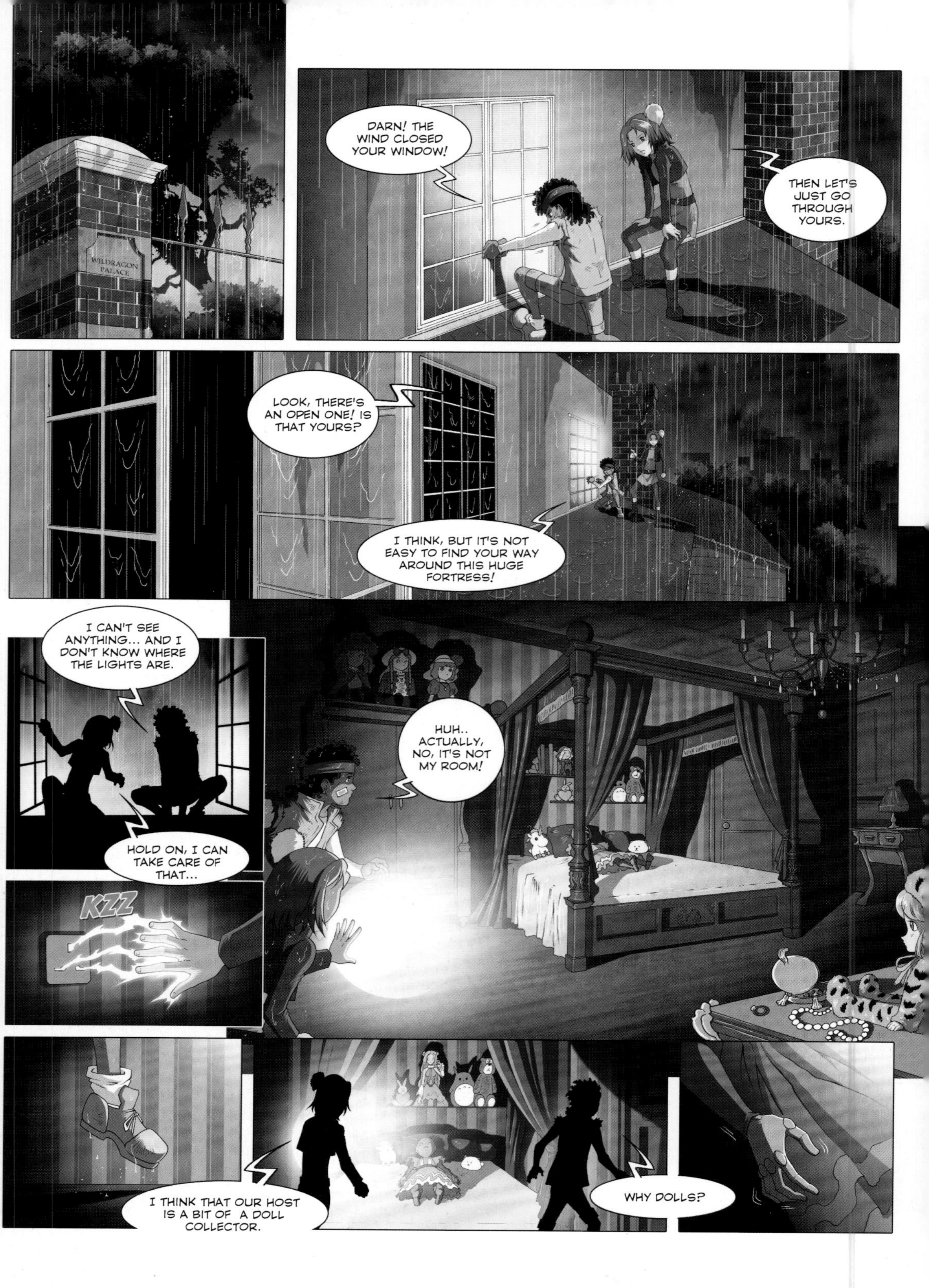
WILDRAGON PALACE
DARN! THE WIND CLOSED YOUR WINDOW!
THEN LET'S JUST GO THROUGH YOURS.
LOOK, THERE'S AN OPEN ONE! IS THAT YOURS?
I THINK, BUT IT'S NOT EASY TO FIND YOUR WAY AROUND THIS HUGE FORTRESS!
I CAN'T SEE ANYTHING... AND I DON'T KNOW WHERE THE LIGHTS ARE.
HOLD ON, I CAN TAKE CARE OF THAT...
KZZ
HUH.. ACTUALLY, NO, IT'S NOT MY ROOM!
I THINK THAT OUR HOST IS A BIT OF A DOLL COLLECTOR.
WHY DOLLS?

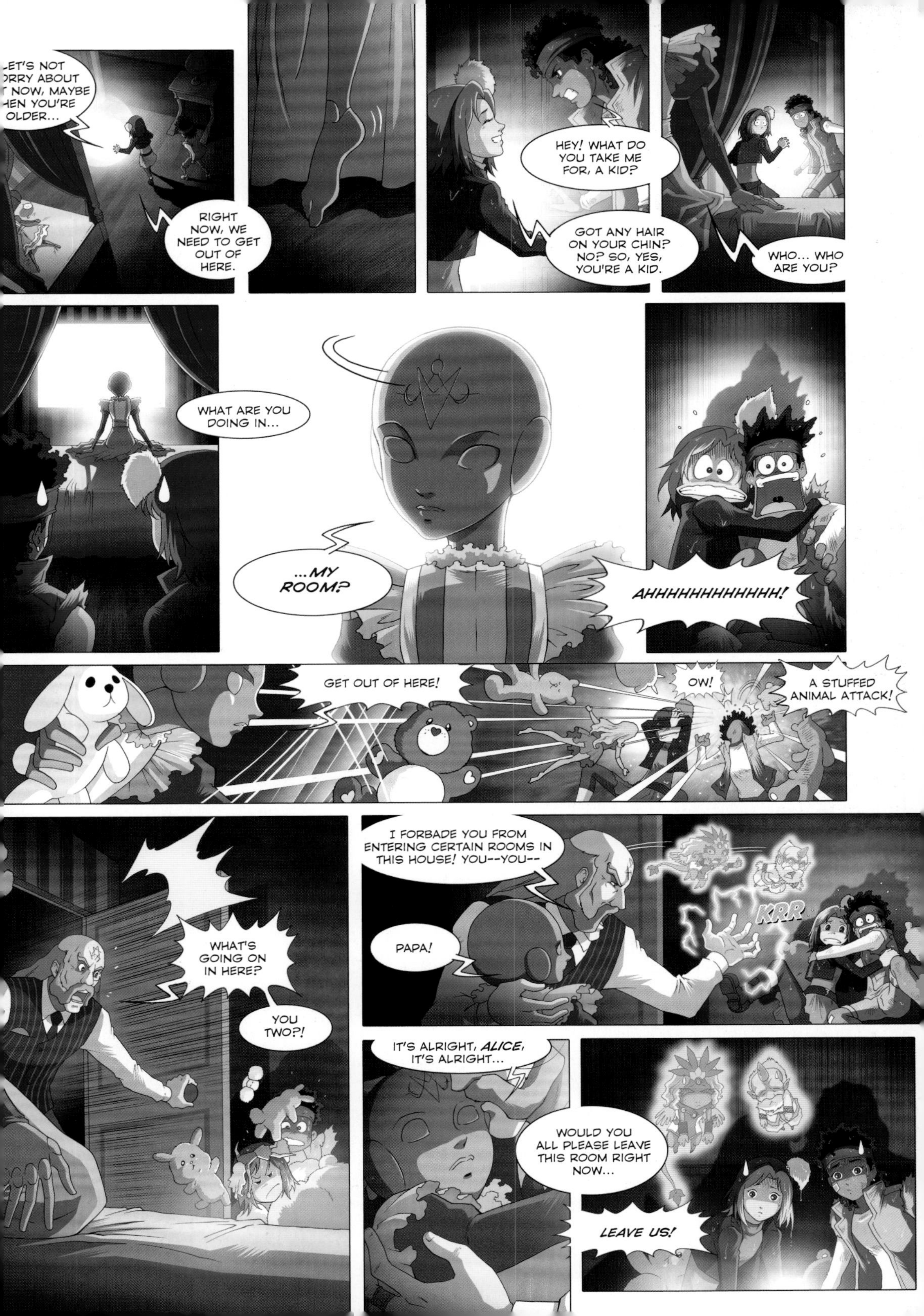
LET'S NOT WORRY ABOUT IT NOW, MAYBE WHEN YOU'RE OLDER...
RIGHT NOW, WE NEED TO GET OUT OF HERE.
HEY! WHAT DO YOU TAKE ME FOR, A KID?
GOT ANY HAIR ON YOUR CHIN? NO? SO, YES, YOU'RE A KID.
WHO... WHO ARE YOU?
WHAT ARE YOU DOING IN...
...MY ROOM?
AHHHHHHHHHHHH!
GET OUT OF HERE!
OW!
A STUFFED ANIMAL ATTACK!
WHAT'S GOING ON IN HERE?
YOU TWO?!
I FORBADE YOU FROM ENTERING CERTAIN ROOMS IN THIS HOUSE! YOU--YOU--
PAPA!
KRR
IT'S ALRIGHT, ALICE, IT'S ALRIGHT...
WOULD YOU ALL PLEASE LEAVE THIS ROOM RIGHT NOW...
LEAVE US!

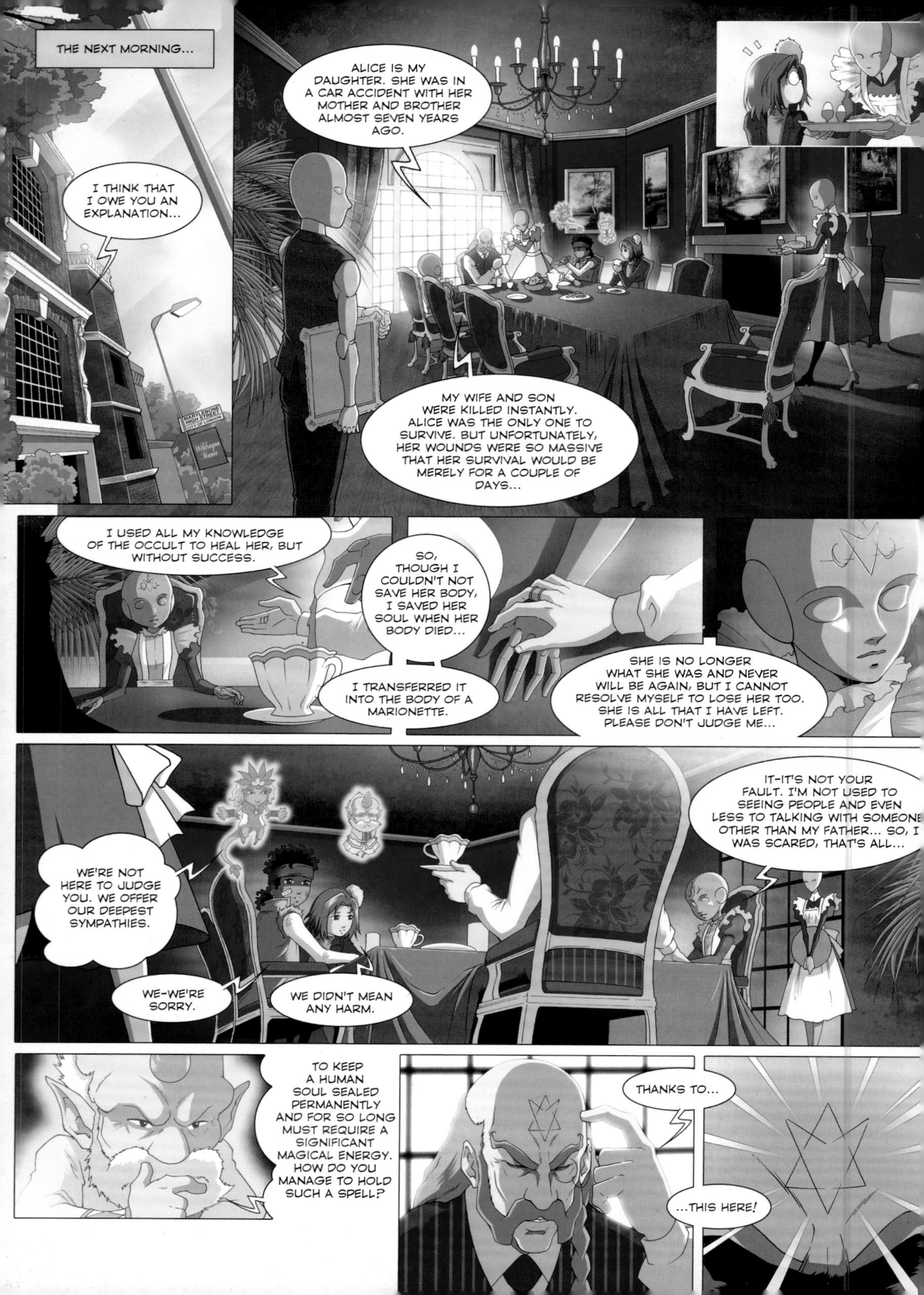
THE NEXT MORNING...
I THINK THAT I OWE YOU AN EXPLANATION...
MARYLEBONE HIGH STREET CITY OF LONDON
ALICE IS MY DAUGHTER. SHE WAS IN A CAR ACCIDENT WITH HER MOTHER AND BROTHER ALMOST SEVEN YEARS AGO.
MY WIFE AND SON WERE KILLED INSTANTLY. ALICE WAS THE ONLY ONE TO SURVIVE. BUT UNFORTUNATELY, HER WOUNDS WERE SO MASSIVE THAT HER SURVIVAL WOULD BE MERELY FOR A COUPLE OF DAYS...
I USED ALL MY KNOWLEDGE OF THE OCCULT TO HEAL HER, BUT WITHOUT SUCCESS.
SO, THOUGH I COULDN'T NOT SAVE HER BODY, I SAVED HER SOUL WHEN HER BODY DIED...
I TRANSFERRED IT INTO THE BODY OF A MARIONETTE.
SHE IS NO LONGER WHAT SHE WAS AND NEVER WILL BE AGAIN, BUT I CANNOT RESOLVE MYSELF TO LOSE HER TOO. SHE IS ALL THAT I HAVE LEFT. PLEASE DON'T JUDGE ME...
WE'RE NOT HERE TO JUDGE YOU. WE OFFER OUR DEEPEST SYMPATHIES.
WE-WE'RE SORRY.
WE DIDN'T MEAN ANY HARM.
IT-IT'S NOT YOUR FAULT. I'M NOT USED TO SEEING PEOPLE AND EVEN LESS TO TALKING WITH SOMEONE OTHER THAN MY FATHER... SO, I WAS SCARED, THAT'S ALL...
TO KEEP A HUMAN SOUL SEALED PERMANENTLY AND FOR SO LONG MUST REQUIRE A SIGNIFICANT MAGICAL ENERGY. HOW DO YOU MANAGE TO HOLD SUCH A SPELL?
THANKS TO...
...THIS HERE!

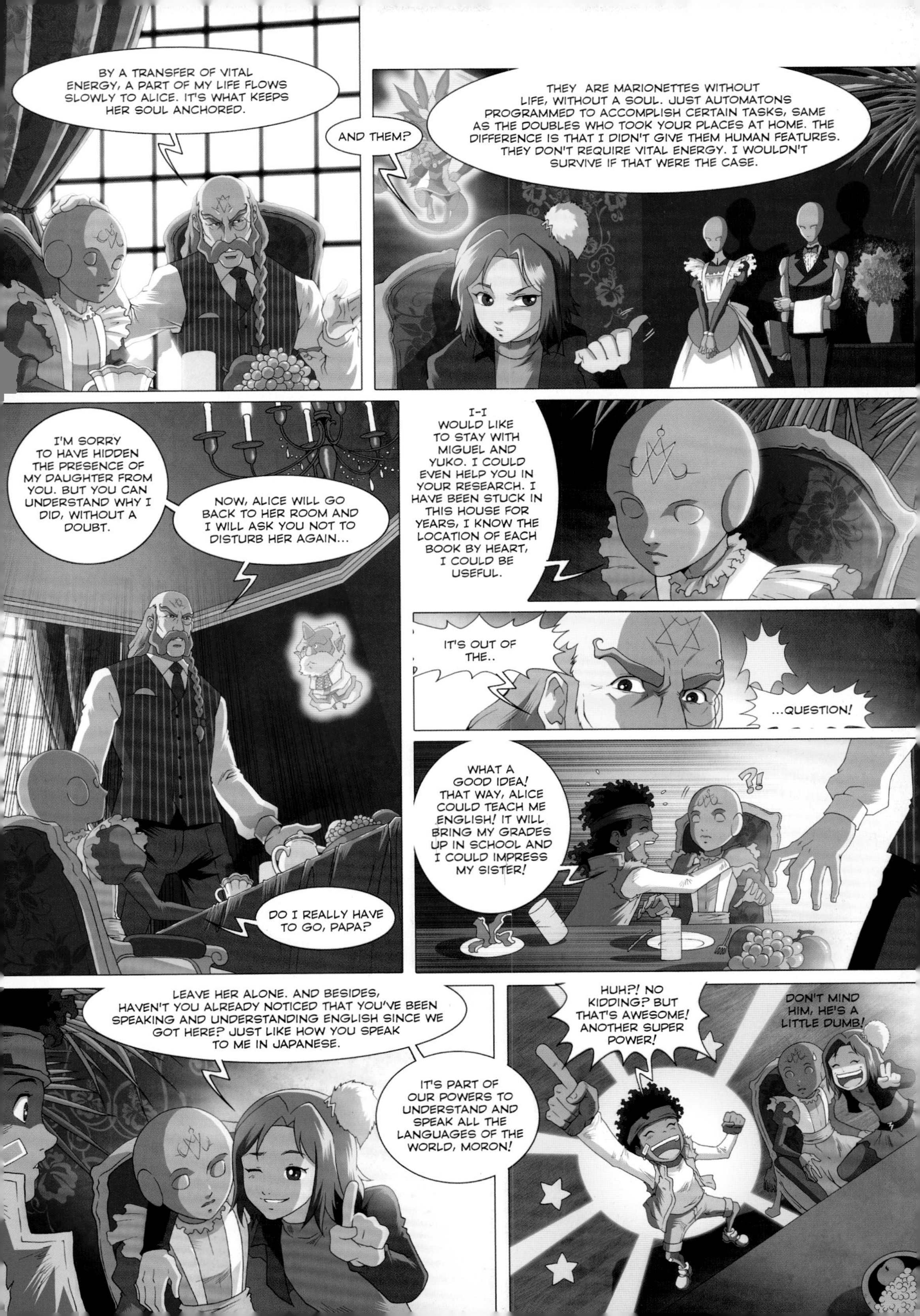
BY A TRANSFER OF VITAL ENERGY, A PART OF MY LIFE FLOWS SLOWLY TO ALICE. IT'S WHAT KEEPS HER SOUL ANCHORED.
AND THEM?
THEY ARE MARIONETTES WITHOUT LIFE, WITHOUT A SOUL. JUST AUTOMATONS PROGRAMMED TO ACCOMPLISH CERTAIN TASKS, SAME AS THE DOUBLES WHO TOOK YOUR PLACES AT HOME. THE DIFFERENCE IS THAT I DIDN'T GIVE THEM HUMAN FEATURES. THEY DON'T REQUIRE VITAL ENERGY. I WOULDN'T SURVIVE IF THAT WERE THE CASE.
I'M SORRY TO HAVE HIDDEN THE PRESENCE OF MY DAUGHTER FROM YOU. BUT YOU CAN UNDERSTAND WHY I DID, WITHOUT A DOUBT.
NOW, ALICE WILL GO BACK TO HER ROOM AND I WILL ASK YOU NOT TO DISTURB HER AGAIN...
DO I REALLY HAVE TO GO, PAPA?
I-I WOULD LIKE TO STAY WITH MIGUEL AND YUKO. I COULD EVEN HELP YOU IN YOUR RESEARCH. I HAVE BEEN STUCK IN THIS HOUSE FOR YEARS, I KNOW THE LOCATION OF EACH BOOK BY HEART, I COULD BE USEFUL.
IT'S OUT OF THE..
...QUESTION!
WHAT A GOOD IDEA! THAT WAY, ALICE COULD TEACH ME ENGLISH! IT WILL BRING MY GRADES UP IN SCHOOL AND I COULD IMPRESS MY SISTER!
?!
LEAVE HER ALONE. AND BESIDES, HAVEN'T YOU ALREADY NOTICED THAT YOU'VE BEEN SPEAKING AND UNDERSTANDING ENGLISH SINCE WE GOT HERE? JUST LIKE HOW YOU SPEAK TO ME IN JAPANESE.
IT'S PART OF OUR POWERS TO UNDERSTAND AND SPEAK ALL THE LANGUAGES OF THE WORLD, MORON!
HUH?! NO KIDDING? BUT THAT'S AWESOME! ANOTHER SUPER POWER!
DON'T MIND HIM, HE'S A LITTLE DUMB!

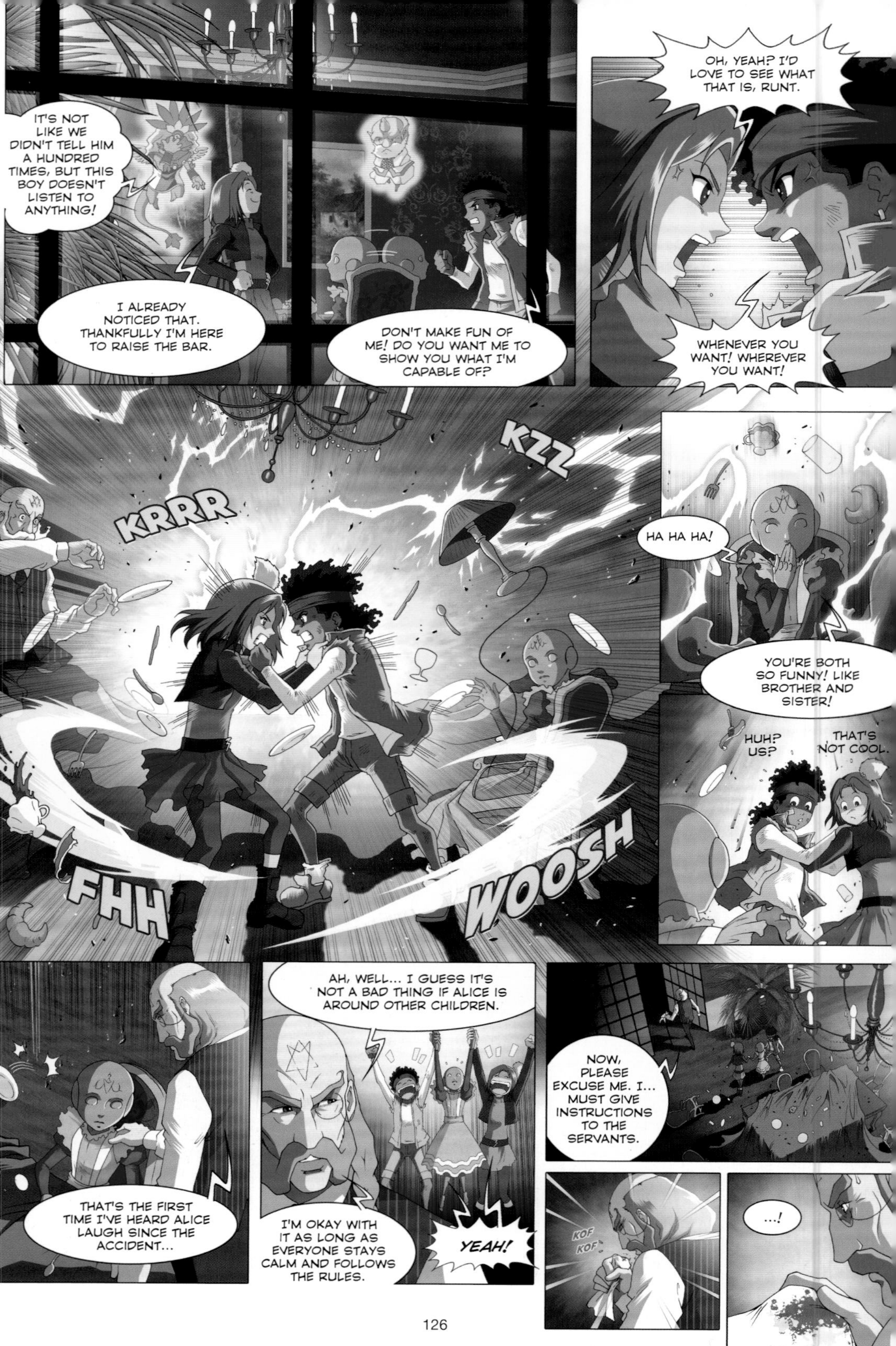
IT'S NOT LIKE WE DIDN'T TELL HIM A HUNDRED TIMES, BUT THIS BOY DOESN'T LISTEN TO ANYTHING!
I ALREADY NOTICED THAT. THANKFULLY I'M HERE TO RAISE THE BAR.
DON'T MAKE FUN OF ME! DO YOU WANT ME TO SHOW YOU WHAT I'M CAPABLE OF?
OH, YEAH? I'D LOVE TO SEE WHAT THAT IS, RUNT.
WHENEVER YOU WANT! WHEREVER YOU WANT!
KZZ
KRRR
FHH
WOOSH
HA HA HA!
YOU'RE BOTH SO FUNNY! LIKE BROTHER AND SISTER!
HUH? US?
THAT'S NOT COOL.
THAT'S THE FIRST TIME I'VE HEARD ALICE LAUGH SINCE THE ACCIDENT...
AH, WELL... I GUESS IT'S NOT A BAD THING IF ALICE IS AROUND OTHER CHILDREN.
I'M OKAY WITH IT AS LONG AS EVERYONE STAYS CALM AND FOLLOWS THE RULES.
YEAH!
NOW, PLEASE EXCUSE ME. I... MUST GIVE INSTRUCTIONS TO THE SERVANTS.
KOF KOF
...!

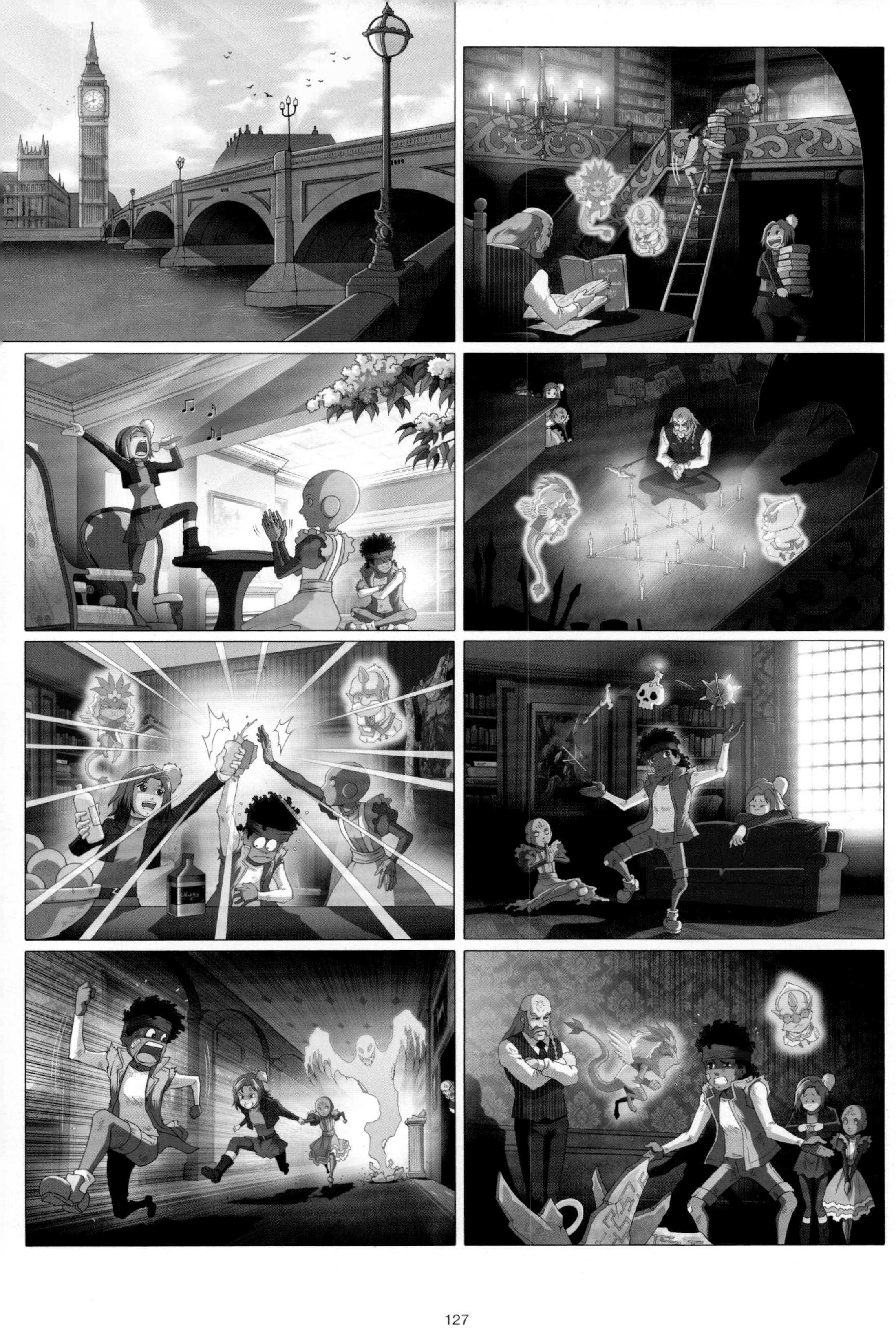

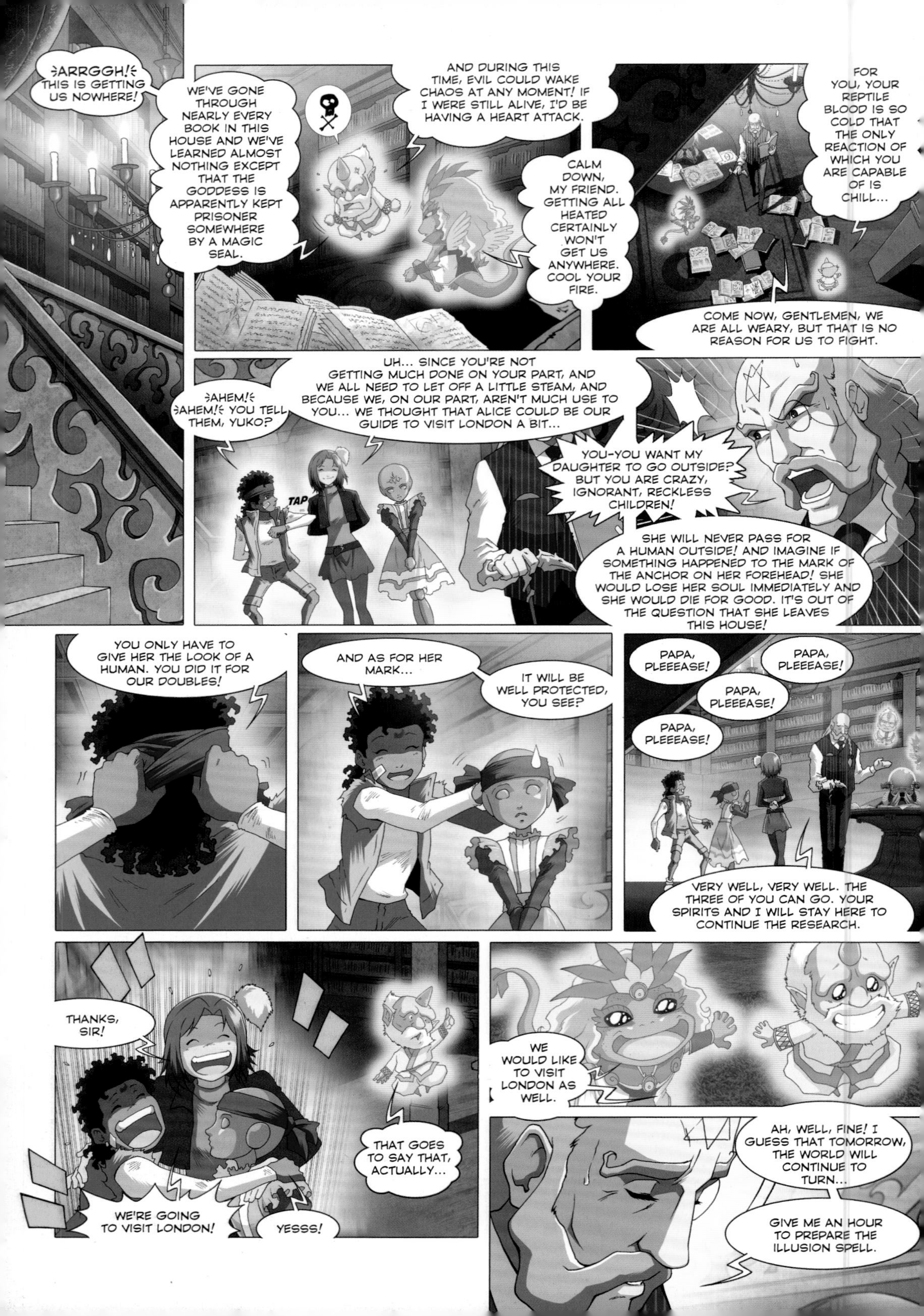
ARRGGH! THIS IS GETTING US NOWHERE!
WE'VE GONE THROUGH NEARLY EVERY BOOK IN THIS HOUSE AND WE'VE LEARNED ALMOST NOTHING EXCEPT THAT THE GODDESS IS APPARENTLY KEPT PRISONER SOMEWHERE BY A MAGIC SEAL.
AND DURING THIS TIME, EVIL COULD WAKE CHAOS AT ANY MOMENT! IF I WERE STILL ALIVE, I'D BE HAVING A HEART ATTACK.
CALM DOWN, MY FRIEND. GETTING ALL HEATED CERTAINLY WON'T GET US ANYWHERE. COOL YOUR FIRE.
FOR YOU, YOUR REPTILE BLOOD IS SO COLD THAT THE ONLY REACTION OF WHICH YOU ARE CAPABLE OF IS CHILL...
COME NOW, GENTLEMEN, WE ARE ALL WEARY, BUT THAT IS NO REASON FOR US TO FIGHT.
AHEM! AHEM! YOU TELL THEM, YUKO?
TAP
UH... SINCE YOU'RE NOT GETTING MUCH DONE ON YOUR PART, AND WE ALL NEED TO LET OFF A LITTLE STEAM, AND BECAUSE WE, ON OUR PART, AREN'T MUCH USE TO YOU... WE THOUGHT THAT ALICE COULD BE OUR GUIDE TO VISIT LONDON A BIT...
YOU-YOU WANT MY DAUGHTER TO GO OUTSIDE? BUT YOU ARE CRAZY, IGNORANT, RECKLESS CHILDREN!
SHE WILL NEVER PASS FOR A HUMAN OUTSIDE! AND IMAGINE IF SOMETHING HAPPENED TO THE MARK OF THE ANCHOR ON HER FOREHEAD! SHE WOULD LOSE HER SOUL IMMEDIATELY AND SHE WOULD DIE FOR GOOD. IT'S OUT OF THE QUESTION THAT SHE LEAVES THIS HOUSE!
YOU ONLY HAVE TO GIVE HER THE LOOK OF A HUMAN. YOU DID IT FOR OUR DOUBLES!
AND AS FOR HER MARK...
IT WILL BE WELL PROTECTED, YOU SEE?
PAPA, PLEEEASE!
PAPA, PLEEEASE!
PAPA, PLEEEASE!
PAPA, PLEEEASE!
VERY WELL, VERY WELL. THE THREE OF YOU CAN GO. YOUR SPIRITS AND I WILL STAY HERE TO CONTINUE THE RESEARCH.
THANKS, SIR!
WE'RE GOING TO VISIT LONDON!
YESSS!
THAT GOES TO SAY THAT, ACTUALLY...
WE WOULD LIKE TO VISIT LONDON AS WELL.
AH, WELL, FINE! I GUESS THAT TOMORROW, THE WORLD WILL CONTINUE TO TURN...
GIVE ME AN HOUR TO PREPARE THE ILLUSION SPELL.

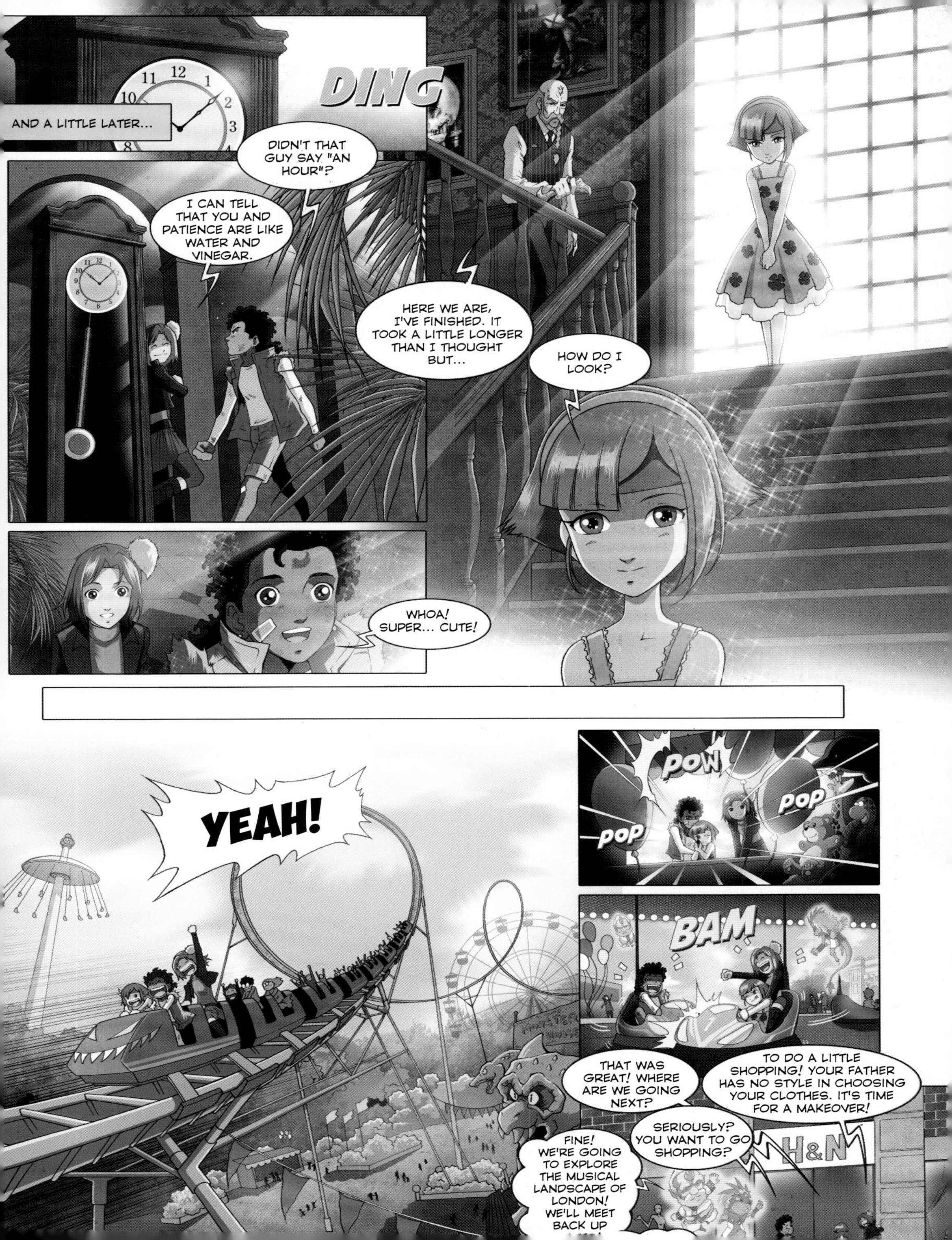
AND A LITTLE LATER...
DING
DIDN'T THAT GUY SAY "AN HOUR"?
I CAN TELL THAT YOU AND PATIENCE ARE LIKE WATER AND VINEGAR.
HERE WE ARE, I'VE FINISHED. IT TOOK A LITTLE LONGER THAN I THOUGHT BUT...
HOW DO I LOOK?
WHOA! SUPER... CUTE!
YEAH!
POW
POP
POP
BAM
THAT WAS GREAT! WHERE ARE WE GOING NEXT?
TO DO A LITTLE SHOPPING! YOUR FATHER HAS NO STYLE IN CHOOSING YOUR CLOTHES. IT'S TIME FOR A MAKEOVER!
SERIOUSLY? YOU WANT TO GO SHOPPING?
FINE! WE'RE GOING TO EXPLORE THE MUSICAL LANDSCAPE OF LONDON! WE'LL MEET BACK UP
H&N

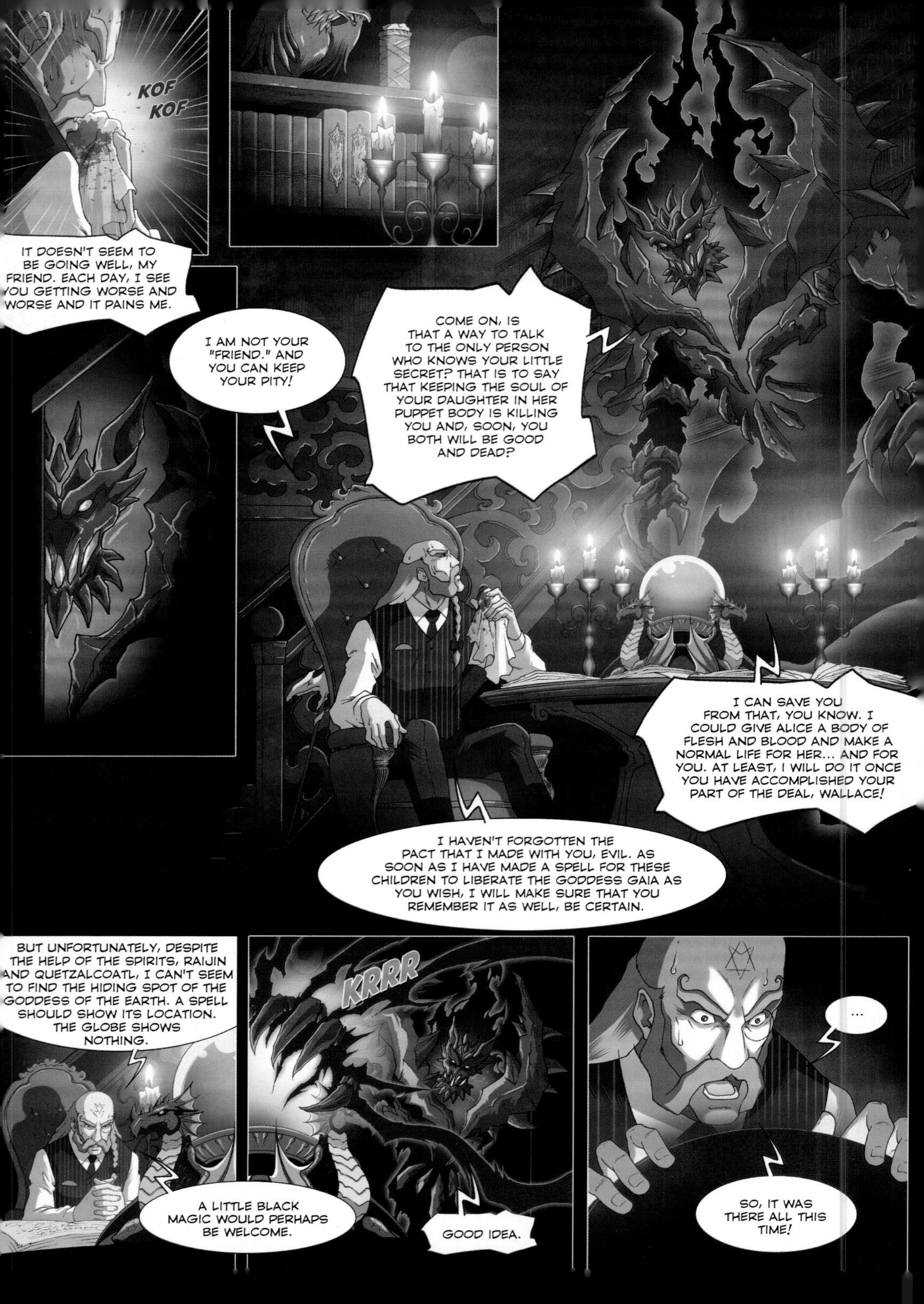
KOF
KOF
IT DOESN'T SEEM TO BE GOING WELL, MY FRIEND. EACH DAY, I SEE YOU GETTING WORSE AND WORSE AND IT PAINS ME.
I AM NOT YOUR "FRIEND." AND YOU CAN KEEP YOUR PITY!
COME ON, IS THAT A WAY TO TALK TO THE ONLY PERSON WHO KNOWS YOUR LITTLE SECRET? THAT IS TO SAY THAT KEEPING THE SOUL OF YOUR DAUGHTER IN HER PUPPET BODY IS KILLING YOU AND, SOON, YOU BOTH WILL BE GOOD AND DEAD?
I CAN SAVE YOU FROM THAT, YOU KNOW. I COULD GIVE ALICE A BODY OF FLESH AND BLOOD AND MAKE A NORMAL LIFE FOR HER... AND FOR YOU. AT LEAST, I WILL DO IT ONCE YOU HAVE ACCOMPLISHED YOUR PART OF THE DEAL, WALLACE!
I HAVEN'T FORGOTTEN THE PACT THAT I MADE WITH YOU, EVIL. AS SOON AS I HAVE MADE A SPELL FOR THESE CHILDREN TO LIBERATE THE GODDESS GAIA AS YOU WISH, I WILL MAKE SURE THAT YOU REMEMBER IT AS WELL, BE CERTAIN.
BUT UNFORTUNATELY, DESPITE THE HELP OF THE SPIRITS, RAIJIN AND QUETZALCOATL, I CAN'T SEEM TO FIND THE HIDING SPOT OF THE GODDESS OF THE EARTH. A SPELL SHOULD SHOW ITS LOCATION. THE GLOBE SHOWS NOTHING.
A LITTLE BLACK MAGIC WOULD PERHAPS BE WELCOME.
KRRR
GOOD IDEA.
...
SO, IT WAS THERE ALL THIS TIME!

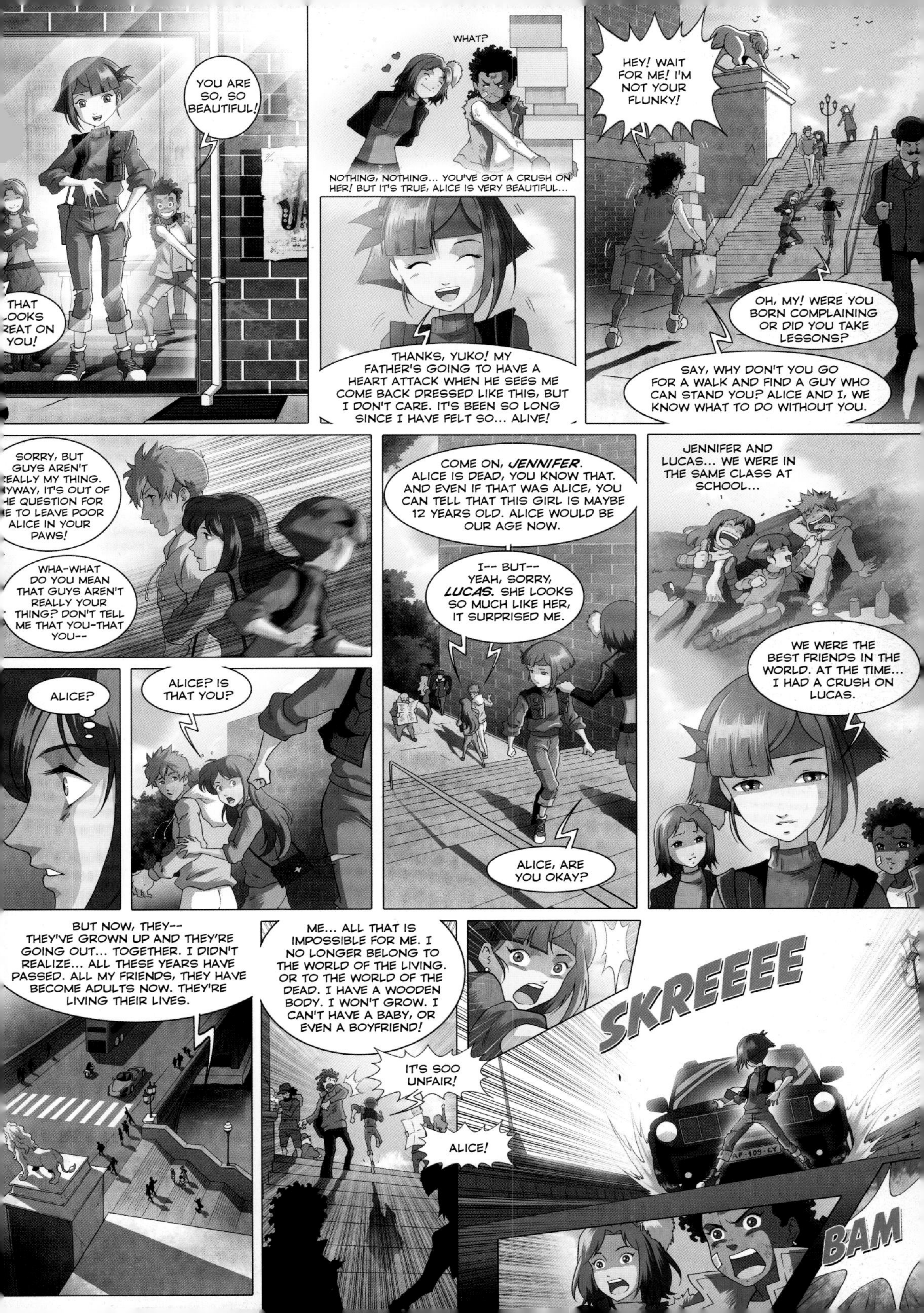
YOU ARE SO, SO BEAUTIFUL!
THAT LOOKS REAT ON YOU!
WHAT?
NOTHING, NOTHING... YOU'VE GOT A CRUSH ON HER! BUT IT'S TRUE, ALICE IS VERY BEAUTIFUL...
THANKS, YUKO! MY FATHER'S GOING TO HAVE A HEART ATTACK WHEN HE SEES ME COME BACK DRESSED LIKE THIS, BUT I DON'T CARE. IT'S BEEN SO LONG SINCE I HAVE FELT SO... ALIVE!
HEY! WAIT FOR ME! I'M NOT YOUR FLUNKY!
OH, MY! WERE YOU BORN COMPLAINING OR DID YOU TAKE LESSONS?
SAY, WHY DON'T YOU GO FOR A WALK AND FIND A GUY WHO CAN STAND YOU? ALICE AND I, WE KNOW WHAT TO DO WITHOUT YOU.
SORRY, BUT GUYS AREN'T REALLY MY THING. YWAY, IT'S OUT OF E QUESTION FOR E TO LEAVE POOR ALICE IN YOUR PAWS!
WHA-WHAT DO YOU MEAN THAT GUYS AREN'T REALLY YOUR THING? DON'T TELL ME THAT YOU-THAT YOU--
ALICE?
ALICE? IS THAT YOU?
COME ON, JENNIFER. ALICE IS DEAD, YOU KNOW THAT. AND EVEN IF THAT WAS ALICE, YOU CAN TELL THAT THIS GIRL IS MAYBE 12 YEARS OLD. ALICE WOULD BE OUR AGE NOW.
I-- BUT-- YEAH, SORRY, LUCAS. SHE LOOKS SO MUCH LIKE HER, IT SURPRISED ME.
ALICE, ARE YOU OKAY?
JENNIFER AND LUCAS... WE WERE IN THE SAME CLASS AT SCHOOL...
WE WERE THE BEST FRIENDS IN THE WORLD. AT THE TIME... I HAD A CRUSH ON LUCAS.
BUT NOW, THEY-- THEY'VE GROWN UP AND THEY'RE GOING OUT... TOGETHER. I DIDN'T REALIZE... ALL THESE YEARS HAVE PASSED. ALL MY FRIENDS, THEY HAVE BECOME ADULTS NOW. THEY'RE LIVING THEIR LIVES.
ME... ALL THAT IS IMPOSSIBLE FOR ME. I NO LONGER BELONG TO THE WORLD OF THE LIVING. OR TO THE WORLD OF THE DEAD. I HAVE A WOODEN BODY. I WON'T GROW. I CAN'T HAVE A BABY, OR EVEN A BOYFRIEND!
IT'S SOO UNFAIR!
ALICE!
SKREEEE
AF-105-CY
BAM

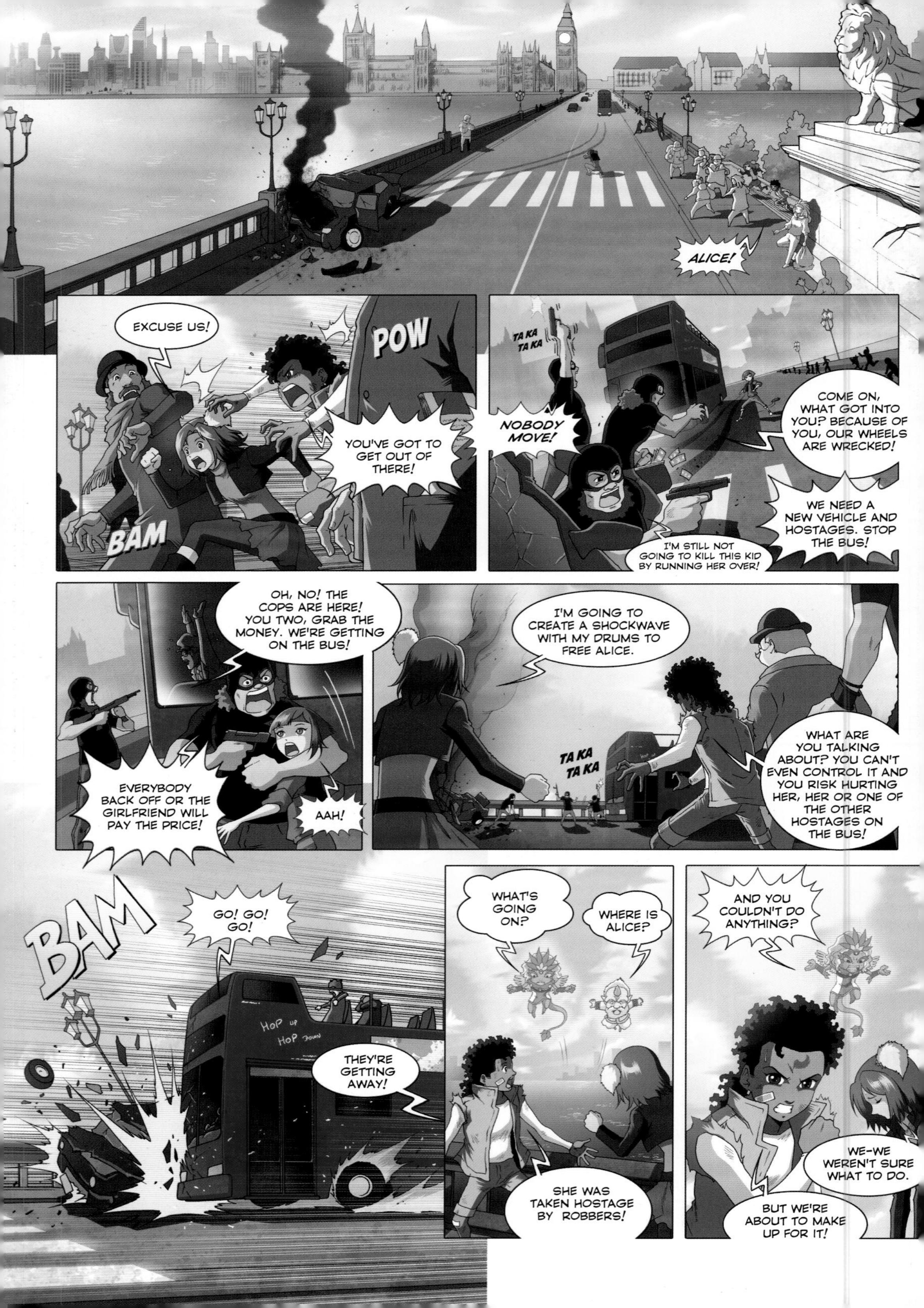
ALICE!
EXCUSE US!
POW
YOU'VE GOT TO GET OUT OF THERE!
BAM
TA KA TA KA
NOBODY MOVE!
COME ON, WHAT GOT INTO YOU? BECAUSE OF YOU, OUR WHEELS ARE WRECKED!
WE NEED A NEW VEHICLE AND HOSTAGES. STOP THE BUS!
I'M STILL NOT GOING TO KILL THIS KID BY RUNNING HER OVER!
OH, NO! THE COPS ARE HERE! YOU TWO, GRAB THE MONEY. WE'RE GETTING ON THE BUS!
EVERYBODY BACK OFF OR THE GIRLFRIEND WILL PAY THE PRICE!
AAH!
I'M GOING TO CREATE A SHOCKWAVE WITH MY DRUMS TO FREE ALICE.
TA KA TA KA
WHAT ARE YOU TALKING ABOUT? YOU CAN'T EVEN CONTROL IT AND YOU RISK HURTING HER, HER OR ONE OF THE OTHER HOSTAGES ON THE BUS!
BAM
GO! GO! GO!
HOP UP HOP DOWN
THEY'RE GETTING AWAY!
WHAT'S GOING ON?
WHERE IS ALICE?
SHE WAS TAKEN HOSTAGE BY ROBBERS!
AND YOU COULDN'T DO ANYTHING?
WE-WE WEREN'T SURE WHAT TO DO.
BUT WE'RE ABOUT TO MAKE UP FOR IT!

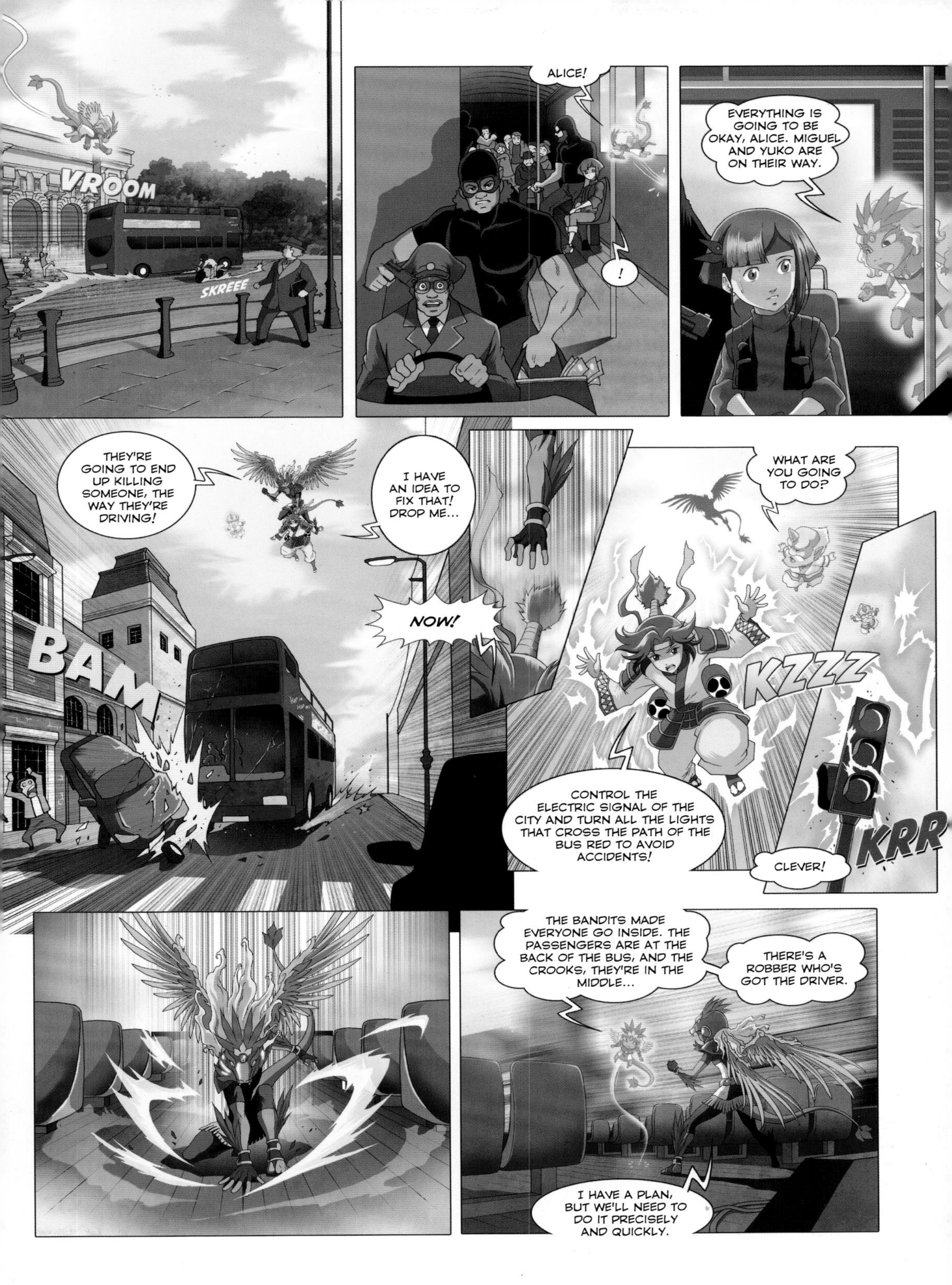
VROOM
SKREEE
ALICE!
!
EVERYTHING IS GOING TO BE OKAY, ALICE. MIGUEL AND YUKO ARE ON THEIR WAY.
THEY'RE GOING TO END UP KILLING SOMEONE, THE WAY THEY'RE DRIVING!
I HAVE AN IDEA TO FIX THAT! DROP ME...
BAM
NOW!
WHAT ARE YOU GOING TO DO?
KZZZ
CONTROL THE ELECTRIC SIGNAL OF THE CITY AND TURN ALL THE LIGHTS THAT CROSS THE PATH OF THE BUS RED TO AVOID ACCIDENTS!
KRR
CLEVER!
THE BANDITS MADE EVERYONE GO INSIDE. THE PASSENGERS ARE AT THE BACK OF THE BUS, AND THE CROOKS, THEY'RE IN THE MIDDLE...
THERE'S A ROBBER WHO'S GOT THE DRIVER.
I HAVE A PLAN, BUT WE'LL NEED TO DO IT PRECISELY AND QUICKLY.

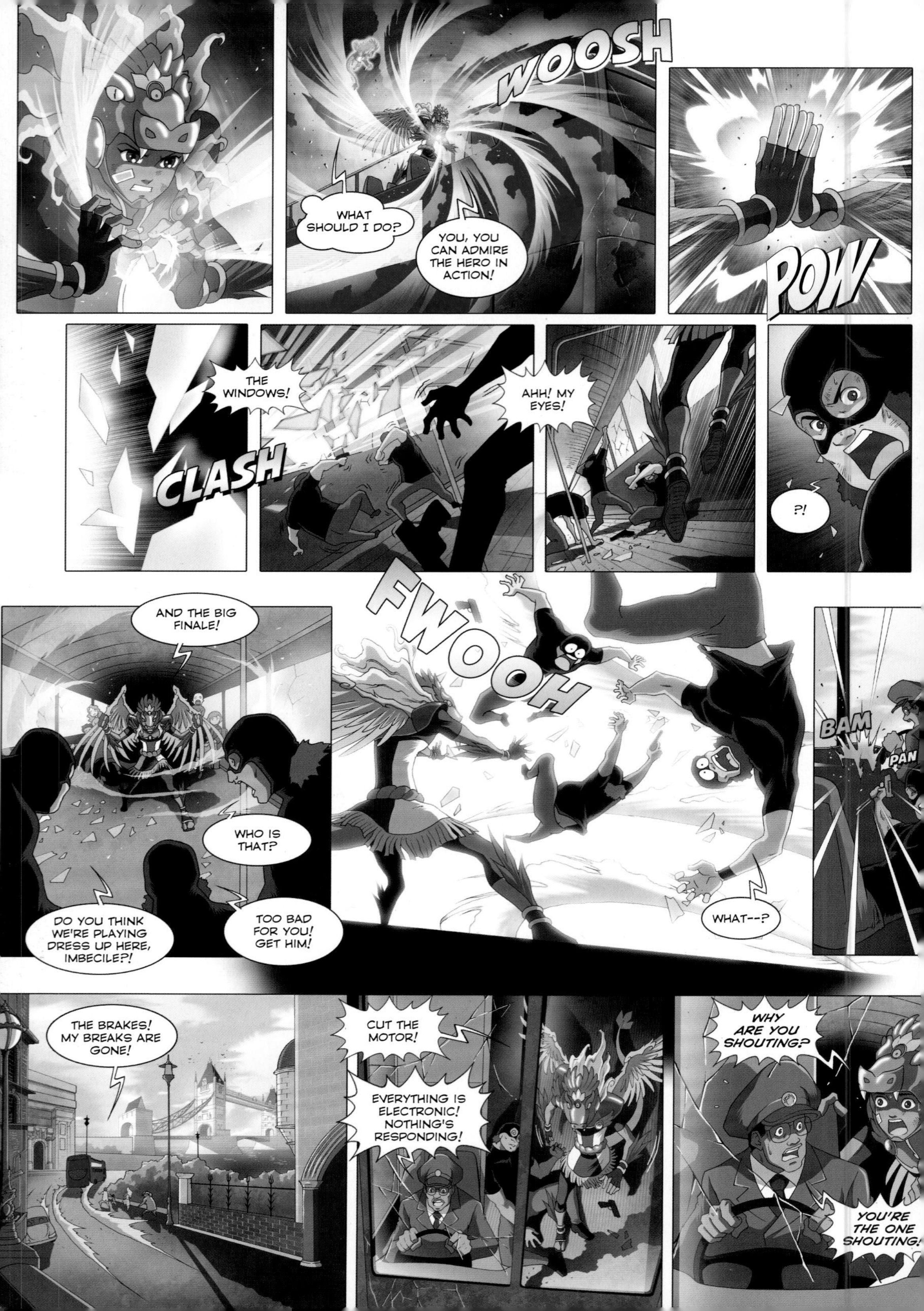
WOOSH
WHAT SHOULD I DO?
YOU, YOU CAN ADMIRE THE HERO IN ACTION!
POW
THE WINDOWS!
CLASH
AHH! MY EYES!
?!
AND THE BIG FINALE!
WHO IS THAT?
DO YOU THINK WE'RE PLAYING DRESS UP HERE, IMBECILE?!
TOO BAD FOR YOU! GET HIM!
FWOOH
WHAT--?
BAM
PAN
THE BRAKES! MY BREAKS ARE GONE!
CUT THE MOTOR!
EVERYTHING IS ELECTRONIC! NOTHING'S RESPONDING!
WHY ARE YOU SHOUTING?
YOU'RE THE ONE SHOUTING!

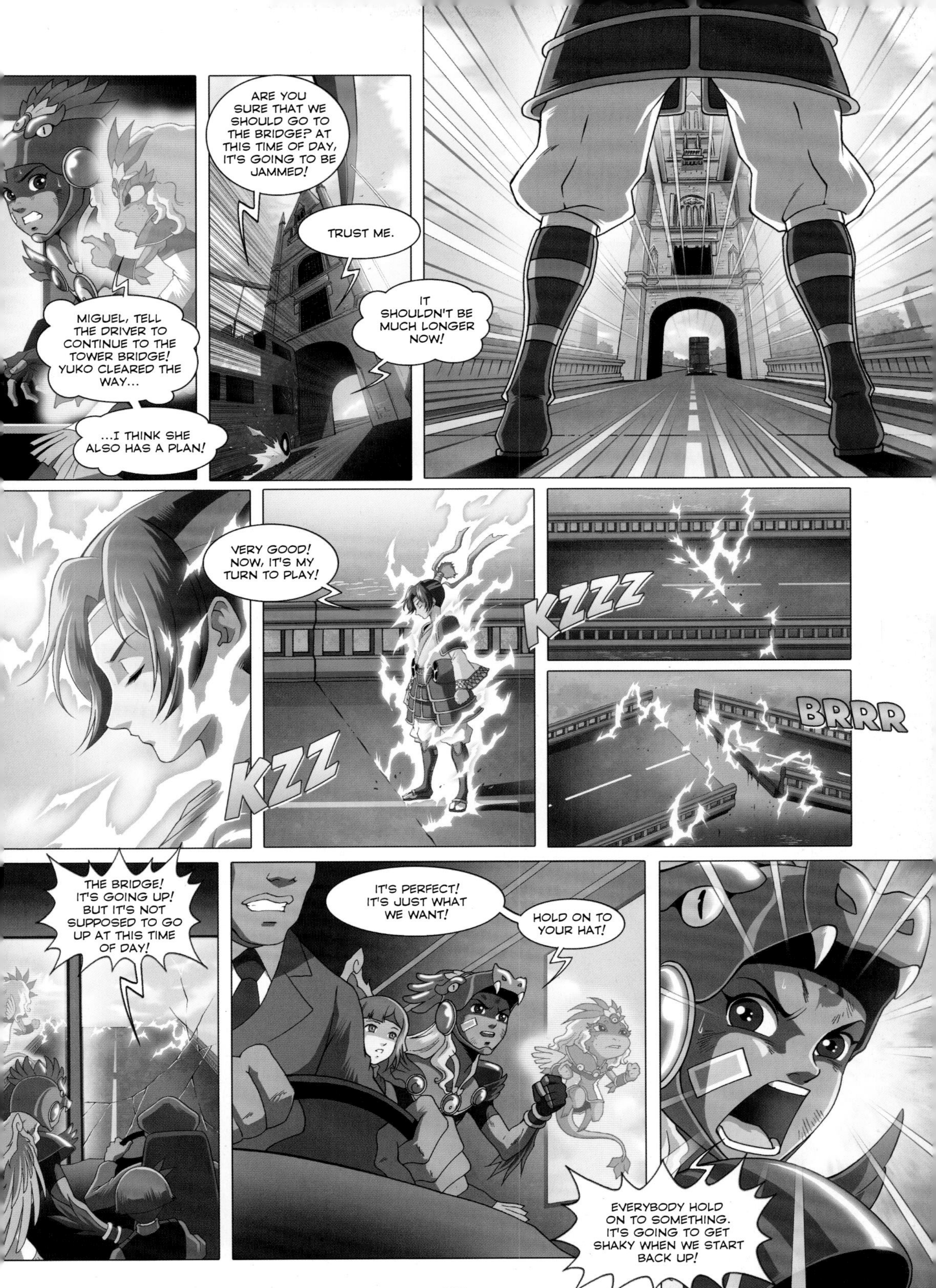
MIGUEL, TELL THE DRIVER TO CONTINUE TO THE TOWER BRIDGE! YUKO CLEARED THE WAY...
...I THINK SHE ALSO HAS A PLAN!
ARE YOU SURE THAT WE SHOULD GO TO THE BRIDGE? AT THIS TIME OF DAY, IT'S GOING TO BE JAMMED!
TRUST ME.
IT SHOULDN'T BE MUCH LONGER NOW!
KZZ
VERY GOOD! NOW, IT'S MY TURN TO PLAY!
KZZZ
BRRR
THE BRIDGE! IT'S GOING UP! BUT IT'S NOT SUPPOSED TO GO UP AT THIS TIME OF DAY!
IT'S PERFECT! IT'S JUST WHAT WE WANT!
HOLD ON TO YOUR HAT!
EVERYBODY HOLD ON TO SOMETHING. IT'S GOING TO GET SHAKY WHEN WE START BACK UP!

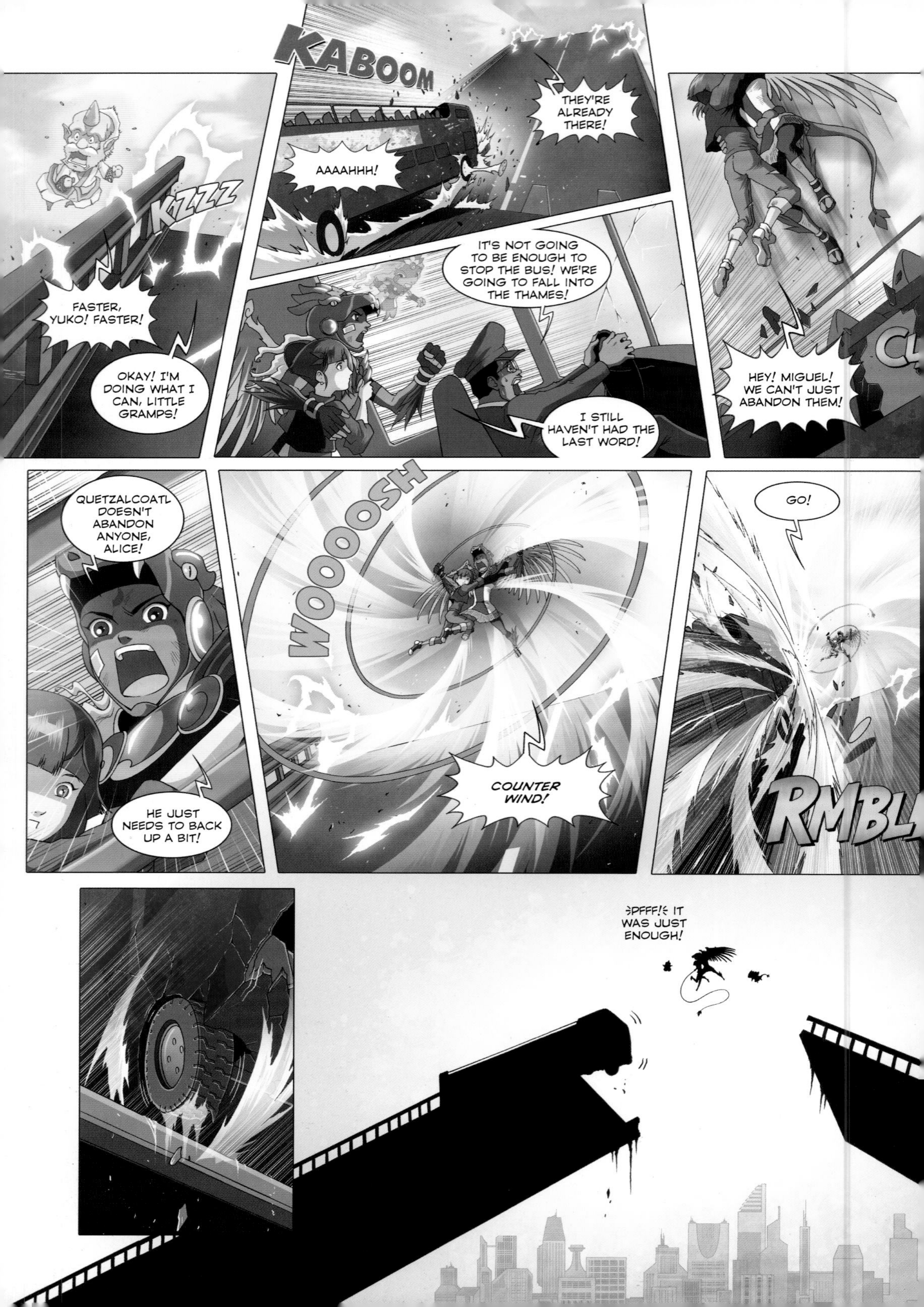
KZZZZ
FASTER, YUKO! FASTER!
OKAY! I'M DOING WHAT I CAN, LITTLE GRAMPS!
KABOOM
AAAAHHH!
THEY'RE ALREADY THERE!
IT'S NOT GOING TO BE ENOUGH TO STOP THE BUS! WE'RE GOING TO FALL INTO THE THAMES!
I STILL HAVEN'T HAD THE LAST WORD!
HEY! MIGUEL! WE CAN'T JUST ABANDON THEM!
QUETZALCOATL DOESN'T ABANDON ANYONE, ALICE!
HE JUST NEEDS TO BACK UP A BIT!
WOOOOSH
COUNTER WIND!
GO!
PFFF! IT WAS JUST ENOUGH!

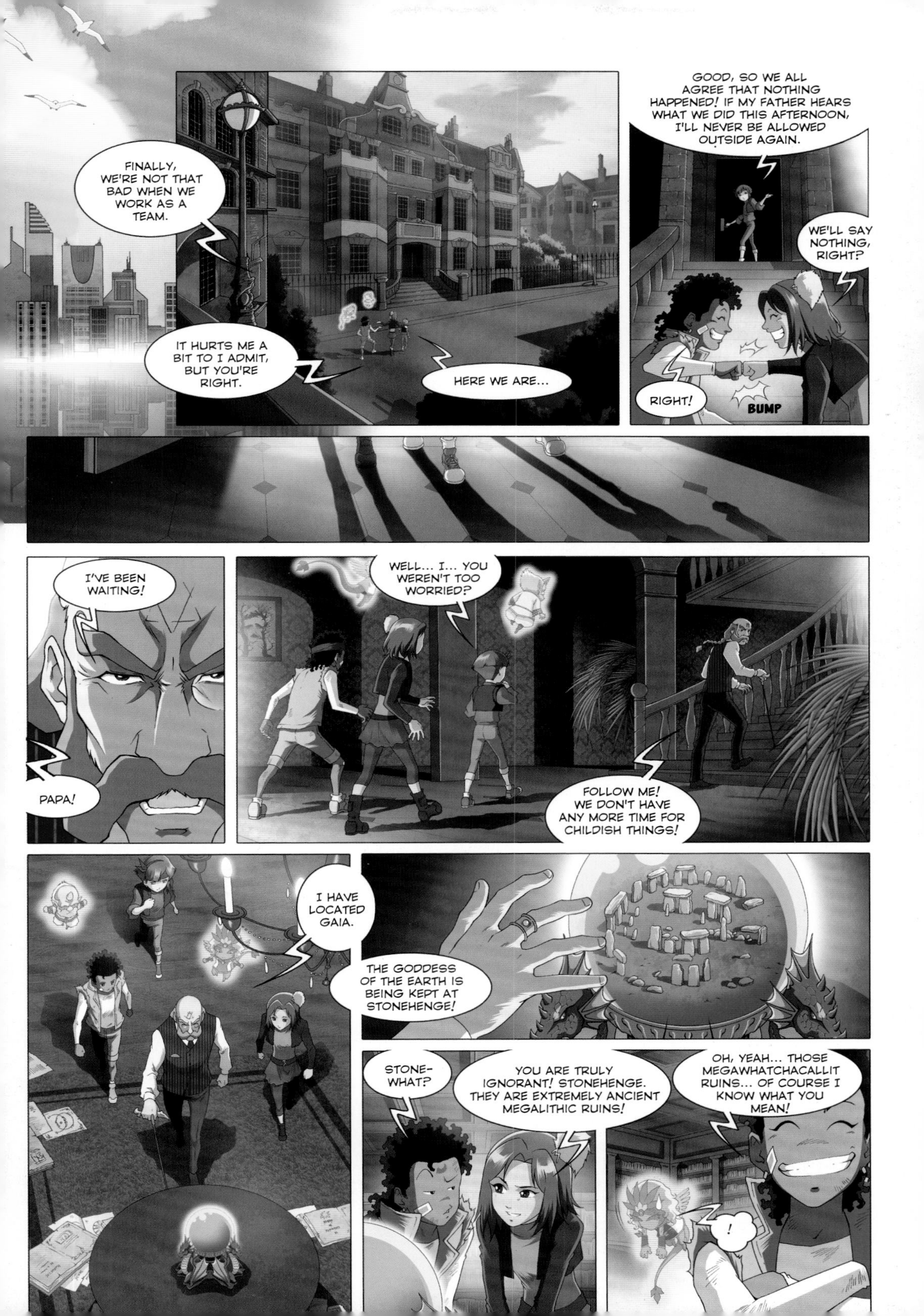
FINALLY, WE'RE NOT THAT BAD WHEN WE WORK AS A TEAM.
IT HURTS ME A BIT TO I ADMIT, BUT YOU'RE RIGHT.
HERE WE ARE...
GOOD, SO WE ALL AGREE THAT NOTHING HAPPENED! IF MY FATHER HEARS WHAT WE DID THIS AFTERNOON, I'LL NEVER BE ALLOWED OUTSIDE AGAIN.
WE'LL SAY NOTHING, RIGHT?
RIGHT!
BUMP
I'VE BEEN WAITING!
PAPA!
WELL... I... YOU WEREN'T TOO WORRIED?
FOLLOW ME! WE DON'T HAVE ANY MORE TIME FOR CHILDISH THINGS!
I HAVE LOCATED GAIA.
THE GODDESS OF THE EARTH IS BEING KEPT AT STONEHENGE!
STONE-WHAT?
YOU ARE TRULY IGNORANT! STONEHENGE. THEY ARE EXTREMELY ANCIENT MEGALITHIC RUINS!
OH, YEAH... THOSE MEGAWHATCHACALLIT RUINS... OF COURSE I KNOW WHAT YOU MEAN!
!

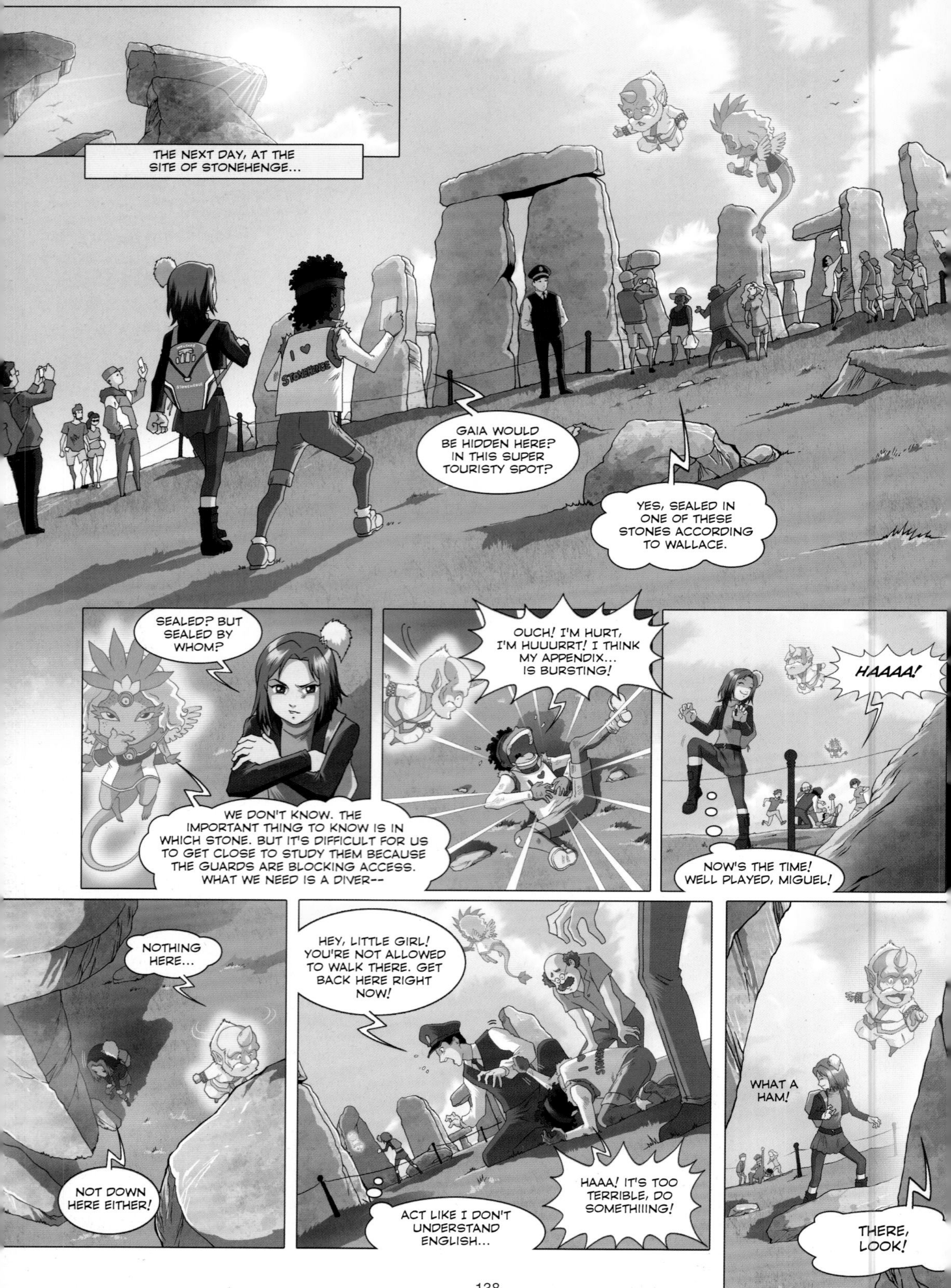
THE NEXT DAY, AT THE SITE OF STONEHENGE...
GAIA WOULD BE HIDDEN HERE? IN THIS SUPER TOURISTY SPOT?
YES, SEALED IN ONE OF THESE STONES ACCORDING TO WALLACE.
SEALED? BUT SEALED BY WHOM?
WE DON'T KNOW. THE IMPORTANT THING TO KNOW IS IN WHICH STONE. BUT IT'S DIFFICULT FOR US TO GET CLOSE TO STUDY THEM BECAUSE THE GUARDS ARE BLOCKING ACCESS. WHAT WE NEED IS A DIVER--
OUCH! I'M HURT, I'M HUUURRT! I THINK MY APPENDIX... IS BURSTING!
HAAAA!
NOW'S THE TIME! WELL PLAYED, MIGUEL!
NOTHING HERE...
NOT DOWN HERE EITHER!
HEY, LITTLE GIRL! YOU'RE NOT ALLOWED TO WALK THERE. GET BACK HERE RIGHT NOW!
ACT LIKE I DON'T UNDERSTAND ENGLISH...
HAAA! IT'S TOO TERRIBLE, DO SOMETHIIING!
WHAT A HAM!
THERE, LOOK!

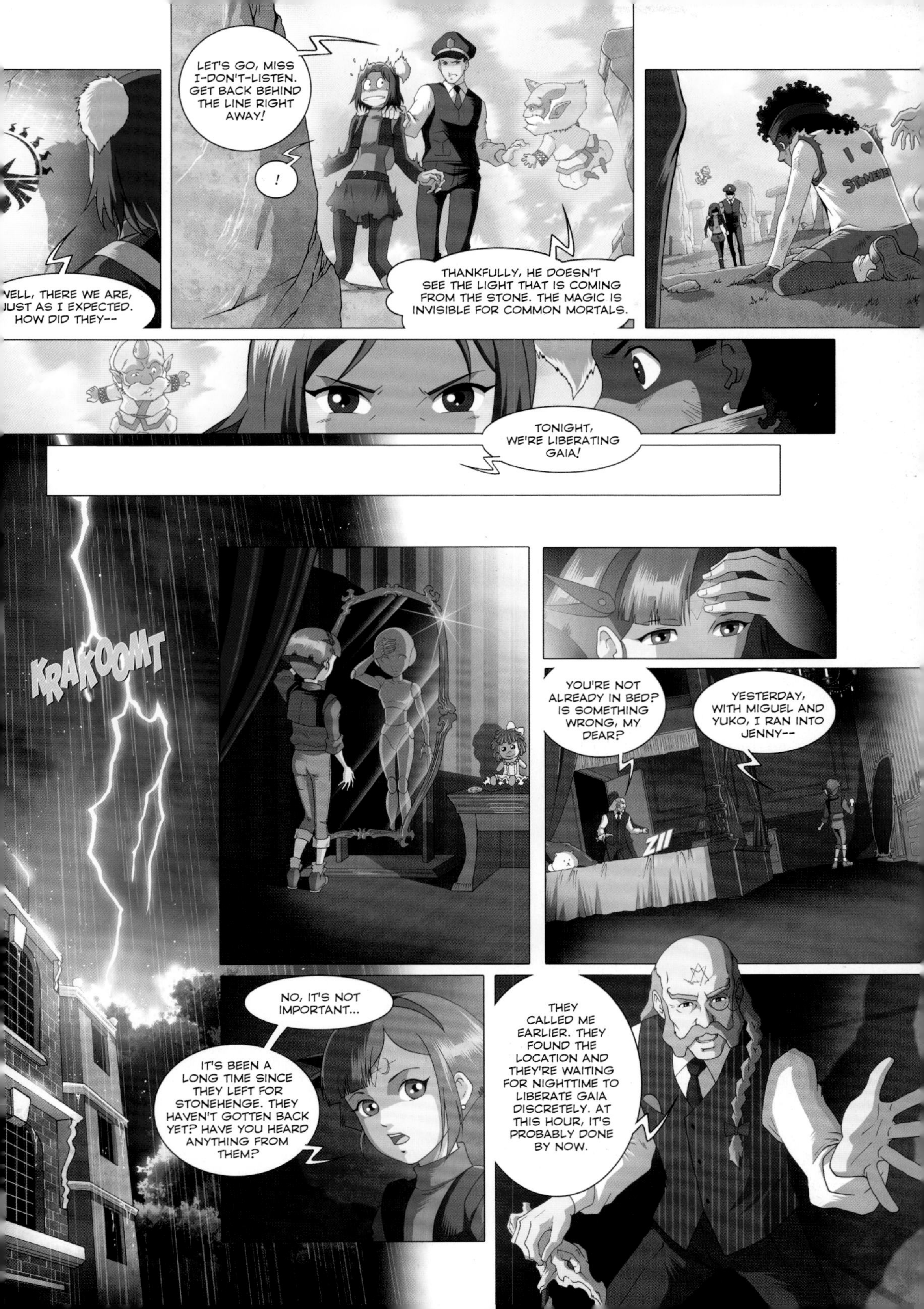
WELL, THERE WE ARE, JUST AS I EXPECTED. HOW DID THEY--
LET'S GO, MISS I-DON'T-LISTEN. GET BACK BEHIND THE LINE RIGHT AWAY!
!
THANKFULLY, HE DOESN'T SEE THE LIGHT THAT IS COMING FROM THE STONE. THE MAGIC IS INVISIBLE FOR COMMON MORTALS.
TONIGHT, WE'RE LIBERATING GAIA!
KRAKOOMT
YOU'RE NOT ALREADY IN BED? IS SOMETHING WRONG, MY DEAR?
YESTERDAY, WITH MIGUEL AND YUKO, I RAN INTO JENNY--
ZII
NO, IT'S NOT IMPORTANT...
IT'S BEEN A LONG TIME SINCE THEY LEFT FOR STONEHENGE. THEY HAVEN'T GOTTEN BACK YET? HAVE YOU HEARD ANYTHING FROM THEM?
THEY CALLED ME EARLIER. THEY FOUND THE LOCATION AND THEY'RE WAITING FOR NIGHTTIME TO LIBERATE GAIA DISCRETELY. AT THIS HOUR, IT'S PROBABLY DONE BY NOW.

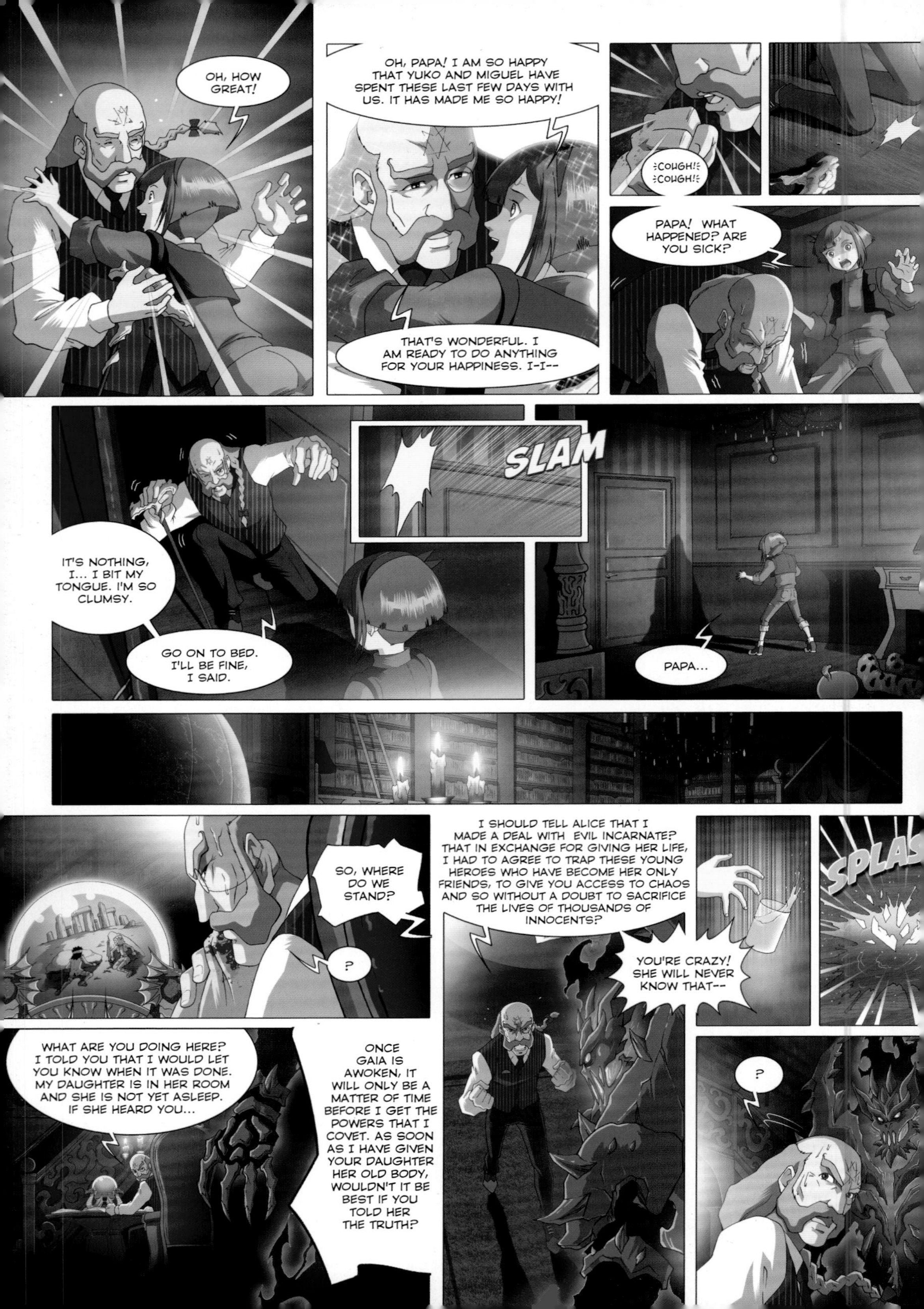
OH, HOW GREAT!
OH, PAPA! I AM SO HAPPY THAT YUKO AND MIGUEL HAVE SPENT THESE LAST FEW DAYS WITH US. IT HAS MADE ME SO HAPPY!
THAT'S WONDERFUL. I AM READY TO DO ANYTHING FOR YOUR HAPPINESS. I-I--
COUGH! COUGH!
PAPA! WHAT HAPPENED? ARE YOU SICK?
SLAM
IT'S NOTHING, I... I BIT MY TONGUE. I'M SO CLUMSY.
GO ON TO BED. I'LL BE FINE, I SAID.
PAPA...
SO, WHERE DO WE STAND?
?
I SHOULD TELL ALICE THAT I MADE A DEAL WITH EVIL INCARNATE? THAT IN EXCHANGE FOR GIVING HER LIFE, I HAD TO AGREE TO TRAP THESE YOUNG HEROES WHO HAVE BECOME HER ONLY FRIENDS, TO GIVE YOU ACCESS TO CHAOS AND SO WITHOUT A DOUBT TO SACRIFICE THE LIVES OF THOUSANDS OF INNOCENTS?
YOU'RE CRAZY! SHE WILL NEVER KNOW THAT--
SPLAS
WHAT ARE YOU DOING HERE? I TOLD YOU THAT I WOULD LET YOU KNOW WHEN IT WAS DONE. MY DAUGHTER IS IN HER ROOM AND SHE IS NOT YET ASLEEP. IF SHE HEARD YOU...
ONCE GAIA IS AWOKEN, IT WILL ONLY BE A MATTER OF TIME BEFORE I GET THE POWERS THAT I COVET. AS SOON AS I HAVE GIVEN YOUR DAUGHTER HER OLD BODY, WOULDN'T IT BE BEST IF YOU TOLD HER THE TRUTH?
?

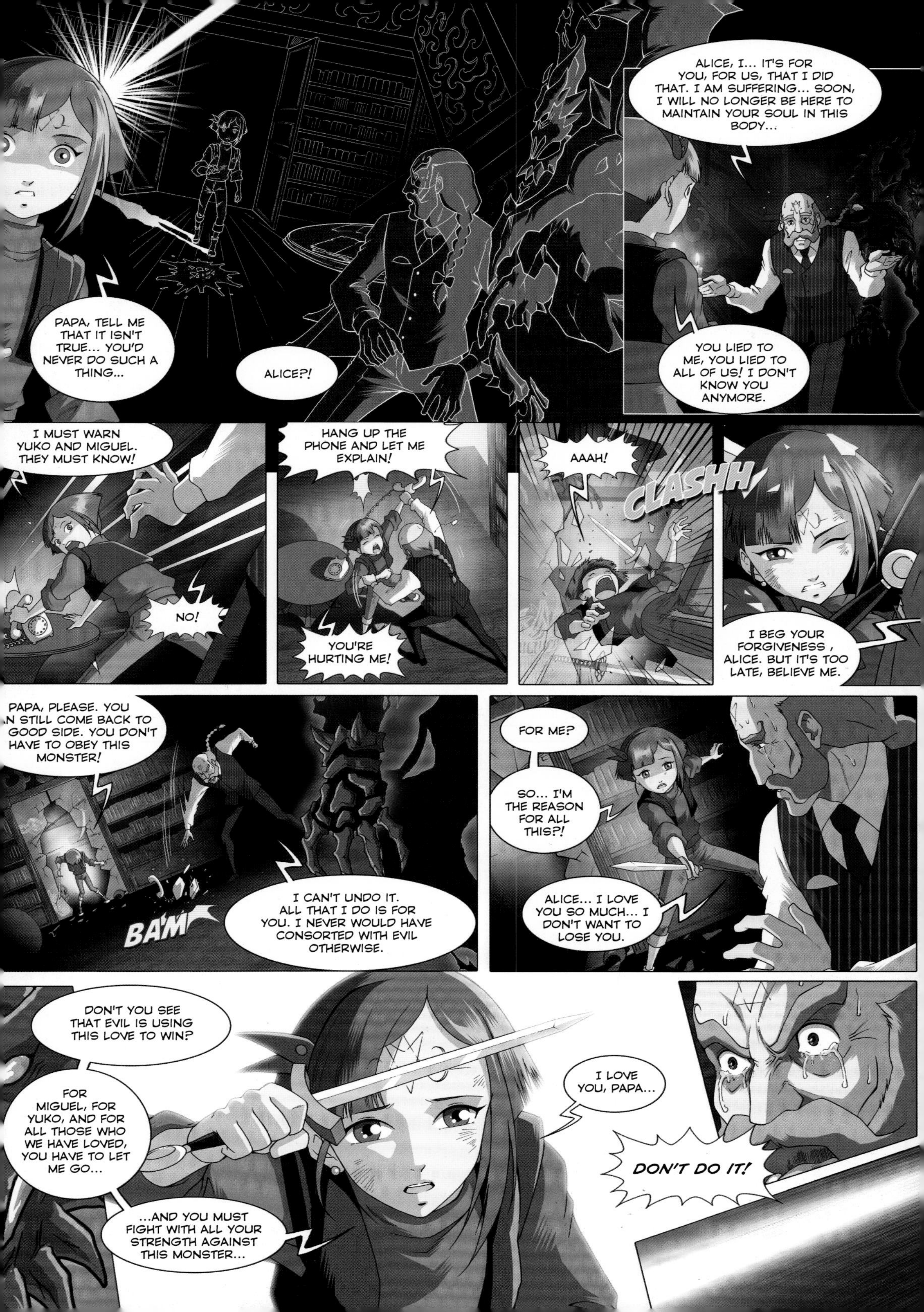
PAPA, TELL ME THAT IT ISN'T TRUE... YOU'D NEVER DO SUCH A THING...
ALICE?!
ALICE, I... IT'S FOR YOU, FOR US, THAT I DID THAT. I AM SUFFERING... SOON, I WILL NO LONGER BE HERE TO MAINTAIN YOUR SOUL IN THIS BODY...
YOU LIED TO ME, YOU LIED TO ALL OF US! I DON'T KNOW YOU ANYMORE.
I MUST WARN YUKO AND MIGUEL. THEY MUST KNOW!
NO!
HANG UP THE PHONE AND LET ME EXPLAIN!
YOU'RE HURTING ME!
AAAH!
CLASHH
I BEG YOUR FORGIVENESS , ALICE. BUT IT'S TOO LATE, BELIEVE ME.
PAPA, PLEASE. YOU N STILL COME BACK TO GOOD SIDE. YOU DON'T HAVE TO OBEY THIS MONSTER!
BAM
I CAN'T UNDO IT. ALL THAT I DO IS FOR YOU. I NEVER WOULD HAVE CONSORTED WITH EVIL OTHERWISE.
FOR ME?
SO... I'M THE REASON FOR ALL THIS?!
ALICE... I LOVE YOU SO MUCH... I DON'T WANT TO LOSE YOU.
DON'T YOU SEE THAT EVIL IS USING THIS LOVE TO WIN?
FOR MIGUEL, FOR YUKO, AND FOR ALL THOSE WHO WE HAVE LOVED, YOU HAVE TO LET ME GO...
...AND YOU MUST FIGHT WITH ALL YOUR STRENGTH AGAINST THIS MONSTER...
I LOVE YOU, PAPA...
DON'T DO IT!

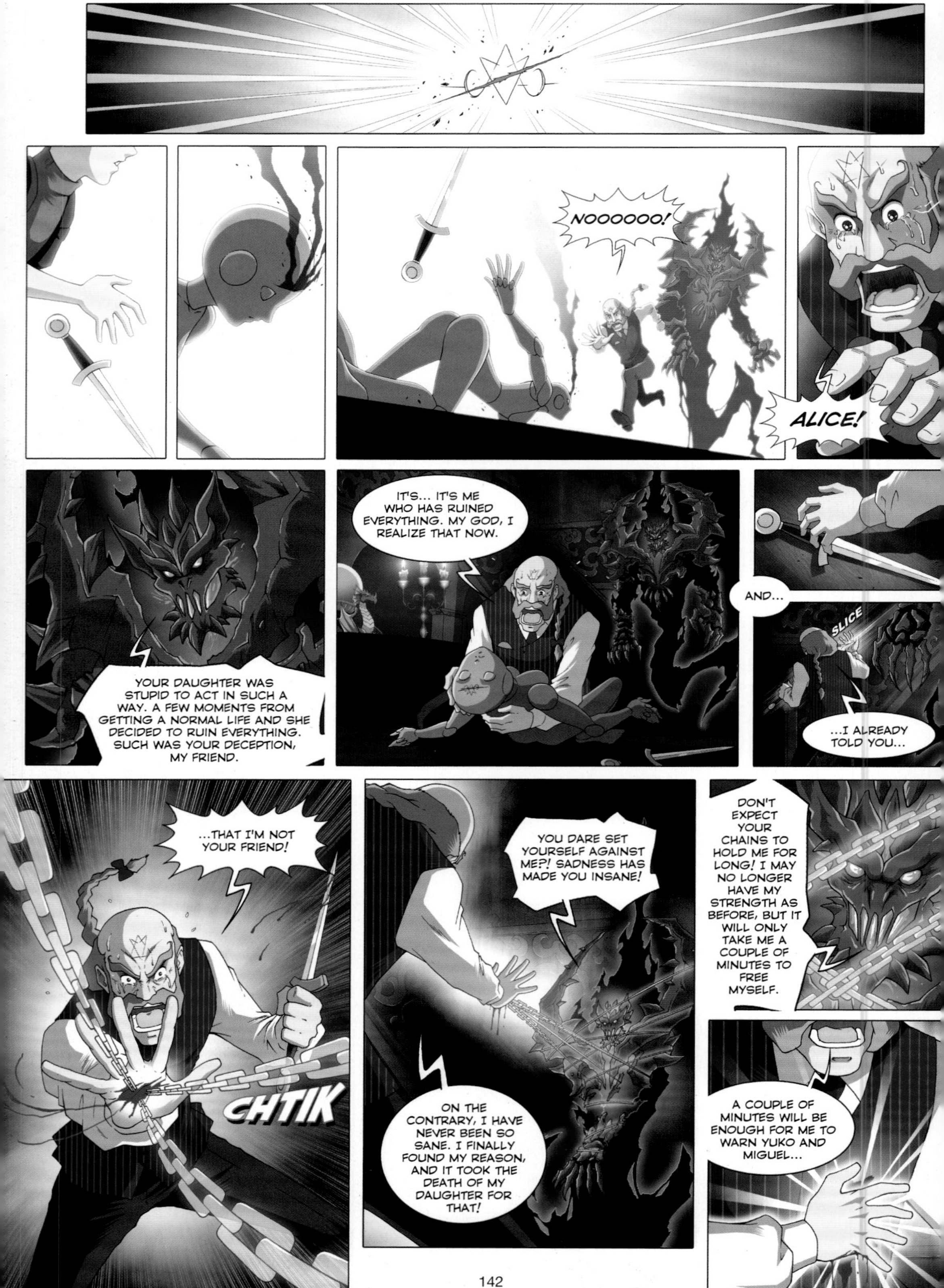
NOOOOOO!
ALICE!
YOUR DAUGHTER WAS STUPID TO ACT IN SUCH A WAY. A FEW MOMENTS FROM GETTING A NORMAL LIFE AND SHE DECIDED TO RUIN EVERYTHING. SUCH WAS YOUR DECEPTION, MY FRIEND.
IT'S... IT'S ME WHO HAS RUINED EVERYTHING. MY GOD, I REALIZE THAT NOW.
AND...
SLICE
...I ALREADY TOLD YOU...
...THAT I'M NOT YOUR FRIEND!
CHTIK
YOU DARE SET YOURSELF AGAINST ME?! SADNESS HAS MADE YOU INSANE!
ON THE CONTRARY, I HAVE NEVER BEEN SO SANE. I FINALLY FOUND MY REASON, AND IT TOOK THE DEATH OF MY DAUGHTER FOR THAT!
DON'T EXPECT YOUR CHAINS TO HOLD ME FOR LONG! I MAY NO LONGER HAVE MY STRENGTH AS BEFORE, BUT IT WILL ONLY TAKE ME A COUPLE OF MINUTES TO FREE MYSELF.
A COUPLE OF MINUTES WILL BE ENOUGH FOR ME TO WARN YUKO AND MIGUEL...

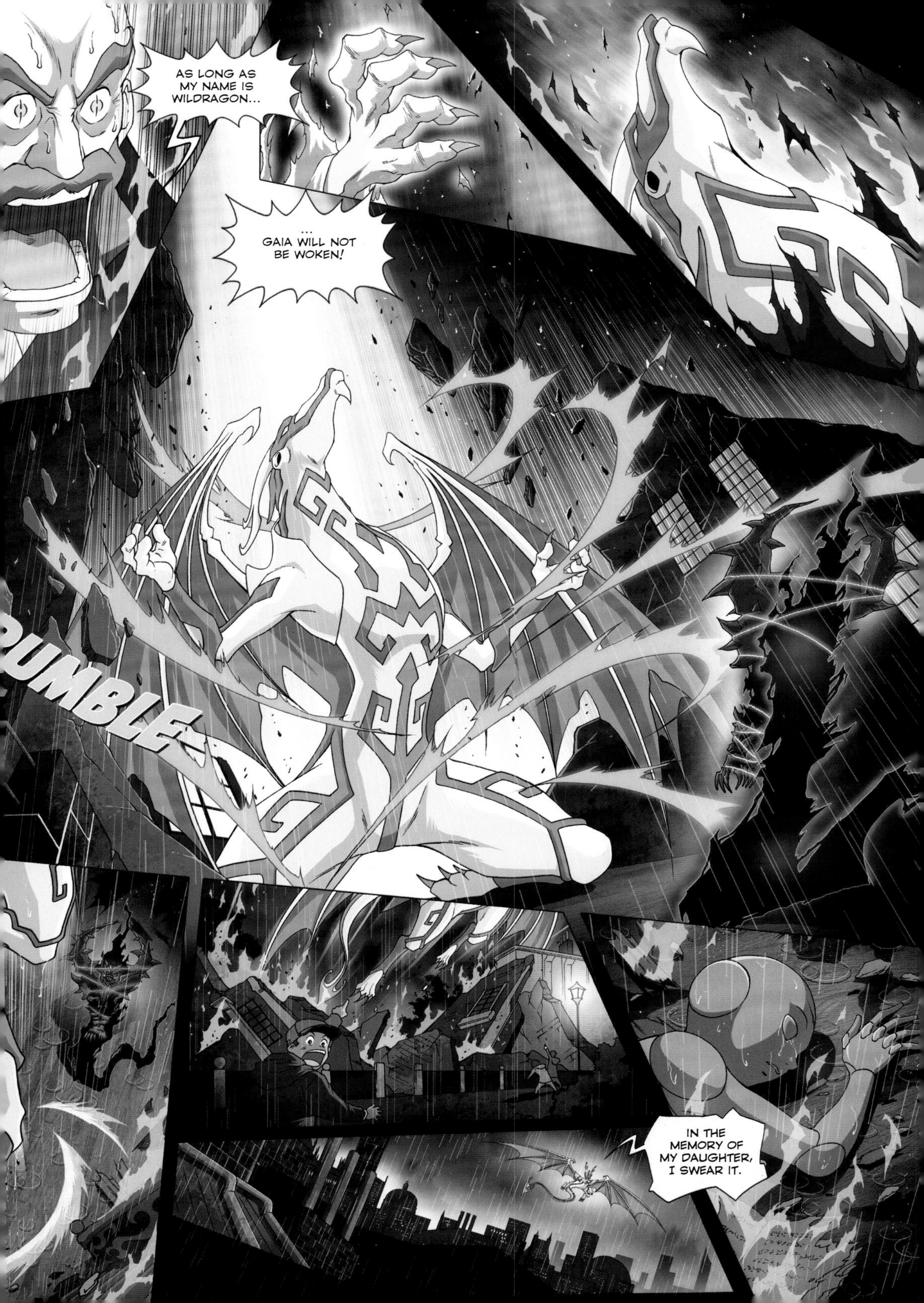
AS LONG AS MY NAME IS WILDRAGON...
... GAIA WILL NOT BE WOKEN!
RUMBLE
IN THE MEMORY OF MY DAUGHTER, I SWEAR IT.

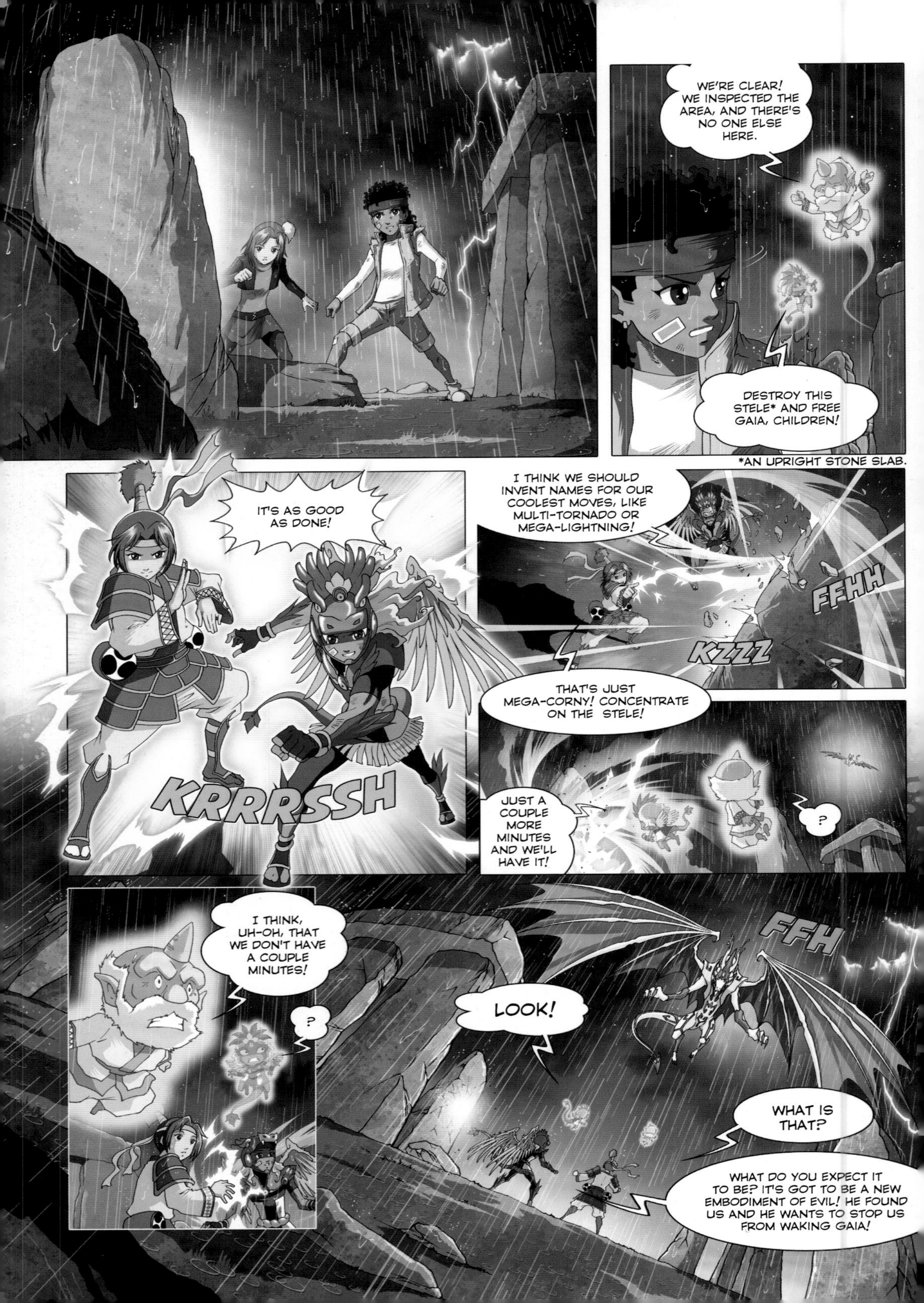
WE'RE CLEAR! WE INSPECTED THE AREA, AND THERE'S NO ONE ELSE HERE.
DESTROY THIS STELE* AND FREE GAIA, CHILDREN!
*AN UPRIGHT STONE SLAB.
IT'S AS GOOD AS DONE!
KRRRSSH
I THINK WE SHOULD INVENT NAMES FOR OUR COOLEST MOVES, LIKE MULTI-TORNADO OR MEGA-LIGHTNING!
FFHH
KZZZ
THAT'S JUST MEGA-CORNY! CONCENTRATE ON THE STELE!
JUST A COUPLE MORE MINUTES AND WE'LL HAVE IT!
?
I THINK, UH-OH, THAT WE DON'T HAVE A COUPLE MINUTES!
?
FFH
LOOK!
WHAT IS THAT?
WHAT DO YOU EXPECT IT TO BE? IT'S GOT TO BE A NEW EMBODIMENT OF EVIL! HE FOUND US AND HE WANTS TO STOP US FROM WAKING GAIA!

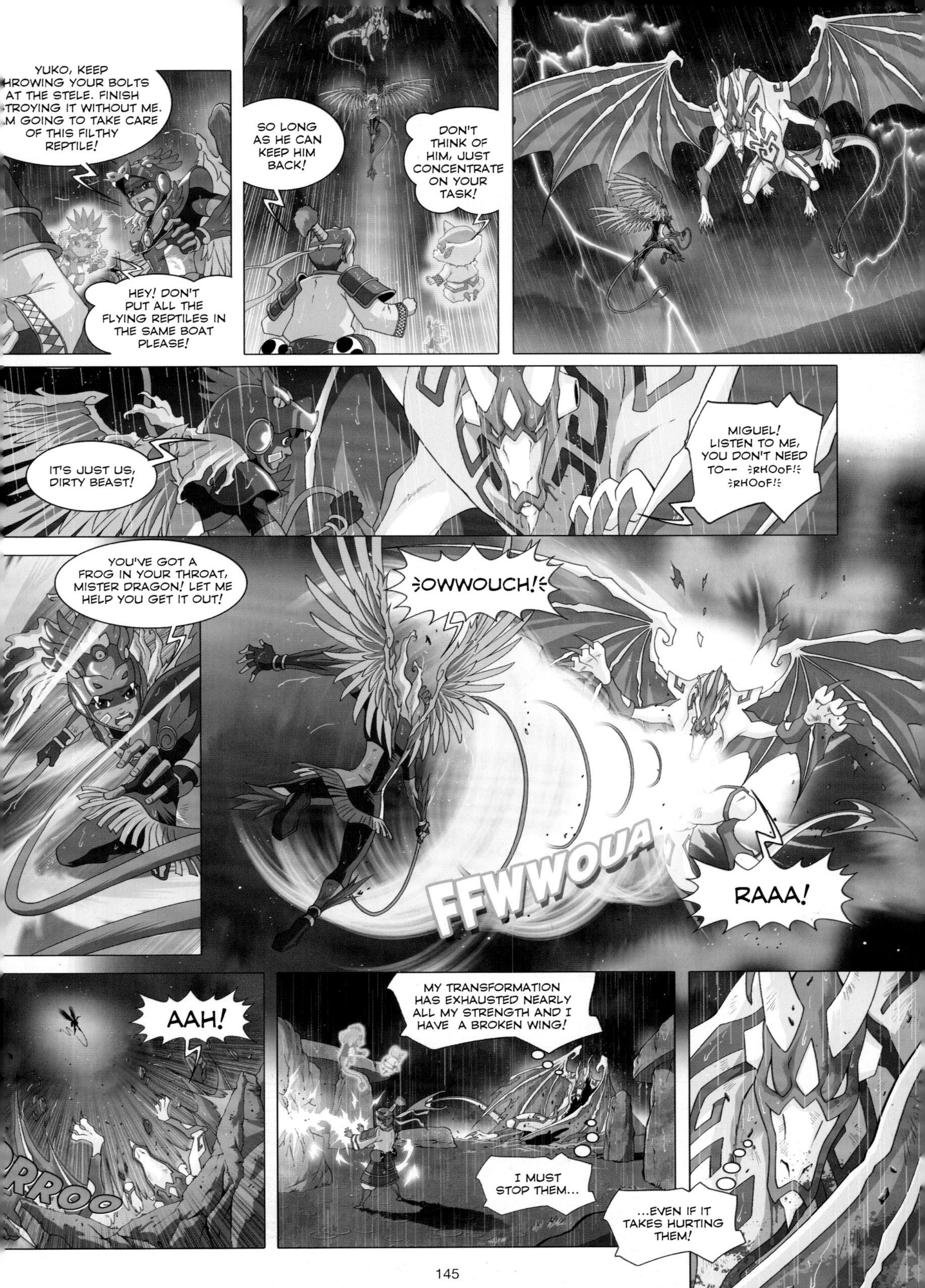
YUKO, KEEP THROWING YOUR BOLTS AT THE STELE. FINISH DESTROYING IT WITHOUT ME. I'M GOING TO TAKE CARE OF THIS FILTHY REPTILE!
HEY! DON'T PUT ALL THE FLYING REPTILES IN THE SAME BOAT PLEASE!
SO LONG AS HE CAN KEEP HIM BACK!
DON'T THINK OF HIM, JUST CONCENTRATE ON YOUR TASK!
IT'S JUST US, DIRTY BEAST!
MIGUEL! LISTEN TO ME, YOU DON'T NEED TO-- RHOOF! RHOOF!
YOU'VE GOT A FROG IN YOUR THROAT, MISTER DRAGON! LET ME HELP YOU GET IT OUT!
OWWOUCH!
FFWWOUA
RAAA!
AAH!
RRROO
MY TRANSFORMATION HAS EXHAUSTED NEARLY ALL MY STRENGTH AND I HAVE A BROKEN WING!
I MUST STOP THEM...
...EVEN IF IT TAKES HURTING THEM!

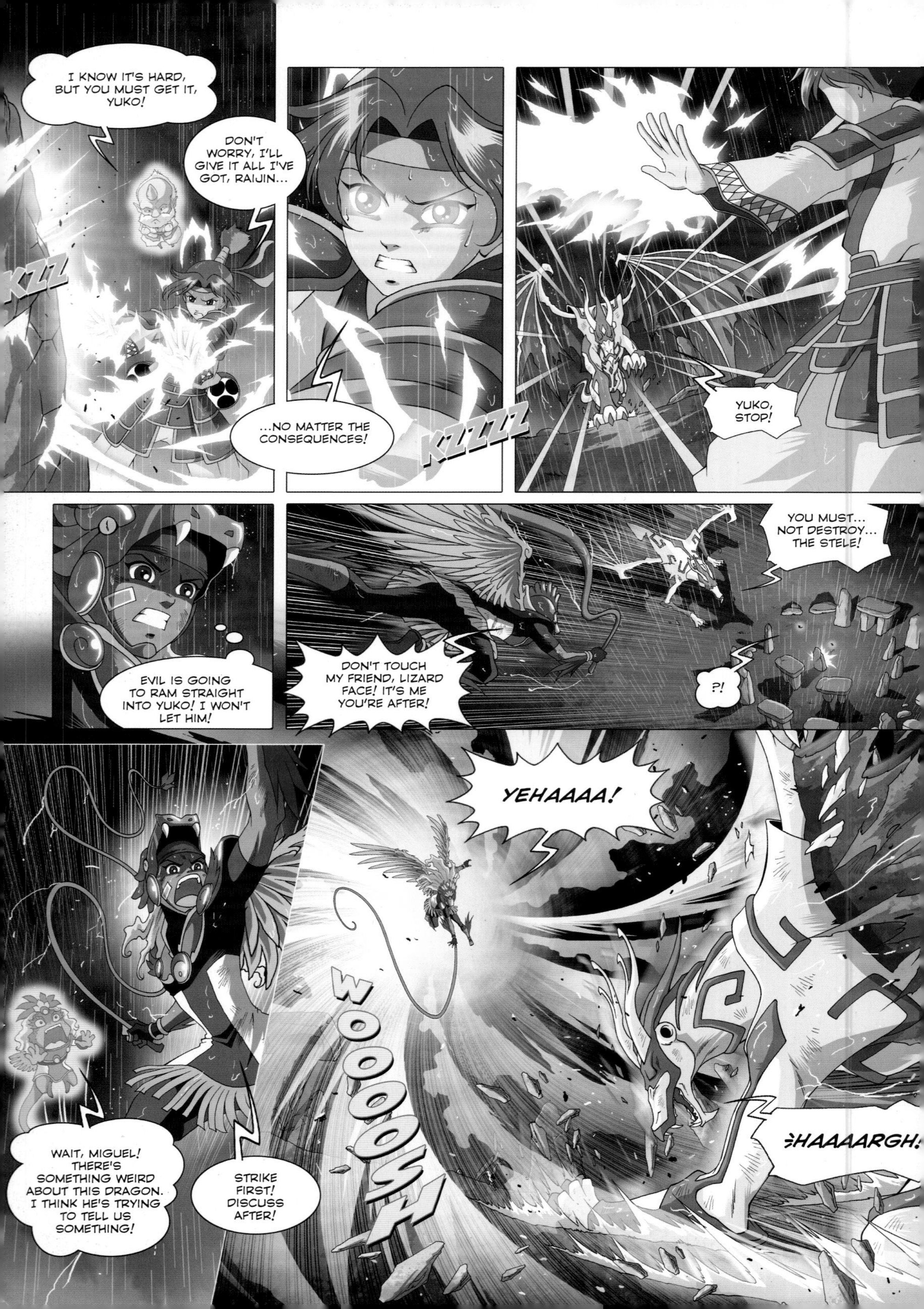
I KNOW IT'S HARD, BUT YOU MUST GET IT, YUKO!
DON'T WORRY, I'LL GIVE IT ALL I'VE GOT, RAIJIN...
KZZ
...NO MATTER THE CONSEQUENCES!
KZZZZ
YUKO, STOP!
EVIL IS GOING TO RAM STRAIGHT INTO YUKO! I WON'T LET HIM!
DON'T TOUCH MY FRIEND, LIZARD FACE! IT'S ME YOU'RE AFTER!
YOU MUST... NOT DESTROY... THE STELE!
?!
WAIT, MIGUEL! THERE'S SOMETHING WEIRD ABOUT THIS DRAGON. I THINK HE'S TRYING TO TELL US SOMETHING!
STRIKE FIRST! DISCUSS AFTER!
YEHAAAA!
WOOOOOSH
HAAAARGH!

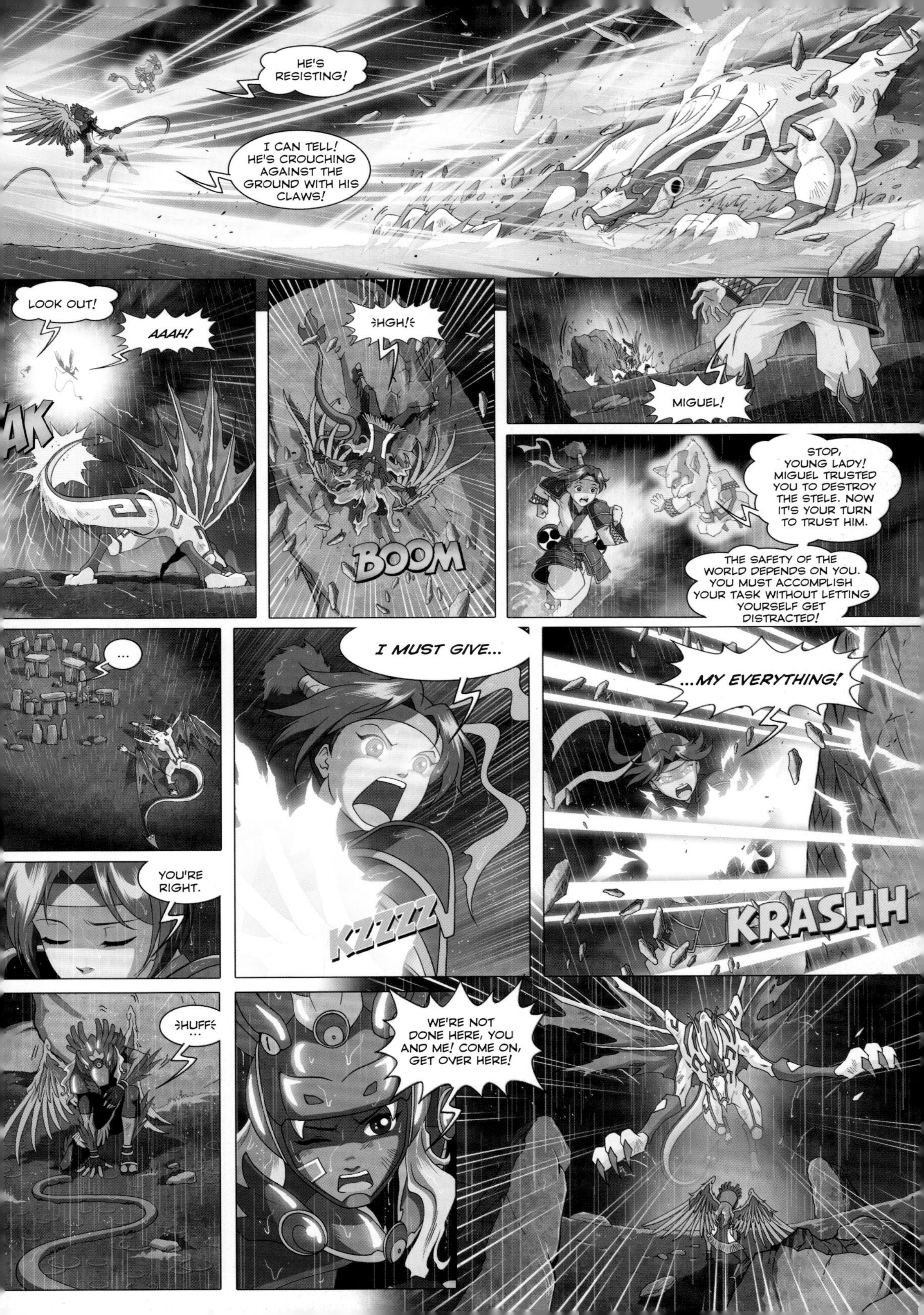
HE'S RESISTING!
I CAN TELL! HE'S CROUCHING AGAINST THE GROUND WITH HIS CLAWS!
LOOK OUT!
AAAH!
AK
HGH!
BOOM
MIGUEL!
STOP, YOUNG LADY! MIGUEL TRUSTED YOU TO DESTROY THE STELE. NOW IT'S YOUR TURN TO TRUST HIM.
THE SAFETY OF THE WORLD DEPENDS ON YOU. YOU MUST ACCOMPLISH YOUR TASK WITHOUT LETTING YOURSELF GET DISTRACTED!
...
YOU'RE RIGHT.
I MUST GIVE...
KZZZZ
...MY EVERYTHING!
KRASHH
HUFF ...
WE'RE NOT DONE HERE, YOU AND ME! COME ON, GET OVER HERE!

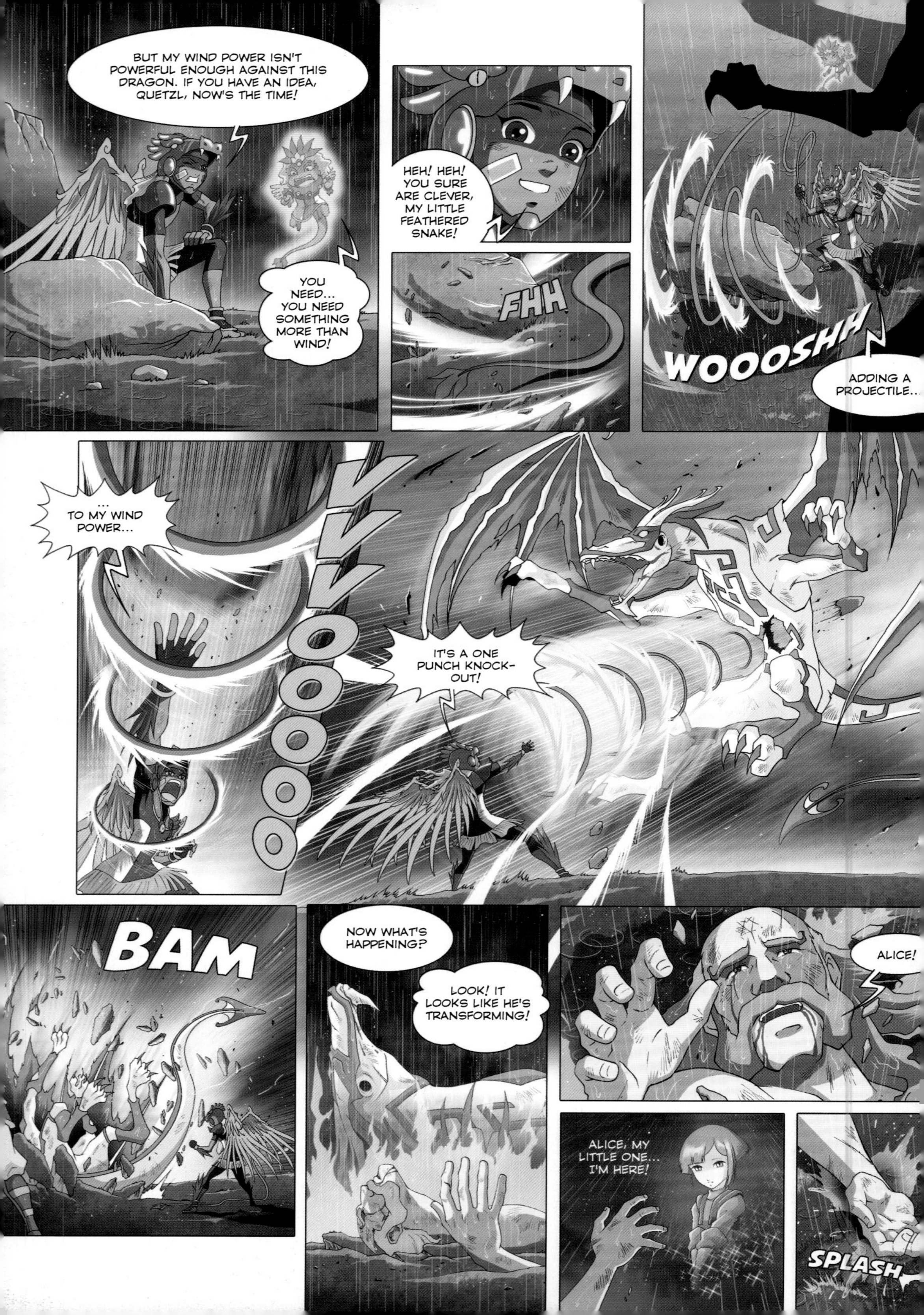

BUT MY WIND POWER ISN'T POWERFUL ENOUGH AGAINST THIS DRAGON. IF YOU HAVE AN IDEA, QUETZL, NOW'S THE TIME!
YOU NEED... YOU NEED SOMETHING MORE THAN WIND!
HEH! HEH! YOU SURE ARE CLEVER, MY LITTLE FEATHERED SNAKE!
FHH
WOOOSHH
ADDING A PROJECTILE...
... TO MY WIND POWER...
VVVOOOOOOOO
IT'S A ONE PUNCH KNOCK-OUT!
BAM
NOW WHAT'S HAPPENING?
LOOK! IT LOOKS LIKE HE'S TRANSFORMING!
ALICE!
ALICE, MY LITTLE ONE... I'M HERE!
SPLASH

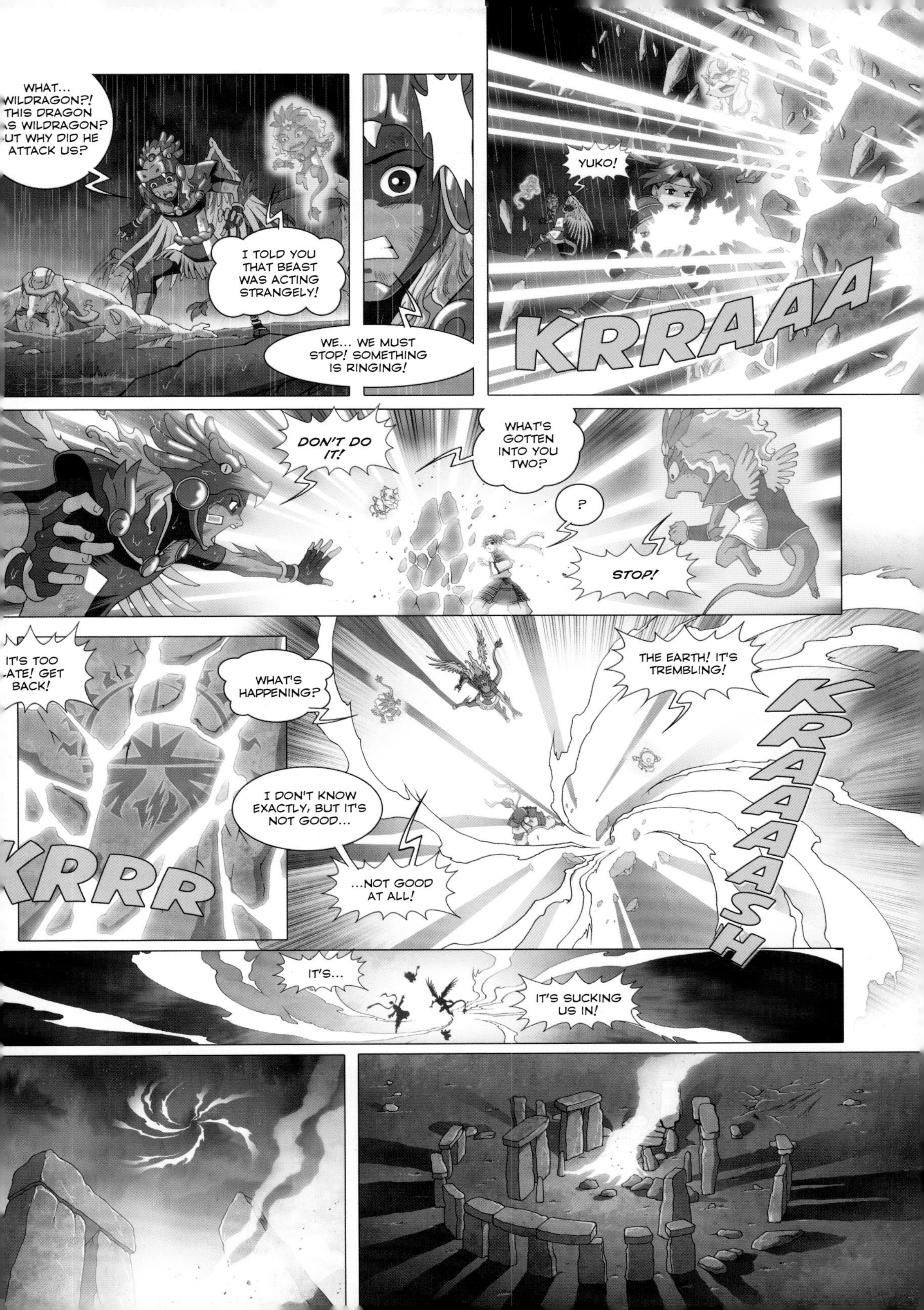
WHAT... WILDRAGON?! THIS DRAGON IS WILDRAGON? BUT WHY DID HE ATTACK US?
I TOLD YOU THAT BEAST WAS ACTING STRANGELY!
WE... WE MUST STOP! SOMETHING IS RINGING!
YUKO!
KRRAAA
DON'T DO IT!
WHAT'S GOTTEN INTO YOU TWO?
?
STOP!
IT'S TOO LATE! GET BACK!
WHAT'S HAPPENING?
THE EARTH! IT'S TREMBLING!
I DON'T KNOW EXACTLY, BUT IT'S NOT GOOD...
...NOT GOOD AT ALL!
KRRR
KRAAAAASH
IT'S...
IT'S SUCKING US IN!

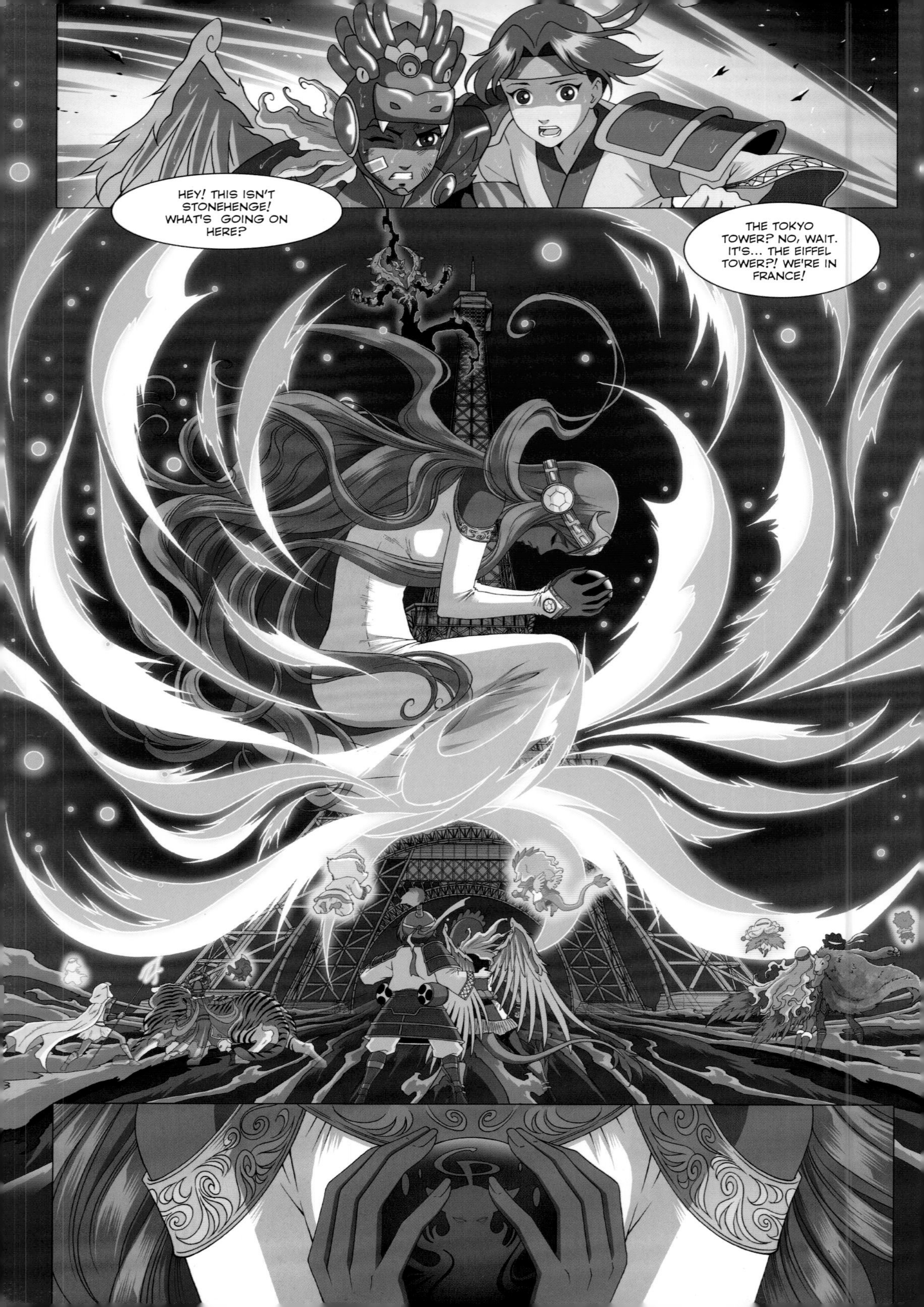
HEY! THIS ISN'T STONEHENGE! WHAT'S GOING ON HERE?
THE TOKYO TOWER? NO, WAIT. IT'S... THE EIFFEL TOWER?! WE'RE IN FRANCE!

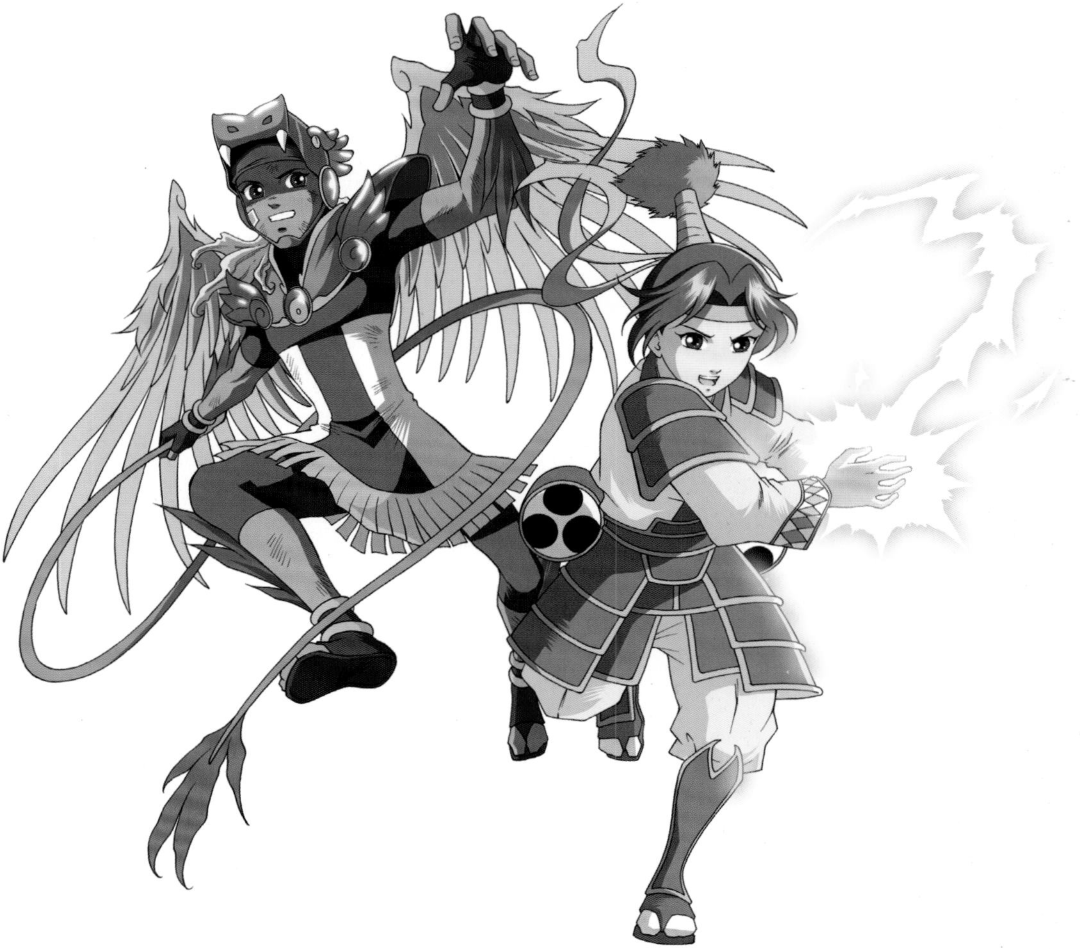

# WATCH OUT FOR PAPERCUTZ™

Welcome to the teeming with team-ups, third volume of THE MYTHICS, "Apocalypse Ahead," by Patrick Sobral, Patricia Lyfoung, Philippe Ogaki, Alice Picard, Jérôme Alquié, Zimra, and Nicolas Jarry, from Papercutz—an editorial super-group dedicated to publishing great graphic novels for all ages. I'm Jim Salicrup, the Editor-in-Chief and Legend in His Own Mind, here to reveal an embarrassing secret…

But before I make my candid confession, a little background information. If you're familiar with Papercutz and the graphic novels we publish, you may've noticed that some of them originated in France or Belgium. Even THE SMURFS, which we've been publishing for years now, many folks mistakenly believe started life as an animated American TV series, but the truth is SMURFS began as comics over 60 years ago, created by Belgian cartoonist Pierre Colliford, better known as Peyo. That misperception is likely to continue as Nickelodeon will soon be introducing a whole new generation to an all-new animated series of THE SMURFS this year. But Papercutz will be re-launching THE SMURFS series as THE SMURFS TALES, to tie-in to the new show and to remind everyone of their real roots. Last year, Papercutz also proudly launched a re-translated ASTERIX, one of the best-selling graphic novel series not only in France, but in the world. ASTERIX, created by René Goscinny, writer, and Albert Uderzo, illustrator, is considered a true national treasure in France. Plus, we publish CAT & CAT, BRINA THE CAT, LOLA'S SUPER CLUB, THE SISTERS, and DANCE CLASS—all from France.

So, here's my deep dark secret: I don't speak French. Yes, *moi*, the editor of so many graphic novels featuring French material, cannot *parle français*. Papercutz publisher Terry Nantier certainly speaks French, he lived there for some time. To make this even more embarrassing, Papercutz Managing Editor Jeff Whitman took up French a mere year ago and he's now virtually fluent!

The question then, is how the heck do I decide which French graphic novels should Papercutz publish? Fortunately, comics are a visual storytelling medium, and when considering various French comics to possibly publish at Papercutz, I place a lot of stock on the visual appeal of the series. If the artwork looks compelling, that's a very good sign. If I'm eager to read the story just from looking at the pictures, then I'm betting it may be good. Also, I rely on Terry's opinions, and now Jeff's as well, since they're able to actually read the stories.

But in the case of THE MYTHICS, there were additional factors involved in deciding to make it a Papercutz series. First, many years ago, I edited many super-hero comics for quite a few years. I love super-heroes, but there are so many great super-hero series published by other publishers, I vowed not to publish any at Papercutz, unless they were unique in some way. The idea of a group of young people who are descendants of the ancient gods from their respective countries coming together to form a super team certainly was a fresh idea. But what really sold me was that THE MYTHICS was co-created by Patricia Lyfoung. Patricia created a series about a swashbuckling female vigilante, THE SCARLET ROSE, that caught Terry's attention when we were launching Charmz, a Papercutz imprint devoted to tales of romance. The series was written and drawn by Patricia and I absolutely loved it. Knowing she was involved in creating THE MYTHICS made me want it for Papercutz, and it's certainly turned out to be an outstanding series.

There. Now you know my secret. Fortunately, it has all worked out well for me. I have Terry, Jeff, as well as translators such as Joe Johnson, Nanette McGuinness, and Elizabeth S. Tieri, to help me if I run into any translating issues. Besides, we also publish comics that come from Brazil, Spain, Italy, and Malaysia and I don't know any of those languages either. There is though a graphic novel coming soon from Papercutz that's from France that I didn't have any trouble reading--it's "THE FLY" by writer/artist Lewis Trondheim. It's the story of a fly, told without any words at all.

Luckily, we do publish graphic novels that are "Made in America," and one of them is "THE ONLY LIVING GIRL," the sequel to the hit Papercutz series "THE ONLY LIVING BOY," by David Gallaher, writer, and Steve Ellis, artist. And it just so happens we have a short preview of that very series on the following pages. *Quelle coincidence!*

All of the above makes me realize that Papercutz is a lot like THE MYTHICS. While they're made up of heroes from around the world, Papercutz is made up of graphic novels from around the world. And speaking of "around the world," be sure not to miss THE MYTHICS #4 "Global Chaos"—and maybe one of our young heroes might shout "Mythics Assemble!" but you'll have to find out for yourself.

*Merci,*

JIM

## STAY IN TOUCH!

EMAIL:              salicrup@papercutz.com
WEB:                www.papercutz.com
TWITTER:            @papercutzgn
INSTAGRAM:          @papercutzgn
FACEBOOK:           PAPERCUTZGRAPHICNOVELS
FANMAIL:            Papercutz, 160 Broadway, Suite 700,
                    East Wing, New York, NY 10038

Go to papercutz.com and sign up
for the free Papercutz e-newsletter!

**Special preview of THE ONLY LIVING GIRL #2**

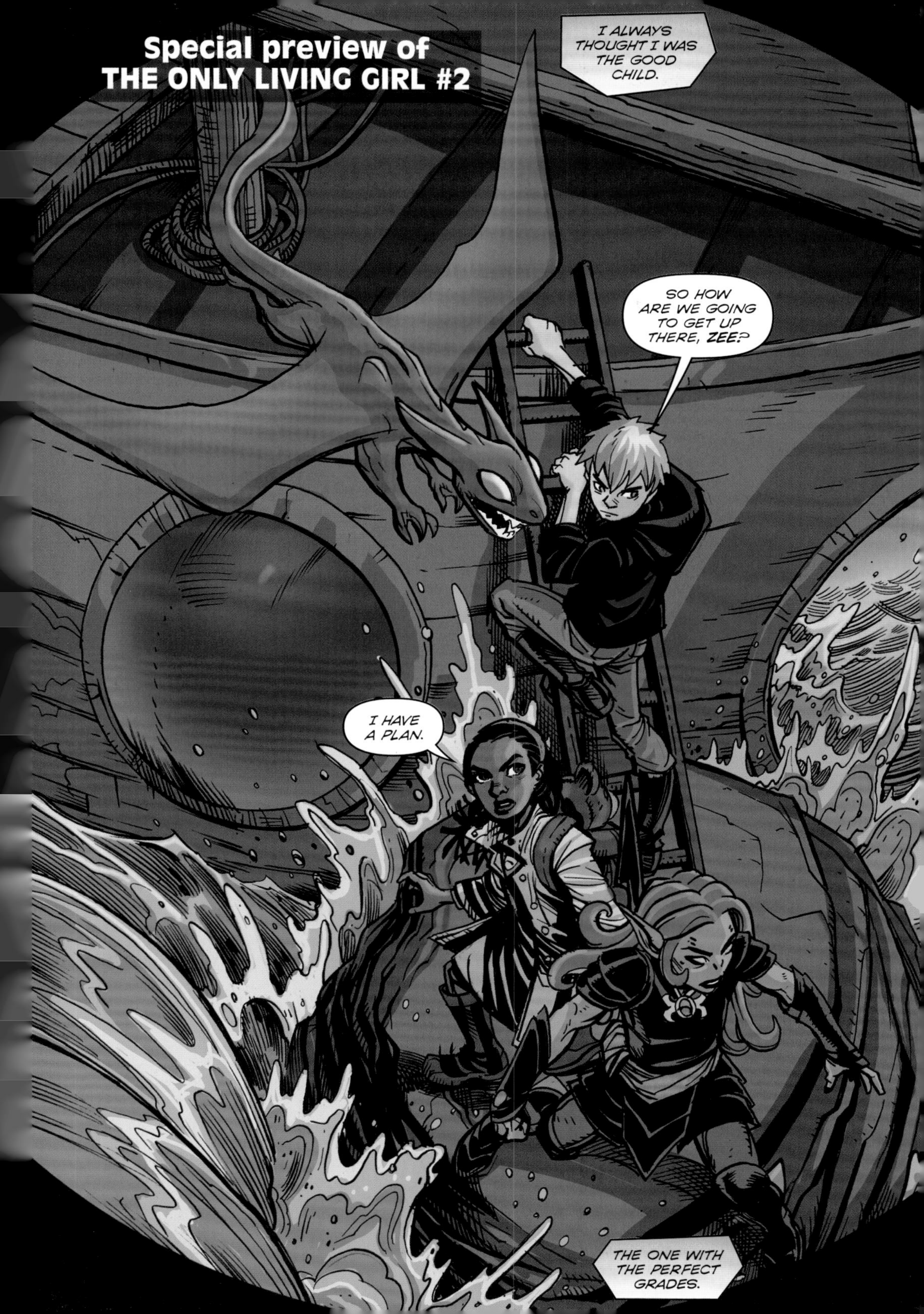
I ALWAYS THOUGHT I WAS THE GOOD CHILD.
SO HOW ARE WE GOING TO GET UP THERE, ZEE?
I HAVE A PLAN.
THE ONE WITH THE PERFECT GRADES.

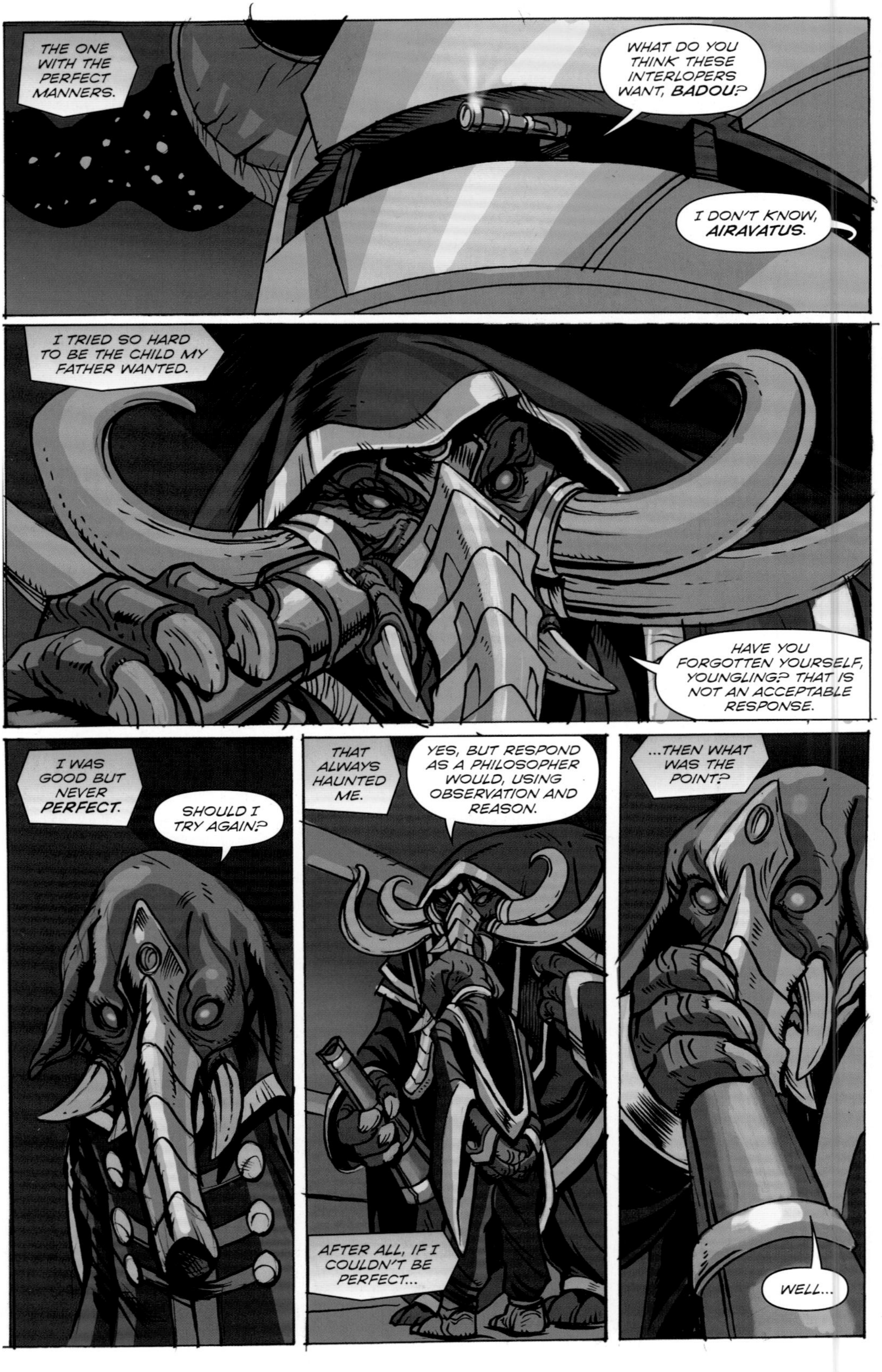
THE ONE WITH THE PERFECT MANNERS.
WHAT DO YOU THINK THESE INTERLOPERS WANT, BADOU?
I DON'T KNOW, AIRAVATUS.
I TRIED SO HARD TO BE THE CHILD MY FATHER WANTED.
HAVE YOU FORGOTTEN YOURSELF, YOUNGLING? THAT IS NOT AN ACCEPTABLE RESPONSE.
I WAS GOOD BUT NEVER PERFECT.
SHOULD I TRY AGAIN?
THAT ALWAYS HAUNTED ME.
YES, BUT RESPOND AS A PHILOSOPHER WOULD, USING OBSERVATION AND REASON.
AFTER ALL, IF I COULDN'T BE PERFECT...
...THEN WHAT WAS THE POINT?
WELL...

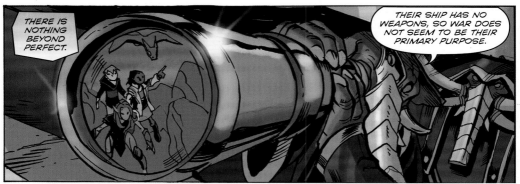

THERE IS NOTHING BEYOND PERFECT.

THEIR SHIP HAS NO WEAPONS, SO WAR DOES NOT SEEM TO BE THEIR PRIMARY PURPOSE.

PERFECTION IS A CONDITION THAT CANNOT BE SURPASSED.

AREN'T YOU OVERLOOKING THE OBVIOUS? TELL ME ABOUT THE CREATURES.

IF YOU CAN'T BE YOUR BEST AT ALL TIMES...

I BEG YOUR FORGIVENESS. I FOCUSED ONLY ON THEIR VESSEL AND NOT THE CREATURES INSIDE.

THERE WERE FOUR CREATURES. AN AQUATIC MERMIDONIAN, I BELIEVE. A WINGED CREATURE OF SOME TYPE... AND... AND...

YOU'RE ONLY GOING TO DISAPPOINT PEOPLE.

THE OTHER TWO... THEY SEEM LIKE HUMANS... BUT THAT WOULD BE IMPOSSIBLE, AIRAVATUS.

IMPOSSIBLE, ACCORDING TO WHOM, BADOU?

AND THAT'S A HEAVY BURDEN TO CARRY.

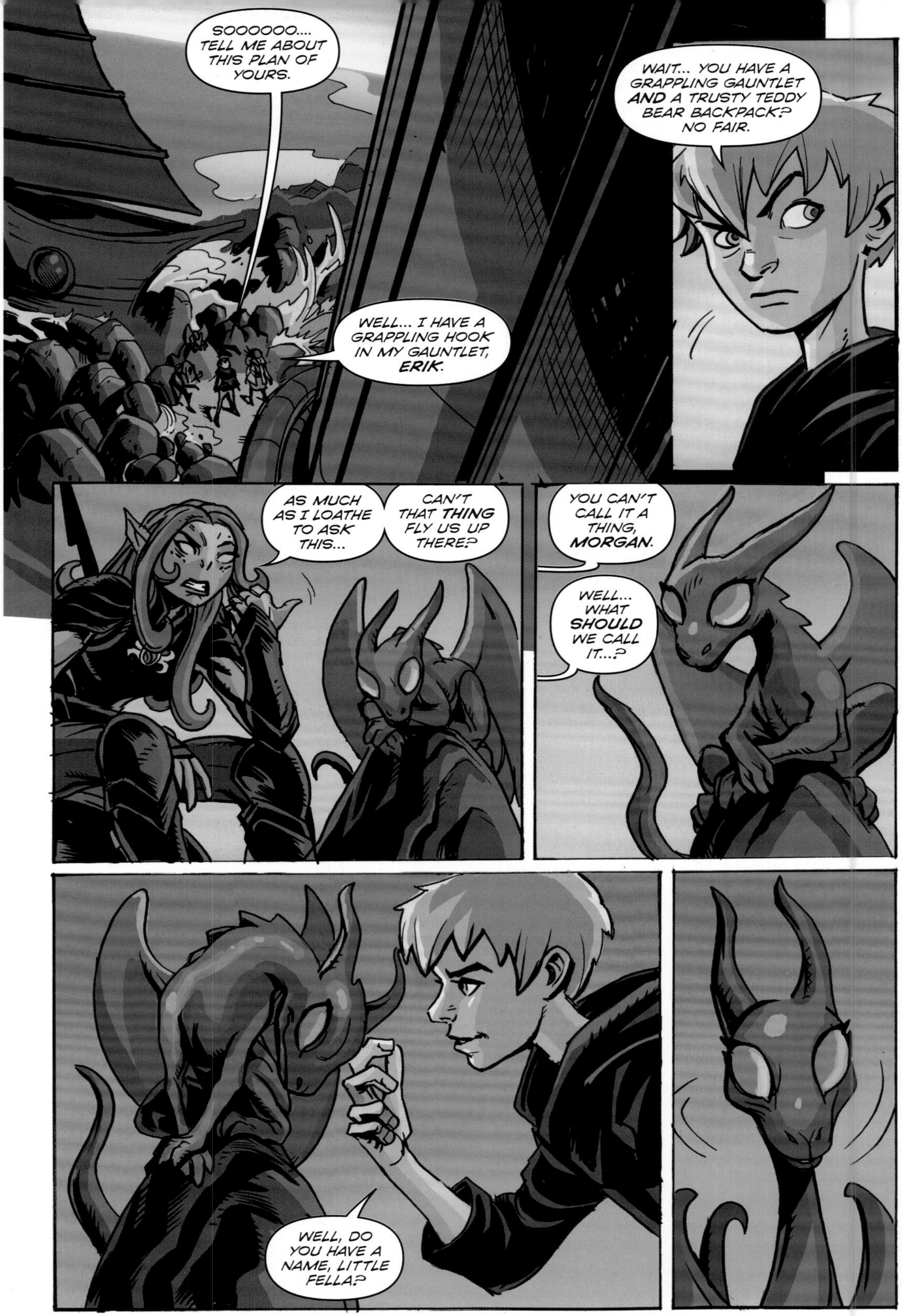
SOOOOOO.... TELL ME ABOUT THIS PLAN OF YOURS.
WELL... I HAVE A GRAPPLING HOOK IN MY GAUNTLET, **ERIK**.
WAIT... YOU HAVE A GRAPPLING GAUNTLET **AND** A TRUSTY TEDDY BEAR BACKPACK? NO FAIR.
AS MUCH AS I LOATHE TO ASK THIS...
CAN'T THAT **THING** FLY US UP THERE?
YOU CAN'T CALL IT A THING, **MORGAN**.
WELL... WHAT **SHOULD** WE CALL IT...?
WELL, DO YOU HAVE A NAME, LITTLE FELLA?

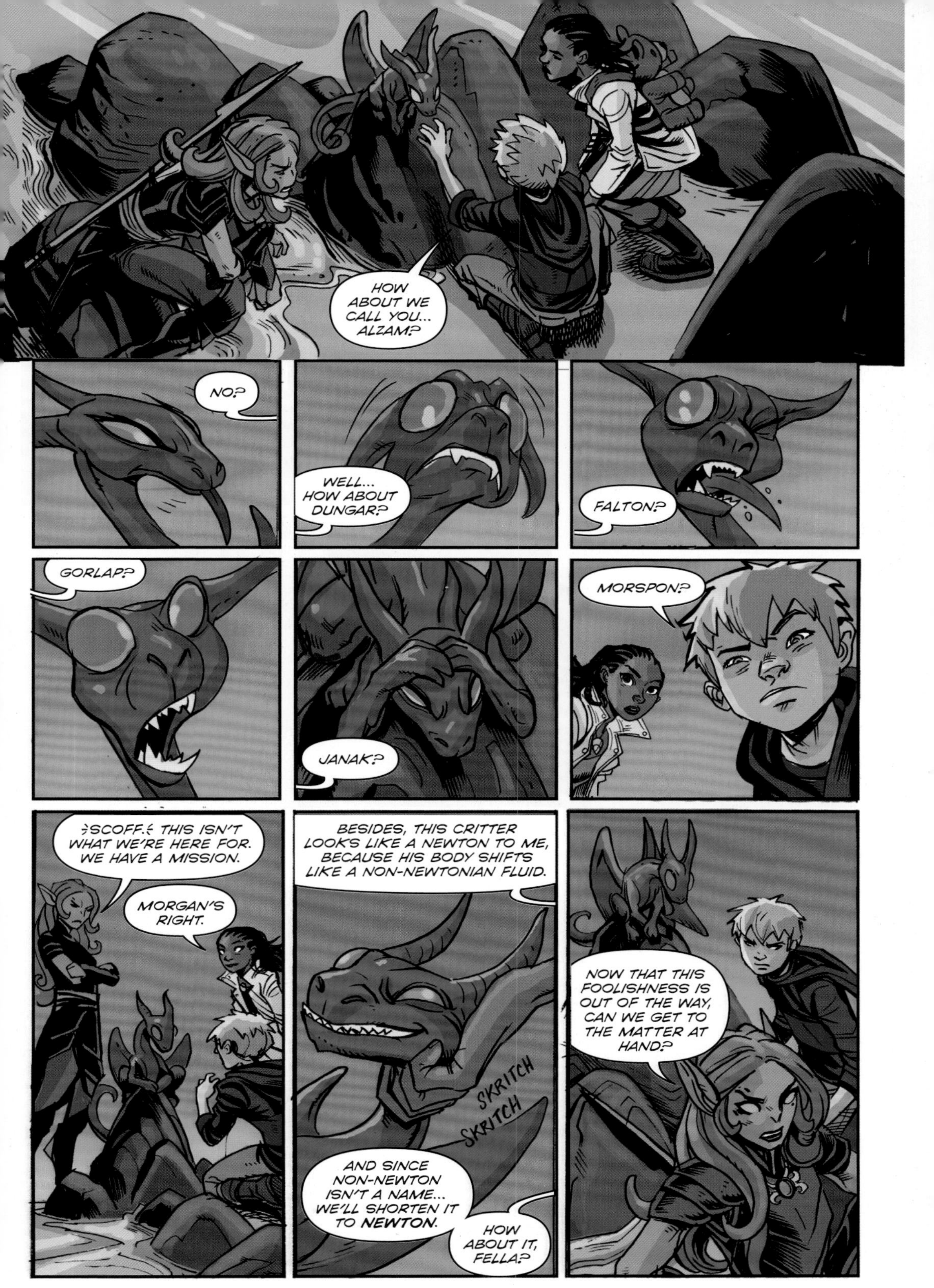

HOW ABOUT WE CALL YOU... ALZAM?
NO?
WELL... HOW ABOUT DUNGAR?
FALTON?
GORLAP?
JANAK?
MORSPON?
*SCOFF.* THIS ISN'T WHAT WE'RE HERE FOR. WE HAVE A MISSION.
MORGAN'S RIGHT.
BESIDES, THIS CRITTER LOOKS LIKE A NEWTON TO ME, BECAUSE HIS BODY SHIFTS LIKE A NON-NEWTONIAN FLUID.
SKRITCH
SKRITCH
AND SINCE NON-NEWTON ISN'T A NAME... WE'LL SHORTEN IT TO NEWTON.
HOW ABOUT IT, FELLA?
NOW THAT THIS FOOLISHNESS IS OUT OF THE WAY, CAN WE GET TO THE MATTER AT HAND?

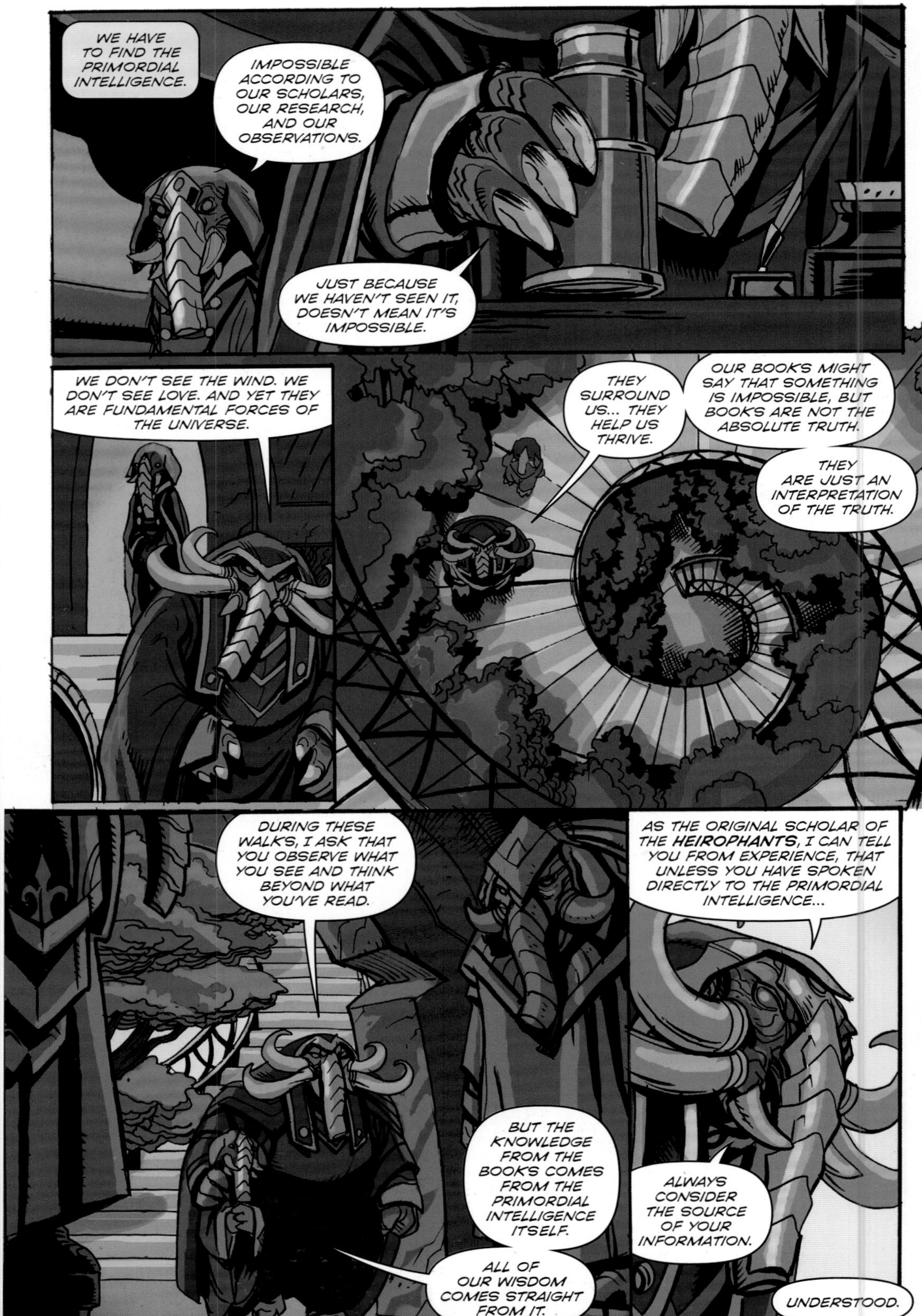
WE HAVE TO FIND THE PRIMORDIAL INTELLIGENCE.
IMPOSSIBLE ACCORDING TO OUR SCHOLARS, OUR RESEARCH, AND OUR OBSERVATIONS.
JUST BECAUSE WE HAVEN'T SEEN IT, DOESN'T MEAN IT'S IMPOSSIBLE.
WE DON'T SEE THE WIND. WE DON'T SEE LOVE. AND YET THEY ARE FUNDAMENTAL FORCES OF THE UNIVERSE.
THEY SURROUND US... THEY HELP US THRIVE.
OUR BOOKS MIGHT SAY THAT SOMETHING IS IMPOSSIBLE, BUT BOOKS ARE NOT THE ABSOLUTE TRUTH.
THEY ARE JUST AN INTERPRETATION OF THE TRUTH.
DURING THESE WALKS, I ASK THAT YOU OBSERVE WHAT YOU SEE AND THINK BEYOND WHAT YOU'VE READ.
BUT THE KNOWLEDGE FROM THE BOOKS COMES FROM THE PRIMORDIAL INTELLIGENCE ITSELF.
ALL OF OUR WISDOM COMES STRAIGHT FROM IT.
AS THE ORIGINAL SCHOLAR OF THE **HEIROPHANTS**, I CAN TELL YOU FROM EXPERIENCE, THAT UNLESS YOU HAVE SPOKEN DIRECTLY TO THE PRIMORDIAL INTELLIGENCE...
ALWAYS CONSIDER THE SOURCE OF YOUR INFORMATION.
UNDERSTOOD.

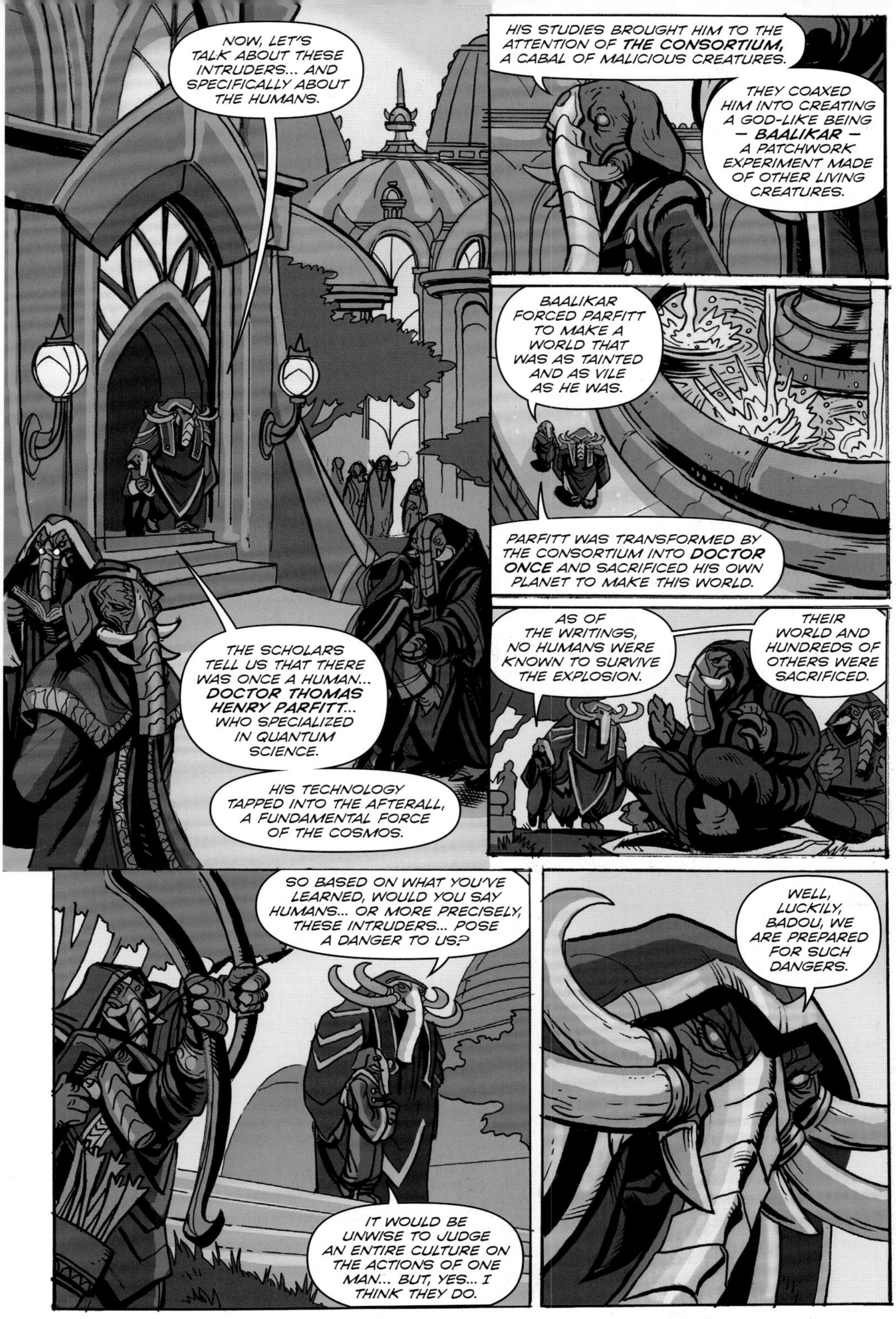
NOW, LET'S TALK ABOUT THESE INTRUDERS... AND SPECIFICALLY ABOUT THE HUMANS.
THE SCHOLARS TELL US THAT THERE WAS ONCE A HUMAN... DOCTOR THOMAS HENRY PARFITT... WHO SPECIALIZED IN QUANTUM SCIENCE.
HIS TECHNOLOGY TAPPED INTO THE AFTERALL, A FUNDAMENTAL FORCE OF THE COSMOS.
HIS STUDIES BROUGHT HIM TO THE ATTENTION OF THE CONSORTIUM, A CABAL OF MALICIOUS CREATURES.
THEY COAXED HIM INTO CREATING A GOD-LIKE BEING — BAALIKAR — A PATCHWORK EXPERIMENT MADE OF OTHER LIVING CREATURES.
BAALIKAR FORCED PARFITT TO MAKE A WORLD THAT WAS AS TAINTED AND AS VILE AS HE WAS.
PARFITT WAS TRANSFORMED BY THE CONSORTIUM INTO DOCTOR ONCE AND SACRIFICED HIS OWN PLANET TO MAKE THIS WORLD.
AS OF THE WRITINGS, NO HUMANS WERE KNOWN TO SURVIVE THE EXPLOSION.
THEIR WORLD AND HUNDREDS OF OTHERS WERE SACRIFICED.
SO BASED ON WHAT YOU'VE LEARNED, WOULD YOU SAY HUMANS... OR MORE PRECISELY, THESE INTRUDERS... POSE A DANGER TO US?
IT WOULD BE UNWISE TO JUDGE AN ENTIRE CULTURE ON THE ACTIONS OF ONE MAN... BUT, YES... I THINK THEY DO.
WELL, LUCKILY, BADOU, WE ARE PREPARED FOR SUCH DANGERS.

**Don't miss the rest of THE ONLY LIVING GIRL #2 available now at booksellers and libraries everywhere.**